Daughters of the Regiment

By the same author

NIGHT IS FOR HUNTING
GLACIER RUN
THE DOLPHIN SHORE

DAUGHTERS OF THE REGIMENT

Phyllida Barstow

CENTURY
LONDON MELBOURNE AUCKLAND JOHANNESBURG

Copyright Phyllida Barstow © 1987

All rights reserved

First published in Great Britain in 1987 by
Century Hutchinson Ltd
Brookmount House, 62–65 Chandos Place,
London WC2N 4NW

Century Hutchinson Australia Pty Ltd
PO Box 496
16–22 Church Street, Hawthorn,
Victoria 3122, Australia

Century Hutchinson New Zealand Ltd
PO Box 40-086, Glenfield,
Auckland 10, New Zealand

Century Hutchinson South Africa (Pty) Ltd
PO Box 337, Bergvlei,
2012 South Africa

British Library Cataloguing in Publication Data

Barstow, Phyllida
 Daughters of the Regiment.
 I. Title
 823'.914 [F]   PR6052.A74

ISBN 0 7126 1427 3

Printed and bound in Great Britain by
Anchor Brendon Ltd, Tiptree, Essex

Acknowledgements

I should like to thank all those who have been so generous with their time, source material and advice on matters linguistic and military during the writing of this book: in particular Barbara Gent, former Librarian of Wellington College; David Lyon; my brother Gerald Barstow; Miranda Lindsay and Colonel Alexander Lindsay; and my husband Duff Hart-Davis, *sine qua non*.

For my mother
Diana Barstow

1

Mr Samuel Hardy of Portsmouth was not one of Fortune's favourites, yet in one respect he was exceptionally blessed. No fewer than six of the nine daughters born to his handsome black-eyed wife, together with a single adored son, had survived the perils of infancy and now looked to their father to launch them upon the world. It was their misfortune that he was by no means as successful a provider as he was progenitor.

A tall man of distinguished looks and scholarly disposition, whose dreamy blue eyes seemed constantly fixed on more noble horizons than those of the daily round, he was better suited to the role of schoolmaster in which he had begun his career than the hurlyburly of Commerce where he now found himself. In matters of business he was cursed with what might be termed the very reverse of the Midas touch. Instead of turning to gold, every commercial venture to which his hand was set ended in failure.

It was while breakfasting with his wife on a bright cold morning in the winter of 1810 that Samuel was obliged to confess the collapse of his latest trading enterprise, and warn her that she should prepare to remove from their large house in Portsmouth's fashionable heart to modest lodgings on the city's outskirts since, as he ruefully expressed it, he found himself with hardly a feather to fly with.

'Sell the house?' exclaimed Mrs Hardy in mingled astonishment and indignation (these emotions largely simulated since she had a very fair idea of the straits to which her husband's bungling had reduced them). 'Indeed, my love, you will do nothing of the kind. How will our girls find husbands if you hide them away in some poky back-street boarding-house? I would rather starve than contemplate such a course.'

'It is the only one open to us, my love.'

'Fiddlesticks!' his wife responded vigorously, with an expressive flash of her large eyes. 'You should be ashamed even to consider it. If you have too much pride to use your interest with friends who might help us, I have not.'

For some moments she pondered, her busy mind checking with clockwork precision through a list of influential acquaintances. Presently she smiled, recalling a glance in which she had discerned some warmer emotion than simple admiration. Since the death of his beautiful Spanish wife Dolores de Alava, whom he had wooed and won in the teeth of her family's opposition when he was a young man attached to Lord Camperdown's embassy in Madrid, Lord Amherst was said to be utterly indifferent to women. Yet with the sure instinct of her sex, Mrs Hardy knew this was not true. Indifferent Lord Amherst might choose to appear, but he was not insensible to feminine charm, and there was no doubt that he had the power to alleviate all their financial troubles. Besides, they possessed a bargaining counter.

'You shall write to Lord Amherst and entreat him to secure you some employment,' she said decidedly. 'When he recalls the service you rendered him, he will not refuse such a request.'

'My love, I cannot,' said Samuel unhappily, '*Bis dat qui cito dat:* his lordship has already been more than generous.'

'You are too modest, my love,' responded his lady briskly. 'He has barely discharged his obligation. Your service deserved a better recompense than mere recommendations, as I am sure his lordship will be only too ready to acknowledge when he is acquainted with the circumstances to which we are reduced.'

Samuel rose and paced the room in agitation, while his wife watched his thoughts reflected in his candid features.

'I cannot do it,' he said at last. 'In all conscience I have already taken enough from my friends without begging for charity.'

'Who spoke of charity? Will it give your conscience less pain to see your family in the workhouse?'

It should be said at once that Mrs Hardy was of a different mettle from her husband. The early need to fight for survival in the dangerous tumult of the French Revolution had tempered her will and marked her character with a force, even a ruthlessness, which Samuel lacked. Though she never forgot she had married beneath her, Mrs Hardy – who had been born Genevieve de la Tour du Pin, and carried in her veins some of the proudest blood of France's old aristocracy – scorned to shrink from any enterprise which might benefit her family. She was keenly aware that her husband's concern for their children was of a less exacting nature than her own, and though she loved him dearly she saw it as her duty to stiffen his resolve, if not with whips and scorpions, at least with the flail of her tongue. Samuel inclined to the philosophy which bade a man take no heed for the morrow, but since he abhorred strife it was rare for him to resist for long any course upon which his wife determined.

Seeing him hesitate, she pressed her advantage. 'If you prefer not to write to him, I will. Only consider how simple a matter it is for a man of his influence to place us in a situation beyond want! When I think of the care and – yes, the *love* – you lavished on that miserable boy of his, and how he repaid you, I vow that nothing you could ask of Lord Amherst would exceed your due.'

'Poor Harry!'

'Fiddlesticks!'

If Mrs Hardy spoke a trifle warmly, it was because the boy in question, the Hon. Henry Churchill, had so far taken advantage of her hospitality when living at their house for the purpose of filling the gaps in his education left by his abrupt dismissal from Winchester College, that he had persuaded fifteen-year-old Clio, her romantically-minded third daughter, to elope with him at night, in a hired carriage. Not only had Samuel lost a night's sleep in pursuit of the truants, but he had also been obliged to pay off the jarvey from his own pocket, a circumstance his wife discovered too late to prevent.

Harry had been banished, Clio whipped and scolded, and the whole lamentable incident hushed up; but Mrs Hardy had not forgotten the debt Lord Amherst owed to their silence, and in the present circumstances she felt fully justified in recalling it to his attention.

'Poor boy,' Samuel sighed again, regretting the waste of a young life. For all his faults, he had retained an affection for the scapegrace Harry, who had fallen at the battle of Talavera on the Peninsula.

Mrs Hardy gave an impatient snort and bustled from the room. Repairing at once to the bureau in her sunny boudoir, she set herself to compose a letter that would awaken Lord Amherst's conscience with regard to his son's former tutor.

Nearly five weeks elapsed before any reply was received, and in those weeks – as is generally the case in a household where money is in short supply – all manner of bills with disagreeable notes appended piled up on Genevieve Hardy's elegant bureau. Even with her Gallic respect for the importance of keeping up appearances, she was a little dismayed by the size of the dressmaker's account – but how were the dear girls to make good matches if they were not becomingly clad?

The surgeon's bill for extracting two of twelve-year-old Louisa's teeth, broken in a fall from the nursery rocking-horse, annoyed her a good deal since the operation removed not only the teeth but the last of the child's pretensions to good looks; and the final straw came when the cook quarrelled with both parlourmaids and left, taking with her the contents of the larder.

Cook's recent departure had afforded another unedifying glimpse into the dark pit of the family's finances. Mrs Hardy, applying herself with her customary energy to the matter of making economies, promptly cancelled a number of weekly orders, only to find the house besieged by angry tradesmen demanding the immediate settlement of their accounts, some of which had remained unpaid for over a year.

Though firm in her conviction that to sell the house would cast an irredeemable blight over her daughters' futures, Genevieve Hardy saw the day of reckoning creep inexorably closer. It was with an eagerness born of desperation that she received the stiff envelope bearing Lord Amherst's crest and tore it open.

Entering her boudoir an hour later, Samuel found her seated at her desk, scribbling furiously. Her cheeks were flushed, her cap awry, and her whole demeanour expressed angry disappointment.

'There!' she exclaimed, throwing down the pen and reaching for a wafer. 'That will teach his lordship not to play games with me!'

'Games, my love?'

For answer she thrust at him the thick paper headed with Lord Amherst's crest.

Dear Madam, he read,
I am writing at Lord Amherst's instruction to express his concern over the difficulties your husband has experienced in obtaining a situation suited to his talents.

It now gives me pleasure to convey to you that his lordship has secured for Mr Hardy an appointment as Deputy Assistant Commissary to the 31st Regiment of Light Horse in the Army of Portugal under the command of Viscount Wellington of Talavera.

Upon receiving confirmation of Mr Hardy's acceptance of this appointment, I am instructed to put matters in hand to expedite his departure for the Peninsula by every means at my disposal.

I beg to remain, Madam,
    Your obedient servant,
        Josiah Triggs
           secretary to the Earl of Amherst

At the foot of the letter was appended in his lordship's impetuous scrawl: *Trust this will keep the wolf from the door. These Commissary rascals generally end up as rich as nabobs. The Roman ruins are certainly very fine.*

'Nabobs! Roman ruins!' exclaimed Mrs Hardy wrathfully. 'How dare he wilfully misunderstand my civil request? To have my letter made the butt of a vulgar jest is something I will not endure. His lordship should be ashamed to mock our misfortune, and so I have not scrupled to tell him.'

Receiving no response to this outburst, she looked with more attention at her husband, and saw he was staring at the letter as if entranced, on his face an expression of absorbed, incredulous wonder. It was plain he had not listened to a word she said.

'Mr Hardy!'

He turned his dreamy gaze upon her with such a look of ecstasy that she received a distinct jolt.

'Rome's oldest province!' he breathed exultantly. 'The land I wish above all others to see. Oh, my love, how shall I ever thank his lordship for affording me the opportunity to realize my dearest ambition?'

Nonplussed, she stared at him. 'You cannot mean to accept this absurd offer?'

'I would die rather than refuse it.'

'You will very likely die if you accept it,' she said sharply. Her ready wrath at what she could only suppose a contemptuous gesture designed to silence any further requests for patronage had blinded her to the possibility that the offer might be made in good faith, or that Samuel might welcome it. His preoccupation with antique remains was incomprehensible to one of her brisk, pragmatic character, and she tolerated it only because it made him happy. For years he had worked intermittently on a history of the Roman legions, which she had supposed would never be finished, but now the design behind Lord Amherst's scrawled postscript became plain. By holding out this lure, he hoped to secure the services of an honest man in a profession which, by his own admission, was largely peopled by rogues. Well, she could forgive him that. What irked her was the blatant attempt to separate her husband from his family, more particularly since in her heart she knew how eager he would be to shed responsibility for his brood.

'Only consider how unsuited you would be for the work of a war commissary!' she said more moderately. 'The hardship! The constant danger! How could I bear to think of you languishing in that terrible climate, a prey to sickness and the insults of rough soldiers? I vow you would not be there above a month before you longed for the comfort of your home.'

He was not listening. 'Segovia, Mérida, the great river Tagus! I shall dedicate my book to his lordship, so generations to come may know of his munificence. What is hardship beside so noble a prospect? You know, my love, since this war began I had quite given up hope of ever seeing the Roman marvels on the Iberian Peninsula. Now the opportunity is handed me on a plate!'

Her husband in uniform? Mrs Hardy compressed her lips to stifle the burning words of reproach which were all too likely to set her husband on an opposite course from the one she wished. Samuel Hardy allowed himself to be led but never driven, and it would go against the grain for him to admit she knew far more of the matter than he did.

Genevieve's own early taste of the devastation of war had given her all too clear an appreciation of the kind of situation her husband was likely to find in Spain, where five years after Bonaparte's first invasion the British were struggling against overwhelming odds to liberate their Spanish allies from the French yoke.

The Revolutionary Armies of France, which had destroyed her own family's fortunes, had now grown into so great an incubus upon the country's revenues that the self-appointed Emperor Napoleon was obliged to extend his conquests ever farther if only to pay his soldiers.

No power on earth seemed able to resist his triumphant progress towards world domination. Since the turn of the century most of Europe had fallen to him: Italy, the German princedoms, the Kingdom of Naples and now Austria were his vassals, the King of Prussia his puppet, and Russia's Czar his reluctant ally. His brother Louis ruled Holland, Jerome was King of Westphalia, and both his sisters were queens. Even his elder brother Joseph, a mild unambitious man of sluggish disposition, had been thrust upon the throne of Spain.

As the creeping fungus of French power spread westward into Portugal, bidding fair to smother the whole of the Iberian Peninsula, the British Government at length decided – albeit somewhat half-heartedly – to intervene on behalf of its oldest ally.

A small, poorly-equipped force had been dispatched to the rocky Atlantic coast of Portugal to confront the French colossus as David challenged Goliath, under the command of a neat spare aquiline-featured gentleman in his late thirties, as plain and precise in his opinions as he was in his dress, whose direct blue gaze, firm-set mouth, and tremendous high-bridged nose wore an expression at once humorous and self-assured.

He was Sir Arthur Wellesley, nicknamed 'The Sepoy General' since most of his fighting had been against the Marathas, and there were plenty of armchair pundits in London clubs who were inclined to criticize his appointment. Fighting a rabble of natives was not at all the same thing as fighting Napoleon Bonaparte. Besides, might not Arthur Wellesley's command be attributed to the influence of his brilliant brother Richard, Marquis of Wellesley?

If Sir Arthur heard these opinions it bothered him not a fig. Immediately upon landing he snatched the strategic initiative from the hot-headed General Junot and defeated him in a swift decisive battle at Vimiero.

Alas, the arrival of two more senior officers, Generals Dalrymple and Burrard, allowed Wellesley no chance to consolidate his victory. Their shameful haste to sign a peace agreement with the French led to a public outcry in England which resulted in all three generals being recalled to face a court martial.

Command of the British force in Portugal was left in the hands of Sir John Moore, but since personal gallantry is only a poor substitute for sound strategy, his ill-advised advance on

Madrid was followed by an appalling midwinter retreat over the most inhospitable terrain in Spain, where men and beasts perished in their thousands. When the emaciated survivors reached Spain's north-westerly extremity and saw British transports standing off Corunna they wept for joy; yet even before they could be embarked they were robbed of their leader by a French shell.

Well might they reflect, as they huddled in the overcrowded holds as the ships battled across the Bay of Biscay, on the truth of the old adage that in Spain a small army is beaten and a large army starves.

Cleared of all blame for the Convention of Cintra, Sir Arthur Wellesley assumed command of the new force dispatched to Portugal in the late spring of 1809, but any optimist who supposed the British Government might have digested the lessons of 1808 would soon have been disabused. Not only was his force half the size of the opposing French, and transport waggons with their animals in desperately short supply, but Sir Arthur's repeated requests for a siege train and guns capable of pounding the massive walls of Spanish fortified towns had been ignored. In a stream of crisply-worded dispatches to Lord Castlereagh, Secretary of State for War, Sir Arthur made plain his displeasure at these deficiencies, and set to work to see what he could do without them.

Very soon the carping of clubroom critics was changed to admiration – even adulation – as Wellesley won a dazzling series of victories each of which was followed by a strategic retreat which over-extended French lines of communication and supply. Though the British were still heavily outnumbered, the whole aspect of the war changed.

Wellesley had forced an audacious passage of the Duero, one of the great rivers running east to west and linking Portugal with Spain, and drove Marshal Soult out of Oporto. Advancing boldly into Spain itself, he confronted Marshal Victor at Talavera and won a resounding victory, despite the obstructionist tactics of his ally the Spanish Captain-General Don Gregorio Garcia de la Cuesta, a stiff-necked elderly incompetent whose unbroken record of defeats made him far more dangerous a friend than foe. A grateful government paid tribute to Wellesley's achievements by awarding him the title of Viscount Wellington of Talavera.

Next year the game of cat and mouse was resumed; a spring offensive being succeeded by a tactical withdrawal to winter quarters in Portugal; but this time there was a difference.

For thirteen months Colonel Richard Fletcher and his engineers had been secretly at work on the Lisbon peninsula, and when Wellington retired thither with Marshal Masséna at his heels in the autumn of 1810, it was to take shelter behind a double chain of superb fortifications stretching the thirty miles between Alhandra at the mouth of the Tagus river, and the Zizandre river on the Atlantic coast, encompassing all the country in between.

Cliffs had been dynamited to render them impassable, rivers were dammed and gullies bristled with palisades. Old forts had new cannon, and a system of signals passed from one hilltop to the next ensured constant surveillance of enemy movements. Into this huge natural fortress poured not only the British army but all the Portuguese from the surrounding countryside – young and old, sick and healthy, rich and poor – bringing with them their donkeys, mules, dogs, oxen, sheep, goats and poultry as well as less welcome concomitants such as parasites and diseases. Furniture was piled on creaking farm carts, food and wine supplies that could not be carried were destroyed. Between Busaco and Torres Vedras nothing was left that might be useful to the French.

Conditions were inevitably crowded but, with the British fleet plying freely between Portsmouth and Lisbon, enough food reached Lisbon to prevent real shortages. In any case after five years of warfare Portuguese peasants preferred short commons with the British to murder, pillage and plunder by the French.

While Lord Wellington spent long hours in his bureau dictating pithy complaints of his men and munitions to the Ministry, and exhorting Lord Castlereagh to send him reinforcements, his officers cast care aside and settled down to enjoy themselves in Lisbon. The theatre was packed nightly and if the standard of playing was hardly what you would find in Drury Lane, at least the girls were pretty, with eloquent dark eyes and hand-span waists; and the gentle sun, delicious fruit and fish, and opportunities for picnics and excursions within the Lines of Torres Vedras filled the mild winter days most agreeably.

What could be more delightful (wrote home the young officers) than to sit at your ease in a pavement café, with a plate of grilled sardines and a jug of hot chocolate before you, and reflect on the plight of Masséna's *Vieux Moustaches* encamped outside the Lines making soup from their own boot-leather or hunting out rats in devastated farms?

For those of more serious inclination, Lisbon's many churches, convents and noble palaces furnished material for historical study, and of course there were Roman remains in abundance...

Mr Hardy sighed ecstatically. 'How truly, my love, it may be said that everything comes to him who waits!'

He caught his wife's hand and pressed it, his face alight with so much of the youthful enthusiasm that had captivated her twenty years ago that she had not the heart to scold. Mrs Hardy had learned her realism in a hard school, and she knew her husband's character too well to doubt that he was in earnest. Samuel seldom made decisions, preferring to drift with the tide, but on the rare occasions when he did oppose her he could be as tenacious as a limpet and obstinate as a mule.

Yet it would be hard to imagine anyone less suited to Commissariat work than her dear husband. Impatient of detail, oblivious to practicalities, scarcely aware of what he ate or drank; how could such a man devote himself to supplying soldiers with their rations, weighing beef, doling out biscuit, keeping accounts?

She sighed, for there was in her household a person ideally suited to all these tasks, though to part with him would be like parting with her own right hand. Auguste Meyer had served her father before the Revolution, and to him she owed not only her escape from the Terror, but much of her security since. As majordomo and faithful friend he had no equal, but she knew she would have no peace of mind unless he accompanied Samuel.

'I shall send Auguste with you,' she said.

Her nimble mind began to leap ahead, assessing how this unlooked-for appointment could be turned to advantage. Though she herself had not the slightest wish to return to the continent from which she had so narrowly escaped with her life, for her beautiful eldest daughter, she thought, a brief sojourn in another country might answer very well. With the flower of the British Army now in Portugal and Peninsular officers all the rage, Lisbon was reputed to be very gay. Amid new surroundings, might not Julia shake off the lethargy that now afflicted her and show a more positive interest in acquiring a husband? Indeed, perhaps she should consider sending Laura with her. Two attractive girls made more than twice the impact of one alone, and in such a climate neither was likely to seek in vain for beaux.

The younger children were another matter. Genevieve's memories of nursing her precious four-year-old Joshua through the dreaded 'Walcheren fever' which had raged through Portsmouth last year in the wake of Lord Chatham's ill-fated expedition were still too fresh for her to contemplate exposing him to foreign infections. Clio was too headstrong and Louisa, Maria, and Clara too inclined to encourage her pranks for there to be any question of sending them beyond maternal control.

'I shall write at once to thank Lord Amherst for his favour and tell him I am ready to leave whenever he wishes,' declared Samuel joyously, with a typical disregard for the inconvenience this desertion was likely to put upon his wife. 'Nor shall I forget, my love, to whom I am chiefly indebted for this good fortune!' He pressed her hand again, planted a kiss on her flushed cheek, and left the room, taking the letter with him.

For a few moments after the door closed Genevieve Hardy sat lost in thought, staring out of the window at the crowded promenade and, beyond it, the forests of masts in the harbour.

Then, with a return of her customary briskness, she tugged the bell and when the sole remaining maid answered, told her to summon the two eldest Misses Hardy to her boudoir.

A brooding silence like the hush before the storm hung over the big shabby nursery which now did duty as a schoolroom.

Nineteen-year-old Julia sat reading, with young Joshua on her lap, but the fact that her mind was not wholly on her book was shown in her apprehensive glances across the room.

Plump rosy Laura, her junior by a year, was trying on bonnets before the looking-glass, but she too stole sidelong glances at the reflection of Clio's stiff shoulders as she sat with her back turned in bitter, furious disappointment.

'I *will* go!' Clio burst out suddenly, swinging round to glare at them both. 'Why should I be left behind with the babies while you enjoy yourselves?'

Beside her tall sisters, Clio looked a changeling. She was dark and small, though neatly-made; but if she lacked their milk-and-roses bloom she more than made up for it by the lustre in her large dark eyes, her quick graceful movements and the flashing brilliance of her smile. For the moment all pretension to beauty was eclipsed by the blackest of scowls. Julia bent her head attentively over her book. She had a good deal of sympathy for Clio, but knew there was little use in arguing with Mamma.

'You are too young,' said Laura with a touch of smugness. She was not ill-pleased that on this occasion the sister who so often outshone her should be deprived of any chance to steal her thunder.

'I am less than a year younger than you!'

'Ah, but I am a young lady, and you are still a schoolgirl.' Laura twirled a fat, glossy ringlet about her finger with an exasperating assumption of superiority. 'There is a world of difference between seventeen and eighteen, as you will discover when you reach my age.'

She preened before the glass, turning her head this way and that to admire the half-poke bonnet that crowned her nut-brown head.

'Perhaps cherry ribbons would be better,' she mused, pulling out a drawer.

'Those ribbons are mine.'

'Surely I may be permitted to *borrow* them?'

'Oh, very well, if you must.' Clio's fingers itched to slap her. The injustice of her mother's decree burned like smouldering coals in her heart. Julia and Laura were to accompany their father to Portugal while she, Clio, the only one of the whole family who truly longed for adventure, was condemned to remain in Portsmouth with Mamma and the babies. It was too bad. It was utterly unfair and insupportable. Somehow she must find a way to make Mamma change her mind. It was no use appealing to her father. In matters of domestic policy, Mrs Hardy's sway was absolute.

'Julia and I will be able to help Papa with his accounts,' said Laura, rubbing salt in the wound. 'You know how impractical he is.'

Clio knew very well. She also knew she was better at accounts than either of her sisters. Laura was too indolent and Julia too absorbed in her private world of Art and Music to be good with figures, but Clio had inherited her mother's business sense.

'I wonder you should be so eager to visit the dreadful place where poor Harry died,' said Laura with a want of tact that could only have been deliberate.

'And *I* wonder that you can bear to contemplate removing so far from the society of Captain Greystone, which you seem to find so agreeable,' flashed Clio. 'Are you not afraid he will find himself another belle in your absence?'

She could not, herself, see anything to admire in Captain Greystone, a thirty-five-year old widower whose reddish eyes and sparse gingery whiskers framing a long pointed nose reminded her irresistibly of the gardener's ferret, but Laura preened herself on this conquest and made no secret of her hopes of becoming the second Mrs Greystone.

'Captain Greystone has been ordered to rejoin his regiment,' simpered Laura. 'He is likely to travel by the same transport as Papa.'

'Then I must be thankful I shall not be obliged to endure his company so long.' This was not true. Clio would have endured the society of a dozen Captain Greystones if it would have secured her a passage to Portugal.

'And I must be thankful he will have no opportunity to discover the sad hoyden I have for a sister.'

'Pig!'

Abandoning all pretence of maturity, Clio seized hold of a ringlet that peeped invitingly from her sister's bonnet and gave it a sharp tweak.

'You – you brat!'

Cheeks aflame, Laura whirled round, and in a moment they were locked in combat in a manner better suited to a beargarden than a young ladies' schoolroom.

'A mill!' cried Joshua delightedly. Slipping down from Julia's knee, he circled his sisters, yapping encouragement like an excited terrier. 'Go it, Clio!' he shrilled. 'Plant her a facer!'

Oblivious to the din, Julia hunched her shoulders and bent her gaze upon her book.

Their mother, entering unexpectedly, had not a moment's doubt where to lay the blame for this disgraceful exhibition, but she understood very well the depth of Clio's chagrin and, being a fair woman, addressed all three girls with equal severity.

'Laura! Clio! Behave yourselves at once. Julia! What can you be thinking of to tolerate such disgraceful conduct?'

The guilty start with which Julia turned to confront her mother showed only too clearly how little heed she was accustomed to pay to her sisters' squabbles. She had so perfected the art of removing herself in spirit from any troublesome situation that when her nose was in a book or a paintbrush in her hand, she was capable of ignoring an earthquake.

'I – I am sorry, Mamma. I was reading....'

'So I observe,' said her mother dryly, 'but that is hardly an excuse for tolerating such a commotion. Why, it could be heard in the street! What were you reading?'

'My Bible, Mamma.'

Such a pronouncement from any of her other children would

have gladdened Mrs Hardy's heart. Coming from Julia, however, it merely deepened her anxiety about her much-loved eldest daughter. Could it be normal or even healthy for a girl to be so *good*?

There could be no doubt that Julia was the Beauty of the family. Tall and slender, with delicately aristocratic features, her looks combined the good bones of her proud French ancestors with the translucent complexion of the classic English Rose. Her figure was graceful, and her large blue eyes shone serenely upon a world which never tempted her to behave with anything but perfect propriety. Her fine silky hair, parted in the centre and falling in loose waves to her shoulders in the manner of a Botticelli angel, was of that ethereal fairness which is seldom retained after babyhood. The elegance of her small hands and feet provoked torments of envy in damsels less blessed by Nature, and the gentle wistfulness of her voice induced young men, and some not so young, to compare it favourably with that of the nightingale.

Julia never romped, or lost her temper, or tore her clothes or spoke saucily to her elders as her sisters were all too prone to do. Yet for all her beauty and serenity, Julia caused her mother more worry than the rest of her brood put together, for she lived in a dream world from which no prince had yet succeeded in waking her.

At first Mrs Hardy had been pleased that her eldest daughter showed no inclination to throw herself away on a Nobody, and evinced little interest in the moonstruck youths who began to lay their hearts at her feet even before her formal emergence from the schoolroom. No callow stripling or red-cheeked farmer's son for my lovely Julia, her mother had thought complacently. She knows she may look higher than that. But seasons came and went without Julia showing the least particularity towards any of her suitors, some of whom – in Mrs Hardy's view – would have done very well indeed.

There was Sir Giles Bowater, whose handsome income from his Hampshire acres would have been highly desirable in a son-in-law; and Mr Rankin, friend of the Prince of Wales himself (not that such a connection was any great recommendation, to be sure) who was so put out by Julia's rejection that he bought himself a pair of colours and disappeared to the Peninsula, where a bout of fever soon terminated his existence.

If Mrs Hardy regretted these handsome catches, the emotion was nothing compared to her mortification when Julia refused her hand to Charles Maybridge. Even now a little moan might escape her lips when she thought how such a prize had been wilfully thrown away.

Lord Maybridge had begged to be introduced to Julia in her third season, when her mother was already becoming concerned at her apparent determination to remain on the shelf. Tall, well-dressed, self-assured, with an open face and winning smile, he was all that any mother could ask for her daughter besides owning Maybridge Hall, a beautiful Palladian mansion on the bank of the Hamner river. Throughout that summer season he had called on Mrs Hardy every day and faithfully escorted Julia to innumerable balls and assemblies. Mrs Hardy had considered the affair as good as settled. She was shocked as well as very much taken aback when Julia calmly informed her that she had refused Lord Maybridge's offer.

'Refused? Why, you goose, what are you thinking of? You cannot know what you are about,' exclaimed her mother with the sharpness born of acute disappointment.

Julia had coloured a little but her tone lost none of its usual composure. 'I know very well what I am about, Mamma. Lord Maybridge made me a civil offer, but he understood perfectly why I was obliged to refuse.'

'Indeed! And why, pray, were you obliged to refuse him?'

'Because I do not love him,' said Julia with the wide-eyed look of one surprised by another's ignorance. 'Papa has always said it is of the first importance to love the man you marry.'

It was on the tip of Mrs Hardy's tongue to respond tartly that love would not pay her brother's school fees nor buy her sisters new dresses, when Julia added with a puzzled frown, 'You must not blame me, Mamma. I did try to love him, you know. But when he was so angry with his poor little dog and beat him for muddying my dress – although I didn't care a fig for that – why, then I knew I could never love a man who was so little master of his passions, and so I told him.'

Mrs Hardy sighed, but recognized that any attempt to reinstate Lord Maybridge in her daughter's affections would be labour lost. For all its gentleness, Julia's character had a core of steel, and she saw no reason why she should please gentlemen if they did not please her.

No such criticism could be levelled at Laura. If anything she was too eager to please gentlemen and the hours she spent rubbing lotions on her face and trimming bonnets could, in her mother's opinion at least, have been better spent improving her mind. Laura was amiable, easygoing, self-indulgent, and her intellectual pursuits seldom went further than studying dress patterns in the fashionable magazines or reading romances. Her single dominating wish was to marry; she did not very much care whom. It was Laura who, on hearing of Lord Maybridge's fall from grace, burst into angry tears.

'You did it to spite me!' she sobbed, fixing her accusing glance on the astonished Julia. 'You wanted to spoil my chances.'

Clio could not help laughing. 'How can Julia's refusal to marry Lord Maybridge spoil *your* chances?'

'You know Mamma would never permit me to marry before her! I shall be left on the shelf until I have lost my looks, simply because Julia does not care if she remains an old maid for ever. Besides,' she added, pouting, 'Lord Maybridge promised to give a ball for me at Maybridge Hall, and his mother would have introduced me at Almack's, and now you have ruined it all.'

Laura was nothing if not resilient, however, and very soon after this disappointment she was able to inform her sisters, in the strictest confidence, that she had made a conquest of Captain Greystone and hoped he would speak to Papa before his regiment sailed. . . .

Now Mrs Hardy fixed her eldest daughter with a fond if critical eye. 'You will have to use your ears to better purpose if you are to be of assistance to your Papa in Portugal,' she observed. 'There will be no time for drifting away in daydreams when you are responsible for running his household.'

'Yes, Mamma.' Julia hesitated a moment, then said with a quiet intensity that spoke of hours of anguished thought, 'Mamma, I beg of you, must I go with Papa? I would so very much prefer to remain here with you. Could not Clio go in my place?'

Clio's mouth opened soundlessly. A look of almost incredulous hope lit her eyes. 'Oh, *please*, Mamma!' she begged. 'I should like it above all things!'

Mrs Hardy preferred her children to be happy, and for a moment she was tempted to agree. Then the memory of Clio's escapade with Harry Churchill stiffened her resolve. Seniority should not be set aside on a foolish child's whim, and the need to get Julia settled was far more urgent than allowing Clio to do as she pleased. In the heady atmosphere of a foreign city, Julia's absurd reluctance to commit herself might soon be overcome. Certainly she had all but exhausted the possibilities at home.

'It seems to me that you are a great deal too eager to see the world before you have learned how to behave in it,' she said repressively to Clio. 'No, do not argue: my mind is made up. When you give me proof that you can be trusted to conduct yourself in an adult and responsible manner I will consider allowing you more freedom, but until that time I prefer to keep you under my eye. Do not mention the matter again unless you wish to vex me.'

Turning to Julia, she added, 'Are you not ashamed to try to shift your responsibilities on to a mere child? You and Laura together should be perfectly capable of managing affairs for Papa, and I shall be very much disappointed if he has cause to complain of neglect. Come, Joshua.'

She took her son by the hand and quitted the schoolroom, leaving Julia crestfallen, Laura complacent, and Clio seething with rebellion.

Had she been able to read her third daughter's thoughts at that moment, there is no doubt that Mrs Hardy would have taken even more stringent precautions than usual to permit no opportunity for the Devil to indulge his favourite pastime, but in the three weeks that followed she was kept far too busy packing, sorting and mending to pay much heed to Clio's unusual quietness. She could only be thankful that due to Lord Amherst's largesse, distributed by way of his punctilious secretary, money was at last available to pay the family's most pressing debts. She was also able to equip Julia and Laura with some of the frills and furbelows necessary to young ladies of fashion, but just when she was congratulating herself that all was going smoothly, with the embarkation three weeks ahead and the consent of Laura's good-natured godmother, Lady Arbuthnot, to act as chaperon to the girls during the voyage easily obtained, an unlooked-for difficulty presented itself. Jane, the nimble-fingered tiring maid who had attended her elder daughters ever since Julia put her hair up, showed uncharacteristic mulishness when told she must accompany her young mistresses to Portugal.

'Sail over the sea? I dursen't, ma'am,' she said, twisting her apron in her thin fingers. 'Not after what became of our Ned.'

'What can you mean?'

Mrs Hardy had supposed that Jane, coming from a fishing village on the east coast, would be well accustomed to the notion of life afloat, but in this she was mistaken. Jane's brother and three of her cousins had perished at sea, giving her so profound a distaste for the element that even the promise of a rise in her wages did nothing to shake her resolution.

'He were drownded, poor Ned, when the *Island Maid* went down, and that not six months after the pressers stole him from home,' said Jane in a shaking voice. 'Fair broke my father's heart it did, ma'am. I vowed then I'd never set sail on a ship, not if Saint Paul himself went on his knees to beg me. I'd as soon set foot in a debtor's gaol as on one o' they accursed hulks.'

'The *Niobe* is nothing like a hulk, foolish girl,' scolded Mrs Hardy, much put out. 'She is a military transport of the most modern description. You would have nothing to fear.'

'Ah, but they gurt storms that do blow up in a twinkling care nothing for modern descriptions,' said Jane shrewdly. 'I see'd them with my own eyes, waves high as a church steeple, tossing ships about like so many driftwood spars. 'Sides' – she blushed suddenly, smoothing her apron – 'Dick Henshaw and I, we hopes to be married come Michaelmas.'

'Married at Michaelmas? And you not turned eighteen? I never heard such nonsense,' cried Mrs Hardy, even more put out by this revelation. 'Why, you can have nothing saved yet, and if you expect Dick Henshaw to support you on a stableboy's pay, you will find yourself greatly mistaken.'

Jane looked at the floor, her lips set in a mulish line. ''Tisn't everyone wishes to live above their station,' she muttered.

Fortunately Mrs Hardy was not attending. 'I wish to hear no more of this foolishness,' she said decisively. 'If I did not think you were a sensible, steady girl I would not have put you in a position of responsibility in my household, but since I have done so, I wish you will show yourself worthy of my trust.' She paused, then added meaningly, 'I am sure Dick Henshaw would not be pleased if I was obliged to dismiss you without a character, now would he? He might even think it advisable to look elsewhere for a wife.'

Though veiled, the threat was there, and Jane's spirit quailed. To be dismissed without a character was the worst that could befall a girl of her calling, bringing shame on her family and ruin upon herself.

'No, ma'am,' she murmured miserably.

'Of course not. You will find when you return home that you are in a better position to marry, and Dick Henshaw will esteem you all the more for it. You need have no fear of losing him to Another in your absence, for I will myself speak to his employer and make the position clear.' She paused, expecting some show of gratitude for this assurance, but Jane kept her gaze obstinately downcast. 'There's not the least need to snivel, girl,' added Mrs Hardy as Jane's apron was again pressed into service. 'Many servants would think themselves fortunate to have this opportunity to see the world. Travel broadens the mind, you know, and I daresay when the time comes you will be as reluctant to leave Portugal as you are now to go there.'

Still the maid's woebegone expression showed she considered herself anything but fortunate.

'Now remember,' warned Mrs Hardy, 'I will hear no more complaints. Miss Julia's sensibilities are very delicate and must not be upset. If I learn that you have been worrying her with your tales of woe, I shall be deeply vexed. Very well: you may go.'

Really, she thought as Jane left the room, servants could be most trying. For every inch you gave them you might be sure they would demand an ell. It was even questionable if it was wise to treat them with the degree of consideration upon which dear Mr Hardy insisted. In her view, a firm hand obtained better service but this, she knew, was a point upon which she and her husband would never agree.

'What *is* the matter, Jane? Why have you been crying?' Seated at her dressing-table for the maid to brush her hair, Clio looked curiously at Jane's red and swollen eyes. 'Have you had a quarrel with Dick?'

Jane sniffed. 'No, miss.'

'Did Cook scold you? Come on, Jane. You know you can trust me.'

'Nothing ain't the matter, miss. Nothing that can be mended, that is.'

Unsatisfied, Clio watched the steady rise and fall of the brush. In her experience maids who wept and refused explanations very soon vanished from the household. She was fond of Jane, whose birthday fell in the same week as her own, making them almost twins, and hoped she would not suddenly disappear.

'Tell me,' she wheedled.

'Your ma wouldn't like it.'

'She wouldn't know.'

Jane shook her head. 'Give over, miss. I've enough to worrit me without your pestering.'

'Are you with child?' asked Clio in a low voice.

Jane banged the hairbrush on the dressing-table's polished

top, making jars and bottles dance. Her face turned a dusky red.

'Indeed I am not! I'm a respectable girl, Miss Clio, as you should know. There's no call for you to go insulting me.'

'I'm sorry,' said Clio, crestfallen but also relieved. 'I didn't mean to insult you. Laura told me –'

'Miss Laura!' exclaimed Jane with a wealth of hidden meaning. 'You didn't ought to go listening to none of her wicked tales.'

'I'm sorry,' said Clio again. 'It was just that when you said. . . .'

'I know very well what I said.' Jane picked up the brush with hands that trembled. She began to brush so hard that Clio flinched, but she was not prepared to let the matter rest.

'You must tell me. Trouble shared is trouble halved, you know. I won't speak of it to my sisters.'

Jane ruminated, working away more in the manner of a strapper than a lady's maid. Her breath caught on a little sob, and to Clio's consternation tears trickled suddenly down her thin cheeks. 'Your ma's sending me away,' she said.

'Sending you away? But that's – that's not fair. I mean, why should Mamma dismiss you if you are not – well, in a delicate –?' Clio floundered, aware that indignation had carried her too close to the forbidden topic.

'Your ma's not dismissing me, miss. Not in so many words, though she did say as how I'd lose my character if I didn't do as she bid me. But now I don't know as how I wouldn't rather lose that than my life in a watery grave.'

She sobbed and sniffed. At last the matter was plain and Clio regarded her with surprise. 'Do you mean you are afraid of the sea? You – a sailor's daughter?'

'Only a fool ain't afraid of the sea, miss.'

'Are you calling me a fool? I can swim. I am not afraid of it.'

'Them as can swim takes twice as long to drown, miss.'

'Oh, Jeremiah!' exclaimed Clio, laughing. 'You won't make me afraid of water, whatever you say.'

'That's 'cause you don't know it, miss,' said Jane obstinately. 'Swimming a stroke or two or catching mackerel from

Auguste's little boat ain't knowing the sea. The more you knows it the more you fears it, and that's a fact.'

Clio considered this. 'Don't you wish to go with my sisters?'

'That I don't, miss.'

'It will be a great adventure,' said Clio wistfully. 'Surely you think it is worth a little risk for the sake of seeing the world?'

'I can see as much as I want of the world without traipsing off to foreign parts,' said Jane. ''Sides, what's my Dick going to think? He wants to be married come Michaelmas. That hussy 'Melia Jones has been a-setting of her cap at him. With me gone, there'd be nought to stop her.'

'Would Dick betray you?' said Clio, shocked.

'Lord, miss, the likes of him don't think it no betrayal,' said Jane with a kind of weary wisdom. 'If Dick wishes to marry and the one he's promised to ain't there, what'll he do? Why, marry another, of course.'

In pensive silence, Clio allowed the hairbrushing to proceed. She could well understand Jane's reluctance to leave her handsome betrothed at Amelia Jones's mercy, yet could not help thinking her a trifle poor-spirited to abandon so easily the chance of adventure. Now if *she* were to be given the choice of going to sea – no matter how rough – or marrying a stableboy – no matter how handsome – she knew without a shadow of doubt which she would choose. But then, she wasn't Jane, nor Jane her.

It was at this point in her reflections that an idea came to Clio: an idea so simple and magnificent that she could only gasp at its perfection.

Would she? Could she?

Jane's face was hidden from her, since she had laid down the brush and begun to gather Clio's dark curls into a single plait. Clio fidgeted, ducking her head as she tried to read the maid's expression.

Would she? Could she?

'Hold still now, Miss Clio, do! I'm all behind with my work, what with gossiping to you,' grumbled Jane, sorry that she had disobeyed her mistress by unburdening herself. Not that she feared Miss Clio would tell on her; it was just that she should have known better than to suppose Clio capable of offering any solution to her problems.

For answer Clio twitched the plait from her fingers and swung round suddenly on her stool, cheeks flushed and eyes alight.

'Listen, Jane!'

She began to talk very fast and earnestly, pounding her fist on the tabletop for emphasis. Jane, with mouth slightly open and glazed eyes, listened as if mesmerized.

'Oh, Miss Clio! You are a one.'

Clio held her gaze. 'Will you do it?'

'I'd lose my place.'

'Would you rather lose Dick?'

Jane considered, her head bent. Clio saw some grand gesture was needed. 'If you'll do it, I'll let you choose anything you like from my jewel-box,' she offered recklessly.

'*Anything*, miss?'

'Anything.'

'I'll do it for your locket, miss,' said Jane, who was less simple than she looked.

Clio's hand flew to her throat. 'I said from my *jewel-box*.'

'There's nothing worth anything there,' said Jane with contempt. 'No, miss, I'll do it for the locket or not at all. You can please yourself.'

For a moment Clio hesitated. Harry had given her the locket, one June evening in the rose garden. How well she remembered the scent of musk-rose and new-mown hay! His dark eyes had been serious for once; his face sombre as he told her he was being sent away.

'Wear it as long as you love me,' he had whispered, and his bony boy's hands had trembled a little as he fastened the chain about her throat.

Equally solemnly she had given her promise. After Harry's departure, her mother tried to make her give up the locket, but unexpectedly her father had intervened.

'A promise is a promise, my love,' he had said quietly but so firmly that Mrs Hardy looked startled and made no further protest.

There the matter had rested. When news reached them of Harry's death, Laura had remarked that there was no need for Clio to go on wearing the locket; but precisely because she knew Laura was jealous, Clio kept it round her neck.

'Please yourself, miss,' repeated Jane, her covetous eyes on the trinket.

'Very well.' Without allowing herself time for regret, Clio unfastened the locket. Her neck felt curiously bare. 'Will you do it, then? Exactly as I say?'

Jane slipped the locket into the bosom of her dress and smiled beatifically.

'Oh, ar, Miss Clio, that I will. Just exactly as you say.'

2

Warmly wrapped in fur-lined pelisses, Julia and Laura leaned on *Niobe*'s rail to watch the lights of Portsmouth fade in the brief February dusk.

'Farewell, dear England!' sighed Julia. 'How many weary months must pass before I next set eyes on thee?'

The words were not intended as a question, nor did they draw a response. Laura had quickly tired of gazing into emptiness; from the tail of her eye she observed the animated group of officers clustered about the stern, their cigars red points in the gloom. The mast-head riding light shed its glow on broad shoulders and excited faces. From time to time a cigar-butt was tossed overboard, to extinguish itself in the dark swell. The rumble of voices was frequently punctuated by bursts of laughter.

It pleased her to see them steal covert glances in her direction, and know that part at least of their animation was due to the presence of females on board. Even before they sailed, word had spread among the male passengers that the newly-appointed Deputy Assistant Commissary to the 31st – 'Hamilton's Horse' as the regiment was generally known – was bringing his daughters to share the perils and glories of Peninsular warfare, and every man among them was resolved to make the voyage an agreeable one.

Warmed by their admiring glances, Laura could almost forget the strange effect the ship's motion was producing upon her insides.

'Come with me, girls. It is time we went below.' Lady Arbuthnot bustled towards them with the breeziness of the seasoned traveller. She was a plump, high-complexioned woman with rather more good nature than good sense, and was making the voyage to Lisbon for the second time, having passed the summer season in London, and remained to supervise the accouchement of her eldest daughter before returning to Lisbon, where her son Hugh, a stout young man with political ambitions, was attached to a diplomatic mission on behalf of the British government. As Laura's godmother and Mrs Hardy's dearest friend, Lady Arbuthnot had willingly agreed to chaperon the girls on the voyage, and so relieve Samuel of any anxiety on this head.

A little unsteadily, Julia and Laura left the rail and followed her down a steep narrow flight of steps within the heaving vessel. A strong and decidedly unpleasant smell assailed their nostrils: the ingredients were hard to define but prominent among them were tar and the odour of close-packed humanity. Laura wrinkled her nose and wished the floor would stop pitching. It was difficult to avoid cannoning into Julia at every step in the narrow passage.

The large airy cabin allocated for the accommodation of passengers had been divided in two equal parts by a canvas bulkhead. One half allowed the ladies ample room to spread their possessions, while Jane and Lady Arbuthnot's maid Johnson were to share a tiny cubbyhole under the companion-way. Into the second half of the cabin were crowded Samuel Hardy and six military men of assorted ranks and regiments, all returning to active service after home leave. The ship's carpenter had made shift to provide for this surplus of male passengers by stacking five bunks in such close proximity that no occupant could so much as sit up in bed without cracking his head against another's mattress. A hammock slung from hooks was allocated to Captain Stanley, an officer whose corpulence made him incapable of entering a bunk and the seventh, most junior member of the mess, a slim subaltern named Jones, was obliged to unroll his bedding in the space between bunks and mess-table and nightly risk being trampled on by his superior officers.

This crowding was borne with perfect good humour; there was not a man on board who would not have put up with far worse conditions sooner than deprive the ladies of one iota of their living room. Yet however hard they tried to suppress them, from time to time groans, exclamations, and muffled oaths penetrated the insubstantial partition, making Lady Arbuthnot flinch and advise her charges to cover their ears.

'Pay no heed,' she said, blushing. 'There are certain emphatic expressions peculiar to military men that ladies do well to ignore.'

Julia was careful not to catch her sister's eye, but Laura had other matters on her mind.

'Where is Jane?' she asked, staring about the cabin as if she expected the little maid to spring from a portmanteau or valise. Their clothes were unpacked; the bunks neatly turned down, but of Jane there was no sign.

'Please, miss, she've taken herself off to lay down,' volunteered Johnson, a sharp-featured middle-aged woman who had served Lady Arbuthnot long enough to be permitted a good deal of licence. She had wiry black hair and an air of smug self-righteousness. 'The idle baggage!' she added, too low for her mistress to hear.

Laura's colour rose. 'She has no business to be resting when I need her. Tell her to attend me at once.'

'Oh, leave the poor girl to sleep,' said Julia, who was herself becoming uncomfortably conscious of the boat's tossing. 'She may feel unwell.'

'That is no reason for her to neglect her duties.'

Johnson nodded vigorously. 'Forgive my speaking plain, miss, but that one don't hardly seem to *know* her duties. Whatever was your ma thinking of to send a raw girl like that to look after you?'

'Jane is an excellent maid,' said Julia rather haughtily.

Johnson snorted. 'Have she been with you long, then?'

'Four years, I suppose.'

'Four years! And she don't even know how to set about laying out a lady's things or turning down her bed!'

Julia and Laura exchanged puzzled glances. Such tasks were performed differently in different households, they knew, but it seemed strange that Johnson should hold their mother's methods in such open contempt.

'Tell Jane to come to us at once,' said Laura.

'Very good, miss.'

Julia shrugged, unwilling to enter into an argument. Her head had begun to ache fiercely. She cast herself down on her bunk without bothering to undress, and closed her eyes.

Johnson returned alone, her mouth compressed in a disapproving line.

'Where is Jane? Why doesn't she come?'

'Please, miss, she won't stir.'

'Johnson!' reproved her mistress.

'It's the truth, my lady. She says,' reported Johnson with the glee of one who sees a fellow heading for well-deserved retribution, 'she says if you wants her you must fetch her yourself.'

'The impudence!' Temporarily bereft of further speech, Lady Arbuthnot sank down on a stool, fumbling for her smelling salts.

'Very well, I *will* go to her,' said Laura with dangerous calm. She hurried from the cabin into the evil-smelling passage.

A curtain hung across the mouth of the dark cubbyhole allocated to the maids. She drew it aside, wishing she had thought to bring a lamp as she peered uncertainly into the gloom.

'Jane?'

A groan answered her.

'What is the matter? Are you unwell?' Anxiety began to tinge the anger in Laura's voice. 'Speak to me, Jane!'

Another groan issued from the back of the narrow space – a groan, or could it be a muffled laugh? Laura began to wish she had not embarked upon this mission. The maid was lying with her buttoned boots towards the opening, so well wrapped in her voluminous dark cloak that nothing of her face could be seen.

Short of hauling her out bodily, there seemed no way of making her emerge. Already Laura was conscious of an interested knot of seamen and passengers gathering at the head of the companionway.

'Listen to me, Jane,' she hissed, grasping the boot nearest to her and shaking vigorously. It kicked in protest, but Laura was a strong girl and held firm. 'If you don't get up and come with me at once, I'll make you sorry for it.'

Silence.

'Very well. I am going to fetch Papa.'

The boot became suddenly still, as if its owner had been given food for thought.

'Are you coming out?'

'How do you expect me to get up when you have hold of my foot?' demanded a well-known and aggrieved voice. Laura released the boot as if it had been red-hot.

'Clio!'

Considerably dishevelled, her shoulders shaking with nervous laughter, her sister emerged from the gloom. 'Oh, Laura! I thought I would die! I meant to keep secret all night, but when I heard you berating poor Jane and threatening to fetch Papa, I couldn't stay quiet another minute. Well! Are you pleased to see me?'

Despite her debonair tone, Clio was not at her ease.

'Are you pleased?' she repeated as Laura's face remained stony.

'Pleased? Why should I be pleased? How could you do such a thing? Have you no heart, no sense of shame? Mamma will be out of her mind with worry when she finds you gone.'

'I left her a letter.'

'A fine lot of use that will be!'

'Don't be cross, Laura. You cannot know how desperately I wished to come with you.'

Clio tried to take her sister's hand, but it was snatched away.

'Haven't I reason to be cross when you, to gratify your own selfish wishes, have deprived me and Julia of our maid? Who is going to dress our hair and mend our clothes when we reach

Portugal? Don't tell me you can do it, or I shall die laughing. What poor Papa will say when he finds how you have disobeyed him and smuggled yourself aboard, I tremble to think.'

'Don't tell him just yet,' pleaded Clio. 'I promise I will go to him and explain everything if you will wait until morning. Just let me keep the secret a few hours longer.'

Laura hesitated. She perceived clearly enough why Clio wished for these few hours' grace, for with every league *Niobe* sailed, it became less likely that Captain Masterman would consent to put about and disembark the stowaway. Yet why should she make herself accomplice to Clio's escapade?

'*Please*, Lulu!'

The unexpected use of the pet name, which Clio had not spoken since Laura quitted the schoolroom, brought a sudden rush of memories of the days before she felt it necessary to stand on her dignity with this younger sister: the time when she and Clio had been friends, not rivals.

'Oh, very well,' she said reluctantly, and was rewarded by a hug and a radiant smile.

'You are the best sister in the whole wide world!'

'Go on! Don't be more of a goose than you can help,' said Laura, not displeased. She gave Clio a friendly shove. 'Lie down and pull the covers over your head, and I will tell Julia I couldn't wake you.' She laughed suddenly. 'Poor Johnson! I wish you could have seen her face when she spoke of your efforts as a lady's maid. It was enough to turn the milk sour.'

'She called me a lazy baggage,' admitted Clio ruefully.

'She will be surprised when she finds out who you are,' observed her sister, and left her.

Feeling a need for fresh air before returning to the cabin, Laura climbed the short flight of steps to the deck. The knot of observers had melted away, and the first figure on whom her eyes fell was that of Captain Edward Greystone. He was standing beneath the riding light, smoking and quietly chatting to a brother officer while keeping a wary eye on the doorway as if he hoped Laura might come through it. Seeing her, both men bowed and extinguished their cigars. His companion made his excuses, and Captain Greystone fell into step beside Laura. They had made half a circuit of the deck before, observing her agitation, he felt emboldened to ask its cause.

Laura had agreed not to reveal her sister's presence to their father, but nothing had been said regarding Captain Greystone. With little hesitation she poured out the story. Already she had begun to regret her promise.

'So you think I should tell Papa? I fear that in concealing this escapade I am throwing away any chance of putting Clio ashore.'

Greystone ruminated, then gave it as his opinion that she had done the right thing. 'Smuggled herself aboard, you say? Dressed in the maid's clothes? Deuced well plucked 'un, your sister, damn me if she ain't!' he exclaimed with a vehemence she could not approve. 'Don't let 'em put her ashore. We can do with plenty of her kind in Portugal, believe me.'

It was not the reaction Laura wished for. Rather distantly she nodded and changed the subject, asking if he did not find himself intolerably cramped in his quarters.

'No, indeed. We shall do very well if it don't blow too hard,' he said, grinning. 'We've a capital mess set up, all right and tight. We elected the Colonel our President, only to be expected, and your father in charge of provisions – good practice, you know! I am to undertake responsibility for cellarage: between us we have some dozens of good wine and porter.'

He rubbed his hands, consulted his timepiece, and announced he must make shift to attend to his duties with the steward, since the gentlemen were to dine in an hour. Laura allowed him to escort her to her cabin and, her dinner hour being long past, could not avoid the wistful reflection that the gentlemen's eating arrangements sounded a good deal more promising than their own.

The prospect of going hungry loomed even larger when, on entering the cabin, she found both Julia and Lady Arbuthnot already prostrate, with Johnson applying cologne to her mistress's temples. Her questions regarding dinner were greeted by faint moans.

'Don't speak to me of food,' begged Lady Arbuthnot.

Since she had no wish to offend her godmother, Laura bowed to necessity and stretched herself on her bunk. Soon a perfect stillness reigned in the ladies' cabin, while from beyond the partition came the agreeable chink of bottle on glass and a steadily rising buzz of conversation.

Few professions are so devoted to the dissemination of gossip as the military, and there are few breeding grounds for rumour more fertile than on board ship. In strict confidence, Captain Greystone regaled his friend Captain Legge of the 4th Dragoons with the story of Clio's escapade. Legge repeated it, embellished to his taste, to young Jones with the soup, and Jones shyly passed it on to Surgeon Hammond with the fish.

By the time decanters of port were circulating among the gentlemen, the tale was known to everyone except Samuel Hardy himself. After drinking toasts to the King and Lord Wellington, Colonel Simpson as President of the Mess rose to thump the table again.

'Gentlemen! In recognition of the honour done us by their presence aboard this vessel, I ask you to join me in a special toast. The Ladies!'

'The Ladies, God bless 'em!' echoed the diners with fervour, draining their glasses. The frail partition trembled.

Captain Greystone, a little top-heavy with wine and good fellowship, hauled himself upright, turning his flushed face towards the President.

'Permit me, sir, to propose a toast to Mr Samuel Hardy, who has left the safety of his fireside to brave the perils of military life, and brought with him to delight our eyes and elevate our hearts three of the fairest jewels old England can boast, that trio of Graces, and the daughters of the Regiment, the Misses Hardy! In bumpers, if you please, gentlemen, with three times three!'

As the cheers died away, Samuel's voice made itself heard above the din. 'Much obliged to you, gentlemen, and you may be sure I will do all in my power to discharge my duties faithfully.' He paused, then added with an air of surprise, 'I must confess myself puzzled by your reference to a *trio* of Graces, Greystone. Only two of my daughters have accompanied me. Are you referring perhaps to their excellent chaperon, Lady Arbuthnot?'

There was a shout of laughter, swiftly hushed.

'If I have been misinformed, sir, I apologize,' said Colonel Simpson a little uneasily.

Captain Greystone, in whom the wine had destroyed all inhibitions, broke into a braying laugh.

'You'll discover three daughters aboard in the morning, sir!'

Samuel looked startled. 'Is this true?'

'Upon my honour, sir. I had it from Miss Laura's own lips,' said Greystone, still laughing. Belatedly he recalled that the matter was by way of being secret and added hastily, 'You must forgive me, sir, if I have spoken out of turn, but so great was my admiration for Miss Clio's spirit that I could not suppress it. Are you not proud of her?'

'Proud?' exclaimed Samuel angrily. 'No, sir, I am not. Far from sharing your sentiments I declare I am quite mortified to find that a child of mine could stoop to such deceit.'

He rose and bowed to Colonel Simpson, and the diners fell suddenly silent. 'Forgive me, sir, for allowing family concerns to spoil a pleasant evening, but I must beg you to excuse me. An urgent matter requires my attention.'

As the cabin door closed behind him a buzz of talk and speculation broke out. Bets were laid on whether or not the ship's master would heed Mr Hardy's demand to return to port, but those well acquainted with Captain Masterman's character were convinced their money was safe enough.

'After waiting ten days for a favourable wind, nothing less than a direct order from Lord Bathurst would persuade him to put about,' was the general verdict. 'We'll keep our Three Graces as far as Lisbon, never fear!'

The painful interview which took place next morning between Samuel and his third daughter was one neither of them would soon forget. However, since Captain Masterman justified the opinion of the officers' mess and refused even to consider disembarking the stowaway, there was little Samuel could do but order Clio to remain in her cabin with nothing but bread and water to eat, and the prospect of being sent back to England by the next boat that sailed from Lisbon.

'Very likely Papa will change his mind when we get there,' whispered Julia consolingly as she smuggled a slice of roast pork to Clio to supplement the punishment diet. 'I will ask Auguste to intercede for you.'

'Thank you,' said the chastened Clio. She crammed the last morsel of pork into her mouth and kissed her sister. The hours of repentance seemed very long as she lay in her berth listening to the chatter and bustle she could not join.

Before long, however, chatter and bustle gave way to groans and plaintive cries of 'Steward!' as *Niobe* announced her arrival in the Bay of Biscay in a manner most uncongenial to her passengers. Overnight the brisk north-westerly which had borne them swiftly from Portsmouth became a gale in which even those who believed their sea-legs acquired were rapidly forced to revise this opinion.

Sails split, timbers creaked and cracked as the ship staggered in mountainous seas. All canvas beyond a storm staysail was hastily run down and the piteous neighs of horses half suffocated in the holds echoed through the boat.

Johnson was the first to retire whey-faced to her lair; then in rapid succession Julia, Laura and Lady Arbuthnot took to their berths. The sounds beyond the partition left no doubt that the gentlemen were in similar straits. Only young Jones, whose frail physique belied a robust digestion, remained capable of independent movement, but his reports on matters above decks were hardly reassuring to the sufferers. Two of the crew were lost overboard when a wave smashed over the bows; the longboat was washed away and the fore topmast splintered.

'The Captain says in all his years at sea he has never encountered a worse blow,' said Jones lugubriously. 'Unless the wind soon moderates, we'll be lucky not to lose all the horses.'

Before this calamity could occur, however, as if in answer to prayer the weather became calmer. Like bedraggled birds, the passengers inspected their plumage and began, cautiously, to preen. Most contented themselves with a mere cat's wash, but Captain Greystone who was something of a dandy (and had not stirred from his berth for three whole days) felt impelled to refresh himself thoroughly with soap and water, a servant standing near at hand with razor and strop, and a clean set of linen at the ready.

With no small difficulty, for the ship still heaved in an erratic swell, he had removed his beard and succeeded in divesting himself of his lower garments when a sudden roll flung him heavily against the canvas bulkhead. Instinctively he clutched at it for support, emitting a startled oath as shaving water upset over his blankets while he strove to regain his equilibrium. Before the servant could come to his aid a second, even deeper roll completed the mischief.

A rending tear was heard as the partition gave way. Lady Arbuthnot, dozing in her berth, opened her eyes just in time to see the unclothed form of an officer she had already characterized as a sad rattlepate catapulted through the air to land head foremost in her god-daughter's bunk.

'Sir!' she shrieked in outrage, while Laura screamed and vainly tried to pull the blankets over her. 'How dare you violate our privacy? Get back where you belong this instant!'

This command poor Captain Greystone was temporarily unable to obey. Stunned by the force of his fall, he lay moaning on top of Laura, who pushed him in the chest with both hands and redoubled her screams.

'Help! Murder!' cried Lady Arbuthnot. 'Look away, girls! Johnson, for God's sake throw some covering over the man!'

Pandemonium reigned in the cabin as more officers sprang to the ladies' aid. The canvas partition to which Greystone still clung did in fact mask some portions of his person from their scandalized eyes, but it was not until Julia, laughing hysterically, had snatched a blanket from her own bunk and flung it over the intruder that some semblance of order was restored to the scene.

The mere removal of the culprit was not enough to satisfy Lady Arbuthnot, who declared that no gentleman guilty of such behaviour should be allowed in a cabin adjacent to young ladies, and demanded that Captain Greystone be banished forthwith. The peacemaking efforts of both Samuel Hardy and Captain Masterman himself were hardly able to convince her of the impossibility of complying with this demand, but eventually she agreed to accept Captain Greystone's apology on condition he forsook his bunk and slept henceforth on the cabin floor.

Nor was this the only punishment meted out to the Captain, for the incident had served to spoil relations between him and Laura. During the rest of the voyage she refused to speak to her former swain, and the jests of his brother officers did nothing to console him for this loss of prestige.

It was with profound feelings of relief in every breast that the passengers gathered on deck just after dawn on the last Tuesday in February, 1811, to watch an enchanted city of gleaming white houses, steeples, towers and gilded domes rise magically from the morning mist as the storm-battered *Niobe* glided to her anchorage in the mouth of the river Tagus.

3

The illusion of enchantment did not survive closer acquaintance with the city of Lisbon. As they jolted up steep narrow streets in a springless cart, followed by another on which was piled their mountain of baggage, the girls looked curiously about them, exclaiming at the tall, close-packed buildings and dark-skinned townspeople, so exotically and strangely dressed. Men of the labouring classes went barefoot, their loose shirts brightly sashed above wide short unmentionables which ended just below the knee. Their betters were better covered but no less curiously attired, strutting in cork-heeled shoes with huge flashing buckles, their sleeves slashed and waistcoat buttons as big as saucers. The brims of their hats were so ridiculously large that the outline presented was that of a mushroom.

As for the ladies....

'Hoops!' cried Clio, nudging Laura's attention to a trio of stately black-clad dames swaying past, their enormous skirts entirely blocking the street. No one had worn hoops in England in their lifetime: it was like seeing a history book come to life.

Less pleasant a reminder of times past was the smell from open gutters and heaps of decaying refuse. The girls held handkerchiefs to their noses and tried to breathe shallowly, but there was no escape from the stench. They eyed the hordes of beggars with horrified fascination. Some were blind, some legless, some so contorted it was hard to believe them human. Sunk in lethargy, they hardly troubled to stretch out a hand for alms, yet Laura noted that the hurrying passers-by gave freely to these unfortunates.

'Poor creatures! They should be locked away where we did not have to look at them!' said Julia, whose vaunted piety had yet to undergo a practical test.

'Would they be less wretched if you could not see them?' asked Laura robustly.

Julia gave her a reproachful look. 'This is the dirtiest place I was in in all my life. I trust Papa does not intend to set up house here.'

'No, no. Ve vill find better lodgings outside the city,' said Auguste decidedly. The Alsatian accent lay heavy on his speech despite his long sojourn in England. Auguste had been a chubby flaxen-haired twelve-year-old when he entered the Marquis de la Tour du Pin's service as a knife-boy, and though he was now near fifty and his hair more silver than flaxen, his blue eyes twinkled as shrewdly as ever and his appetite for life's good things had increased rather than diminished with the years. Nor could his worst enemy accuse him of lack of energy in pursuit of his comforts. Auguste had many faults, but his overriding virtue was devotion to the family he had adopted as his own. As soon as he heard of Samuel Hardy's appointment he made it clear that he expected to accompany him.

Though of limited education, he wrote a clear hand and his exceptional dexterity with figures made him an admirable purveyor to any organization, civil or military. In this respect he was better qualified for the post of Deputy Assistant Commissary than his master, and it must be admitted that Mrs Hardy had watched his departure with almost more regret than her husband's, since for as long as she could remember, Auguste had been the household's mainstay.

To Clio he had made no secret of his motives. 'The man who holds the key to the stores holds the key to his fortune,' he grinned. He rubbed thumb and fingers together in a characteristic gesture. 'To feed this great army it vill be necessary to buy constantly, and each time a commissary spends gold a trifle sticks to his fingers. It is the custom.'

'Do you suppose Papa knows of this custom?' Clio found it hard to imagine gold sticking to her father's fingers. In her experience it had the habit of slipping through them like sand.

'Ah!' Auguste shook his head indulgently. 'It vill not be necessary to trouble your Papa about such small matters.'

She was glad of this assurance. Between her father and Auguste there existed a respect based on complete lack of understanding. Samuel thought Auguste an admirable fellow; it was a puzzle to him how he could keep the family supplied without needing money to do it. 'I don't know where we'd be without Auguste,' he often said. 'In Queer Street, most likely!'

On his side, Auguste reserved for his employer the indulgence usually accorded to the half-witted, and saw it as his duty to protect Mr Hardy from the worst consequences of his high-minded improvidence. Diametrically opposed in temperament, they suited one another very well.

It was Auguste who made himself responsible for extracting the family's baggage from the hold and hiring carts to carry it. Auguste, likewise, had discovered in conversation with other officers' servants where the best lodgings were to be had. Now he directed the muleteers to drive beyond the city's bounds, and as they left the crowded noisome streets and trotted down a white dust road bordered with white laburnum, all the cart's occupants breathed more freely.

After their cramped life on board *Niobe* the sun and sweet air were intoxicating. Among the glistening dark leaves of lemon and orange trees, fruit hung like golden lamps on some branches, whilst from others white blossom filled the air with a heady, incomparable perfume. Even the humblest house they passed had its trellis of vines over the verandah, and the small gardens were neatly cultivated with vegetables and bright flowers. Compared with England's winter-grey landscape, it seemed a paradise.

To the girls' regret, the first two lodgings recommended by Auguste's informants proved unsatisfactory. Wilting in the unaccustomed warmth, they watched the ominous lengthening of his upper lip; the firm, decided headshake.

'This is no good, sir,' he said confidentially to Samuel.
'Why not? It seems quite adequate to me.'
'Adequate is no good.'
'Oh, I don't know.'
Auguste said with great firmness, 'An officer who is not vell lodged is not vell respected. This house is too small. The furniture is poor and the servants cannot be trusted.'

Certainly the cook and maidservants were old and ill-favoured. How Auguste could deduce their degree of honesty from their looks was something he did not divulge.

Samuel sighed, but followed his usual practice of leaving decisions to others. With a curt nod towards the owner of the house, Auguste commanded the muleteers to drive on.

The second house belonged to a priest and pleased him no better; but when the carts halted for the third time at the end of a chestnut avenue guarded by a high iron gate, neither Samuel nor his daughters could repress cries of pleasure. The elegant white *quinta* with its mosaic courtyard and tinkling fountain seemed more like a fantasy from the Arabian Nights than a mere billet. Hardly daring to glance at Auguste for fear he would find hidden faults, Clio, Laura and Julia hurried to explore the cool airy rooms, handsomely appointed with polished oak and olive furniture. There was a rose-trellised arbour and a charming small cloister.

It was the summer residence of a Portuguese nobleman who had fled to Brazil with the Prince Regent shortly before the French invaded his country. Though deserted by its owner for the best part of four years, the *quinta* showed no signs of neglect: the garden was well tended and the floors shone. In the library were enough leather-bound volumes to keep Samuel happy throughout any number of winter evenings, and thither he vanished, leaving Auguste to his tour of inspection. With majestic tread he processed from stables to coach-house, from bakehouse to vineyard while the girls waited anxiously for his verdict.

'Oh, it is perfect! If Auguste will not let us stay here I will die!' exclaimed Julia.

Happily no such dramatic measures were called for. In the

cool, high-ceilinged kitchen they found Auguste beaming approval at a handsome dark-eyed cook, whose husband stood behind her in a pleasing attitude of subjection. Three little maids completed the domestic staff: all were young and pretty.

'Ve stay here, sir. These are good people and the young ladies vill be comfortable. I do not think ve find better lodgings in Lisbon,' said Auguste, and the girls sighed with relief.

'So long as you think it suitable, I am prepared to accept your choice.' Samuel tore his eyes briefly from the copy of *Antiquitas Romana* which he had taken down from its shelf. The matter of where he laid his head was to him of no more moment than with what he filled his belly. So long as the one was rested and the other satisfied, he was perfectly indifferent to how it was done. The girls were more open in their enthusiasm.

'It is beautiful – quite a palace!' said Julia, forgetting the shortcomings of Lisbon in her pleasure at taking possession of this new home. 'I vow I should like to remain here for ever.'

Under Auguste's energetic direction the baggage was soon unloaded, rooms opened up and more servants engaged. Two days later, Samuel rode his new horse to report to the offices of the Commissary-General, where Assistant Commissary Matheson, a florid jovial Scotsman, greeted him warmly and invited him to partake of some breakfast while he outlined his immediate duties.

'I own I am delighted to see you, Mr Hardy, for since my poor colleague Mr Smallbone died of the ague my staff has been overwhelmed with work.'

The British Army had withdrawn from Spain to Portugal the previous autumn and for the past four months had been cantoned in and around Lisbon, protected from the encircling French by the defensive Lines of Torres Vedras.

'I will not disguise from you, sir, that Lord Wellington's policy in obliging the Portuguese to desert their homes and lay waste the countryside presents the Commissariat with peculiar problems,' went on Matheson, hospitably loading his visitor's plate. 'Since there is hardly a bullock left within a hundred miles, I have to rely largely on our own ships for supplies, and though there can be no doubt – no doubt at all – that the French army's situation is very much worse than our own, I confess I am puzzled to know how we may maintain our people here another week, let alone another month. As for keeping the outposts supplied – which is my particular concern – why, it would be hard to exaggerate the perils and exertions of bringing them the bare minimum to support life!'

Despite this scarcity, the Assistant Commissary's own table was handsomely charged with ham, sausages, a roast goose, confits, white bread, and a large silver pot of chocolate simmering over a spirit-lamp. Auguste eyed the room's appointments with open admiration. Clearly Mr Matheson enjoyed a high standard of comfort in return for his perils and exertions.

While the officers breakfasted, Auguste took himself off to the servants' quarters and acquired much useful information.

Samuel emerged pensive and somewhat bewildered from his interview.

'I am to relieve Mr Wilson as Deputy Assistant Commissary in charge of the depot at Mafra, and keep the observation posts beyond it supplied,' he said in reply to Auguste's question. 'As soon as a general advance is ordered, I must be ready to march to Rio Maior, and am charged with assembling a train of mules and bullock-carts with their drivers, to carry biscuit to the outposts at Arruda. There are waybills to be checked and accounts to be signed.... Upon my soul, Auguste, I hardly knew what I was undertaking when I agreed to this appointment!'

It was clear to Auguste that Assistant Commissary Matheson had been indulging in the time-honoured practice of impressing a new recruit. It would be necessary to strike a balance between allowing his master to think his duties easy, and seeing him despair at difficulties.

'*Ne vous inquietez pas, monsieur*,' he said soothingly. 'It is natural all seems complicated at first. In a few days ve vill know more exactly how matters stand.'

'Where in the world am I to find bullock-carts?' said Samuel distractedly.

Auguste smiled. 'Leave it to me. If there are carts to be found, you may be sure I vill find them.'

'You are a good fellow, Auguste,' said Samuel with relief. 'Damn me if I'd know what to do without you.'

Auguste was as good as his word. A pleasant routine soon established itself, whereby Samuel Hardy visited the interesting sites and antiquities in the neighbourhood of Lisbon and made careful sketches, while his clerk took charge of all commissariat duties.

Delicate attentions and well-judged compliments to Senhora Lopez, the handsome cook, rapidly made Auguste a favourite, giving him access to an apparently limitless tribe of her cousins, nephews and brothers-in-law to run errands, chop wood, and keep the household supplied with fresh food and garden produce denied to most British officers. They also supplied him with information.

The reservoir of goodwill felt by the Portuguese towards their liberators, which had overflowed so bountifully when the British Army entered their country in 1808, had by the spring of 1811 fallen dangerously low. Though it was generally recognized that the British did not rape and plunder like the French, and were under strict orders to pay for the goods they wrested from the peasants, yet a certain cold superiority of manner, a tendency to mock at customs differing from their own and to take as their right what was offered from generosity ensured that even if respected they were not loved. Besides, they were heretics, condemned to burn in eternal flames. Goodwill became reserve, which in turn was replaced by sullen resentment as the British troops stayed on and on.

Auguste's manner was neither stiff nor self-righteous, and it did not escape Senhora Lopez and her friends how regularly he attended Mass. A little flattery, a judicious dispensation of trifles such as scissors and cutlery which the Commissariat would never miss was soon repaid with information about all sorts of useful commodities which the prudent Portuguese had hidden from their allies.

Auguste did not make his master party to this information:

far from it. From time to time he would quietly absent himself from the *quinta*, always returning with a few laden mules or an extra bullock-cart whose driver was prepared to work for the British in return for a dollar a day.

Samuel knew better than to question Auguste's coming and going, and was content to regard the spoils of such forays as manna from Heaven. Clio yearned to know how Auguste obtained the unobtainable but he would not enlighten her.

For Clio the weeks after their arrival in Portugal were disappointing and frustrating. Caught in the awkward age between schoolroom and ballroom, she watched with envy as Julia and Laura were swept into Lisbon's social whirlpool where Julia floated like a beautiful butterfly, buoyed up by gauzy wings, and Laura swam strongly, with encouragement and support from her godmother.

Lady Arbuthnot knew everyone, went everywhere. Nothing, she declared to Samuel, would give her greater pleasure than to take his elder daughters under her wing, for two more charming, pretty-behaved girls she had never seen. Clio? No. She would prefer not to feel responsible for Clio.

The large imbalance between unattached young officers in Lisbon and females to entertain them would ensure, she said, that neither Julia nor Laura knew a moment's dullness. In this she was right. The girls were inundated with invitations to parties, balls, dinners and military reviews, assemblies and plays, besides the unending round of social calls.

'How can you bear to see the same people at every ball?' Clio taunted. 'It sounds very tame to me.'

'You would not think so if you were allowed to come,' responded Laura. 'Only imagine! We have not been here above three weeks and already I have received four proposals.'

Poor Captain Greystone had never recovered the ground lost by his unlucky vaulting act. Now it was Hugh Arbuthnot, her godmother's son, who led the field among Laura's suitors; Julia's heart remained as untouched as ever.

Unable to bear the smug self-satisfaction on Laura's face, Clio ran away to talk to the maids in the kitchen. Already she could understand most of what they said, and her linguistic efforts were encouraged by her father and Auguste.

'If we are ordered up-country, a knowledge of Spanish and Portuguese will be of great value,' said Samuel, and supplied his daughters with grammars and a dictionary.

'*I* have no wish to travel up-country in a dirty, screeching bullock-cart,' said Laura, tossing her head. 'I shall ask Lady Arbuthnot if I may stay with her if Papa is obliged to leave Lisbon.'

For the moment, at least, such a move seemed unlikely. Outside the defensive Lines of Torres Vedras, Marshal Masséna's army waited like a pack of wolves – starving wolves, indeed, could not have ravaged the countryside more savagely. Everything that could be eaten had been eaten, for every convoy of supplies dispatched from Madrid to Masséna's troops fell victim to guerrilla bands long before it reached the hungry French. Yet Masséna's soldiers seemed able to live on air. Despite all reports of the privations they were suffering they refused to withdraw.

No more had been said about sending Clio home, but she was careful to avoid attracting her father's attention. This was not difficult: wrapped in his dreams of Roman legions, he paid little heed to his daughters' doings beyond asking if they had yet visited this or that aqueduct or Roman theatre.

The awe with which Commissary Matheson had filled him on his first visit had soon evaporated. Thanks to Auguste's success in discovering food where none was thought to exist, Mr Matheson changed his tune towards his new colleague and no longer sought to burden him with the worst of the work. Instead he was devious enough to try to lure Auguste into his own service, but the ruse misfired. An urgent appeal to Lord Amherst resulted in a stinging rebuke to Matheson, soon followed by his departure.

He was replaced by a man of very different calibre, Assistant Commissary Gregory, a stooping, mild-mannered Londoner whose interest in classical remains bid fair to rival Samuel's own. Still more responsibility drifted into Auguste's eager hands as the two scholars neglected the present for the past. It was a state of affairs that suited all parties.

Alone in the rose-trellised arbour one morning, Clio looked up from her grammar on hearing a most welcome, if unexpected, voice.

'Clio! By all that's wonderful! I was told I might discover you here.' He approached and stood before her. 'Don't tell me you have forgotten me or I shall die of vexation,' he said, laughing. She looked up and saw a tall, well-set-up young officer dressed in the striking dark green uniform of a Light Dragoon.

'How could I forget you? I am so very pleased to see you, Robert,' said Clio, clasping his hand warmly. 'I did not know you were in Lisbon.'

'I rode over as soon as I heard you were here.' His smile faded. He said, 'I wanted to see you alone, to... to offer my condolences. How well I understand your loss!'

Tears sprang to her eyes. Since Harry's death no one had spoken so frankly of it to her. 'A loss you and I share,' she said in a choked voice.

The young officer nodded gravely, his long face falling into sombre lines. Though the two were as unlike as chalk and cheese, Robert Cole had been Harry's greatest friend, the faithful follower in all his mad enterprises and ally against authority. Orphaned at an early age, Robert had inherited a large fortune and the responsibility for several brothers and sisters, all of which had given him an air of unchildish solemnity when Clio first knew him. Contact with Harry had changed that, and while his exuberant spirits encouraged Robert to take life more lightly, the latter had in his turn acted as a brake on Harry's recklessness. When their schooldays were over, they had joined the 23rd Light Dragoons together, and it was Robert who had carried Harry from the ravine at Talavera after the disastrous cavalry charge.

He had changed a good deal in the two years since she last saw him. The gangling, uncertain boy had become a handsome man whose frogged and braided uniform suited him well, though his dark vulnerable eyes and sensitive mouth remained just as she remembered.

'You don't mind my speaking of Harry?' he said anxiously.

'On the contrary, you cannot imagine how glad I am to hear his name. It was strange: when he was killed, no one would speak to me about him. It was as if they preferred to pretend he had not existed. I never heard anything about the battle – or how he died.'

'Shall I tell you? I saw it all, you know.'

When she nodded he took her hand, and sat beside her on the wooden bench. He said with remembered anger, 'It was a bad business. If the Spaniards had supported us as they promised we should not have suffered half the losses. Even before we reached Talavera de la Reyna our men were on half rations and our poor horses could hardly raise a gallop after marching for a month. Where was the food and forage they had sworn to deliver? Empty promises!'

With an effort he mastered his indignation and went on more moderately, 'Lord Wellington saw that Talavera could be his sole defensive position, for beyond to Madrid the ground is perfectly flat. He swore he would not continue towards the capital unless he received the supplies promised to us, and halted at Talavera. What did that damned old stiff-necked fool General Cuesta do then?'

'I cannot tell you,' she said, smiling despite herself.

Robert said a trifle guiltily, 'I beg you will excuse my language. After so many months soldiering, a man's tongue runs away with him.'

'I assure you that after ten days aboard a military transport nothing you can say will shock me! Pray continue. What did General Cuesta do?'

'Why, he continued to march alone with his ill-disciplined rabble of an army,' said Robert disgustedly. 'We took up our position on the bank of the Portina stream, between the town and the mountains, and before the day was done, back came Cuesta and his Spanish rabble, howling that the French were at their heels. Half of them fled through the town and that was the last we saw of them. The rest were persuaded to take up a secure position flanked by our fellows, but that didn't stop four of their regiments breaking and running when they heard the first cannonade – even though it came from their own guns!'

'Are they such cowards?'

'Not so much cowards as badly led. Between pride and mulishness and sheer ignorance of the most basic military tactics, the behaviour of the Spanish High Command is beyond belief. Harry used to say the men would fight bravely enough if they could be relieved of their generals, and of course he understood them better than most.'

After the mention of Harry's name he fell silent, regarding her a little anxiously; when she showed no further inclination to weep but merely nodded encouragement, he took up his tale.

'We of the 23rd Light Dragoons were with Anson's Brigade on the Northern Plain, facing the stream. The French attacked at daybreak, but we were held in reserve until late in the afternoon, and damned hot it was, without water or shade, waiting for the trumpet to sound. Harry had his best mare, Black Bess. Do you remember Bess? My charger was lame, so I rode a Portuguese remount I called Dobbin, a handsome enough beast but with no turn of foot. There we waited most of the day. What with the smoke and dust and turmoil it was hard to see what was happening to our right, but at last an aide brought the message that though the Guards and the Legion were badly mauled, the 48th under General Hill had held the French attack in the centre. We gave them a cheer.

'Soon after came the order to charge and clear the valley before us. Harry and I started knee to knee, but before we went half a mile poor Dobbin was outpaced, and I could only watch what followed. I saw the Colonel on his grey, with Harry hard on his heels, going hell for leather at the French who had formed into a square when, without warning, the front of our line suddenly vanished! A gully concealed by long grass lay right across our path. Some horses flew it, some pulled up short and refused to leap, but a good many of our poor fellows plunged in head first, with Harry among them.'

'Did you see him fall?'

'The dust was too thick, but when I reached the spot it was clear enough what had happened. Old Dobbin, for all his slowness, was a clever beast and he managed to scramble over and join the survivors as they re-formed under Colonel Elley and Major Ponsonby.'

'Was the charge abandoned?' she asked as he fell silent.

He looked at her with a faraway stare, reliving the heat and thunder of that day. 'Abandoned? Not a bit of it! It's strange what you remember in a battle. When we rode forward again to charge the square, I wondered why the fellow beside me sat his horse so ill. Then I saw his head had been carried away by a shell. We broke through the infantry and put the Chasseurs supporting them to the right-about. When the guns on the heights opened up we knew our charge had carried the day, though at terrible cost to us.'

'And Harry?'

'I found him in the gully with his legs broken, stripped bare by those Spanish devils before he was dead. I had him carried to one of the churches used as a hospital, but after that I lost sight of him.'

'You lost him?'

He said sombrely, 'Unless you have been in a battle you can have no idea of the chaos. Friend and foe, prisoners and wounded, horses, mules, oxen and baggage, ammunition – all are mingled in the most indescribable confusion. When I saw Harry a week later he had been taken to a convent, but fever had set in and he hardly knew me.'

'Then he – he died there?'

Robert nodded to spare her further pain. What good would it do to tell her Harry had died deserted by his comrades and abandoned by their allies? 'Take me with you, old fellow,' he had pleaded, his eyes fever bright, when Robert came to bid him farewell. 'That way I'll have a fighting chance, at least. Don't leave me for those French devils to kill as they please.' He had tried to raise himself but the effort was beyond him. He fell back with a groan. 'Take me with you, like a good chap!'

But the order had gone out. All British wounded were to remain in the care of the Spanish authorities while the British withdrew to meet Soult's new threat in their rear. There could be no question of carrying wounded on such a march. Better to let Clio believe Harry had died of his fever than admit the truth: that no sooner had the British withdrawn than the Spaniards abandoned Talavera, leaving the wounded from both armies to be massacred by the French.

Clio was silent for a while and he wondered if he had said too much. But when she finally turned her face to him he knew he had been right to tell her. Harry's ghost was laid.

'Thank you,' she said softly. 'I should always have wondered.... I am glad to know a friend was by him when he died.'

He did not disillusion her. Instead he picked up her book and rifled the pages. 'A Portuguese grammar!' he said in astonishment that was not wholly feigned. 'Am I to understand that you have become a bluestocking, Miss Clio?'

The ruse succeeded. Her melancholy vanished in a flashing smile. 'I hardly think I aspire to that description! The truth is I am so confoundedly dull here. Laura and Julia think of nothing but picnics and balls, and Papa is occupied with his affairs. I have been driven to learn the language as a means of passing the time.'

'With what success?'

'Oh, pretty fair! I understand most of what I hear, though writing is another matter.' She added longingly, 'I would like to converse with people outside the house, but Papa and Lady Arbuthnot are so determined to give me no chance to *get into mischief*, as they call it, that I am hardly allowed to leave the *quinta*.'

'For shame! Have you not visited Caluz, or Cintra, or the famous convent of the White Friars at Belem? We must remedy that at once. Permit an old friend to suggest some entertainment your Papa cannot disapprove. I will hire a riverboat and invite a party of friends to join me in a visit to the Palace of Cintra. Now, would not that be agreeable? We will glide along the

Tagus at our leisure and see life displayed along its banks.'

He was rewarded with another smile that transformed her elfin features into an elusive, fleeting beauty. A dryad, he thought distractedly, or a naiad? Some wild and altogether pagan spirit; he could not precisely decide which. His heart lurched in a most unsettling manner and he looked at her with new eyes.

In their past acquaintance, Harry had monopolized Clio's attention, and Robert had been content to stand aside, obeying his injunction to 'Make yourself agreeable to Miss Laura, there's a good fellow, while I talk to Clio, or Laura will be for ever interrupting us.'

Compared to Clio, Laura was an undemanding companion, and Robert would good-naturedly sit beside her and engage her in conversation, or allow her to lead him about the garden; and thus a myth had grown up that Mr Cole had an interest in Laura. But it was Clio who gave him that strange lift of excitement, sending his pulses racing when she looked at him. Clio with her sharp wits and ready tongue. She was made for Harry, of course... but with Harry dead affairs wore a different complexion.

'Oh, Robert! I should like it above all things!' she said with shining eyes.

'Then if I may call on you again, I will arrange the party without delay.'

'An old friend need not ask permission,' she said, laughing. 'You are welcome whenever you call. How long will the army remain in Lisbon? I own, I had not supposed soldiering to be so dull.'

He laughed at that. 'I daresay you will see enough action to please you before long. Though a poor captain can hardly hope to read the Commander-in-Chief's mind, there are signs that our days here may be numbered.'

'What do you mean? Has Lord Wellington ordered an advance?'

'I mean that even a French army cannot survive without supplies for ever. God knows what Masséna's poor devils have been eating these past months: their horses and mules, most likely. I spoke with Captain Coghlan this morning at his outpost. He had a report from some Portuguese peasants that the French were retreating, but he told me it must be a hum, since he could still see their pickets quite plainly through his glass.'

'Perhaps Captain Coghlan's glass requires a polish! My father's clerk, Auguste, says the peasants' reports are generally true.'

'Well, Coghlan has sent out a patrol. We shall hear soon enough if there is any truth in the rumour. So Auguste is with you? How well I remember him! The regiment which is fortunate enough to secure his services may expect to live on whatever fat there is in this poor land!'

He took his leave, promising to return very soon, and rode away firmly resolved that soon he would find more to share with Clio than memories of Harry.

4

Clio was right. Captain Coghlan's glass had indeed misled him, but the dozen straw-filled dummies dressed in French uniforms did not long deceive his patrol.

When their report confirmed that Masséna had stealthily withdrawn his army and was in retreat over the mountains towards Spain, the British followed at a respectful distance. Hungry and ill-equipped though they were, the French were still superior in numbers, and even with the reconstructed Portuguese regiments to support him, Lord Wellington preferred not to force a major engagement on Napoleon's wiliest marshal.

Behind the French army a hideous trail of devastated villages, murdered peasants and mutilated, hamstrung animals bore witness to the savage mood of Masséna's men.

'The devils! The cruel, barbarous devils! Can even God forgive them this?' exclaimed Samuel Hardy, his voice shaking with pity and horror as he halted one evening in the square of the pretty village of Vilha Nova in the hills beyond Cartaxo.

A week after the French began their retreat, the British commissaries had ventured to forage beyond the Lines of Torres Vedras. Auguste's informants spoke of Vilha Nova as a place likely to escape French depredations owing to its remote situation among inhospitable cliffs, and thither he and his master had ridden with a small escort and a saddlebag of gold, hoping to replenish Cartaxo's depleted stores.

Shadows were lengthening in this hour before sundown, and a cursory glance suggested that the people gathered in the cloistered square were celebrating a religious festival. Priests in rich embroidered vestments flanked a flower-decked carriage in which was seated an image of the Virgin, draped in tinsel robes, before whom men, women and children knelt in silent homage. More people thronged the cloisters and wrought-iron balconies around the square, leaning on one another's shoulders as they craned towards the procession.

An unremarkable scene such as you might see on any one of Portugal's numerous saints' days. It was only on closer approach that the utter silence and stillness of the packed figures struck a chill in the observer; only when he touched one of the stiff, unresponsive bodies and smelt the miasma of corruption hanging over the square did one realize that of the hundred or more persons gathered there, not one was alive.

Horses, humans, mules... even the cats and dogs had been butchered and arranged to form the gruesome tableau.

Samuel sat his horse rigidly, shocked as much by the mockery of death as by death itself. Behind him the escort muttered curses, their stolid British faces pale beneath the tan, while their horses snorted and fidgeted.

Auguste alone preserved his self-command. 'Search the houses,' he ordered, seeing Samuel needed time to recover. 'Bring out any food you find.'

'Them Frenchies won't have left enough to feed a flea,' muttered the corporal. He was rebuked with a steely flash of Auguste's light eyes.

'Fool! It is because the French could find nothing that they perpetrated this crime. Search everywhere. Pour water on the ground, and where it soaks in quickly, dig! Go on!' he snapped as they hesitated. 'Are you soldiers or children?'

Unwillingly they obeyed, shouting to keep up their spirits as they plunged through dark doorways and up narrow stairs. Auguste led the hunt, his senses keen as an animal's as he tapped on walls and examined the soil for signs of disturbance.

'Look at 'im! Sniffs out food like a bloody blood'ound,'

muttered a seasoned trooper, torn between disgust and admiration.

Samuel sat his horse without moving, transfixed by the horror of the square.

It was not long before Auguste's information proved correct. Hidden beneath a stack of timber, a dry well was discovered: sacks of grain and barrels of oil filled it to the brim. Auguste gave orders these should be hauled up and loaded on to the pack-mules. While it was being done he hurried to the church where Samuel, recovered from his shock, was examining the frescoes with a connoisseur's eye.

Auguste set busily to work to lever the lids off tombs, in the hope of finding more corn concealed, but in this he was disappointed. He looked around for further hiding places.

Before the altar lay a handsome gilded coffin; from the disordered state of the flowers surrounding its trestle base, it appeared that the mourners had been interrupted before they could commit the coffin to its last resting place. Curiosity impelled Auguste to pry up the lid and peer at the occupant.

Occupants, rather: for the young woman dressed in rich brocade who lay in the satin-lined interior clasped an infant to her breast. Lifting her veil, Auguste saw fine emeralds at her ears and throat and a diamond ring on her finger. His eye brightened. Though the features of the corpse bore the unmistakable ravages of smallpox, Auguste's hands stole towards the jewels as if drawn by a powerful magnet. With a swift wrench, he pulled the ring from the left earlobe. As he did so, the infant stirred and uttered a mewing cry.

Even Auguste's robust nerves were not proof against such manifestations. Uttering a startled oath, he sprang back, and the coffin lid descended with a crash.

'What is the matter, Auguste?' Samuel gazed at him with mild inquiry. Receiving no reply, he strolled over to the coffin and lifted its lid.

'Poor soul!' he said, gazing with pity at the young mother. Then he saw that an earring was missing; his expression hardened. 'Did you steal that jewel? Put it back at once. For shame, Auguste, to rob the dead!'

'What use are jewels in Heaven?' protested Auguste. Even as his fingers clutched the stolen emerald in his pocket, they itched to recover its pair.

'Restore it to the coffin or you leave my service today,' said Samuel with unusual severity.

Inwardly cursing, Auguste tossed the jewel into the satin interior; again the child cried. Hastily he slammed the lid shut, hoping his master had not heard, but Samuel had too large an experience of crying babies to mistake the sound.

'That child is alive!' he cried in astonishment. 'Open the coffin at once.'

When Auguste did not move but stared at him blankly, Samuel lifted the lid once more himself and gently took the little bundle from its mother's arms.

'Sir! I beg of you, do not touch it. It vill kill us all!' cried Auguste, who had a morbid horror of disease.

'How can you call yourself a Christian?' demanded his master. 'Would you leave the poor creature to die?'

'It vill die in any case. What purpose is served by prolonging its sufferings?'

'My daughters will care for it,' said Samuel, and tucked the infant in the bosom of his voluminous coat. Without another glance at his servant he carried the last surviving native of Vilha Nova out of the church and gave the order to mount.

Auguste waited only long enough to see him disappear before snatching the remaining jewels from the corpse. He hurried after the troopers as they rode away down the steep track towards Cartaxo.

To everyone's surprise it was Laura who elected to take charge of the orphan. Instead of shrinking away as Julia did when told where the baby had been discovered, she took the little bundle (now whimpering and decidedly damp) from her father without hesitation, saying, 'Give him to me. No, Clio, you have not the least idea how to hold a baby. Poor little thing! Why, he is no bigger than a doll!'

Since Laura had never shown the smallest interest in her own younger brother and sisters, it was by no means clear why she should consider herself an expert on babies, but in their astonishment no one felt disposed to question her. Apparently the orphan's helplessness had woken some latent maternal instinct.

'I will care for him and my maid Luisa shall help me,' she said firmly. 'She has children of her own.'

'How can you bear to touch it?' shuddered Julia, drawing aside her skirts as if the baby could contaminate them from a distance of several feet. 'Auguste says it is too young to survive, and the mother died of smallpox.'

'Much he knows!' said Laura with disdain. She was not one of Auguste's favourites and welcomed any opportunity of proving him mistaken. She swept from the room, calling for her maid, leaving Julia amazed, Clio amused, and her father serenely conscious that, having acted as a Christian gentleman should, he was now relieved of further responsibility in the matter.

Like a log-jam freed from stagnation, the British Army streamed out from behind the Lines of Torres Vedras, driving the French to the Portuguese border. As one regiment after another received its marching orders, Deputy Assistant Commissary Hardy and his clerk worked to assemble the stores they would carry up-country.

It was late April before they set forth: Samuel, Auguste, Julia and Clio, together with six Portuguese servants. Laura's determination to remain in Lisbon had found a staunch ally in her godmother. 'My dear Mr Hardy, of course Laura may stay with me and I hope she will consider my home her own until you return. Such a charming girl! I have come to rely on her so much I should consider myself bereft were you to deprive me of her company.'

'Dear ma'am, you are too kind.' But Samuel's attempts to add Clio to the Arbuthnot household were less successful.

'No, no. A child of that age is better under her father's eye,' said Lady Arbuthnot so firmly that he recognized it would be fruitless to persist. Like it or not, he must take Clio with him.

The mountain of stores would be carried upriver as far as Abrantes and there transferred to bullock-carts which had preceded them by the land route. Turning north from the valley of the Tagus, they would then follow the road through the mountains to Sabugal, where Samuel had been ordered to take charge of a stores depot serving not only his own regiment but several others deployed on the Spanish–Portuguese frontier.

With such mild courtesy had Assistant Commissary Gregory framed these orders, prefacing each one with a 'Pray, sir, oblige me by...' that Samuel – unaccustomed to military discipline – was inclined to treat them as requests. He had by no means exhausted his interest in the antiquities of Lisbon, and would have dallied there long after he should have taken up his duties in Sabugal had not Auguste made all the arrangements for departure.

'The interior has less to offer in antiquities,' he complained. 'Why should I travel up-country before I have completed my survey of the coast? Mr Gregory will perfectly well understand my reasons for delay.'

This was very likely true, but soon stiff messages began to arrive from the Commissary-General in Almeida, demanding why the clerk at Sabugal had not yet been relieved.

'Much as it grieves me to forego your amiable company, Mr Hardy, I believe you would be well advised to expedite your departure,' said a pink and flustered Mr Gregory on receiving the second of these communications in a day. 'The Commissary-General threatens to hold me responsible for any delay.'

Reluctantly Samuel consented to leave, but he gazed wistfully upon the great aqueduct as the riverboat glided over the Tagus's shining surface, and refused to take any interest in the quantity and disposition of his stores. When Julia ventured some question about the way-bills, she received a surprised stare.

'What do I know about them? Auguste may be relied on to

deal with such matters. Admirable fellow! I trust him absolutely.'

Julia and Clio exchanged worried glances. During their stay in Lisbon each had learned enough about the system governing the commissariat to realize that their father's cavalier attitude might land him in serious trouble. As a civilian employed by the Treasury, but under military discipline, a commissary was financially responsible for the stores he carried and would be called to account for the money he dispensed. Stories abounded of rascally bullock-drivers who absconded with their loads, and river captains who demanded tribute. Vigilance on the commissary's part was essential if his supplies were to arrive at their destination; it was neither safe nor sensible to expect Auguste to bear the responsibility alone.

'You must allow me to check your accounts, Papa,' said Julia tactfully. 'It will be good practice for when I have a household to run.'

'Bless you, dear child! I could not permit you to concern your pretty head about such trifles. I tell you, Auguste will deal with it,' he added with the air of one reciting a well-known lesson. 'Where would I be without him? In Queer Street most likely, my dears.'

For the first time Clio understood the irritation she had seen her mother display on hearing these words. Hitherto she had thought them simply proof of her father's good nature. Now she began to see how deeply indolence was rooted in his character.

'We must do all we can to assist Auguste,' she said privately to Julia. 'If Papa will not exert himself to look after the stores, we must. Queer Street, indeed!'

Still frowning, Julia nodded. 'Captain Barnard told me that any deficit in a commissary's accounts must be paid from his own pocket. I wonder Papa will not take more care.'

'I will tell Auguste he may count on our help,' said Clio. 'He cannot watch day and night unaided.'

So a conspiracy was born between Auguste and the girls as the little fleet advanced slowly upriver. At night, when they tied up by the bank, fires were kept burning through the hours of darkness and, unknown to the peacefully-sleeping Samuel, his daughters took turns to stay awake, ready to rouse Auguste at the least hint of disturbance.

After five days' travelling they arrived at Abrantes, where a pleasant discovery awaited them.

'Is it not the most fortunate of chances?' exclaimed Julia, returning flushed and animated from a tour of the town. 'Captain Cole tells me he is riding to join his regiment at Celrico, and has volunteered to escort us as far as Sabugal!'

Clio was inclined to think this owed less to chance than careful planning, but she was as pleased as her sister. The question of how to stand guard over a train of bullock-carts several miles in length had begun to worry her a good deal, but with Captain Cole commanding their escort fears of losing their stores en route could be laid aside.

'It is indeed fortunate,' she agreed.

To her, Robert made no secret of why he had sought this duty. 'I could not bear to think of any other fellow escorting you!' he said with his shy smile. 'Harry and I explored this country pretty thoroughly when we were on detachment, and I can undertake to show you every Roman remain between Abrantes and Almeida.'

'Papa will be glad to hear that!' she said with a slight grimace.

'Oh, it is not your father I wish to please.'

She looked at him in surprise. Had he not realized that her interest in Lisbon's antiquities had been feigned to give her a chance to escape from the *quinta*? Wishing to make the matter plain, even at the risk of wounding his feelings, she said, 'I must tell you that the beauties of Nature are more to my taste than any Roman site! I find flowers more interesting than emperors, you know.'

'Then I will bring you flowers! Before we reach Sabugal I promise we shall have collected enough to fill an album.'

He could not understand that she preferred to see those flowers growing wild, and insisted upon picking and dissecting and pressing them for her. His long features lit with enthusiasm as he spoke of the habitat and characteristics of his botanical specimens, and his grumbling troopers were ordered to bring him any unusual flowers they found.

Clio soon wished she had never expressed an interest in them; but she had to admit that Robert's enthusiasm for learning was a godsend in keeping her father happy, and he was a conscientious officer who took care of the convoy in his charge.

The first week passed pleasantly as the long train of bullock-carts wound its slow way up the mountain roads to the screeching accompaniment of ungreased axles and the drivers' low, monotonous chant: '*Munto Santa-a-a, munto bonita nossa Senhora Maria-a-a-a!*'

'How can they bear the din?' Julia would cry, stopping her ears with her fingers. 'It is enough to drive one mad.'

Clio laughed. 'Without the music of the axles, they say their bullocks would refuse to budge an inch.'

'Music!'

'I daresay we shall soon grow used to it. At least you cannot deny the scenery is beautiful. How I wish I could sketch like you!'

Julia looked pleased and made no further complaint.

Each evening when they halted to make camp, Julia would wander away with her sketchbook, little Dolores her maid trotting behind well laden with cushions, shawls and anything else she might require, and spend an hour or two sketching in some idyllic spot. Children would gather round her, pointing and exclaiming. Sometimes they could be persuaded to pose.

This carefree nomadic life delighted both girls, for few countries are so beautiful in springtime as Portugal. Dark blue lavender and thyme blanketed whole hillsides; ravines were frogged with golden broom and laced with creamy honeysuckle and giant cistus like some fantastic uniform dreamed up by Marshal Murat. Riding on narrow tracks above clear mountain streams one might catch the blue flash of a kingfisher or see chestnut-crested hoopoes dancing amid the racemes of white laburnum. At midday the warm air was heavy with the scent of balsam and eucalyptus, but when darkness fell they were glad of a blazing fire to counter the mountain chill.

The sense of waste and frustration Clio had felt in Lisbon quickly melted away. Here on the march she was no longer conscious of the three-year gap in seniority between herself and Julia. Indeed, as in most large families, those closest in age tended to be bitterest in rivalry. Without Laura to thrust a wedge between them, Clio and Julia dealt famously – at times Clio even felt herself the wiser of the pair.

She thought it prudent, for example, not to draw Julia's attention to their cook's habit of breaking eggs into his leather apron and beating them with his fingers before pouring them to set on the mess of onions, red peppers, bread and oil which constituted the Portuguese notion of a meal. Like her father, Julia had little interest in the minutiae of domestic life: so long as her meals arrived regularly, it was unlikely she would feel an urge to see how the food was prepared.

It was true that she sometimes winced when she saw her delicate lawns and muslins being vigorously beaten against the stones of some mountain stream and then spread on the gorse bushes to dry, but if the servants were heavy-handed at times they more than made up for it by their obliging cheerfulness and thought nothing too much trouble to ensure their masters' comfort.

'Laura was quite mistaken in supposing the journey would be disagreeable. We are as snug as we ever were in Lisbon,' said Clio contentedly one evening as they sat round the campfire with the appetizing smell of roasting turkey wafting across from the servants' encampment.

'This is only the beginning. When we reach the Serra you may wish you had stayed in Lisbon after all,' warned Robert.

'Croaker! I don't care for cold.'

He smiled at her confidence. 'There are wolves in the mountains, you know.'

'Why should that worry us when you are here to protect us?'

Wolves were not the only danger, as Robert well knew, but there was no sense in meeting trouble halfway and he said no more. Bullock-carts travelled slowly and were an easy target for robbers, bandits, deserters or even the *guerrillero* bands now haunting the hills; but nothing on earth would induce bullocks or their drivers to progress beyond three *leguas* or nine English miles a day.

Of them all, it was only Robert who fretted at this leisurely rate of advance. It was not that he wished to curtail by so much as a moment his time in the Hardy sisters' company, but Samuel had delayed so long before starting for Sabugal that Robert feared his own commanding officer might take a poor view of his prolonged absence from headquarters.

Since bullocks could not be hurried, the accompanying riders had ample time to visit places of interest along the route – an opportunity of which Samuel was not slow to avail himself. He had bought horses in Abrantes for himself and the girls, and often rode ahead of the convoy, leaving Auguste on his sleek black mule to superintend the bullock-carts and keep them moving. His roars of '*Arrivo!*' urging the drivers to greater efforts, mingled with the axles' hideous squeals.

Julia preferred to ride in the foremost cart which, being drawn by a pair of white mules, was quieter and more manoeuvrable than the lumbering waggons, but Clio generally accompanied her father for the dual purpose of seeing the country and keeping a link between him and the convoy. Left to himself, Samuel might have forgotten both the time and his duties.

At night the carts would be drawn up in a circle, their shafts pointing outward, and the oxen unyoked to graze in the centre. Samuel and his daughters would withdraw to a suitable spot and encamp with their own servants, leaving Auguste and Captain Cole to see to the feeding of animals and posting of sentinels. When these matters had been arranged to his satisfaction, Robert would generally join the family at supper, and many a convivial evening they passed in the shelter of some cork grove, with the fire throwing fantastic shadows on the stumps of hollowed-out trees, guitars throbbing softly from the muleteers' encampment, and the red points of the men's everlasting cigars glowing like fireflies in the dusk.

As the convoy climbed higher into the mountains the weather became unpredictable. Heavy storms drenched the travellers and the girls were hard put to it to dry one set of clothes before another was soaked. For those accustomed to the gentle drizzle of an English spring the violence of Iberian downpours was a new and uncomfortable experience. Just as a bantering exchange among the servants might turn without warning into a deadly quarrel, a sunny smiling landscape would suddenly vanish beneath sheets of torrential rain and stabbing lightning.

'Vere is your sister?' asked Auguste one evening after prolonged study of a cloudless sky.

'Sketching, I suppose.' Clio spoke abstractedly, absorbed in the ticklish business of untangling burrs from the coat of a small shaggy mongrel which had attached himself to the convoy.

'Find her and tell her to come back to the camp. It is going to rain.'

'Oh, Auguste! She is not made of sugar, you know. A little rain won't hurt.'

'Do as I say, *petite*.'

'Oh, very well.'

Reluctantly she rose and shook the burrs from her skirt.

'Hurry!' called Auguste as she wandered away. The afternoon sun was hot and she felt no inclination to bestir herself, but sensing his eyes on her she quickened her pace until she was out of sight.

Julia was never pleased to be interrupted in her work, but Clio had a fair idea where she was likely to be found. Half a mile back along the track they had passed the ruins of a Moorish castle perched on a cliff and commanding a fine view of the surrounding countryside.

A deep gully separated the road from the path that led to the castle gate. Rather than go the long way round, Clio bunched up her skirts in a way that would have scandalized her mother and took a flying leap across the ravine's narrowest point, scraping her knees against rock as she landed and hearing the ominous rip of a flounce caught on brambles.

Steps had been cut from the rock, and up these she scrambled, arriving somewhat out of breath to be rewarded by the sight of Julia perched on a canvas stool in the shade of the castle wall, a vast panorama of olive groves spread out below her, sketching with deep concentration.

'Oh, it's you,' she said without raising her eyes from her paper. 'I hope you have not come to disturb me.'

'Auguste sent me to tell you to come back.'

'Surely supper cannot be ready yet?'

'He thinks it is going to rain.'

'What nonsense! I never saw a more beautiful evening.'

'Are you coming?' asked Clio after a few moments' silence during which Julia showed no inclination to move.

'I don't suppose another ten minutes will matter to Auguste, but they will make all the difference in the world to my picture,' murmured Julia, shading away as if her life depended on it.

Clio recognized her mood and settled down quite happily to watch the lizards sunning themselves on the walls of the keep until Julia's fever of creation was exhausted. The warm stone was comfortable against her back after the long day in the saddle; bees buzzed in the clumps of wild thyme and only the tinkle of sheep bells and drip of water broke the evening calm.

Clio closed her eyes and must have dozed, for she woke with a start some minutes later as a large drop of water splashed her cheek. Ten yards away, Julia still sketched busily, unaware of the threatening cloud of deepest indigo which had crept up behind her and was about to blot out the sun.

A little dizzy, Clio scrambled up. 'Come, Julia. Auguste was right. There is going to be a storm.'

'Just one more minute.'

'Look behind you!' said Clio so sharply that involuntarily her sister obeyed.

'*Oh!*'

Without further protest she began to pack away her materials. Even before she had them safely stowed and the paper rolled the sky grew suddenly dark, like a room when the curtains are drawn. There was a moment's hush during which Clio was unpleasantly aware of the thudding of her own heart, then with a roar the storm burst upon them.

In less than a minute they were both soaked to the skin, hats drooping and ruined, muslin dresses clinging round them in chilly transparent folds. Rain beat down with a violence they had never dreamed of, striking the ground so hard that it rose again in a spray. The sudden drop in temperature chilled them to the bone.

'Quick! Under the arch!'

As they ran for the relative shelter of the gateway the rain turned to hail the size of marbles. Blindly they splashed through spreading puddles, trying to protect their faces from the stinging fusillade. Thunder growled and lightning stabbed the earth in vicious forks. Shivering, they clung to one another.

'My sketch!' moaned Julia.

In her haste she had allowed the scroll to slip from her grasp and it lay in the centre of the courtyard, rapidly turning to pulp under the rain's furious onslaught.

'I'll fetch it.'

'No, no! It does not signify.'

But Clio broke free from her restraining hand and darted out to rescue the sodden object. When she regained the shelter of the arch her hair was plastered flat to her skull and the starch had stuck the folds of her petticoats together so movement was almost impossible.

'We – we can't stay here,' she said between chattering teeth. 'Wait until it clears a little.'

At the end of ten minutes the rain ceased as suddenly as it had begun. The storm passed on eastwards, the sun shone out and their wet dresses began to steam. But when they slipped and stumbled in their ruined shoes down the winding path from the castle, a new difficulty confronted them. The stream which Clio had skipped across so easily had been transformed into a raging torrent several yards wide, but there on the opposite bank, to their vast relief, stood Auguste and Captain Cole, wrapped in their great boat-cloaks, shouting instructions to make for the bridge half a mile downstream.

'Waste of good spirits,' grumbled Samuel Hardy when he saw his half-drowned daughters' hands and feet being chafed with brandy to restore the circulation, but even he had been worried by their absence during the cloudburst, and added his voice to Auguste's scolding.

'Let this be a lesson to you,' he said sternly. 'Portugal is very different from England and it is no use thinking you can behave just as you would at home. If Auguste has cause to complain of your conduct to me again, I shall send you back on the next boat. Is that understood?'

'Yes, Papa,' they murmured, chastened by their experience though they knew the threat was an empty one. Julia pressed her sketch between two thicknesses of linen and laid it in the sun to dry. Privately she agreed with Clio that it was her best work since arriving in Portugal, and though it would have seemed immodest to say so, she thought it well worth the drenching.

It was as they prepared to cross the Serra das Mesas, no more than three days' march from Sabugal, that Samuel proposed an alteration in their route. Careful study of Robert's maps had shown him how close they were to Meimao, site of a former temple to Jupiter, and the thought of passing by without visiting it was one he could not bear.

'It will delay us no more than half a day,' he argued, 'yet it would be of great value to me to see it. I shall be far too busy at Sabugal to think of visiting antiquities! This is an unique opportunity.'

Robert considered, drawing thoughtfully on his cigar. 'I see no reason why we should not make a detour, sir,' he agreed. 'I have not had occasion to ride that way myself, but even if the road is steep I expect the bullocks are equal to it. Judging by the map we shall save several leagues on the valley road.'

'Where the Romans lead, we follow,' said Samuel, delighted to have carried his point.

Next morning, when the road junction was reached, orders were sent down the line that the drivers should leave the valley and turn their beasts' heads to the hill.

This command was badly received. The leading driver halted

his team, and in no uncertain terms declared his reluctance to proceed. Finding their way blocked, the following vehicles also stopped.

'What in the world is the matter?' fretted Samuel, looking back from his vantage point halfway up the hill to see the long snake of convoy stationary at the crossroad. After waiting a few minutes he left his post and trotted back downhill.

Auguste was arguing with a noisy, gesticulating circle of drivers while Robert watched silently, his hand on his sword. Clio caught the word '*Demonios*' and saw the drivers cross themselves as they glanced fearfully up the mountain road.

'They say the temple is a dangerous place, full of spirits who will destroy them and kill their cattle,' reported Auguste.

'Superstitious nonsense! Tell them we will protect them. We are not frightened of evil spirits.'

A sullen silence fell when Auguste translated this, but still the drivers refused to lead their beasts forward.

'Tell them that any man who will not proceed loses his wages,' snapped Samuel. 'Truly their priests have much to answer for! By wilfully promoting superstition they keep these poor peasants under their thumbs, fearing whatever they do not understand. Demons!' he said angrily, slashing with his whip at a tall thistle as if he would cut down Beelzebub himself. '*Sanctus! Sanctus Romanorum!*'

These pronouncements had little effect on the drivers, but the threat to curtail their wages brought an instant outcry and wails of '*Jesús! Misericórdia!*' Poor men with large families could not afford to lose the money they had earned since leaving Abrantes.

'Tell them I will give an extra dollar to each man who follows me,' said Samuel, seeing them hesitate.

'Too much!' whispered Auguste, scandalized at such waste. 'Two piastres would be enough.'

'Offer them a dollar.'

Auguste obeyed, though it went against the grain. Even this largesse met with little enthusiasm. The drivers continued to mutter among themselves until Samuel, losing patience, turned his horse and began to ascend the hill again. 'Tell them they can take it or leave it,' he called over his shoulder. 'I am going to the temple.'

His departure threw the drivers into fresh confusion, some prepared to risk the demons for the sake of an extra dollar, some still reluctant to proceed. At last their leader picked up his goad and pricked his beasts into motion, while the others followed, grumbling. Robert and his troop fell in behind to discourage straggling, and the long convoy moved forward. As if in echo of the prevailing mood, rain began to fall heavily.

There were many times that day when Clio wondered if she would ever be warm and dry again. Rain beat down relentlessly and the convoy moved at a crawl. Again and again it was forced to halt when a waggon stuck in a rut or between two boulders, which was strange because the road, though steep and rough, was no steeper or rougher than others they had traversed without difficulty, and in general the drivers were far too skilful to misjudge their distances. Once a yoke broke and the bullock lumbered away up the hillside. Another time a load which should have been securely corded mysteriously slipped off its waggon, obstructing the whole track, and whenever front, middle, or tail stopped moving, the rest of the convoy stopped too. Continuous and strenuous efforts by Robert and his troopers were needed to set them going again, and Auguste became hoarse from cursing in three languages.

'Upon my soul, I can't understand what is wrong today,' grumbled Samuel. After four hours' march they had barely covered a *legua* and the temple still lay at some distance. Following his usual practice when irked by difficulties, he rode off by himself to find it, leaving the rest of the party to struggle with the waggons.

As the convoy left the shelter of the cliffs and reached the top of the hill, the full force of the wind struck it. Though it was only two hours past noon the sky was dark as night and Clio and Julia, huddling together beneath a blanket in the mule-cart, heartily wished they had never left the valley road. Stinging hail drove into their faces and the bleak wild moorland promised no shelter for miles. The bullock drivers had ceased their plaintive song and only the squealing axle-music and wailing wind broke the silence.

Julia rubbed her cold hands together and strove to divert her mind from bodily discomfort by repeating passages from *Paradise Lost* in an undertone.

'What are you mumbling about?' asked Clio, irritated by the half-heard monologue.

'Nothing you would understand.'

'How do you know if you don't tell me what it is?'

Julia did not reply. Clio hunched her shoulders and concentrated her thoughts on the vexed question of supper. The Portuguese cook, Joachim, had only two dishes in his repertoire and would serve these relentlessly on alternate evenings unless otherwise directed. Samuel and Julia were quick enough to complain of their monotonous diet, but since they refused to bestir themselves to improve it, it fell to Auguste and Clio to prod poor Joachim to greater culinary achievement. Generally Auguste could be relied on to discover something appetizing along the route to vary Joachim's everlasting eggs with onions or bacon with lentils, but in this wilderness the choice of victuals would be limited to what they carried.

Perhaps I can prevail upon Papa to open a keg of beef, she thought. Beef in a broth with onions and dried peppers, with bread baked in the ashes, providing we can make a fire. Not a feast, precisely, but a substantial meal. How I wish Julia would take some interest in domestic affairs!

But the hope was vain and she knew it. Food was altogether too mundane a subject for Julia's consideration, and if Clio did not wish to starve herself she must shoulder the burden of directing the servants. As the mule-cart jolted on over the bleak moorland Clio thought of her mother's calm mastery of all matters relating to her household, and wished not for the first time that Mrs Hardy was with them on this journey.

When Samuel rode back to them he was in excellent spirits and seemed as oblivious to their discomforts as he was to his own sodden cloak and sadly dripping hat.

'Just as I thought! A superb example from the second century, perfectly preserved. There is a good camping ground just beyond. If we press on we will be there before nightfall.'

This optimistic forecast failed to take into account the perverse mood of the bullock-drivers. The rain stopped at last and a magnificent sunset did its best to compensate for the wet day, but despite all Samuel's efforts to speed their progress they were still half a mile from the temple when darkness obliged them to make camp.

The heavy waggons began to lumber into their accustomed formation. As each passed him, Samuel threw the driver the promised dollar from a bag held by Auguste, whose face was a study in disapproval. The bullocks were unyoked and allowed to graze in the middle of the circle formed by the wains, and their drivers, each wrapped in his round blanket-cloak, took shelter beneath them, lighting the cigars which were their consolation against life's hardships. With sombre dark eyes they stared at the ground in silence.

'Will you camp here, Papa?' asked Julia, shivering with cold and wet.

Samuel stared about, frowning. 'No. Tell the servants to go on as far as the temple. There is better shelter.'

The girls drove away, and Auguste went off with them. Samuel turned to Robert.

'When you have finished your duties I hope you will join us for supper?'

The young officer hesitated, tempted, then shook his head. 'Thank you, sir, but I must ask you to excuse me.' He added in a lower voice, 'The truth is, I don't care for these fellows' looks. I think they mean mischief.'

'Mischief? My dear fellow, what mischief can they get into here? You cannot suppose they are planning to abscond with our stores? Why, we should catch them in half an hour if they tried such a trick!'

Robert smiled, but said he preferred to remain where he could keep them under his eye.

'Oh, very well,' said Samuel, somewhat piqued. 'If you conceive it your duty to spend the night in the open, I cannot prevent you, but I warn you my daughters will be disappointed.'

'I am sorry for that, sir, but I think I should stay.'

In the next hour Robert posted his pickets and returned to the miserable smoky fire his servant had kindled. As he munched his hard biscuit and beef he could not help looking across with a certain regret at the distant flames flickering beside the temple, and imagining the savoury stew which Auguste's minions would prepare. He thought of Clio's eager, vivid face lit by the firelight's glow and was half inclined to stroll across to join them despite his fears, but a certain presentiment of trouble made him stay where he was.

At ten he made his rounds and found the pickets at their posts. One put something behind his back on hearing Robert's approach.

'What's that you have there, Jenkins?'

'Nothing, sir. Leastways,' said the man reluctantly, 'it's nobbut a drop o' grog the Portugee give me to keep out the cold.'

'You know you should not drink on duty.'

'Yes, sir.'

'You are fortunate I did not see you do it.'

'Yes, sir. Thankee, sir.'

Robert returned to his smoky fire. The rain had begun to fall again, and the wind was rising. He felt chilled to the marrow of his bones.

'Who's there?' he challenged, seeing a shadow move near him.

'Manoel, *senhor*.' A boy stepped into the firelit circle and he recognized the youngest of Mr Hardy's servants. He held out a flask. 'Señor Commissary send this for you.'

Robert put the flask to his lips. A warm glow spread from his throat to his stomach. 'Convey my thanks to the Commissary, Manoel,' he said gratefully.

'*Sí, senhor. Boa noch', senhor.*'

The boy melted into the shadows. Robert drained the flask and wrapped himself in his boat-cloak. Then he lay down to sleep.

Clio awoke to bright sunlight and an eerie stillness. For a moment after opening her eyes she lay listening, but apart from birdsong and the far-off braying of an ass, all was quiet. Too quiet. She had a strong impression of having slept past the usual hour and this, also, was strange since the servants were accustomed to rouse her long before she had her sleep out.

Leaning over, she shook her sister's shoulder. 'Julia! Wake up! What has happened?'

For a moment she experienced an absurd fear that her father had forgotten their existence and ridden away without them, but a glance through the tent-flap reassured her. Samuel's ruffled, grey-flecked head was plainly visible at the opening of his tent. As she watched, he turned over, yawning, and settled back to sleep.

'Where are the servants? Why has no one brought us tea?'

Julia was now awake, infected with the same unease. Normally the camp was astir soon after dawn, and they dressed to the sounds of jingling harness, shouts, groans, bellows, creaks, and roars as the bullocks were yoked for the day's march.

Clio shook her head and voiced the thought in both their minds. 'I fear they have run away.'

Pulling on their clothes, the girls went across to Samuel's tent. He was breathing stertorously and did not rouse even when Julia shook his shoulder.

'Wake up, Papa! You must wake up! The servants have abandoned us.'

Samuel raised his head from his rolled cloak, sighed deeply, and went back to sleep. The girls looked at one another in dismay.

'Do you suppose he has been *poisoned*?'

Clio sniffed the dregs of the goblet that stood on the camp table and pulled a wry face. 'Drugged, rather. Those devils! To think they could do this to Papa!'

Not only to Papa, as they quickly discovered on making a tour of the camp. Auguste lay rolled in his boat-cloak, snoring heavily, dead to the world. Exploration farther afield in the convoy's encampment revealed the grim truth of their situation. The great wains remained where they had been parked, their contents intact, but the drivers had stolen away in the night taking their beasts with them.

It was several hours before Robert and his troopers could be roused from their drugged torpor. Each told the same tale: a drink gratefully accepted... then oblivion. No purpose would be served by reprimanding men for a fault of which their officers had been equally guilty, but a desire to even scores with the culprits had the troopers saddled and mounted almost as soon as they had been dragged back to consciousness.

'We will teach them to play such a scurvy trick! We will drive them back here like whipped curs before nightfall,' promised Robert wrathfully.

'I vill eat my best hat if you do!' muttered Auguste, who had a better appreciation of the wily ways of Portuguese bullock-drivers.

'Take your time, my dear fellow, take your time. You could not be leaving us in a place more to my taste,' Samuel assured him. 'Upon my soul I feel almost grateful to those rascals for gaining me another day here.'

He exchanged his round hat for one of unbleached linen, settled himself on a folding stool on a slope overlooking the temple ruins and began to sketch with great exactitude, leaving Auguste and his daughters to restore the camp to some semblance of order since there was not a servant left to cook, wash, clean or serve their meals.

All the fine horses Samuel had bought in Abrantes had vanished along with their staff. Only Auguste's sleek black mule remained at his picket, and this more likely because of his well-known skills in biting and kicking than from any feelings of delicacy on the part of the thieves.

Presently Auguste mounted him and rode away to discover what the neighbourhood could offer in the way of victuals, leaving Clio and Julia in charge of the encampment.

'What will we do if the French come while you are away?' asked Julia nervously.

Auguste assured her there was no French regiment nearer than Casillas de Flores, twenty miles to the east.

'All the same, I trust Captain Cole will not be away too long,' said Julia.

'I tell you, there is no danger here. *Petite idiote!*' scolded Auguste. 'You would discover something to worry about in Paradise itself!'

For a time after he rode away the girls amused themselves picking flowers and catching the brilliantly coloured butterflies that abounded in the long grass, but soon the sky grew dark once more and they retired to shelter. Samuel joined them, shaking drops of rain from his unfinished sketch. He asked for food and was put out to hear the servants had taken all they possessed.

'Damned barbarians!' he grumbled.

'I could open one of the store-barrels,' offered Clio. 'It seems foolish for a commissary to starve in the midst of his stores.'

But Samuel forbade any violation of his barrels on the ground that they were government property for which he would be called to account. Cold and hungry, they wrapped themselves in damp blankets and waited for the sound of returning hoofs.

When Auguste rode back he was not alone. A sturdy friar in a brown habit marched with him through the rain, matching his stride to the mule's.

'Father Ignacio of the convent at Santa Olalla has been kind enough to offer us shelter,' said Auguste. 'This is Brother Gonzales, who has undertaken to conduct you and the ladies to the convent vile I remain here with the stores.'

'Impossible, my dear fellow! It is my plain duty to stay here until Captain Cole returns,' said Samuel, thinking how much he wanted to finish his sketch of the temple undisturbed. 'You go with the girls to the convent, Auguste, and leave me here. Go on!' he added with a smile. 'Don't you think me capable of mounting guard? I can do it as well as you if I have a mind to!'

'Very vell, sir. I vill come back early in the morning. In the meantime, here is something to refresh you.' He handed his master a wineskin and piece of ham which he had procured at the convent, and wished him a good appetite. Then, putting his mule into the light cart and throwing in a few necessaries, he bade the girls mount, and they drove away behind the silent friar, leaving Samuel to finish his drawing as he pleased.

5

Captain Cole did not return that night and at the convent Auguste learned something that disturbed him a good deal. It was true there was no French regiment within twenty miles, but that would have been less dangerous than the brigands much closer at hand.

Perched on a frowning outcrop of the Serra das Mesas, not half a league from Santa Olalla's convent, stood a fortress known as the Castelo Rubio. A few months earlier it had been made the headquarters of a company of deserters from the French army led by the notorious Sergeant Marcel Legrue, a veteran of the Revolutionary Army whose record of violence together with his flaming red beard had earned him the soubriquet of 'Barbarossa'. Since installing themselves in this stronghold, Barbarossa and his evil band had terrorized the region, and it was fear of falling into his hands that had prompted the bullock-drivers' flight.

'My master must hear of this at once!' exclaimed Auguste when he understood the peril of Samuel's situation. Not without difficulty, he persuaded the Abbot to lend him a dozen men and teams of oxen, with permission to bring the store-waggons into the protection of the convent walls. Father Ignacio's fear and horror of Barbarossa was evident, and he dreaded the bandits discovering the convent's part in the work of salvage. At length however he agreed, on condition that in return the British would rid the district of the scourge of Barbarossa; a promise Auguste gave as readily as if he had power to implement it.

Next morning at first light he set out for the temple with his ox-teams, leaving Clio and Julia in the Abbot's charge. Clio pleaded to go with him, but Auguste was firm in his refusal. The business was too urgent and dangerous to brook the presence of ladies.

'How I wish I was a man!' sighed Clio.

Auguste smiled and did not reply.

The girls passed an anxious, fragmented day taking turns to crane from the high window of the cell they shared to watch the comings and goings in the courtyard. Three times the great studded doors were thrown wide to admit Auguste and a dozen waggons filled with barrels of beef and boxes of biscuit. Three times the oxen were unyoked and led back for another load.

Before leaving for the fourth time Auguste came to reassure the girls that all was going well. Though his blue uniform was dusty and his eyes looked sunken with fatigue he was in good spirits.

'Ve vill have all our stores safe before nightfall, mark my vords!' he told them, gulping down a goblet of wine.

'Where is Captain Cole?' asked Clio. 'Why has he not returned?'

Auguste rolled his eyes. 'The good Lord alone knows! I told him he would have his vork cut out to find even one runaway in these hills, let alone fifty, but who listens to old Auguste? *Tant pis!* Tomorrow ven the coast is clear I vill ride to Sabugal and bring fresh oxen and a strong escort.'

He made a hasty meal and left them, waving cheerfully from the gate as he led his men out.

An hour or so later Clio thought she heard shots in the hills to the north, but it might as well have been thunder. Not wishing to alarm Julia, she kept her fears to herself. Her sister was occupying her time by working up sketches, and Clio envied her ability to ignore present anxieties. She could settle to no employment, but paced restlessly up and down the narrow cell, now and then springing on to the single chair to stare through the grille.

'Sit down, Clio. You are as jumpy as a cat! Have you nothing you can read?' asked Julia.

But as the shadows lengthened, even Julia became aware that this journey had taken far longer than the earlier ones. Their supper was brought by a scared-looking lay brother, who would not answer Clio's questions.

'Oh, to be a man!' she exclaimed again as he scuttled away.

'I have not the smallest wish to be a man,' said Julia primly.

'At least they are not compelled to endure this waiting and wondering....'

'Hush! Someone is coming.'

The soft slap of sandalled feet halted outside their cell, and a moment later Father Ignacio came in, carrying a lantern. A glance at his face confirmed their fears. The men had not returned.

'What has happened, Father? We are so worried,' blurted Clio in her stumbling Portuguese. 'Where is my father?'

He regarded her with compassion. 'I regret I bring you bad news, *senhorita*,' he said slowly. 'The French have attacked your camp and seized your stores.'

Both girls turned pale and Julia gave a faint cry.

'And our father? What of our father?'

'*Senhorita*, I am sorry to tell you he and his clerk are Barbarossa's prisoners.'

The Abbot was apologetic but firm. The English ladies must not be discovered at the convent. By sheltering them he put his own people at risk, and their fate if Barbarossa captured them would be too terrible to contemplate. He regretted it infinitely but for their own safety they must leave at dawn.

'Where shall we go?' asked Julia when she grasped the fact of this dismissal.

'What will become of Papa's stores?' asked Clio.

Father Ignacio was reassuring. The stores he held would be safe until the British could send a strong escort to fetch them. As for the ladies, he was prepared to lend them one of his servants to guide them over the hills to the nearest British outpost.

'No!' cried Clio with such vehemence that they stared at her. 'We cannot run away and leave Papa and poor Auguste. Father' – she fixed the Abbot with a look of entreaty – 'I beg of you to help us. Who else can we turn to?'

'My child, if it was in my power to help you, I would.'

Of necessity the conversation was conducted in the simplest terms, for Clio's grasp of the language was elementary.

'Then who will help us?' she said piteously.

The Abbot considered the question in silence. At last he said gravely, 'There is one man alone who would have the power to storm Barbarossa's stronghold.'

'Who is he? Where can we find him?'

He smiled a little. 'El Forastero has as many names as he has lairs, but I have heard it said he was baptized with the name Don Enrique Monte de Laiglesia. I will make inquiries among my servants. It may be they can direct me to him.'

He would promise no more, and left them. An hour later he returned to say he had found a guide. He looked doubtfully at their clothes and said the way would be too long and hard for them. They had better send a message.

'He thinks we are like Spanish ladies, who never set foot to the ground,' murmured Clio. She had no desire to leave negotiations in the hands of a stranger.

'Truly, Father, we can walk as well as any man.'

A glimmer of amusement lit his grave face. 'Then you would be well advised to dress as men tomorrow. I will give orders for clothes to be found. Good night, ladies, and God speed.'

He blessed them with uplifted hand and left them to an uneasy sleep.

Some time before dawn a lay brother brought bread and olives with a jug of water, and placed on their stool a bundle containing loose shirts such as the peasants wore, short pantaloons ending at the knee, and two sleeveless jerkins in russet frieze. Straw shoes and neat, three-cornered caps completed their attire. Clio put on hers and took prancing steps about the cell, delighted by their easy lightness. Julia's long silky hair was a problem.

'It is no use, we shall have to cut it,' said Clio when the cap fell off for the third time. 'Call for a pair of shears.'

'No!' Julia could not have been more horrified if it had been her head Clio wished to cut off. She damped her hair from the water jug and plaited it tightly, winding the braids round her head and planting the cap on top.

'It looks very strange,' said Clio, surveying her. 'I suppose it must do.'

There was no time for further experiment. A knock at the cell door heralded their guide, a little wizened nut-brown man like a gnome. His name, they learnt, was Tomás. He wore the snuff-coloured velveteen jacket with large silver buttons of the *serranos*, the mountain men.

He looked so old and bent that Clio felt perfectly confident of outwalking him; but when they had been ferried across the river and set their faces to the opposite hill, she soon formed a different estimate of his powers. He led them at a pace they could not match.

'*Arrivo!*' he urged when they begged him to halt. 'This is a dangerous place. Barbarossa is near. *Arrivo, senhoras.*'

Thorns caught at their clothes and flies buzzed maddeningly round their unveiled faces.

'My complexion!' mourned Julia, feeling tenderly at her reddening nose. 'Oh, why must he go so fast?'

The straw sandals afforded their feet little protection from the rough ground. Being too broad, they soon rubbed sores on the girls' feet.

Pride kept them going as far as the top of the first hill and into the valley below. There, when the sun was high, in a hidden dell among great clumps of cistus and golden broom, their guide at last allowed them to rest.

'Water!' exclaimed Clio, and flung herself face down to drink from the stream. Julia sank down on the sward, too tired even to slake her thirst. Tomás eyed her thoughtfully. He brought hard greyish bread and harder cheese from a pouch at his waist, and handed Julia a blackened wineskin.

'*Boa*,' he encouraged, and made a mime of drinking. With some reluctance she put the bag to her lips.

'*Obbrigado*.' Face screwed up at the sourness, she turned to hand it back to him, but without a word of explanation or farewell he had vanished.

'Where did he go?' she asked, a little frightened. The disappearance had been so swift it smacked of magic.

Clio looked up from her drinking. She surveyed the quiet dell with attention but nothing moved among the broom and cistus. 'Father Ignacio would not allow him to abandon us,' she said uncertainly.

Nevertheless, as the sunny hours crawled past, various unpleasant possibilities occurred to them. What if the Abbot had deceived them? Foreigners were not to be trusted. Might he have ordered his servant to desert them in this wilderness? A wilderness it undoubtedly was. No sound of human or domestic animal reached their straining ears as they sat in the little glade, with eagles wheeling overhead and the sad story of the Babes in the Wood uncomfortably prominent in their minds.

What if...? What if...?

What if their guide was a traitor who planned to sell them to the French?

'Perhaps we should make our way downstream,' suggested Clio. 'Streams lead to rivers and people live beside rivers.'

'If we did, we should very likely fall over a cliff and break our necks!' The instinct that leads one to blame others for present misfortunes made Julia add, 'If only you had not forced this mad scheme upon us! Without your interference we would be safe at a British outpost by now.'

'Leaving Papa and Auguste to their fate.'

'I daresay Captain Cole will rescue them,' said Julia, and shut her mouth tight.

'With only sixteen men?'

'Sixteen British soldiers are worth more than a hundred Spanish bandits! Why do you suppose this *guerrillero* chief will listen to you?'

Clio was spared the need to answer as her ears caught a distant jingling of harness. Julia heard it too, and turned very pale. Without a word she reached for her sister's hand and drew her into the shadow of the overhanging cliff, where a great tangle of honeysuckle hid them completely.

With palpitating hearts they crouched low, feeling the slight tremor in the ground as a small file of men and mules came down the rocky path and entered their glade. There were six mules, four laden and two saddled, led by bearded, ruffianly-looking men clad in mountaineers' russet, their wide leather belts stuck full of pistols and knives. On their heels shuffled Tomás, the guide; and at the sight of him they shrank back still further in their scented hiding place.

The file halted and the old man glanced about, evidently surprised.

'*Senhoritas!*'

The two girls pressed against the rock, still as death.

'Come, *senhoritas!*'

One of the bearded ruffians pointed down the path. They conferred in low tones, and padded back and fro with eyes on the ground, examining tracks.

Hope flared briefly in the girls' hearts as the mules began to move away down the path, but it was quickly quenched. The last man in the file turned abruptly and darted back, plunging into the undergrowth and seizing Julia.

'Let me go!' Julia struggled, so deathly pale that Clio feared she would faint. There was no further point in concealment. She stepped forward to confront Tomás, her voice trembling as much with anger as fear. 'Why did you leave us?'

'Quiet, *senhorita*!' snapped the leader of the muleteers with none of the deference usual in men of his calling.

'Who are these men? Why have you not brought us to El For-Oh!' she ended with a gasp of outrage as a soft cloth was slipped over her mouth, stifling the flow of words. Strong arms lifted her bodily and deposited her on a mule saddle. A rope was passed around her wrists from behind, then from one ankle to the other, under the beast's belly.

The leader gave a soft command and for a moment men and mules stood utterly still, listening intently. Then the file wheeled and began to move briskly back the way it had come with the girls helpless and indignant in the middle and the pack-mules bringing up the rear.

The ground was rough and the pace fast. Clio shifted from one side of the wooden saddle to the other, no more comfortable in mind than in body. I wanted an adventure, she reflected ruefully, and now I've found it I don't care for it. If only we had done as Julia wished, and ridden to the nearest outpost! Tales of Spanish treachery were rife among British soldiers: despite the heat she shuddered.

The jolting worsened as her mule was pulled off the path and urged to clamber over boulders. Clio clung to the back of the saddle with her unbound fingertips, too intent on keeping her balance to speculate about this sudden diversion, but when she was dumped on the ground beside Julia with no more ceremony than if they had been two bundles of washing, she saw the reason for it. Fifty yards below, on the path they had just left, a small party of horsemen had appeared – horsemen whose tall shakos and green tunics were at once unfamiliar and unmistakable. They were the first French soldiers Clio had seen, and she observed them with a mixture of interest and apprehension.

The solitary officer was olive-complexioned but undeniably handsome, sitting his bay horse with an easy, unconscious swagger. Nor were the troopers who accompanied him the ill-favoured child-eating monsters of English popular imagination, though they had the weathered leathery look of men who spend much time in the saddle. They rode closely grouped, the officer no more than a pace or two in front, and as they entered the narrow defile where the Spaniards had left the path the troopers glanced uneasily up at the rocks.

At least our captors do not mean to sell us to the French, thought Clio with a rush of relief. She nudged Julia to communicate this reassurance, but her sister did not respond. She was gazing at the approaching Frenchmen with an expression of horrified anticipation.

Puzzled, Clio looked below her. A movement close to the

path caught her eye, and she recognized the glint of a musket's barrel poking out between two rocks. Her heart began to race. Far from hiding while the Frenchmen passed, the muleteers were about to spring an ambush. Just as a herd of deer may emerge from empty moorland as the eye learns to distinguish minute variations of shade and shape, so rocks turned into crouching men, and every tree had one straight branch that was a musket.

Eight, she counted, nine and ten... Most of them must have been lying already concealed before Tomás's party arrived, waiting for the Frenchmen to ride into their trap. There was a horrible avidity in those tense figures poised to attack an unsuspecting foe and, enemies though they were, every fibre of Clio's being cried out to warn them.

The little troop came nearer. Now she could see crusted sweat dried on the horses' necks, and the men's long boots were dull with dust.

The officer turned, frowning, to address some remark to his companions, and the movement undoubtedly saved his life, for the musket ball that would have struck his head cracked into the wall of rock behind him, sending splinters flying.

Before the echoes had finished crashing round the narrow defile, a deadly hail of lead poured from both sides of the path upon the luckless troopers. Five collapsed over their pommels with the first volley. The rest wheeled and would have fled, but their way was blocked by a mule-cart flanked by grim-faced *guerrilleros*.

'*A moi!*' shouted the French officer, and his remaining men gathered about him in a tight knot.

Thrifty of their ammunition, the bandits closed in for the kill: from the look of fiendish exultation on their faces it was plain that memories of murdered children, burned villages and violated wives would only be expunged by French blood.

'Oh!' moaned Julia into her muffling gag. 'Oh! No!'

The quiet hillside echoed to screams and yells as men sprang from among the rocks. Some leapt on to the troop-horses' haunches, poignarding the riders from behind; some dragged the victims from the saddle and cut their throats even as the Frenchmen begged for quarter.

The young officer fought desperately, his shako fallen and his uniform rent in a dozen places as he hacked and stabbed, his horse curveting to avoid the murderous Spanish blades. When he alone of all the troop remained alive, he drew the horse back until its haunches were bunched like a coiled spring then, giving the animal its head, leapt the blockading mule-cart as if it had been a two-foot pole. With a wild yell he clattered away up the track like a man pursued by demons.

'That one will not go far,' grunted Tomás.

Some of the bandits gave chase while the rest turned their attention to stripping the dead. The time for silence was over: each man seized whatever finery caught his fancy while ransacking the troopers' saddlebags.

The girls huddled together, shuddering. 'Don't look!' mumbled Clio, burying her face against Julia's shoulder. Her stomach heaved and the bright afternoon darkened, but no matter how tight she clenched her eyelids it was impossible to erase the image of a French soldier's pale body swinging limply by the heels from a solitary pine tree; and nothing could shut out the sickening grate of steel against bone as the bandits ran it through with their swords.

Sick with horror, she could not tell if it was minutes or hours before a rough hand pulled away her gag and a wineskin was forced between her teeth, trickling fiery spirit into her mouth. The harsh voice of the muleteers' leader was calling his men to order. Unwillingly she opened her eyes.

The mule-carts had gone and with them all trace of the battle except for a heap of valuables piled on a flat piece of ground near the path. Gold chalices, crosses, richly embroidered ecclesiastical robes and censers set with precious stones lay jumbled together along with more prosaic treasures such as canteens, knapsacks and flasks. It was strange and repulsive to see a man with bloody hands raise a crucifix reverently to his lips before stowing it among his garments, but she could not doubt that these spoils from some plundered monastery would some day be restored to their rightful owners. The captured horses were examined for wounds, then roped together for sale in the nearest town; French uniforms were distributed piecemeal among the bandits, and finally the girls' own bonds removed.

'Mount, ladies,' said Tomás curtly as they stretched their cramped limbs. 'The way is long and we must hurry.'

'Where are you taking us?'

He laughed and spat. 'Have you lost your wish to meet with El Forastero, *senhorita*?'

Clio said nothing. The recent sickening scenes had stifled her appetite for adventure.

'Hurry!' snapped Tomás; when Julia was too slow in rising, he seized her hands and pulled her to her feet with shocking familiarity.

Julia did not appear to resent or even notice the discourtesy. Though her complexion was waxen, a spot of colour burned on either cheek and her eyes glowed with a faraway light.

'A paladin!' she murmured. 'Fighting all alone, like a paladin of old!'

Had the sight of so much violence affected her wits? As the mules moved off along the path, Clio watched her sister anxiously, but she said nothing more. Julia's head was so full of fancies that it was sometimes hard to know if she belonged in the real world.

Daylight had begun to fade and billows of mist filled the valley below them before the bandits halted in a grassy bowl high on the mountainside. Their leader set a horn to his lips and blew a long note; after a moment it was echoed from within the hill.

A strange misshapen figure, almost a dwarf, with wide square shoulders and arms hanging close to his knees, emerged from the shadow of the cliff and greeted the newcomers with a guttural burst of questions; then he turned and limped rapidly ahead of them through a cleft in the rocks so narrow it hardly admitted the passage of the mules.

It opened into a grassy space surrounded by high peaks, with the black entrances of caves looking out on a long trench filled with glowing embers over which were slung two cauldrons supported on tripods. A trio of ancient women, so bundled in shawls that they appeared grotesquely stout, stooped over the pots, stirring with long-handled spoons. A rich smell of meat and onions rose on the air and Clio sniffed hungrily. At the convent they had tasted little but bread and lentil soup.

Without a word Tomás helped them to dismount and led the mules away, leaving Clio and Julia to watch the ritual of the bandits' homecoming.

It was a scene wild enough to satisfy any romantic's heart: Julia sighed deeply and reached for the sketchbook which was her constant companion but Clio, too much her mother's daughter to be romantic, could not help noticing the heaps of refuse and dung that littered the ground where they sat and the pitiful thinness of the mangy dogs scratching fleas by the fire.

There were other smells decidedly less appetizing than the stew, and the wolfish way in which the bandits fell upon their food without any attempt to satisfy their captives' needs brought home to her how much she and Julia were at their mercy – if, indeed, they knew the meaning of the word.

'I hope they will offer us some food,' she murmured, but Julia was too absorbed in her work to attend.

Clio looked from one fierce dark face to another, wondering which was El Forastero. The Abbot had implied that he was a gentleman but she saw no one here to merit the description.

'It is too bad of Father Ignacio to put us in this situation,' she went on, trying to bolster her courage, for the thought of spending the night among these rough uncivil men was more daunting than she cared to admit.

'You put us in this situation,' said Julia, her hand moving busily, 'but I am glad you did. How fortunate that I have brought my sketchbook!'

There were a hundred things Clio wished for more than a sketchbook. 'If they do not offer us food, I shall take it for myself,' she said, and was in the act of rising to carry out this resolve when a woman spoke behind her.

'Who are you, and why have you come to trouble us?'

They turned. A tall woman, her proud pale face set in an expression of haughty distaste, surveyed them coldly. Her full but graceful figure was dressed in rustling black silk and tortoiseshell combs set with brilliants flashed like stars against her thick, high-piled hair.

'Pedro!' she called imperiously. 'Who brought these women?'

The burly leader of the muleteers hurried to her side. 'They came with Tomás, Doña Mercedes,' he said respectfully.

'Tomás?' Her plucked eyebrows rose.

'We came to seek help from El Forastero,' said Clio.

'What is the matter? What does she say?' Julia pulled anxiously at her sleeve.

'You are English?'

'Sí, *señora*.'

'Who told you of El Forastero?'

'The Abbot of Santa Olalla. Our father has been captured by the French and we need El Forastero's help to rescue him.'

'French?' said Doña Mercedes with contempt. 'There are no French here. You had better seek help elsewhere.'

'My father is Barbarossa's prisoner,' said Clio, trying to speak calmly although her temper was rising. She could not understand this woman's hostility but it would not help to alienate her further.

'Why should El Forastero save an Englishman?'

'Because you are our allies. We are fighting to save your country.'

'Father Ignacio should not have sent you,' said the woman coldly. 'You have wasted your time. El Forastero is not here.'

It was bitter news. 'Then where may – ?' Clio began, but before she could frame the question a commotion at the mouth of the passage diverted attention from her.

'Look, Mother! See what we have brought you!' cried a rough voice.

Three men dragging another by the heels thrust their way through the crowd and flung down their burden at the feet of the old crone tending the fire. At the sight of the green and gold uniform, Julia gave a little cry.

Cackling with delight, the beldame and her companions left their work and bent over the prisoner.

'See how the pretty Frenchman sleeps. Let us wake him to sport with us.'

They slapped the unconscious man's cheeks and poured water over his head, but he did not stir.

'They have killed him,' said Julia in a flat voice.

For several minutes it seemed this was indeed the case. The crones redoubled their efforts, pinching and slapping. They propped the prisoner against a wall and forced the neck of a wineskin between his teeth. He spluttered feebly, a response which delighted them beyond measure.

The *guerrilleros* crowded round, watching eagerly, but made no move to interfere as, with every appearance of tenderness, the crones coaxed the young officer back to consciousness, crooning endearments.

'Come, pretty Frenchman, wake and speak to us. We want to play with you. What a gallant fellow you look in your little uniform. Surely you would be more comfortable without it? Here, Jorge, help us put our visitor at ease.'

Grinning, the misshapen sentinel who had guarded the entrance scuttled forward to divest the prisoner of his tunic.

'Hold him up, Jorge! Let us admire our guest. Now, little soldier, show us how a Frenchman can dance!'

'Animals!' exclaimed Doña Mercedes in disgust. She pulled aside a goatskin curtain and withdrew into a cave.

'They mean to torture him,' whispered Julia, watching with round horror-struck eyes as the old women thrust long metal forks into the fire. When these were red hot they waved them menacingly before the prisoner's face. Conscious now and fully aware of what lay in store, he shrank back against the wall of rock.

'*Por piedad, señores!*' he moaned. '*Clemencia, por Dios!*'

The plea evoked a roar of laughter, and the uglier of the crones stepped forward and swept a mocking curtsey.

'You shall taste of the mercy you showed my children, Frenchman!' she cried, and lunged with the red-hot fork. The prisoner screamed as it sizzled against his skin.

'The devils!' exclaimed Julia.

Before anyone guessed her intention she ran forward and snatched the instrument of torture from the old woman's hand. Swinging the iron wildly from side to side, she placed herself in front of the prisoner, shielding him with her body.

'Leave him alone!' she cried in English. 'Have you no mercy or Christian charity, you who torment a helpless man?'

A low growl of displeasure burst from the throats of the *guerrilleros*. The ancient crone tried to seize back her weapon but with a recklessness totally at odds with her gentle looks Julia swung the smoking metal and held her assailants at bay.

'You shall not touch him!'

Julia's hair had escaped from its plait and cloaked her to the waist. She looked tall but fragile, like a willow in a storm, as the angry mob closed about her. Clio tried to go to her assistance but was held back by a dozen hands.

Then at the height of the tumult, a stillness fell on the company. Heads turned towards the entrance and a name rippled through the crowd like a wind through standing corn.

'*El Forastero!*'

The result was immediate. Pedro, who had been urging on the mob, resumed his seat, and the old women bent over the fire. The girls were ignored, the French prisoner forgotten as disjointed phrases flashed from mouth to mouth: 'A fight... wounded... the French in pursuit....'

A litter was carried in and Doña Mercedes hurried to bend over it, uttering a low wail as she saw the cloak-shrouded figure on its rough framework. Blood-stained bandages obscured most of his face, so only a portion of cheek and a single dark eye were visible, but that eye was very much alive.

'Mercedes?' he murmured.

'I am here. You are safe. Hush, do not speak.'

Slowly the eye ranged round, coming to rest on the Frenchman, with Julia in her boy's clothes, long hair tumbled about her shoulders, standing protectively over him.

Clio, watching intently, saw it register anger – anger and a kind of shock.

'Who brought that woman here?'

His voice was a low, hoarse whisper. Doña Mercedes spoke quickly, bending over the litter. 'There are two, Enrique. Two English girls. Father Ignacio sent them....'

'The damned old fool. Does he want my hideout known to all the world? Get rid of them. *Por Dios*, I will have something to say to that meddling priest.'

He moved his head painfully, and the eye came to rest on Clio. She flinched under the intensity of that dark, sombre stare; then, uncertainly, she smiled. He was only a man, and wounded. There was no need to be afraid of him.

'*Señor* –' she began, and would have moved towards him but her captors held her back.

'Pedro!'

Though the voice was weak it carried authority. The burly lieutenant straightened and sprang to the head of the litter.

'I am here, Don Enrique.'

'I gave orders that prisoners were to be well treated.'

'*Sí, señor.*'

'Let me see how my orders have been obeyed.'

The Frenchman was pulled roughly to his feet and brought to the foot of the litter, with Julia clinging to his arm. Clio stared in fascination at that solitary dark eye. For a long moment it surveyed them in silence. Then the laboured voice said, 'Put them in the inner cave and set a guard. If any harm comes to them you will pay for it.'

'*Sí, señor.*'

The eye closed, as if the effort of speaking had eclipsed its last energy. Faintly the whisper came: 'Where's that damned horse-doctor? Get him to cut out this bullet....'

6

For two days El Forastero hovered between life and death, and the captives whiled away the hours of their confinement as best they could.

Colonel Jean-Gabriel de Rochefort – adventurer, womanizer, and Masséna's most trusted spy – had been in many tight spots since he joined the Revolutionary Armies of France at the age of fourteen. He was now twenty-eight: a lean dark daredevil cavalryman with bright narrow eyes under level brows and a cool calculating head. The papers he carried declared him to be a simple sergeant of Dragoons, Etienne Simon, and tucked away in the sole of his boot was a secret letter to the Governor of Almeida, besides a confidential list of persons prepared – for payment – to assist the French invaders.

These last documents he now proceeded to abstract from their hiding place, chew to a pulp and swallow, since he knew they could very well prove his death warrant. It was a slow and distasteful business but necessary to his survival. Not until the last was consumed did he feel free to turn his attention to his fellow captives, but when he did so it was with enthusiasm, for Colonel de Rochefort was a connoisseur of beautiful women and the blonde ethereal looks of the elder Miss Hardy were very much to his taste.

With amusement but also some concern, Clio observed her dreamy sister fall head over ears in love. It was hardly necessary for the Frenchman to lay siege to her heart, for the battle had been won when first she clapped eyes on him. Julia's romantic fantasies had found a focus at last. When Rochefort thanked her gracefully for coming to his aid, and compared her courage to Joan of Arc's, she blushed vividly and shook her head.

'Indeed, *monsieur*, you must not call me that,' she protested in stilted schoolroom French. 'Anyone would have done the same.'

He took her hand and brushed it with his lips. 'Accept the expression of my eternal gratitude, *mademoiselle*. If it is in my power to serve you, I beg you will ask it.'

'You do me too much honour, *monsieur*,' responded Julia shyly, but if her tongue was stiff her beautiful eyes were eloquent, and Rochefort smiled approval. A Beauty, indeed, and quite unspoiled. In any other circumstances he would have enjoyed introducing so ravishing a creature to the arts of love. It was a tragedy that the presence of the guards and her sister – not to mention his own uncertain position – made any ambitions in that direction impracticable.

Nevertheless, he set himself to captivate her, reasoning that a friend in the enemy's camp is worth two in one's own.

Clio, excluded from their charmed circle of mutual attraction, passed her time listening to the gossip of their guards. In her mind she rehearsed the speech she would make as soon as El Forastero recovered sufficiently to receive them. She felt sure he had the power to rescue her father if only he could be persuaded. Plainly the fifty or so men gathered here were only a portion of the forces at his command.

His followers regarded him with a mixture of pride and fear. She ignored their more blood-curdling tales, guessing they were trying to frighten her.

I would act harshly to persons who invaded my country and imprisoned my king, she thought. When you consider the wrong the French have done the poor Spaniards, it is no wonder they thirst for vengeance.

On the third day of their captivity a summons came from behind the goatskin curtain, but Clio's hopes were disappointed. The Frenchman alone was ordered into El Forastero's presence.

Rochefort approached the interview with fair confidence, reasoning that if the *guerrillero* chief had intended to kill him he would have done so before now. Compared with other patriotic leaders such as El Empecinado – the dweller by the stream – and the brutal Don Julián Sánchez, El Forastero enjoyed a reputation for clemency. Now his secret documents were destroyed, Rochefort believed his story would convince any ignorant peasant or overbred *hidalgo*.

El Forastero sat with his injured leg propped on a stool. One arm was in a sling and his head still swathed in bandages so that the only section of face plainly visible was pale and stubbled with three days' growth of beard. He looked neither ignorant nor overbred.

'Name and rank?'

'Etienne Simon, *señor*. Sergeant in the —th Chasseurs of the Imperial Cavalry.' Rochefort, who spoke Spanish as well as his native tongue, bent his head humbly and assumed a hesitant, stumbling speech as he added, 'I have to thank you, señor, for sparing my life. Believe me, I am grateful.'

'My men have no reason to love the French,' said El Forastero curtly. 'At times they become over-enthusiastic. It is hard to convince them that prisoners can be more valuable alive than dead.'

He means to sell me to the British, thought Rochefort.

'Where were you bound when you were captured?'

'To Nave Redonda, *señor*, with dispatches for Colonel Leclerc,' replied Rochefort readily.

'Let me see them.'

Rochefort took from his jacket the sheaf of false papers that constituted his cover. To his surprise, El Forastero gave them only the briefest of glances before tossing them to the floor.

'You chose a strange route from San Felices to Nave Redonda.'

'It was the route I was ordered to take.'

Rochefort settled his features in an expression of dull passivity, but his mind was racing. How had the bandits known he came from San Felices? He had taken such care to cover his tracks. It was crucial to his story that they should believe him bound for the French outpost at Nave Redonda. If they guessed that his real mission was to the beleaguered French garrison at Almeida, now surrounded by British troops, his hopes of claiming a six-thousand-franc reward for delivering Masséna's message to the governor there would vanish.

Chronically short of money and ever ready for adventure, Rochefort had volunteered for this dangerous mission, together with two brother officers. The three were to travel by different routes, and a salvo of cannon fired from Almeida at five-minute intervals would be the signal that one, at least, of them had slipped through the British blockade and gained entry to the fortress.

'Tell me,' said El Forastero, 'since when has Masséna found it necessary to employ colonels to carry his movement orders?'

Startled, Rochefort raised his eyes. The look that met his seemed less than ever ignorant or overbred. He saw he must be careful.

'I do not understand, *señor*. I am only a sergeant.'

El Forastero tapped ash from his cigar. 'Tell me, sergeant, have you reason to complain of your treatment here?'

'No, *señor*. I have been well treated.'

'You have received a fair ration?'

'*Sí, señor*.'

'Then perhaps you will tell me why you found it necessary to swallow so many papers? Was this hunger, or had you another reason?'

He had been observed! Rochefort cursed inwardly, but replied coolly enough, 'I was obeying orders, *señor*. If captured, couriers are ordered to destroy military documents.'

'Why not destroy these?' El Forastero pointed at the papers on the floor. 'Were they less important, perhaps? Less sensitive? Or is the whole story you have spun me a pack of lies?'

'I am telling the truth, *señor*.'

'Then explain the meaning of this.' From his pocket the outlaw drew another paper and held it up for Rochefort to see. With dismay he recognized the list of ciphers which had been concealed in a secret pouch in the pommel of his saddle. When he was dragged from his horse there had been no time to remove them.

Having nothing to lose, he put a bold face on it and said in his rough assumed accent, 'I regret, *señor*, I cannot tell any letter's meaning since I have never learned to read.'

'This was hidden in your saddle. If you did not place it there, who did?'

'Ah, *señor*, that is easy to answer. The saddle belonged to poor Colonel de Rochefort, God rest his soul. I bought it in the sale of his possessions, not ten days since. Undoubtedly the paper was placed there by him.'

The eye narrowed. 'You deny that you are Colonel de Rochefort?'

'I deny it absolutely.'

'*Qué lástima!* What a pity!' said El Forastero gently. 'I hoped I might be able to save you. You see, if you were indeed Colonel de Rochefort, it would be my duty to deliver you into the hands of the British. However, since a humble sergeant can know nothing that might be of interest to Lord Wellington, I see no reason to deprive my men of the pleasure of killing you by any means they prefer.'

There was a moment of silence. Then Rochefort said stiffly, 'Let me see the paper, *señor*. It may be that I can remember something Colonel de Rochefort told me concerning it....'

'Something is not enough, *amigo*. Unless you can swear that you are Rochefort in person, I will watch you die with no compunction.'

The Frenchman fell to his knees. '*Piedad, señor...!*'

'Do not speak to me of mercy,' snapped El Forastero in sudden anger. 'I have seen too much of French mercy to spare you any of mine. Pedro!' he called. 'Take the prisoner away and do as you please with him. He is no use to me.'

Too much of a realist not to recognize defeat, the Frenchman rose, shrugging. 'Very well. I admit I am Colonel de Rochefort, *señor*. I will tell your British allies all they wish to know.'

'I congratulate you on your good sense, *mon Colonel*.' El Forastero's eye gleamed as he smiled. 'Pedro will be disappointed, of course, but I believe the assistance you can give our allies will compensate for that. I wish you good day, Colonel.'

He gave rapid orders to the guards, and held himself upright until the curtain swung shut behind the Frenchman. Then he flung himself back on the pallet with a sigh.

Hang it, I'm as weak as a kitten! thought Don Enrique Monte de Laiglesia, better known to his friends as Harry Churchill. So much for Rochefort! Now, what in God's name am I to do with those girls? Of all the damned unlucky chances that brought them here! Clio's no fool. Even if she doesn't see my face, she'll know my voice the moment I speak out, and I can't go on whispering for ever. Then the game will be up before it's properly begun, and two years' work gone to the deuce. Damn that meddling Abbot, and damn Tomás as well! He should have known better than to bring strangers here.

Through a gap in the goatskin partition he had a clear view of the captives in the inner cave. Julia's blonde head was bent close to the Frenchman's in whispered converse. Clio sat a little apart, her pointed chin propped on her fist, staring into the fire. He considered her gravely, noting the changes, the fining down of face and figure, the elfin beauty he had not known she possessed. Or didn't I see it before? he mused. Has she changed, or have I?

He wondered if she still wore his locket, and felt a stab of regret that promises made in those far-off days would never be fulfilled. Better that Clio should think him dead than know him dishonoured. He had chosen his path; there was no going back.

'Why are you watching those prim English misses?' whispered Mercedes, entering on silent silk-shod feet. 'You should have allowed Pedro to have his fun with them.' She wound soft arms about his neck and bent to kiss him but he did not respond. All of a sudden her sensuality repelled him.

'What is troubling you, *querido*?' Her rich musky scent wafted over him and he felt a sharp longing for English lavender and the smell of new-mown hay. Spanish beauty ripened early. Though Mercedes was barely older than he was, she seemed overblown.

That was unfair, and ungrateful besides, he rebuked himself. He owed everything to Mercedes. Courage and devotion such as hers were rare among their Spanish allies. She risked her life every time she stole out of French-occupied Ciudad Rodrigo to bring him news of French movements, or made a pilgrimage her excuse to visit him in the hills. She deceived her pompous elderly husband, Don Sebastian – who made no secret of his admiration of the French – and encouraged the advances of the town's loutish French Governor so she might pass on his plans to her lover.

She had stolen Harry's honour, but he owed her his freedom and his life. If life without honour sometimes seemed a bleak affair, at least it was better than no life at all. Or so he had thought until Clio came here.

Mercedes's brother, Don Alvaro, had led this guerrilla band, and her support secured Harry the leadership after Alvaro was killed. She alone knew Harry's true identity: to the rest of the band he was El Forastero, the Stranger – which to these hill-peasants meant any man born beyond their own mountain range. The Spanish learned at his mother's knee came readily enough to his tongue... though sometimes he wondered if Pedro Gonzales suspected the truth. He was a sly, sadistic fellow, and his delight in tormenting the prisoners they captured had earned him more than one rebuke from Harry, who had the English dislike of cold-blooded torture. In this matter he was aware that his men's sympathies were with Pedro.

Mercedes stretched herself on the pallet beside him, cradling his head against her bosom. '*Mi Enrique*, I love you so much. If you were killed I should die of grief.'

He forced a smile. 'Who talks of dying? *I* have no intention of being killed.'

'Pedro says you take too many risks. One day the French will trap you. They have orders to spare no efforts to catch El Forastero. While you live, no convoy or courier is safe in these hills.'

Harry grinned and pulled himself to a sitting position. 'That is how I wish it. Let them waste their time looking for me – they will not find me. All the same,' he added, frowning, 'Father Ignacio must learn to be more circumspect if he wishes to enjoy my protection. I do not want my lairs known to all the world.'

'Tomás will not do it again. Sleep, now, *querido*, and heal your wound.'

He shook off her hand. 'In a while. First I must speak with Tomás and Pedro.'

'You are weary, *mi Enrique*. Wait until morning.'

Her lustrous hair fell across his face, her rich warm scent encompassed him. Again he thought of English lavender. He said harshly, pulling a little away, 'By morning it may be too late. Send them to me now.'

After three days of inactivity, Clio slept fitfully on her straw palliasse. From time to time she heard groans from the sleeping *guerrilleros* as terrible memories woke terrible dreams.

'*Jesús, María!* Have mercy!' cried one.

'My children! My poor wife!' moaned another.

Towards dawn she drifted into a sounder sleep and woke with a jolt of pure terror, her senses muffled by a cloth hood which had been slipped over her head.

'Quiet!' growled a voice in her ear. 'One sound and you die.'

The cloth was drawn so tightly over mouth and nose that she could hardly breathe. Panic seized her when she found her wrists and ankles securely tied. She could not move or make a sound. Hands gripped her arms and legs; she felt herself lifted and carried through darkness along a tunnel so narrow that hips and shoulders scraped the walls.

Where are they taking me? Where is Julia? Does El Forastero know of this? The memory of that solitary dark eye brought fresh fears flooding in. While it was open it had seemed to promise protection, but who would protect them when it closed?

Air struck cool on her hands; even through the hood she sensed they were in the open, though the darkness remained impenetrable. Her captors dumped her roughly on the ground and conferred in low tones.

'Why not kill the bitches here and save ourselves a journey?' urged Gonzales. 'If we hide the bodies El Forastero will never know. *Caramba!* He is too soft with his prisoners. They have seen our stronghold. Who can say they will not lead our enemies to it?'

Tomás hesitated, tempted. He had not relished El Forastero's rebuke for bringing the girls to the cave, but Father Ignacio had ordered it, and how could a man obey two masters? Nothing would have pleased him more than to plunge his dagger into the Frenchman's heart, but even as he contemplated this pleasure he remembered the suffused face of young Diego Aranda, who last week had dared disobey El Forastero's order. Diego's gargling cry as the breath was choked out of him still rang in the old man's ears. El Forastero might be too soft with his prisoners, but he demanded absolute obedience from his followers. In matters of discipline, even Don Alvaro had been less harsh.

'Put them on the donkeys and hold your tongue, fool!' he said curtly. 'If Don Enrique discovered we had killed them, nothing would save us.'

'Who would tell him? How would he know?'

Tomás shook his head. 'You may be tired of this world, *amigo*, but I wish to live as long as God permits. Do as I say.'

Captain Cole's shock at discovering the campsite by the Roman temple abandoned and broken barrels of biscuit and beef strewn around like Gargantua's picnic was nothing to his agony of mind when he learned at the convent that Clio and Julia had been gone three days in search of the guerrilla chief.

'That brigand!' he exclaimed in horror.

'El Forastero is a man of honour,' Father Ignacio assured him.

'Your notions of honour have little in common with mine,' snapped Robert. 'How could you trust the safety of defenceless females to such a rogue?'

'What else could I do, Señor Capitán?' cried Father Ignacio distractedly. 'Had Barbarossa discovered I was sheltering them, he would have torn the convent apart stone from stone.'

'Why did you not send them to the British outpost at Castaneheira?'

'Believe me, Señor Capitán, that would have been no safer. With Barbarossa's patrols on the road, they would not have escaped him. Besides,' he said simply, 'they would not go. The little *señorita* – *la morena* – insisted on seeking help.'

'So to save your skin you dispatched two delicate females to a den of thieves. No doubt Pontius Pilate would have done the same.'

Father Ignacio stiffened. 'Do not seek to blame me for what is your fault, señor,' he said with stern dignity. 'Had you not strayed from your route and abandoned your convoy there would have been no need for my intervention.'

Robert recognized the justice of this. 'Forgive me, Father. Indeed, I am grateful for your care of them. If you will be good enough to tell me where El Forastero may be found, I will ride at once in search of him.' He turned to gaze out at the snow-capped hills, adding almost to himself, 'Pray God I get there before harm befalls them. Well?' he added rather impatiently when the Abbot remained silent, 'where is he to be found?'

'My son, I could more easily tell where the mountain wolf lays his head,' said Father Ignacio apologetically.

'The villagers must surely know?'

'Assuredly.'

'Pray inquire of them.'

Father Ignacio smiled at such simplicity. 'The Prince of Essling's men burned twenty children from this village before their fathers' eyes, yet they would not tell where El Forastero was hiding. Why should they tell you?'

'*I* would not harm their children!' Robert had been in the country three years and heard countless tales of atrocity, yet they still had the power to sicken him.

Father Ignacio said sadly, 'El Forastero would if they betrayed him. It is the law of the jungle, my son.'

'Then how shall I find him?'

This tall troubled young man with his hesitant speech and melancholy dark eyes had an indefinable air of gentleness, in marked contrast to most British officers whose arrogant assumption of superiority greatly offended their Spanish hosts. Also the shrewd Abbot suspected that his interest in the missing girls was not wholly inspired by duty. Taking pity, Father Ignacio told him his best hope of finding the *guerrilleros* was to ride into the sierra and let them come to him.

'But where?' Robert surveyed the vast inhospitable landscape of rock and forest outside the convent walls. 'How will they find us?'

'They will find you, my son, never fear. Not a mouse moves in his territory without word of it reaching El Forastero.'

'*Anywhere?*'

It was hardly an enticing prospect. Robert reflected gloomily on what his Colonel would say when he heard that a troop of his horse had vanished into the sierra in direct disobedience of orders. Might as well be hanged for a sheep as a lamb, he mused. Having lost the stores, there was nothing to stop him losing his troop too: one could only be court martialled once. The thought of Clio suffering Heaven knew what torments at the hands of the *guerrilleros* stiffened his resolve. He straightened his shoulders.

'Very well,' he said. 'If that is the only way to find El Forastero, I must take it.'

'May God in His infinite mercy guard and protect you, my son,' said the Abbot gravely, raising his hand in benediction. To Robert the blessing had a sinister ring. He tried to rid himself of the notion that this was a trap and Father Ignacio knew that without the intervention of the Almighty his mission was already doomed.

All next day they followed a winding track into the hills, and bivouacked on a bare windy plateau studded with smooth boulders as if giants had just abandoned a game of marbles. Huddled into their boat-cloaks against the driving rain, the troopers cursed monotonously, while their horses hunched their tails towards the wind and hung their heads low. Since there was neither food nor firewood to be had, they supped off raw rations and rolled in their damp cloaks to sleep.

Robert, sitting a little apart from the men, stared into the immensity of landscape and allowed despair to overwhelm him.

This was the bleakest, most barren terrain he had ever encountered, a very abomination of desolation. Ridge upon ridge of bare serrated mountain peaks faded into misty distance, each one criss-crossed with perilous goat-tracks which might or might not lead to the edge of a precipice. Time and again that day his troop had been forced to retreat and seek a new way round some natural obstacle. Most of the watercourses were already dry and thirst was a constant menace.

His maps were useless here. Before darkness fell he had tried to reconcile the country before him with the printed sheet, but in vain. Neither tracks nor streams, mountains nor valleys were charted more than vaguely. A thorough search for two girls in such a wilderness was impossible.

Nevertheless, while his men made camp, Robert occupied himself in tracing as best he could the features of the country they had traversed. It was a shock to discover when he sought to complete his work next morning that both his mapcase and drawing instruments were missing.

Nor was this loss the only evidence of an unfriendly visitation while they slept. Six of their pack-mules had vanished as well, along with their loads, yet none of the troopers had heard a sound.

It was a serious blow to lose half their rations, but far more serious was the effect on the men's morale. Robert ignored as best he could their frightened looks and rebellious mutterings, but when his sergeant came to report two men sick and unable to ride, his own feeling of foreboding exploded in anger.

'Sick? They are no more sick than I am! You may inform the men, Sergeant, that any malingerers will be left here with a day's rations to wait our return, and their horses will be distributed among the rest of the troop.'

'Very good, sir,' said Sergeant Matthews woodenly and saluted.

Twenty minutes later, when Robert gave the order to march, he noted sardonically that the threat of being abandoned without their horses had wrought a miraculous cure. Though the men eyed him sullenly, every saddle was filled.

All that grilling day they marched into the wild heart of the sierra without seeing a living soul, yet Robert knew they were watched, and the knowledge preyed on his nerves as no visible danger would have done.

A stone would rattle down the scree, kicked by an unseen foot; a tree rustled and sighed without a breath of wind to stir its leaves. Once he seemed to hear mocking laughter, but when he looked round sharply the only movement was an eagle wheeling in lazy circles above the rocks. He was haunted by the fear that the girls were already dead and his mission a vain one. Impartially he cursed Father Ignacio, the bandits, and the whole godforsaken country with a rancour quite foreign to his nature.

They left the barren plateau and descended steeply to a wooded gorge which looked the very place for an ambush. The men sweated in their tight tunics and their horses stumbled so badly that Robert was obliged to order frequent halts to rest them. As the sun sucked the vitality from them, Robert's anxiety focused into a burning hatred for El Forastero. What was the damned fellow planning? Why wouldn't he make himself known?

Darkness closed in on them, and he ordered the horses and mules tethered in a small circle, the stores in the centre and a double guard set round. He withdrew to his tent, telling the sergeant to summon him at the least disturbance and, loading his pistols, lay down with one within reach of his hand, to rest, but not to sleep.

The stars were fading and the first pearly filter of light heralded the dawn before his vigilance was rewarded. He sensed rather than saw a movement in the tent, and felt a smooth cool touch against his cheek. Breathing steadily, while his wide-open eyes probed the dim corners of the tent, his right hand stole out to grasp the pistol.

It was not there.

'Keep very still, *señor*,' breathed a voice behind him, and again his cheek felt that smooth touch. It pressed harder, colder into the flesh and he knew it for his own pistol.

'Who are you?' he whispered. 'What do you want?'

'I bring a message from El Forastero.'

There was a rustle as a paper was laid at Robert's side. Stealthily he felt for the second pistol beneath his pillow.

'Where are the English *señoritas?*'

'That you must find for yourself,' replied the man insolently.

'Tell El Forastero to bring them here. I will not leave without them,' said Robert steadily, and was answered by a mocking laugh.

'Then your bones and theirs will lie on the sierra, a warning to those who disobey El Forastero,' said the man, and laughed again.

The sound scraped Robert's raw nerves. Without pausing to consider the consequences, he drew out the second pistol and fired at the darker patch of shadow, feeling a fierce joy as the man screamed.

'To me!' shouted Robert, springing up to seize him. 'Here, Sergeant! Catch this fellow and clap irons on him.'

For an instant the squirming figure was in his grasp, then he stared and cursed as, with an eel-like twist, the visitor shed his cloak and was gone up the hillside, leaving Robert grasping thick folds of material.

'After him! He must not escape!'

The troopers tumbled from their bivouacs, stringing out in a line across the hill as the hunched figure of the fugitive scrambled from rock to rock above them. From his gait it seemed plain that he was wounded: steadily the soldiers gained on him, with the long-legged Robert in the lead.

Once he turned and fired at his pursuers, but the ball went wide. He flung away the pistol and continued his ascent, his movements weaker as he neared the summit.

Now we've got him! exulted Robert, forcing his aching legs still faster.

Gasping, he surmounted the last ridge and looked around, but the fugitive had vanished. Instead, Robert's gaze fell on three long bundles wrapped in hessian, roughly tied, which lay on the saddle of the ridge. He stood transfixed, staring at them while his heart pounded his ribs.

Sergeant Mathews arrived at the summit, blowing like a foundered horse. 'Gawd!' he said heavily, seeing the ominously shaped bundles.

The rest of the men came up, panting and cursing. They fell silent, casting furtive glances between the bundles and Robert's stony face.

'Open them up, Sergeant,' he ordered, and despite his effort at control, his voice shook.

'Bateson! Wilkins! Vickers! Open up them sacks. Look sharp!' snapped Sergeant Mathews as the men hesitated. To Robert he muttered, 'Can't be the ladies, sir, seeing as how there'm three on 'em. Likely it will be some trick by them devils to get us away from our camp.'

Too late Robert recognized the truth of this. He was hesitating, reluctant to split his small force but still more reluctant to suffer any further depredations at the bandits' hands, when a shout from Trooper Bateson brought his heart to his mouth.

'It – it moved, Sarn't.'

Bateson, a fresh-faced farmer's boy, stood staring in horror at the body he had just unwrapped from its cocoon of dirty hessian.

'Well, get on wi't, lad. Get rest o' they rags off'n the poor devil,' said Mathews impatiently.

He knelt and thrust a hand inside the victim's shirt, feeling for a heartbeat, while Bateson cut the strings of the hood.

A boy, thought Robert dully, looking down at the slight body. Quite a young boy. What can he have done for the *guerrilleros* to punish him like this?

Then Mathews withdrew his hand sharply, as if he had been stung, and Robert saw a dusky flush spread over his weathered face.

'It – it's a woman, sir,' he muttered, and scrambled awkwardly upright.

'A *woman?*'

'That it is, sir. Lookee.'

Gently Bateson pulled the hood clear, and Clio blinked

dazzled eyes at the sunlight. Pale and grimy though she was, Robert thought her the most beautiful sight he had ever seen.

'Clio! My dearest girl!'

'Give us your knife, Sarn't.' With swift strokes Bateson cut the gag and the twine which bound her ankles and wrists. Clio tried to move her cramped limbs and cried out.

Heedless of the interested looks of his men, Robert took her in his arms, cradling her head against his chest. 'Hush, my dearest. Don't try to speak just yet. You are safe now.'

She nodded and smiled, but tears of weakness welled up in the eyes he had never expected to see again.

'Julia?' she whispered.

He had forgotten Julia. He turned to see Trooper Wilkins pull away the hood from the second long bundle. She was alarmingly pale and the silky golden hair tumbled about her shoulders gave her the look of a drowned Ophelia, but her breast rose and fell steadily and when the gag was removed she uttered a faint moan.

With a surge of pure thankfulness, Robert saw that Julia, too, was alive.

7

Jean-Gabriel de Rochefort brooded between his guards. He had no intention of ending his meteoric career in a British prison hulk. By the time an exchange of prisoners was arranged, the war in Spain might well be over and his professional hopes blasted. This was countryside he knew well – no more than ten *leguas* from Ciudad Rodrigo as the crow flew. He watched his captors across the little plaza and planned an escape.

This village where Captain Cole had halted for the night was en fête for a wedding, and the English visitors occupied seats of honour on a dais garlanded with flowers and ribbons.

Fresh muslin dresses, countryfied though they were in style, had done much to restore the girls' self-respect after their rough treatment in captivity. Captain Cole's generosity had not stopped at dresses. He had halted for a whole day in the first sizeable town they came to and insisted on Julia and Clio purchasing shoes, bonnets, night apparel and all the other items necessary to a lady's travelling wardrobe, together with two stout brassbound trunks to contain them.

Fortune had further favoured them when a clean, decent-looking young woman named Manuela offered her services as abigail, and in this capacity Robert was glad to engage her. Servants and baggage-boys had been added to the column, as well as half a dozen bullocks to provide meat on the hoof. It was an altogether better-equipped convoy that took the road next day, and its progress over the hills towards the frontier had been unmarred by any further accidents.

From his makeshift prison Rochefort surveyed the festive party sardonically. It was easy to see the gallant captain was over his ears in love with *la petite* – what did they call her? – Clio; *drôle de nom*, and from what he heard her father was *un drôle de type* who would never have been entrusted with a commission in any rational army, let alone put in charge of a regiment's food supplies. These English! They broke all the rules of warfare, but one had to admit there was method in Milor' Wellington's madness. The defences he had constructed so secretly at Torres Vedras had changed the whole course of the war. Even Masséna, the old fox, had not dared to beard him in that den.

So the chance of pushing the leopards into the sea, as Napoleon had ordered, was lost and now – it seemed – the pendulum had begun to swing in favour of the British, with these damned guerrilla bands springing up in every sierra to harass French convoys and patrols.

El Forastero was undoubtedly the most dangerous of them, Rochefort reflected dourly. Not the most brutal – that distinction must belong to El Moreno, whose amusement it was to see how many captured Frenchmen he could maim with each discharge of his enormous blunderbuss – but certainly the most cunning. His inclination to cooperate with the British made him a particular threat. Most guerrilla leaders were too fiercely independent to submit themselves to British orders, but Rochefort had heard rumours that El Forastero consulted regularly with Granto El Bueno, Major Colquhoun Grant, one of Lord Wellington's daring Intelligence officers.

As soon as I escape I shall make it my business to trap El Forastero, vowed Rochefort. That will be the way to retrieve my fortunes with Masséna. But first I must find a way to rid myself of these *maudit* shackles.

Again he looked across the plaza and his keen narrow eyes rested on Julia.

In a cleared space before the dais a Spanish couple of exceptional handsomeness were dancing a spirited fandango for the pleasure of their guests. The woman was full-figured and supple-waisted, with dark flashing eyes, and wore a wonderfully flounced and tiered skirt which floated round her ankles as she stamped and twirled. Her partner, slim as a sword in his tight black breeches and flowered waistcoat, moved with arrogant grace, now pursuing, now retreating in a mime of courtship that brought gasps of lust from the British troopers.

'Downright indecent, that's what it is!' muttered Sergeant Mathews, licking his lips. 'Didn't ought to be allowed, not afore those young maids' eyes.'

Despite his complaints, his own eyes remained riveted to the dancers, and the villagers smiled in amused contempt at the effect of the spectacle upon their susceptible guests.

'Bravo!' called Captain Cole, clapping enthusiastically at the conclusion of the dance, and Clio turned shining eyes upon him.

'Oh, was it not beautiful? Such grace! Such fire! What would I give to dance like that!'

Julia shook her head. 'I own I found it a trifle shocking. Such . . . such passion! Only imagine the outcry if such a dance were performed at Almack's!'

The notion made them all laugh.

'What does very well in one country will not do at all in another,' agreed Robert. 'Observe our gallant lads! I bow to no one in my conviction that they are the best soldiers on earth, but they are also certainly the worst dancers. Look at Mathews!'

With but a token show of reluctance, the staid sergeant had allowed a pretty dark-eyed girl to encircle his waist with her arm as she attempted to teach him the steps they had just witnessed. Fired by liberal potations of strong wine, Mathews embarked on the lesson with a good deal more enthusiasm than grace. Pretty soon all the troopers were similarly engaged with village damsels, while the guitarist obligingly struck up a new tune.

Robert and Clio smiled at the ludicrous spectacle, but Julia wore an expression of distaste.

'I beg you will excuse me, Captain Cole,' she said after a while. 'I find myself a little tired. No, do not disturb yourself,' she added as Clio moved to accompany her. 'Manuela will help me. What a treasure she is! We were lucky to obtain her services in so primitive a place. I am sorry to leave so soon, but I feel a headache coming on.'

'I hope you will soon be well,' said Robert civilly.

'Oh, do not concern yourself, I am sure I shall.' She smiled bravely. 'I know I can leave my sister in your care. You have been so kind! I think of you almost as our brother.'

Clio's eyes were full of laughter. 'Would you care for a stroll, dear brother?' she asked when Julia had departed.

'With pleasure.' He took her arm, saying ruefully, 'She means it as a compliment, I know, but the truth is I don't in the least wish you to regard me as a brother.'

With mock demureness she lowered her lashes. 'May I ask how you would prefer to be regarded, Captain Cole?'

Robert looked down at her and his heart lurched unsteadily. So often in imagination he had rehearsed the way he would declare his love but now the opportunity was offered, his carefully prepared words deserted him.

'Don't pretend you don't know, minx!' he said gruffly, holding her arm tightly to prevent his own shaking.

'Truly, Robert, I haven't the least idea.' She thought a moment, then added, 'Unless you wish me to regard you as Harry's best and most loyal friend, and therefore mine as well.'

'Harry's friend!'

She looked at him in astonishment: for a moment his expression was quite wild. Seeing he had frightened her, he continued more quietly but with great intensity, 'No, I do *not* wish you to think of me as Harry's friend. I love you, Clio. Can you truly be unaware of that? I have loved you ever since I first saw you.'

'But did you not know I loved Harry?' Her hand moved to her neck in the gesture she had not yet succeeded in banishing, but the locket was gone just as Harry was gone, and suddenly her eyes sparkled with tears.

How could I not know when every word, every movement proclaimed it? he thought bitterly. Aloud he said, 'Yes, but I loved you all the same. I'm a dull fellow compared to Harry, I know –'

'Papa does not think so! He says you were the best scholar he ever taught, and would have made yourself a name in the ... the groves of Academe if Harry had not dragged you into the army.'

He smiled at the tribute, but wished the conversation would not revert so constantly to Harry. 'Be that as it may, I am happy in my career. I would be happier still, I own, if I knew you liked me for my own sake – not just as an appendage to Harry. Oh, I don't deny I used to hero-worship him just as you did, but there comes a moment when a man must stand on his own.'

'I do like you for yourself!' She could not bear the hurt look in his dark anxious eyes, and hated to feel she was the cause of it. To comfort him she said, 'When I saw it was you come to rescue us, and not the French, I truly believed I was in Heaven.'

'I would be in Heaven if you would consent to marry me,' said Robert fervently.

Clio looked at him uncertainly. 'You ... you are funning.'

'I was never more serious in my life. I have always loved you, Clio, but only when I thought you were lost did I realize how very precious you have become to me.' He put his hands on her shoulders, turning her to face him. 'Say you will marry me, Clio, and I swear you will never regret it. My only wish is to make you happy.'

It was the first proposal of marriage Clio had received and she considered it with care. Harry had not asked her to marry him: he had simply taken it for granted that she would, which was not at all the same thing.

Certainly she was fond of Captain Cole, but she had never thought of him as a lover. She had supposed, if she thought of it at all, that his interest was in Laura.

How pleased Mamma would be! she thought irrelevantly. Mrs Hardy had never approved of Harry, but for Robert she entertained great affection and, since he lacked a mother of his own, treated him almost as another son. Clio tried to imagine herself married to Robert, and knew instinctively that he would make a much better husband than Harry. Robert was kind, clever, considerate and extremely rich. Even Laura would admit he was something of a catch. Though he had not Harry's dash, he was far from ill-looking, and the thought of any man eager to devote himself to making her happy was undeniably attractive. Why, then, did she hesitate?

'Is there... someone else?' asked Robert as the silence lengthened.

'No. Only –'

The shadow of Harry loomed between them. Clio's hand strayed again to her neck. She bit her lip.

'He would be glad for us.' Robert willed her to meet his eyes, but her lashes remained obstinately lowered.

She said disjointedly, 'I had not thought – You must forgive me. This comes as a great surprise.'

Yet for months Robert had been paying her the most particular attention. Why else should he single her out to the exclusion of other young females? She must have been naïve indeed not to recognize the purpose behind his attention.

He looked so lost and anxious, awaiting her reply, that her heart went out to him. He said in self-rebuke, 'I have been too hasty. You need time to consider... to talk with Julia, perhaps. What a monster I am to hurry you! It is just that I have been hoping so long....'

She raised her head and smiled. Remembering Harry's contempt for 'shillyshallying females who keep a man hanging round to please themselves', she said impulsively, 'Thank you, Robert. I – I shall be honoured to become your wife.'

He let out a whoop of delight and caught her to him in a display of emotion so unlike his usual gravity that she was startled. Passing Spaniards raised supercilious eyebrows as he kissed her enthusiastically, but Clio did not mind.

Perhaps he is not such a sobersides after all, she thought; and the shadow of Harry retreated a pace.

'Until I can buy you a ring, will you wear mine?'

'Willingly,' she said, laughing as he fumbled in haste to pull the signet from his finger. It hung too loose on her, and he clicked his tongue in vexation.

'It will fall off.'

'I will hang it round my neck,' she promised, banishing the

thought of what had hung there before. One must look forward, she told herself fiercely. Harry is dead and I have promised to marry Robert. The signet ring was heavy. She felt a quite unwarranted sense of betraying a trust.

'You have made me the happiest man on earth,' Robert assured her as they stood at the door of the house in which the girls were lodging. From the vine-covered verandah behind it came the throbbing of a guitar and a tenor voice raised in a plaintive love-song.

Robert was disposed to linger. 'I swear you will never regret it.'

'I am sure I shall not.' Clio suppressed her urge to hurry his departure. She wanted to be alone. She allowed him to kiss her again, but when he began to outline plans for their future she hushed him firmly.

'It is late. We must not wake Julia.'

'When will you tell her of our betrothal?'

Clio hesitated. 'You must allow me to decide that,' she said, and Robert looked abashed.

'Forgive me. I cannot help wishing all the world to know of my good fortune.'

'The world will know soon enough,' she assured him, smiling, and softly closed the door.

Moonlight streamed through the shutters of the best bedroom which the owners of the house had surrendered to their visitors. She stood on the threshold a moment, listening to Julia's breathing, then tiptoed to discard her clothes and creep beneath the covers. In a very few moments she was asleep, unaware that Julia was lying rigid beside her, staring into the darkness and wondering what she had done.

When Julia made a headache her excuse to leave the plaza, she walked towards her lodging via the alley where the French prisoner was confined with his two guards. There were several streets leading in the same direction. To say she *chose* this one would lay too much emphasis on a conscious decision. Rather she was drawn to it, the magnet in this instance being the burning gaze of Colonel de Rochefort.

All through the evening's festivities he had dominated her thoughts. She felt it unjust that he should languish in fetters while they made merry, and had even remonstrated with Captain Cole, urging him to accept the prisoner's parole and allow him more liberty.

'He would be ready to give his word, I am sure,' she said earnestly.

'I have no doubt you are right about that,' said Robert, laughing. 'The obstacle is that I have no authority to accept it.'

'You cannot intend to keep him bound and fettered until we reach Fuentes de Oñoro.'

'Why not? If our positions were reversed I am sure he would not dream of untying *me*.'

'But it is cruel! Barbaric!'

Robert frowned. 'My dear Miss Hardy, may I recommend you to attend to affairs which concern you and leave me to deal with mine?'

Julia flushed a deep pink. 'Surely it is the duty of any Christian to see that captives are honourably treated, Captain Cole?'

'If Rochefort has cause to complain of his treatment, let him do it himself. I am sure he is capable! Only consider: a fine cake I should look if I accepted the fellow's parole and he absconded!'

'How can you speak so and call yourself civilized?'

'Miss Hardy, while the prisoner is my responsibility he will remain in fetters. Oblige me by saying no more on the subject.'

Julia was temporarily silenced, but it did not stop her worrying about her paladin. Though his guards were under orders to protect him from any display of animosity on the part of the Spaniards, it seemed to her they took their duty lightly. On entering this small village, she had seen the prisoner jostled, jeered at and spat on, while the troopers guarding him looked on grinning and made no effort to chase away his persecutors.

As she walked down the alley she could see the guards sitting in the open doorway of the hovel which served as a gaol, craning to watch the spectacle in the plaza, while behind them the pinioned Frenchman sat on the earth floor, resting his head on his knees in an attitude of despair. Her heart went out to this caged eagle she had once seen proud and free.

'A pleasant evening,' she greeted the guards, pausing to adjust her shawl. At the sound of her voice Rochefort raised his head and sent her a look of such pleading intensity that her knees felt weak.

'Pleasant enough for them as is free to enjoy it, miss,' said Corporal Vickers belligerently. He was a sharp-faced, vinegar-tongued fellow, always ready with a grumble. 'It ain't so pleasant for us stuck 'ere with 'im to guard.'

'Oh, I am sorry,' said Julia in her gentle way. 'Of course it must be dreadfully dull to watch the dancing without being able to join in.'

'You're right there, miss. Cruel 'ard it is to watch 'em drinking and enjoying theirselves while we rot 'ere and no one takes a blind bit o' notice.'

He gave her a leering, meaning look and Julia's heart began to beat fast.

'Would it help if my maid brought you some refreshment?'

'Ah, that it would miss, that it would,' said Vickers with satisfaction. His companion, Corporal Jones, looked shocked by his impertinence.

'Very well, I will see what can be done. Pray inquire of the prisoner what he would like me to bring.'

'No need to bother with the likes of 'im! Bread and water are all 'e deserves and all 'e'll get from me.'

Julia said reprovingly, 'Certainly he must have some refreshment. No Christian would deny a captive such small comfort.' She raised her voice, asking, '*Monsieur le Colonel, qu'est-ce que vous voulez que je vous apporte à manger et à boire?*'

A light sprang into his eyes. He leaned forward eagerly. '*Je ne veux qu'une lime, mademoiselle, je vous en prie. Rien qu'une lime.*'

Lime? The word was unknown to her. Was it lime-juice he wished for? Lemonade?

'*Du citron?*' she said uncertainly.

'*Une lime pour couper mes fers, petite imbecile!*' he said in a low fierce tone. Suddenly the message got through. He wanted a file to cut his fetters. He trusted her to help him escape.

Heady excitement surged through her – excitement mixed with pride.

'Comme vous voulez, monsieur,' she said as calmly as she could; he bowed his head to hide his triumph.

'Vous êtes trop bonne, mademoiselle.'

' 'Ere, miss, that's enough o' that Frenchifying!' broke in Vickers. 'Doesn't do to act soft wi' these devils.'

'Were you in his place you might be glad of a word in your own tongue,' said Julia in gentle rebuke. She felt elated, lighter than air. 'We should all do as we would be done by, Corporal. Come, Manuela!'

Leaving the gaol, she hurried back to her lodging to find her purse, and dispatched Manuela to the nearest *posada* in search of bread and wine. While she was gone, Julia approached the owner of their lodging and begged the use of a file.

He looked surprised at the request. Julia, a notably truthful girl, listened aghast as her tongue glibly explained how a padlock on her valise had jammed, and she wished to sever the hasp.

Though he seemed disappointed that she would not accept his assistance to break the lock, he supplied the tool with a good grace and resolutely refused payment.

'De nada, señorita,' he insisted, smiling. 'It is of no value.'

'Muchas gracias, señor.'

When Manuela returned with the victuals, Julie took the opportunity to conceal the file in a long loaf. Bearing the loaded tray, they set out once more for the gaol.

Night had fallen but every little street and alley was illuminated by torches. These cast flickering shadows on the wine-flushed faces of the British soldiers and the grave most dignified Spaniards leaving the plaza. In any other circumstances Julia might have been fearful of walking at such an hour accompanied only by her maid, but tonight her romantic desire to save her paladin banished fear and she stepped out boldly.

Corporal Vickers's eyes brightened when he saw them. He

abandoned his lounging posture and moved smartly to take the wine jug and earthenware goblets from Manuela.

'Much obliged to you, miss, I'm sure. Allow me to drink your very good 'ealth.'

Julia had on her arm the basket containing three long loaves. She distributed these to the soldiers, being careful to keep her hand on the one in which the file was concealed.

'I will give this to the prisoner,' she said, but as she moved towards the dark interior of the cabin, Vickers's arm shot out to bar her way.

'Sorry, miss. No one's to go near 'im. Captain's orders.'

'But that is absurd!' she protested, retreating a pace. 'How else may I give him his food?'

'I'll give it 'im. 'Ere, you!' He plucked the loaf from her grasp. ''Eavy as lead. Them bakers should be shot,' he grumbled, and lobbed it carelessly towards Rochefort, while Julia watched in agony lest the file fall from its hiding place.

With extraordinary agility Rochefort leaned sideways and caught the loaf between his manacled hands before it could touch the floor.

'Merci, mademoiselle. Merci mille fois!'

The smile that accompanied his thanks was ample recompense for the risks she had taken. Later that night, with Clio sleeping peacefully beside her, the memory warmed Julia's heart. With growing excitement she waited for morning, and news of the prisoner's escape.

Two days later, in the crushing heat of noon, Captain Cole called a halt near the gorge where the swift-flowing Coa joins its turbulent waters to the Nocine's more placid stream. The river was wide and shallow. Whooping like boys released from school, the troopers unsaddled and rode their horses bareback into the frothing water, while the baggage-boys scurried about collecting forage and the servants prepared a hasty meal.

Clio and Julia, who felt no appetite for tough beef and ship's biscuit, withdrew a few hundred yards upstream to rest in the shade of a cork grove. Faintly to their ears came the men's splashing and laughter. Apart from Manuela's quiet presence they were alone.

Julia loosened her clothes and eased the slippers from her feet. She lay back with a sigh and closed her eyes. Clio watched her, fidgeting with the ring around her neck. She had waited in vain for her sister to remark on it or to give Clio some opening to broach the subject. Robert had begun to eye her reproachfully and ask why she did not tell Julia, but with every day that passed it became more difficult to gain her attention.

'Don't go to sleep just yet,' she said coaxingly after a moment or two's silence.

'Oh, I am too tired to talk.'

'There is something I must tell you. Something of the first importance.'

Julia yawned without opening her eyes. 'Oh, Clio, surely it can wait?'

'Please listen! I have been trying to speak to you ever since we left Covilhao, but you were in one of your dreams and would not attend.'

'Was I?' Julia was guiltily aware that lately she had paid even less heed than usual to her sister. All her thoughts had been fixed on the Frenchman, wondering why he made no move to escape. Once she had tried to speak to him, but he had looked at her so coldly that she blushed and hurried away.

'I must tell someone, and if you will not listen, who will?'

Julia settled herself more comfortably and yawned again. 'A secret? How charming! I am all ears.'

Clio looked despairingly at Julia's perfect profile against the dark tree trunk. This was the only moment of privacy they might expect today. In his haste to deliver his prisoner and the precious ciphers which El Forastero's gnome-like messenger had given him to Lord Wellington's headquarters, Robert had forced his men at a killing pace over the rough hill-tracks of the Serra de Estrela, and now with headquarters no more than a short day's ride away, he was unlikely to dawdle.

'Tell me your secret and then let me have a few minutes' peace,' said Julia.

'Captain Cole has asked me to marry him and . . . and I have accepted.'

Julia's eyes snapped open. She stared at her sister in frank astonishment. 'To *marry* him? No, surely not! It was Laura he wished to marry, but she threw him over. If this is one of your teases, Clio. . . .'

'Of course it is not a tease. Look, he has given me his ring.'

Julia examined the heavy signet ring with its engraved swan and bells. 'It seems most improper. . . . That is not an engagement ring.'

'It was all he had. Oh, Julia, do say you are pleased!'

Julia recovered herself. 'How can you doubt it? Why, it is splendid news!' she said, and embraced her warmly. Anxious to atone for her earlier lack of interest, she added, 'I have the greatest regard for Captain Cole. He is everything a gentleman should be. But is not this very sudden? I had not the least idea you felt more than friendship for him. Forgive me – I do not mean to pry – but do you truly love him?'

This was a question which weighed heavily on Clio's mind. 'I think I do,' she said after a moment's hesitation. 'Not in the way I loved Harry, of course; but yes – in a different fashion I do love him. He is so kind, you know. So eager to please me. He *needs* me, more than Harry ever did.'

Julia looked doubtful. This lukewarm declaration did not accord with her romantic ideals. Nevertheless she said, 'Then I wish you happy with all my heart. Only think how pleased poor Papa would have been!'

'Do not speak as if he was dead. Depend on it, Auguste will find a way of escape, and we shall all be together again.'

Julia sighed. She was about to question Clio further when a confused shouting in the distance made them both sit up. A moment later they heard a volley of shots.

The girls started to their feet. 'Whatever is happening?' cried Julia.

'*Los franceses vienen!* Hide yourselves!' Manuela exclaimed. She picked up her skirts and ran. Thunderstruck, they saw her vanish into the trees.

'What shall we do?' said Julia in extreme agitation.
'Hush! Listen.'
They strained their ears to interpret the confused sounds coming from the camping ground. Men shouted, horses neighed, bullocks bellowed. Hoofs pounded this way and that.

Julia struggled to force her swollen feet into her slippers. 'Run, Clio! It is the French,' she said faintly. 'Our men have been surprised.'

'Wait!'

Clio listened intently, then turned with a smile of relief. 'It is only the bullocks loose again. No need for alarm. Listen, you can hear the drivers rounding them up.'

'Wretched beasts to give us such a fright!' Pink with indignation, Julia sank down on the turf again, propping her back against a tree trunk.

The devastated state of the country made it necessary for every detachment to carry its own meat ration on the hoof, and this was not the first time that the half-dozen bullocks accompanying Captain Cole's troop had broken out of their makeshift corral of ropes and stakes. On a previous occasion four of them had stampeded through the bivouacs at dead of night, uprooting picket-lines and causing general havoc before the soldiers and muleteers combined to capture them. One had even succeeded in swimming the nearest river and escaping altogether.

'At least they will be easier to catch in daylight,' observed Clio, seating herself beside her sister and spreading out her skirt. Sunlight filtered through the leaves of the pretty grove. It was cool and quiet and she felt a twinge of pity for the men pursuing the escaped steers.

'*Mes hommages, mesdemoiselles!* A charming tableau.'

Startled, they looked up. Out of the dark shadow a familiar lean figure in a green Chasseur uniform was approaching. He rode a handsome chestnut charger and led two more horses, whose hoofs made little sound on the soft turf.

'Colonel de Rochefort!' exclaimed Julia.

'Those are Captain Cole's horses,' Clio accused, recognizing the distinctive white blaze of Robert's favourite charger.

The Frenchman bowed, smiling. 'Perfectly correct, *mademoiselle.*'

'What has happened? You have not – not hurt Captain Cole?'

'*Mais non!* The gallant Captain is quite unharmed, I assure you. I have merely taken the opportunity of liberating his cattle to create a diversion, and requisitioning his horses. The fortune of war, you know.'

'Fly, fly before your escape is discovered!' cried Julia, revealing all too plainly where her sympathy lay.

'How could I fly without first rendering thanks to my charming benefactress?' said Rochefort coolly.

'Benefactress?' Clio turned to her sister, whose vivid blush confirmed her guilt.

Rochefort smiled at Julia and she seemed to blossom like a flower touched by the sun. 'Oh, take me with you!' she pleaded. 'I will go anywhere, endure any hardship, if you will take me with you.'

'Certainly you shall accompany me, *ma belle*, and your sister too. That was my purpose in seeking you here. Allow me to assist you to mount.'

'Julia! Have you lost your senses?' demanded Clio. She stared from one to the other, appalled by the understanding between them. Steadily the sounds of the muleteers beating through the thicket came nearer.

'Come, *mademoiselle,* to horse!' said Rochefort urgently. 'We have no time to lose.'

'I don't wish to go with you.'

'Believe me, your wishes are of no importance.'

'I won't go.'

'Much as I regret to inconvenience you, I must insist. I need your help to recover certain property before we leave,' said Rochefort.

Dismounting with a quick spring, he strode purposefully up to her, and Clio felt the cold round muzzle of a pistol pressed against her heart.

'Be very careful, *mademoiselle,*' warned Rochefort in a low menacing tone. 'Guns are dangerous toys. I would be sorry to be obliged to hurt you.'

'Leave her,' whispered Julia. 'I will come with you and she will not betray us.'

'No, it is necessary to take her too. Come, mount. No argument.'

Obediently Julia turned towards one of the led horses, but as Rochefort helped her into the saddle, Clio picked up her skirts and dodged behind the nearest tree.

'Sacré Dieu!' growled Rochefort, and darted in pursuit, while Julia, clinging to the pommel as if in a trance, moaned softly.

Rochefort feinted round one side of the tree then lunged the opposite way, grasping at Clio's sleeve. 'Little fool! Come back or it will be the worse for you.'

'Come and get me,' retorted Clio, scared but defiant. Robert's men were close at hand. If she could give the alarm Rochefort might yet be recaptured. The shameful knowledge of Julia's treachery burned her mind: Julia was in thrall to her own romantic dreams and would obey any command the enchanter gave her.

Rochefort cast a glance over his shoulder, alive to the danger of the approaching muleteers. He debated whether to pursue his objective or to escape with the bird in hand, but his innate recklessness drove him on.

'Help! Murder! Help!' screamed Clio as he made another lunge towards her, but her voice sounded small and thin, lost in the general tumult. She could hardly believe her ears when, faintly, came an answering shout.

'I am coming!'

The voice was Robert's. With a leap of hope she turned towards the sound, and the momentary distraction proved her undoing. Again Rochefort pounced, this time succeeding in catching her arm.

'Let me go!' gasped Clio as his sinewy fingers bit into her flesh. She struggled unavailingly as he drew her towards him. One arm was pressed across her throat, muffling her cries; with the other he held the pistol to her head.

'Do not move, *mademoiselle*, unless you wish to die.'

Robert crashed through the thicket and into the open space beneath the cork trees: tunic unbuttoned, shirt ripped, eyes wild. In his hand was a sabre, but what use was that against the Frenchman's pistol?

'Let her go, Rochefort,' he commanded, but his eyes were afraid. 'The game's up. Put down your pistol.'

Rochefort held Clio before him like a shield. 'On the contrary, *mon Capitaine*,' he said coolly, 'it is now my turn to give orders. Oblige me by returning my ciphers. If you refuse, she dies.'

'You would never harm a woman.'

Rochefort laughed in open contempt. 'What an exalted view you have of French chivalry, *mon Capitaine!* I should have thought recent experience would have taught you otherwise. Believe me, I will shoot her with no more compunction than I would a rabbit. Give me the papers immediately. Come, no argument.'

'First let her go.'

'Do you take me for a fool?'

'Not a fool, Colonel, but a man of honour.'

'Bah! What children you English are! War is not a game to be played with petty rules and courtesies, *mon Capitaine*. Perhaps this will convince you that I am in earnest,' said Rochefort lightly, and discharged his pistol so close to Clio's head that she felt the ball scorch past her cheek and powder blackened her skin. Deafened by the blast, she screamed in terror, but Rochefort merely laughed. He replaced the pistol and drew out its twin. 'My next ball will be through her head,' he promised. 'Come, my papers.'

With a shaking hand Robert drew the packet from its hiding place in the breast of his tunic. Since obtaining the ciphers he had kept them with him constantly, now he cursed himself for not leaving them in his baggage. He tossed them across the intervening space to Rochefort, who stooped swiftly to retrieve them.

He began to back towards the horses, dragging Clio with him.

'Let her go,' said Robert angrily. 'I have done as you asked. Now you must keep your bargain.'

'Who spoke of a bargain?' jeered Rochefort. 'These ladies are my hostages. Their survival depends upon you, *mon Capitaine*.'

'You cannot make hostages of women!'

'Why not?' Rochefort shrugged. 'If you expect me to sacrifice my sole assurance that you will not pursue me, you are very much mistaken. Come, *mademoiselle*, to horse.'

'You will pay for this,' vowed Robert, watching helplessly as Clio was thrown up to the saddle of the spare horse. 'If you harm so much as one hair of their heads, I will never rest until I have destroyed you.'

'Empty threats,' said Rochefort with a mocking smile, and turned the horses' heads towards the river.

8

Manuela had been briefed for such an emergency. True to her trust, she rode her donkey through the hills all night in search of El Forastero. She found the guerrilla band far from home, preparing to storm Barbarossa's stronghold, but by then it was far too late to catch Rochefort and his hostages.

'Where has he taken them?' demanded Harry, his mouth tight and grim. Though his wound was healing, he still wore a sling. Manuela had never seen him so angry.

'To Ciudad Rodrigo, *señor*. Already they must be within its walls.'

Harry cursed freely.

'I came as quickly as I could, *señor*.'

His black brow lightened. 'I am not angry with you, only with those damned bone-headed English sentries, God rot their slovenly ways. Tell me again, how did the Frenchman escape?'

As he listened to her description of the events leading up to it, Harry was left in no doubt who had furnished Rochefort with the means of removing his fetters.

'Never have I seen a woman so foolish with love,' said Manuela, rolling her eyes. '*Está locamente enamorada*. The quiet ones are always the worst. When they love it is serious, a disease. They make heroes in their dreams and will not see that men are not heroes.'

Harry was inclined to agree. He too had sensed banked fires smouldering under Julia's cool façade. What a moment for them to catch ablaze! Rochefort was a notorious womanizer, guaranteed to cause unhappiness to anyone who loved him.

'And the dark one? *La morenita?* She did not go willingly?'

'Most unwillingly, *señor*. She fought like a tigress, *la pobrecita!* She called for her betrothed – her *novio* – to help her, but when he came it was already too late.'

'Her betrothed?' Harry frowned again.

A certain harshness in his voice puzzled Manuela. Why should El Forastero, beloved of so beautiful and passionate a woman as Doña Mercedes Cortes, concern himself with a thin, dark-eyed English girl who was not even pretty? Yet she had something, the little *morena* – some power of attraction that brought men buzzing round like wasps to a jar of honey. It was as well that she was pledged to the English officer. Doña Mercedes was famous for her jealous rages, and if she and her lover were to quarrel, the future of the whole band would be in jeopardy.

Manuela shrugged. 'She wore his ring,' she said simply. 'I know they were betrothed, for she spoke of it to her sister.'

I should be glad, thought Harry. Since I cannot marry her myself I should be glad she has chosen Rob. Good old Rob! He is the best fellow in the world and I ought to wish him happy.

But a sense of loss possessed him, a burning aching rage against war, and fate, and everything that had conspired to ruin his career and make him outcast from the society of decent women. It burned in his stomach like bile, and among the objects of this rage he could not help including Doña Mercedes.

Poor Rob! he thought. It would have been a feather in his cap to turn in Masséna's most trusted Intelligence officer, but now the best he can hope for is a reprimand for losing his prisoner and his girl as well. Rob should have stayed at home with his books and his Grecian busts, and married a good sensible English girl, not a wild flighty changeling like Clio. What a dance she will lead him!

At the thought of the dance she was likely to lead the French garrison at Ciudad Rodrigo, his mood lightened a little. Remembering various escapades of her not-so-distant childhood, he grinned reluctantly. Colonel de Rochefort could hardly have known the trouble he was bringing on himself when he forced Clio to ride away with him. Behind the enemy lines she would be worth as much as an infantry battalion to Lord Wellington in the matter of demoralizing the French.

Shaking off his sense of loss, he commended Manuela's courage and faithfulness.

'It was nothing, *señor*,' she murmured but her eyes glowed.

'I wish you to return to Ciudad Rodrigo in Doña Mercedes's household,' he said. 'You will be safe enough there. Keep your eyes and ears open, and if you hear of prisoners being exchanged, or sent to Madrid, be sure to report it to me.'

'*Sí, señor.*'

He gave her money and detailed instructions of how messages were to be passed along the guerrilla network so as to reach him with the least delay. El Forastero's band was on good terms with Don Julián Sánchez, the hate-driven Castilian farmer whose guerrilla band dominated the area around Ciudad Rodrigo. Sánchez had made the French pay in blood many times over for their murder of his wife and children: he could be counted on to join with enthusiasm in an attack on a Madrid-bound convoy. But first there were plans to be made for the punishment of Barbarossa and for Samuel Hardy's release from captivity.

Harry grimaced at the prospect of telling his old tutor about the disappearance of his daughters, and decided it was a task he must leave to Robert Cole. Old Samuel was more acute than one expected. It was vital he should not be allowed any chance to recognize his rescuer.

Dismissing Manuela, he gave orders that Pedro, his lieutenant, was to command the attack on Barbarossa's lair. Pedro was capable enough: it would do him good to bear responsibility for once. His worst fault was his cruelty, but in the matter of Barbarossa he could please himself, provided Commissary Hardy and old Auguste escaped unharmed.

These Hardys, thought Harry, picking up his pen to draft tomorrow's order, what trouble they cause! Clio and Julia prisoners, and Laura setting Lisbon society by the ears! What the deuce could have prompted Samuel to bring his daughters with him to the Peninsula?

An hour later Doña Mercedes came to him as he sat in the darkening parlour, gazing out across the valley, the pen unmoving in his hand.

'Enrique! What are you thinking of?' She pulled his head back to rest against her bosom and he felt the quick, insistent beating of her heart.

'Do not waste the precious moments we are together by sitting here in the dark! Come to my bed and warm me,' she whispered.

He followed her upstairs and responded to her passion as she desired, but even as he lay pressed to her voluptuous body in the enveloping softness of the farmer's best feather bed, his thoughts were of an English rose garden at dusk, the scent of new-mown hay, and a slim girl's laughter.

Samuel Hardy was a single-minded man. Finding himself a prisoner within the walls of a Moorish castle in a remarkable state of preservation, and recognizing the ruins of a Roman town beneath its battlements, he wasted no time in bemoaning his fate but set to work at once to sketch the castle and discover the secrets of its construction. 'Escape?' he scoffed when his gaolers protested. 'Why should I wish to escape? This fortress is a jewel. I am perfectly content to remain here.' His enthusiasm was contagious. As a teacher, his greatest gift had always been his power to communicate his passion for a subject to even the dullest of his pupils. Pretty soon the guards became curious, and finally eager to assist. They helped him draw plans and measure stones. In his excellent French he gave them the benefit of his highly individual view of Spanish history.

'Spain has been ruined by her riches,' he declaimed to the men mixing plaster for the scale model he had begun to construct. 'If her *conquistadores* had stayed at home to lift their country out of the slough of superstitious ignorance and broken the power of the priesthood, she might now be a thriving modern state instead of lagging two hundred years behind the rest of Europe.

When the floodgates of easy wealth opened to them, the Spaniards neglected domestic trade, manufacture and husbandry. Only when the Peninsula can break the golden fetters that bind her to the New World will the rays of science and of truth which have illuminated other nations shine on wretched Spain.'

Such speeches were wholly to the taste of the French deserters of Barbarossa's band; even the brutal ex-sergeant himself was amused by his eccentric captive. He sent a message inviting him to dine.

Samuel shuddered. 'Tell him I will be glad to accept his invitation if he will permit my clerk to prepare the meal,' he responded. 'I am not a strong man, and the abominations that pass for dishes among Spaniards play the deuce with my constitution.'

Barbarossa graciously gave his permission, and soon Auguste, released from his bonds, was engaged in his favourite activities of baking and roasting, ordering fine wines to be brought up from the cellar and the tenderest young vegetables and salads from the garden. The excellence of the resulting dinner was enough to convince Barbarossa that these prisoners must be treated with respect.

Night after night, the two would sit over their wine in the Castelo Rubio's great hall, Barbarossa's pockmarked face and coarse red beard turned eagerly to Samuel as he demanded further stories of the valiant Roman legions.

'And what did Tiberius do then? And Claudius? *Racontez-moi encore.*'

Lacking all education and unable even to write his name, he had an almost mystical reverence for a man like Samuel Hardy who knew the secrets of the past. Samuel loved the sound of his own voice and never before had Fate given him such an opportunity to exercise it. Military history, Greek mythology, politics and archaeology – he held forth on them all to the spellbound Barbarossa.

'Don't stop. Tell me more,' he would urge when Samuel at last fell silent.

'Do you take me for Schéhérazade? How can I talk when my throat is as dry as dust?'

His glass would be filled and away he would go again, until Barbarossa's eyes glazed and his head fell forward in his plate. Weaving top-heavily, swearing eternal friendship, Englishman and Frenchman would stagger away to bed.

So pleasant this life seemed to Samuel and so congenial the company that he was far from pleased to be roused one night in the small hours by a bearded desperado slung about with weapons and ammunition, who ordered him brusquely to get up and follow since the castle was mined and about to be blown sky-high. Pedro's guerrillas had taken Barbarossa completely by surprise.

'It is a great deal too bad of you, Cole,' Samuel grumbled, after a bullock cart had deposited him and Auguste safely back in Robert's camp. 'You, of all people, in whom I hoped I had instilled a proper veneration for the treasures of antiquity. Barbarossa was an excellent fellow, and between us we were making a valuable contribution to archaeological research. Now you have ruined it all. You should be ashamed. You are no better than a Vandal.'

Politely Robert disclaimed responsibility for his rescue. He pointed out that the *guerrilleros* had acted at the request of Mr Hardy's daughters.

'Then *they* should be ashamed,' said Samuel vigorously. 'Interfering baggages! What have I done to deserve such children? Upon my soul, I cannot imagine why I agreed to bring them. They cause me nothing but worry and annoyance.'

The news that two of his daughters were captives of the French hardly moved him as much as the destruction of his beloved Castelo Rubio. Robert wondered whether, in his anxiety to spare the bereaved father pain, he had not made clear how dangerous was the girls' situation.

'Oh, I daresay they will be well enough treated,' said Samuel with marked indifference. 'The French are a civilized people. I would be a good deal more anxious had they fallen into Spanish hands, for all that *they* are supposed to be our allies.'

'I am ordered to return to Lisbon, sir. May I offer you my escort? No doubt you will wish to acquaint Miss Laura with the whole story in person.'

Samuel raised his eyebrows. 'I wish I could take so light a view of my duties as you do of yours, Captain Cole,' he said severely. 'Upon my soul, whatever next! Were I your commanding officer, I should have an exceedingly poor opinion of a military man who preferred dallying with the belles of Lisbon to facing the enemy.'

Poor Robert, still smarting from his Colonel's rebuke over the bungled affair of Masséna's spy, could only gape at this attack.

'But, sir –'

'As a war commissary on active service, my place is with my regiment,' continued Mr Hardy. 'A letter to Laura will do very well. Perhaps you will oblige me by seeing it is delivered? Now, Captain, if you will provide horses for me and my clerk, and direct me to the Commissary-General's office, I have the honour to bid you good day.'

'Please, dearest Godmamma, just one more! See how prettily she smiles! I swear on my honour this will be the very last.'

'My dear Laura, this is the fifth time you have made that promise,' said Hugh Arbuthnot, looking with disfavour at the dirty scrap of humanity cradled in his guest's arms. 'Really, you have tried my mother's patience far enough. Return that filthy brat to its parents and be done with it. You are making yourself ridiculous. Pretty soon every beggar in Lisbon will think he has only to knock at this door and all his wants will be supplied.'

'I wish they could be,' said Laura forcefully. 'Poor souls, you can have no idea what they suffer. Remember, it was we who made them leave their homes. You cannot be surprised that they look to us now to relieve their afflictions. Compared to us, they want so little.' She looked meaningly at the breakfast table burdened with ham and eggs, sausages and kidneys, the loaf of white bread, confits and fruit, the big silver chocolate pot on its spirit-lamp and the smaller teapot. Finally, accusingly, she allowed her gaze to rest on the pastry charged with quince conserve which Lady Arbuthnot was in the act of conveying to her mouth.

'All this child's mother found to eat yesterday was a rat. We should be ashamed to feast while these poor creatures starve.'

Lady Arbuthnot replaced the pastry on her plate. 'Really, Laura, you quite spoil my appetite,' she complained. 'Give the child to your maid and come and tell us about the play you saw last night. Forget this nonsense. The world is full of injustice but you cannot right it single-handed, you know.'

'Then may I keep her?' Laura's face lit up. 'Dearest Godmamma, you are an angel.'

'Keep her if you must,' said Lady Arbuthnot reluctantly, 'but I warn you she must be the last. After this, I will accept no more beggar children, no matter how pitiable their tale.'

Hugh's long upper lip expressed disapproval. He was a thickset, jowly young man with sandy eyelashes and an air of unconquerable superiority. At first he had felt himself attracted by this handsome, lively protégée of his mother's, and looked with indulgence upon the waifs she seemed incapable of turning from the door. Scabby, diseased, and so undernourished that they were mere bundles of bones, the children were deposited at the Arbuthnots' house and Laura took them in. Hugh had given secret orders to the butler that no more beggars were to be admitted, but it made no difference. The parents simply waylaid Laura in the street, and another starving child would join the household, smuggled in beneath Laura's cloak or in her maid's basket. There must be ten or a dozen of them now, he thought, all eating their heads off at my expense. It is too bad of Laura.

To begin with her philanthropic dabblings had been a source of mild amusement – even admiration – to Hugh's cronies. They were inclined to think better of him for permitting her to fill his house with the unfortunate flotsam of the war.

'You're a good fellow, Arbuthnot, damn me if you ain't,' declared his friend Major Reed of the 19th Foot, recuperating from Guadiana fever. 'Everyone should do his bit for these poor devils, but it beats me how you stand 'em in the house with you.' He had grinned. 'I should guess Miss Laura's pretty eyes have something to do with that, eh, you dog?'

But now Hugh felt the matter had gone quite far enough. Laura's eyes, however pretty, were insufficient compensation for the trouble and expense they were causing him. Hang it, he thought, Laura got the credit but *he* was the fellow at whose expense all these beggars were fed and housed. He had had enough of it, and so Laura must be made to understand.

He said stiffly, 'No, Mother. You forget, I am master here and I say that child must be returned at once to its parents. I will not tolerate one more vagabond under this roof. Do I make myself clear?'

'But – but you told me you admired me for helping these unfortunates. You did! You cannot deny it.' Laura's voice shook: she went very pale.

'There is a vast difference between helping two or three and helping a dozen. Why, there is hardly a room in the house where one does not stumble over these wretched objects of your misplaced charity, and my servants spend far too much time tending them.'

'That is not true in the least! My children have never caused you the smallest inconvenience,' said Laura hotly. 'From the first I gave strict orders that you were not to be troubled with them, and they were never to be placed where the sight of them might offend you.'

'Out of sight is hardly out of earshot, my dear Laura,' said Hugh dryly. 'No, Mother, I must ask you not to interfere in this. It is high time Laura was brought to her senses.'

'It is you who have lost your senses, and I am *not* your dear Laura!' she cried, starting up from the table. 'Very well: if my children are unwelcome in your house, I shall take them to someone who will be *glad* to accommodate them. Someone with a better heart than you, Hugh Arbuthnot. Someone who means what he says instead of mouthing worthless platitudes and laughing at me behind my back!'

Where she would find such a person she had not the smallest idea, but Laura's tongue had always been inclined to run ahead of prudence, and in her anger at Hugh's betrayal she did not pause to consider the consequences of antagonizing him.

Lady Arbuthnot, who dreaded dissent within her household, tried to pour oil on troubled waters, but she could not help wondering sadly what had become of the gentle, prettily-behaved young female she had taken under her wing.

'Pray, do not say anything so dreadful, my dear. Of course you are welcome here and it is very wrong of Hugh to speak to my guest in such a way. Hugh! Oblige me by apologizing to Laura at once.'

'No, he is right. I have imposed upon your hospitality too long,' said Laura, who had her share of pride. 'Believe me, ma'am, I would not have stayed unless I thought you approved my efforts to save these children. Now I see you do not, I will find them other quarters without delay.'

'My dear child, there is no need –'

'Where will you go?' cut in Hugh, who had no intention of letting this opportunity slip.

Where, indeed? Laura cast her mind over the list of her acquaintance. Surely there must be one among them who would welcome her ragamuffin troop?

'God will provide,' she answered, with a disregard for reality worthy of Samuel Hardy himself.

Hugh gave a snort of disbelief. He folded his news-sheet and left the room.

'You should not take too much notice of Hugh,' said his mother confidentially. It was true her spirits had soared at the prospect of seeing the last of Laura's brood, but now as she surveyed her god-daughter's white angry face, her kind heart smote her. She reflected on the scandal it would cause if it got about that she had turned Mr Hardy's daughter out of doors.

'Gentlemen are seldom fond of small children, and in many ways Hugh is very like his father. He will come round in time, you may depend on it.'

'Dear ma'am, I would not dream of abusing your hospitality further,' said Laura. 'Now if you will excuse me, I will see what is to be done.'

Four hours later, hot and dishevelled, Laura returned to the Arbuthnots' house with her spirits at a low ebb. She had made numerous calls upon numerous friends – all without the smallest success. Politely but very firmly each had declined to house her orphans. It was a shock to discover how specious were the promises, how shallow the goodwill of her English acquaintances the moment she was obliged to ask practical assistance. While they believed her tucked securely under Lady Arbuthnot's wing, the Misses O'Connor and Carberry, Mesdames Sykes and Westfield had been glad to play with the pretty Portuguese waifs when they made their morning calls. They delighted in petting, dressing, feeding, and even washing them. In her innocence, Laura had believed they took the same interest as she did in the children's rehabilitation. Now, as one lady after another explained how impossible it would be for her to offer them shelter, Laura was rudely disabused of this belief. It was only a game for them, she thought, like playing with dolls. Oh, whatever shall I do? Thirteen children and nowhere to take them.

For despite her promise that little Maria-Rosa should be the last, she had not returned empty-handed from the morning's walk. The latest recruit to her family, a starvling sparrow of a toddler less than two years old, was clasped in her arms as she climbed the steep steps to the Arbuthnots' door, hoping she would not meet Hugh. The child had been thrust at her in the main plaza by a hollow-eyed young mother, with the words: 'Take him, *senhora*, for the love of all the saints. I cannot feed him and he will die.'

How could I refuse? she thought; and then with sudden anger: How is it that Miss Carberry and Miss O'Connor can turn their eyes from these unfortunates while I cannot?

As she reached the front door it opened and a man in uniform came out, his back towards her as he bade farewell to Hugh. Laura drew back to the shadowed wall, unwilling to confess the failure of her mission.

The door shut. The officer turned and came down the steps; with pleasure and a certain surprise she recognized Captain Cole.

'Ah, Laura! The very person I wished to see!' he exclaimed, and his long serious face lit with a smile. 'I have been waiting an hour, and had just given you up. But who is this?' He bent to examine the child in her arms. 'What a beautiful boy – but so thin! These poor Portuguese. So many of them are starved. Is it true that you have rescued a number of these poor waifs and taken them into your care?'

'I do what I can for them,' she admitted.

'Then I congratulate you. It is all too rare to hear of our countrywomen taking a practical interest in the problems war has brought to this nation. You must be tired, carrying him in this heat. Allow me to hold him for you.'

'No, no. He is far from clean and probably verminous as well! He will certainly spoil your uniform.'

'Nonsense!' He took the small bundle, cradling him expertly against his shoulder and laughing at her surprise. 'Never fear, I will not drop him. I know just how babies should be held.'

He rang the bell and they were admitted.

'May I ask where you came by this knowledge?' she asked, smiling shyly. Of a sudden he seemed younger and more carefree than she had known him.

'Oh, that is too long a story.' As he recalled his errand, the laughter left his face.

'I am so glad to see you, Captain Cole. Is it too much to hope that you can give me news of Papa, and my sisters?'

'No, indeed. That was the purpose of my call.'

'I hope they are well?'

Robert hesitated. 'As to that, I can hardly say.' He pulled a letter from his pocket and handed it to her, saying, 'Your father entrusted me with this letter which he asked me to deliver in person. I fear – I fear it contains news that will distress you.'

Laura bit her lip. Without another word she took the letter and he waited, absentmindedly rocking the sleeping baby, while she read it.

When she looked up, he saw tears sparkling on her lashes. 'This is terrible news,' she said. 'Julia and Clio prisoners? I can hardly believe it. What use could two girls be to the enemy?'

Robert could think of several uses, none of them suitable for her ears. 'It is seldom easy to divine French motives,' he said somewhat lamely. 'Perhaps they wish to make an exchange of prisoners.'

'What can we do to help them?'

He leaned forward earnestly. 'Everything that can be done has been done, believe me. A letter has been sent under flag of truce to the Governor of Ciudad Rodrigo, demanding their safe return. That was more than a week ago. It may be they have already been released.'

'I hope with all my heart you are right! Poor Julia!'

'Are you not equally sorry for Clio?' said Robert defensively.

'Oh no! Clio will think it a splendid adventure, but poor Julia will be scared to death.'

'On the contrary, everything points to the fact that Julia herself engineered the prisoner's escape, while Clio did all in her power to detain him,' said Robert with an anger he could not suppress. His raised voice caused the baby to wake and cry loudly. 'If only I had reached them more quickly,' he went on, hardly seeming to notice as Laura took the screaming bundle from him. 'I might have been able to save her. She had promised to marry me, you know.'

Laura shook her head, bewildered. 'Julia promised to marry you?'

'No, no. Your sister Clio.'

'But –'

The urgent need to silence the baby before his cries reached Hugh Arbuthnot's ears made Laura say hurriedly, 'I am sorry. I must leave you. The Arbuthnots do not care for children. They think they should be seen but not heard.'

'How many have you? May I see them?'

She cast a flurried glance at him. 'No, better not. I would not wish – You would not be interested.'

'I assure you I would. Come, lead the way.'

'Oh, very well,' she said ungraciously. She preceded him down a maze of corridors and covered ways to the wing where the children were installed. By rights, this should have been the quarters of Lucia, the cook. Though she had good-naturedly turned them over to Laura's growing 'family' it was part of Hugh's complaint that since Lucia now lived with her mother in the stableyard, her cooking had lost its quality.

With an air of mingled resignation and defiance, Laura flung open the door of a long light room, packed with humanity. There was a moment's startled silence, then she was engulfed in a tidal wave of children, who ran at her and swirled round her skirts, clamouring to be picked up.

'Laura!' they shrilled. 'Mama Laura!'

'Good God!' said Robert faintly, taking a step backwards. 'How many are there?'

Laura hugged one after another. 'Pepe! Pedro! Manolito! Quiet, children, let me look at you.' Though her Portuguese was poor, they understood her and fell silent. 'Here is a gentleman come to see you. Are they well, Madalena?' she asked the smiling woman who put aside her sewing and came to greet her. 'Did little Silvia sleep all right? How is Susannah's leg? See, children, I have brought a new brother to play with you.'

She crouched down to show them the baby, who had stopped crying and stared back at them, black eyes solemn in his little pug's face. Robert caught his breath. The spoilt, peevish young woman he remembered was transformed into a Madonna.

Absorbed by the children, she did not see him leave. On his way out he encountered Hugh Arbuthnot standing by the fountain in the tiled courtyard, an expression of deep dissatisfaction on his freckled face.

'Why, Cole!' he said in surprise. 'I thought you left some time ago. Laura has returned, if you still wish to speak to her. I heard another of those damned brats yowling just a moment ago.'

'Thank you – I have already seen her. Is it not splendid what she is doing for those poor children?'

Hugh gave him a suspicious glance and his scowl became more pronounced. 'What she is doing is making me a laughing-stock and my house a den of thieves.'

'Surely you cannot deny that the poor creatures deserve her charity?' said Robert with raised eyebrows.

'*You* may call it charity. I call it damned bad form to fill my house with a pack of beggar-brats and feed them at my expense. If it wasn't for my mother, I'd turn the whole lot out in the street and be damned to 'em.'

'Indeed?' said Robert politely. 'Would you include Miss Laura in this exodus?'

Hugh glared at him, belatedly aware of expressing his irritation too freely before a comparative stranger. 'Of course not. It's easy enough for you military men to look down your noses. You don't have to live with the consequences of your fighting and laying waste the country, as we unfortunate civilians are obliged to.'

'Precisely. That is why I find Miss Laura's efforts so admirable,' said Robert firmly, and bade him good day.

He repaired to the lodgings he had hired, still bemused by the extraordinary change Portugal had wrought in Laura. She deserves my help, he thought, and by God! she shall have it. I shall spare no effort to see she does not have to endure the slights and sneers of that oaf Arbuthnot another day.

As he began his search for a house commodious enough to shelter Laura's entire brood, he felt happy for the first time in weeks, and the image of Clio carried away to captivity faded from his mind.

9

Julia strolled arm-in-arm with Colonel de Rochefort in the formal garden of the fortress at Ciudad Rodrigo, overlooking the Roman bridge across the Agueda river. Clio had declined to accompany them.

'*Chère amie,* I must bid you farewell,' he said, and she turned on him a look of anguish.

'Where are you going? Oh, do not leave me, I beg! You cannot be so cruel.'

He smiled at that. Putting a hand beneath her chin, he kissed her lightly on the lips. She clung to him, repeating, 'Oh, do not go. I shall die if you leave me.'

'Do not blame me, *ma petite,*' he said, gently detaching himself. 'The Governor has been warned of an attack, and means to send you to Madrid for your own safety. Do not cry: we shall not be parted for long. I will make it my business to visit Madrid very often. I will take you to theatres . . . balls. . . . Ah, that pleases you?'

'Shall we be married there?' whispered Julia, gazing at him with her heart in her eyes. Not for the first time he wondered how the myth had arisen that English women were cold. Certainly this lovely creature was far from cold, though her innocence made him smile. Her thoughts of love were coupled with those of marriage; yet she was a peach ripe for the plucking. Were it not for her little termagant of a sister, he thought ruefully, he would have bedded the lovely Julia weeks ago. It amused him to see her restrain her ardour for fear of Clio's scolding tongue. No doubt she was watching them now, preparing to berate Julia for consorting with the enemy. He grinned.

'As to marriage, we shall see. Come, *ma belle*, smile for me! Let us make the most of the time that remains to us.'

He drew her into his arms, unable to resist a glance of triumph at the window above as Julia willingly lifted her lips to his. Mademoiselle Clio might protest as she pleased, thought Rochefort, her sister belonged to him, body and soul, and he intended to enjoy her to the full.

'You let him kiss you,' accused Clio the moment Julia returned. The room that served as their living quarters and prison was a somewhat bleak apartment, furnished in the Spanish style with massive wooden furniture, black with age, its only touch of comfort provided by a well-upholstered chaise-longue of French design.

On this Julia stretched herself, gazing at Clio through half-closed eyes. 'You should not play Peeping Tom. It is quite permissible to kiss the man one is going to marry.'

'How can you even *speak* of marrying a Frenchman?'

'Oh, Clio, what a child you are! Haven't all the greatest lovers belonged to opposing sides? Romeo and Juliet – Dido and Aeneas – Paris and Helen – Antony and Cleopatra....'

'That man does not love you,' said Clio brutally.

'Of course he does. He is sending us to Madrid – for our own safety, you know – and there we will be married.'

'You ninny!' scoffed Clio. 'Don't you see he merely wishes to add you to *Le Bordel Ambulant*? He thinks it will enhance his prestige to have an English mistress.'

'Why can't you speak English? I haven't the least idea what you are talking about,' said Julia, but her colour had risen.

'Then I'll explain. *Le Bordel Ambulant* – The Travelling Brothel – is what French soldiers call King Joseph's army. Auguste told me so.'

'Auguste should mind his tongue. Mamma would be angry to hear you use such language.'

'Each general officer, from the Marshal down, takes his *chère amie* to war with him. On his staff, you know – it is quite the thing! He dresses her in a fancy uniform and lets her follow the rabble. How charming you will·look on your little pony among the camp followers!'

It was a rather different picture from the one Rochefort had painted.

'I won't listen to your nonsense,' said Julia, close to tears. 'You don't know what you're talking about. He *does* love me.'

Turning her back, she took up a sketch of the castle garden, but Clio saw her shoulders were shaking.

She has become an enemy herself, she thought sadly. That man has bewitched her. If only El Forastero had killed him when he had him in his power! Still, the news that they were to be moved was cheering. Anything would be better than sitting in this gloomy fortress with nothing to do but bicker with Julia.

Perhaps I will get a chance to escape, she thought, though it is useless to expect Julia to help me. If I escape, it must be alone.

Rochefort had lied when he blamed the decision to move them upon the Governor. It was his own idea: the product of a devious brain and long musing on the subject of how to catch El Forastero.

Every day that passed brought news of fresh depredations by the principal guerrilla chiefs in the region, Don Julián Sánchez and El Forastero. Convoys were ambushed and robbed; couriers murdered. Captured dispatches, often stained with the courier's blood, would arrive at British military headquarters and it was clear that Lord Wellington's uncanny prescience when it came to frustrating French plans and blocking their manoeuvres was largely due to the activities of the guerrillas on his behalf.

Rochefort had been charged with the special mission of putting an end to these losses against which French military might seemed powerless. The first step must be to catch and destroy the guerrilla chiefs.

As he reviewed for the hundredth time his own brief meeting with El Forastero, an idea came to Rochefort. At first it seemed preposterous ... but as he mulled it over, it fitted with a number of known facts about the guerrilla: the high degree of discipline among his followers. His strange leniency towards captives. Last, but not least, there was his soubriquet: El Forastero: The Stranger.

Rochefort lit a cigar and considered the customary weaknesses of Spanish guerrilla chiefs. By and large they were boastful, unpredictable and cruel, and there was a certain pattern to their operations which made them vulnerable. They would only attack poorly guarded convoys. They would ambush, but seldom pursue. Above all they were too jealous of one another to cooperate in combined manoeuvres, even when cooperation would more than double their strength.

El Forastero was dangerous because he had none of these weaknesses. Might it therefore follow that he was not a Spaniard at all? Not a Spaniard, but a *forastero* – an alien – in short, a British officer.

This could explain why the guerrilla chief had never spoken directly to the English girls. His Spanish was fluent, certainly, but there were so many variations of speech here in the mountainous border country between Portugal and Spain that an accent went unremarked.

I shall put it to the test, thought Rochefort with the surge of excitement he used to feel when a shy roebuck, patiently stalked, ventured at last within musket range. Like an animal he relied on his instincts and they seldom failed him. His thoughts leapt ahead as the plan took shape: a valuable convoy – an insufficient escort – the English girls as bait....

That will tempt him, thought Rochefort, and threw away his cigar. The escort will look weak, but I shall be there. This time El Forastero shall not escape me.

The Colonel asked the Governor for an escort. The Governor grumbled, but had to agree. He aired his complaints when he dined with his friend Don Sebastian Cortes and his beautiful wife, Doña Mercedes. The wines were delicate, the food sumptuous. The Governor looked across the table at his hostess's splendid bosom and dark brilliant eyes glowing in candlelight, and unburdened himself of his troubles.

'That damned fellow Rochefort is demanding an escort to take his loot to Madrid. Rot the blighter! How he expects me to spare him a troop when half my horses are lame and the other half foundered from chasing the damned guerrillas, he doesn't say. These Intelligence types are all the same. Expect you to hand them the moon on a silver plate, and you can whistle for thanks!'

'It is too bad of Colonel de Rochefort,' said Doña Mercedes in the low thrilling voice that sent shivers up the Governor's spine.

Her husband said stiffly, 'Why should you take orders from a mere Colonel? What is so important that it needs an escort to Madrid?'

'Nothing but a few cartloads of ecclesiastical loot and those damned English girls. Skinny little pieces. Can't think why he bothers to keep 'em!' The Governor looked with frank admiration at his hostess. 'If they were fine handsome women like your wife,' he said to Don Sebastian, 'it would be another matter.'

'I fear you are a flatterer, *señor*,' said Doña Mercedes with delicious coyness. Her dark eyes promised a thousand delights. 'When does this convoy leave?'

From his vantage point in a church tower, El Forastero surveyed the convoy inching across the barren uncultivated wilderness between Ciudad Rodrigo and La Bercola. The golden broom which had bloomed in glory a month ago was over now and only a few late-flowering cistus relieved the grey-brown monotony of the landscape, but what it lacked in beauty it made up for in natural cover. Though the ground appeared flat, an army could have hidden among the dry hummocks of rockrose and broom. Harry put the glass to his eye and scanned the area on either side of the road where his men lay in ambush, but not a movement or gleam of metal betrayed their presence.

Satisfied, he returned to his examination of the convoy. A closed carriage on springs, drawn by four sleek Andalusian mules, was clearly the girls' conveyance. Fore and aft of it were a dozen country carts piled with boxes and chests: French plunder on its way to France. At the head and tail of the convoy rode armed Chasseurs. Harry counted them: less than twenty all told. An easy target. Too easy a target?

A shadow crossed his mind: a fleeting suspicion. Would even the hard-pressed Governor of Ciudad Rodrigo permit a convoy to travel with so weak an escort? Could it be a trap? Then he pushed the suspicion aside. If Clio and Julia were taken to Madrid, all hope of saving them was gone. This was his chance and he must make the most of it.

Clio had been surprised, Julia indignant when instead of being handed into the comfort of the sprung carriage they were made to crouch on the uneven floor of a country cart, surrounded by sacks and boxes piled so high they could not see out.

'You have made a mistake. *That* is our conveyance.' Julia pointed to the sprung carriage.

The sergeant of the escort shrugged. '*Non, mademoiselle.*'

'It is. It must be. You cannot expect us to travel all the way to Madrid in this dirty vehicle.'

'Those are my orders.'

'Then you have mistaken them,' said Julia in her laboured French. 'Summon Colonel de Rochefort.'

'He is not here, *mademoiselle*.' The sergeant grinned.

'He must be here. Call him at once or I shall report you.'

The man made a rude and explicit gesture and turned away. 'Mount. March!'

'I *shall* report you,' cried Julia in a fury, but the waggon started with a jolt and further protest went disregarded.

The girls settled themselves as best they could among the sacks and boxes. They drew muslin veils over their mouths after the manner of Portuguese women, having learned by experience that this was the best defence against the choking dust, and prepared for long hours of discomfort. At the end of sixty minutes their backs ached; as the sun rose higher hammers beat at their temples and their mouths tasted of sand. It was better not to talk.

At noon they halted for an hour, and then resumed their

march. Julia, lulled into a stupor by the heat and monotonous creaking of the wheels, lay comatose in her nest of sacks. Clio gazed at the blue arc of sky and conversed with Harry's ghost.

She did not often permit herself this indulgence. It was a secret vice – a weapon saved for those moments when discomfort and misery threatened to overwhelm her. Soon after he had sailed with his regiment for the Peninsula she had begun to use him in this way to bolster her spirits in adversity, and even when she knew he was dead the habit persisted. Lately she had tried to put an imaginary Robert to the same use, but he was less effective in the role of spine-stiffener. He lacked the ghostly Harry's astringency.

'Oh, poor Clio!' the imaginary Robert would say when tears of helplessness or frustration threatened. 'What a terrible time you are having.'

'What, crying again?' Harry would jeer. 'Proper little fountain you are, these days.'

'*You* would cry if your sister betrayed you, and your father was dead, and you were hot and tired and lonely and thirsty....'

'I wouldn't! I'd plan how to get even with that rotten frog-eater. I'd make him pay for abducting me. If Julia's too besotted to help, as you say, you'll have to help yourself, won't you? Turn off the tap and do some thinking for a change.'

All Clio could think today was that if she had never been fool enough to agree to run away with Harry, he would not have joined the army instead of going up to Oxford, as his father wished him to. If he hadn't joined the army, he would not have been killed. In a way, she was responsible for his death.

Harry must have travelled this road. On the way to Madrid they would pass through Talavera de la Reyna, scene of the fatal charge. Did Harry's ghost still hover over the field?

A violent jolt interrupted her musing. A moment later wild yells rent the air.

'*Los guerrilleros vienen! Vamos fugir!*'

As one man, the drivers flung away their whips and fled.

Clio shook Julia's arm. 'Julia, wake up! We have been attacked!'

Unable to see what was happening, Clio scrambled to the top

of the boxes that formed their travelling pen, then ducked sharply as shot rattled against the wood. She peered with more caution through a gap between two crates, but the field of vision was too limited to give much idea of what was going on. The attack had thrown the carts into indescribable confusion compounded by noise and the choking clouds of dust. She saw arms rise, swords flash, horses rear, and the sporadic deafening explosions of muzzle-loading guns made her clap her hands to her ears.

The attackers were cutting the traces, letting the carts in the convoy crash down on shafts or tailboard as they dragged the horses and mules away. Some they overturned, spilling out goblets and candlesticks, tapestries, books, and rich embroideries. The Chasseurs of the escort fought grimly, hacking and stabbing the nimble foes swarming round the carts, but they were outnumbered.

'Heaven save us!' Julia clung to the tailboard as their cart rocked like a ship in a storm. A moment later a concerted heave from the guerrillas capsized it. Sacks rained down on top of the girls. The lid of a chest burst open and gold coins rolled into the dust.

'Quick, Julia! Now's our chance!'

The guerrillas flung themselves off their horses to grovel among the hoofs and wheels. Clio tugged at her sister's hand, but Julia held fast to the tailboard, moaning, 'Leave me alone. I won't go.'

There was no time to lose. Any moment one of the grovelling men might look up and see them. Clio gave one last unavailing tug to Julia's hand, then picked up her skirts and ran for cover. Heedless of scratched legs and ripping clothes, she plunged into the thick tangle of undergrowth from which the *guerrilleros* had emerged, and flung herself to the ground.

'Fool!' she sobbed. 'Why wouldn't you come?'

No one had followed her. The fight was hottest round the closed carriage which the mounted escort defended as best they could until the tide of *guerrilleros* forced them back. As they retreated, a slim figure in russet leather leapt down from his horse and wrenched open the carriage door.

'*Clio! Julia! Come out!*'

Afterwards Clio wondered if she had imagined the words. Why should a *guerrillero* speak English, and how did he know their names? For a moment he stood poised on the step, peering into the darkness within. Then an arm reached out and dragged him into the carriage. The door slammed shut.

'Treachery!'

The carriage walls bulged and shook as a titanic struggle took place inside. Next minute the whole vehicle seemed to disintegrate as men burst from it – six, eight, nine armed men – in hot pursuit of the russet *guerrillero*.

'That's him. Don't let him escape.'

Rochefort's shout pierced the din. The mounted Chasseurs wheeled as if by prearranged signal, encircling the russet figure, cutting him off from his companions. For a few hectic moments he dodged them, doubling on his tracks like a frantic hare; then, finding himself surrounded, he flung up his hands.

A groan burst from the *guerrilleros*'s throats. As if by common consent the fighting ceased, and eyes were fixed on Rochefort as, holding his pistol steadily aimed at the *guerrillero*'s breast, he strode forward to claim his surrender.

'El Forastero? We meet again.'

The russet bandit said nothing. His hand dropped towards his belt, but a sharp command from Rochefort arrested it.

'Throw down your sword.'

The weapon clattered on the road.

'Your pistol.'

The silver-mounted gun followed the sword. Warily Rochefort surveyed his captive. He had not expected him to surrender so easily. He signed to two of the Chasseurs.

'Arrest him.'

From the tail of her eye Clio caught a movement on the edge of the ring of Chasseurs. A young ragged boy, curious to see what was happening, had edged his way through the throng until he stood just behind the wall of French horses. Trailing on a halter-rope he held a worn-out pack-pony, its drooping head and tangled mane witness to years of neglect though the delicate dished face spoke of Arabian blood.

The Chasseurs closed in on the prisoner.

'My lord! Your steed!' shouted the boy. He dropped the halter and darted back the way he had come, vanishing in the crowd.

Steed? thought Clio. *Steed?* That bag of bones couldn't raise a trot.

The effect on the russet bandit was instantaneous. One moment he was standing with bowed shoulders, defeat in every line; the next he had dropped to hands and knees and squirmed beneath the belly of the nearest charger.

'Catch him!' shouted Rochefort, his voice sharp with alarm.

Too late. Before the Chasseurs could wheel their horses, the prisoner emerged from their encircling wall and the hands that stretched to catch him closed on air.

In two strides he reached the pony, whose drooping head came up with a jerk as he landed astride it bareback. As Clio watched, astonished, the bag of bones was transformed into an Arabian thoroughbred, a creature of fire and grace with speed in every muscle and finely-tuned sinew.

'*Vaya, Francisco!*' cried the russet bandit, bending low over his neck, and the pony bounded forward so lightly that his hoofs barely touched the ground. The ranks of *guerrilleros* opened to let him pass through, and an instant later the whole mass of them streamed away along the road with the white pony at their head.

They were gone. Nothing but a dust cloud remained to mark where they had vanished. Clio rolled on the ground, hugging herself with delight, stuffing her fist in her mouth to stifle wild laughter. She could hardly believe what she had just seen.

The voice of Rochefort, raised in passion, recalled her to a sense of her own danger. Very soon her absence would be discovered. Before that happened she must put as much distance as possible between herself and the Frenchmen. With a last regretful glance at the cart where Julia still cowered, she eased herself down the bank of a dry gully and hurried in the direction the *guerrilleros* had taken.

*

Night found her still walking. All hope of catching up with El Forastero and his men was long gone, but she knew she was travelling the same way for at a fork in the track she found evidence of their passing in the form of a drift of scalloped lace, cobweb-fine, sparkling with a thousand diamonds and perfectly-graded seed pearls.

It was a mantilla, one of the priceless ceremonial vestments in which images of the Virgin were arrayed on feast-days. It must have been stolen by the French, recovered by the *guerrilleros*, and dropped in their headlong flight. Clio wrapped it round her shoulders for the night air was cold, and trudged on. Though the empty tussocky plain appeared limitless, she reasoned that sooner or later this track must lead to human habitation where she could beg food and shelter. Before she arrived at one, however, weariness overcame her. Curling up at the roots of a clump of cistus, she shut her mind to the thought of snakes and wolves and fell into an exhausted sleep.

She was woken by a gentle but insistent tugging at the Virgin's mantilla which she had spread over herself like a blanket.

'Oh, it is pretty – so pretty!' said a childish voice. 'It is fine enough for the Mother of God.'

Clio sat up, groaning. Her feet were sore and every bone ached from the buffeting it had received when the cart overturned. She met the curious gaze of a young goat-herd – a pretty, gipsy-looking girl clad in bright tattered clothes. She seemed no more than twelve or thirteen years old, with a smooth olive-flushed complexion, delicate aquiline features, and the dark liquid eyes of her Moorish ancestry.

A short distance away, three dogs moved like shadows as they herded a milling, bleating flock of sheep and goats to the stream to drink.

'Who are you?' asked the girl, her thin brown fingers plucking at the mantilla. 'Why do you sleep here?'

In the towns, popular sympathy often favoured the French, but in most country districts they were hated. Clio took a chance.

'I am English,' she said.

The bright curious gaze showed no emotion. 'English? Why are you wearing the Virgin's mantilla?'

'The French soldiers stole it, but it fell in the road. I found it. I am taking it back to Her.'

'*Franceses!*'

With relief Clio saw the pretty face twist in disgust.

After a moment the girl said wistfully, 'I wish I had been the one to find it.'

'I am hungry. Have you any food?'

'Give me the mantilla and I will give you food.'

It seemed a fair exchange. Clio handed her the priceless cobweb and the thin hands closed on it avidly. She shook it out and turned it this way and that, making the jewels flash. Clio wondered if the Virgin would ever recover Her property.

'Food,' she reminded.

The girl produced bread and cheese and salty olives from a pouch, and offered a sip from a blackened wineskin. While Clio ate, the girl ran to the stream and, draping the mantilla over her dark locks, knelt to admire her reflection.

'Oh, I am beautiful!' she exclaimed. 'I look like the Holy Virgin.'

Clio did not contradict her. The sparkling jewels would have lent beauty to the plainest of women: against this child's vivid face the effect was dazzling.

'What is your name?' she asked when her hunger was blunted.

'Pepita Aruzo, *señorita.*'

'Where are you taking your sheep?'

A shadow crossed the girl's face. 'The French are coming. I am taking the sheep from our village in the mountains to hide.'

'May I come with you?'

'I shall be glad of your company, *señorita*,' said Pepita with as much courtesy as if she had been a queen and Clio a visiting potentate. She adjusted the sparkling lace about her head and knelt once more to admire it.

'Oh, I am beautiful! Wait till Ignacio sees me!'

All that morning they drove the flock towards the distant

hills. The pace was slow, to spare the young lambs. By degrees Clio's stiffness wore off and she moved freely once more. The few villages they passed through were deserted: word of the French approach had gone before them. Pepita cast frequent anxious glances over her shoulder; as the shadows were beginning to lengthen, Clio's ears caught the sound of distant hoofbeats.

'Listen!'

At once Pepita knelt to put her ear to the ground. She rose with the colour draining from her face.

'Horses, coming fast. We must hide.'

She whistled to her dogs, who worked swiftly to turn the flock off the road and into a nearby dell where they were hidden by steep overgrown banks. Just as Clio thought them safely out of sight, one scrawny ewe and her lamb evaded the dogs and made a dash back to the road.

'*Madre de Dios!*' moaned Pepita.

'Leave her. Let her go.'

'No, no. I dare not. It is the Alcade's ewe. He will make me pay for it.'

Pepita leapt up the bank in great bounds, racing to cut off the truants. The mantilla streamed out behind her, a dazzling cloud emitting a kind of radiance. It looked, thought Clio, very like a halo.

'Come back!' she called, but Pepita paid no heed. Intent on capturing the runaway sheep, she ran down the dusty road with the dog at her heels, straight into the path of an approaching party of Dragoons.

Sick with fear, Clio crouched on the slope above the dell while the animals stood pressed together in perfect silence, for all the world as if they realized that a single bleat might betray them.

Bleats there were in plenty from the truant ewe and lamb as they were spitted on the Dragoons' lances and borne away, but more dreadful still was the sound of Pepita's screams and prayers diminishing in the distance and fading at last to silence.

Two of the sheepdogs slunk up the slope, ears and tails low, bellies to ground. Their amber eyes, disconcertingly wolf-like, were fixed on Clio's face and they whined softly, but she did not move.

As night was falling the men of Pepita's village came down from their mountain hideout in search of their missing flock. A solitary sheepdog, hobbling on three legs after a Dragoon's sabre had carried away the fourth, had warned them of disaster. Now it led them to where Pepita's body lay broken and abused at the road's edge. The Dragoons had stripped her naked, but one thin stiffening hand still clutched a fragment of cobweb-fine lace, sparkling with pearls and diamonds.

The men stared in silence. Two of them picked up the body and, with the dog hopping and whimpering behind them, carried it back up the hill. The others went on warily, scanning each gully and dell, searching for the missing sheep. When they saw the girl hunched on the slope below the road, her head bowed on her knees, their first thought was that she must be dead, too.

Miguel Alvarez, headman of Manzanares, tossed a pebble down the slope and Clio, looking up to see silent figures silhouetted against the sky, filled her lungs and began to scream.

The men looked at each other and nodded.

'*Por Dios!* This is too great an affair for us,' said Miguel Alvarez heavily. He turned to his son. 'Go, Ignacio. Saddle my mare and ride into the mountains. El Forastero must hear of this.'

10

'You!' said Clio faintly. She stared at the apparition with incredulous eyes. 'I thought – they told me you were dead.'

'Don't make a row,' said Harry curtly. 'I *am* dead as far as the army's concerned.'

'What do you mean?'

'Dishonoured. Dead as a doornail. Same thing.' He glanced over his shoulder but there was no one in earshot. 'Gave my parole and broke it. Serious matter.'

'What utter nonsense!'

Nevertheless a chill touched Clio. Men were such stupid creatures about matters of honour. For them war was a game which had to be played according to certain rules. If you broke the rules you weren't allowed to play any more, and the rules about parole were strict. An officer who broke his promise not to escape forfeited his honour.

'How did you escape?'

Harry grimaced, touching his temple where a white streak ran through the dark hair. 'I don't care to speak of it.'

'But I wish to hear. Come, Harry,' she coaxed as he hesitated. 'You owe me an explanation, at least! Let me judge for myself the kind of monster you are.'

His black eyebrows drew together. In the *guerrillero* dress he looked altogether foreign, as if his Spanish blood had submerged all the Englishness in him. 'No, dammit, you won't get round me that way. I don't remember the half of it. I was taken prisoner when the Spaniards abandoned the wounded after Talavera. Gave my parole. Later... I escaped.'

She knew he was lying. That was Harry all over. As in his boyhood scrapes, he wanted to get out of this mess alone. He didn't trust her to help him. Tears stung her eyes and she blinked them away. If he called her a fountain she would strike him. She waited, half hoping he would, but he said nothing.

She said scornfully, 'Half the French officers we capture escape after giving their parole. I've never heard of *them* being disgraced. On the contrary, the Emperor welcomes them back!'

'Different code. Different kettle of fish. What does for Napoleon's army won't do for us. You should know that.'

Oh, she did, she did! Yet still she thought it absurd. What was the use of fighting if you didn't try to win? Why should you allow the enemy an advantage you wouldn't take yourself? She thought of the sharpshooter whose lucky shot had broken General Junot's nose. Lord Wellington had given the man a severe reprimand and sent an apology to General Junot. *She* would have promoted him!

It exasperated her to see Harry bound by such nonsensical rules. 'You might as well hand the Peninsula to Boney and be done with it,' she said scornfully. 'Throw in England as well. While you're about the business, give him the New World and all our colonies.'

'That's what I like about you, Clio. Your sense of logic. Now listen, if you don't want to ruin the whole show. You're my prisoner and don't you forget it.'

'*Prisoner?*' She couldn't believe her ears.

'You don't suppose I can let you run about the countryside blabbing to everyone you meet that Don Enrique is a renegade Englishman? What do you suppose my life would be worth then?'

'I wouldn't blab.'

'I can't risk it.'

'Don't your men know you are English?'

'Only half English! Doña Mercedes knows the truth, but I can trust her.'

'Doña Mercedes? But she is *afrancesada!*' exclaimed Clio in dismay. 'She is the Governor of Ciudad Rodrigo's doxy – the last person you should trust.'

'Doña Mercedes serves her country better than any man I know,' snapped Harry. 'What she does is not for you to criticize.' Seeing her bewilderment, he added more gently, 'How do you think I heard of your departure from the fortress? You owe Doña Mercedes and Manuela more than you can repay. Do not speak slightingly of them to me.'

'Manuela, too?' Clio's brain whirled. 'How could I know they were your creatures?' she flashed. 'I suppose you have spied on me since I entered the country?'

'Do not flatter yourself,' said Harry crushingly. 'I sent Manuela to look after you because I could not hope you capable of looking after yourself.'

'And Doña Mercedes?'

'Manuela is her abigail.'

Who took orders from Harry. A sharp pang pierced Clio as all she had glimpsed through the goatskin curtain of the guerrillas' cave took on a new significance.

'Do you love her?' she demanded.

'Is that your business?'

Clio blinked at him, astonished. 'You *know* it is.'

'I think not,' said Harry with a cool finality that forbade further discussion.

She saw he had changed a great deal. A bitter maturity had taken possession of the careless boy she once loved. Harry had risen from the dead, but a different Harry. He frightened her: she, who used to know his innermost thoughts, now found herself a stranger. She did not know what to make of him.

Though he had worn a chequered headcloth drawn over mouth and nose in the Moorish manner when he rode into the mountain village at the head of his *guerrilleros*, she had no trouble in recognizing the slim russet-coated bandit who had escaped from Rochefort and his Chasseurs. Watching from the window of the house where the Alcade had lodged her, she had been struck by the degree of respect the villagers accorded him.

He might have been a prince. Gifts were heaped on the *guerrilleros,* the horses loaded with sheep, chickens, hams, vegetables and fruit until they looked less like a fighting band than a travelling market. Four of El Forastero's men wore French bearskin helmets, front to back, and the imperial eagle adorned their horses' tails. Pepita had been avenged.

'Your people must leave the mountain, Don Miguel,' she heard the russet *guerrillero* say. 'You know Masséna's custom. Reprisals will fall on every soul within ten leagues when the Dragoons' bodies are found.'

Miguel Alvarez thanked him gravely. 'We will return to our village,' he agreed. 'My people are in your debt, Don Enrique. Whatever you ask of them, they will do.'

'Keep me informed of everything you learn concerning the French. That is all I ask.' He dismounted, handing his horse to a boy to hold. 'Now I will speak with *la inglesa.*'

His face had been in shadow as he entered the hut, and for a moment he stood looking at her as the light from the open door fell on her features. Then he sighed and unwrapped the long headcloth. He had held out his hand, saying, 'Well, Clio! What a troublesome little creature you are! Popping up here and there like a jack-in-the-box. One never knows where one will find you next.'

'Harry!'

The shock was too great. Abruptly her knees folded and she slid to the floor in a faint. When she came to he was slapping her hands and cheeks with a vigour more suited to reviving a drunken soldier than a lady in a swoon.

'Damn it all, Clio, don't pull tricks like that,' he said in mingled annoyance and concern. 'You've put me to enough trouble without behaving like a Bath Miss.'

'I've put *you* to trouble? *You?*' she said dazedly, beginning to shake all over with fury; and from there the conversation had followed a downward path, with little satisfaction to either party.

'Allow me to felicitate you on your betrothal,' said Harry now, and she looked at him blankly. Robert had vanished from her thoughts.

'Oh, but now you have –'

'Robert is the best fellow that ever breathed. I shall hold you responsible for his happiness.'

The words had a menacing ring. He should have wished me happy, thought Clio with resentment. She thanked him with equal stiffness, while from the depths of her heart she wished both Robert and Doña Mercedes Cortes to the Devil.

Judging by her expression when they dismounted at the *guerrilleros'* hideout a few hours later, Mercedes's sentiments matched Clio's exactly. Nor did she scruple to voice them.

'Why have you brought that – that creature here?' she demanded in a furious undertone. 'You should have sent her into Portugal. Why have you kept her?'

Harry shrugged. 'She saw me, *querida*. She knows who I am. I cannot risk returning her to the British Army.'

'Fool! Why did you let her see you? I demand that you get rid of her.'

'I regret that is impossible.'

Mercedes's breast heaved. 'Impossible? You speak to me like this? *Trágalo, perro!*' She raised a hand to strike him, but Harry's fingers closed on her wrist.

Without raising his voice he said, 'Since when have you given me orders, *señora*? There is only one leader here. If you wish to usurp my position you will have to depose me first.'

Mercedes's black eyes flashed. 'Do you forget who gave you your command?' she said softly.

'I have not forgotten, but neither will I have my command challenged, least of all by you.'

'Can you not see this girl is a danger to us all?'

'She would be more dangerous still if I let her take her knowledge to the British camp.'

'Then kill her,' Mercedes hissed. 'While she lives she puts us all at risk.'

They had been speaking in soft rapid Spanish, unaware that Clio understood. At these words she moved forward to confront them.

'Let me go,' she said quietly, 'I won't betray you. You know you can trust me, Harry.'

For a moment he appeared to consider, then shook his head. 'I can't risk it. Not for the next two months, at least. If my plans succeed – well, then we'll see. Until that time we must keep you hidden. Spaniards have a queer notion of honour, you know. If they suspected I wasn't the man they think, my life would not be worth a brass farthing.'

Two months! thought Clio. How can I live here all that time, seeing him, knowing he loves that woman? It is too much. I almost wish I had never found him.

Two months, thought Mercedes. My condition will show by then. She stared at Clio with narrowed eyes and her fingers caressed the jewelled dagger at her waist. She loves him – oh, that is easy to see! She is not beautiful, no; but there is something about her – something to turn the foolish heads of men. Why couldn't that thick-witted English officer keep better watch over her? Why must she turn that look of hers on my Enrique? He is mine – mine! Before she came he had forgotten his life in England. He was happy . . . but now the memories are stirring. It would be best for us all if *la inglesa* vanished as suddenly as she appeared.

Two months, thought Harry. By then my *guerrilleros* will be ready to strike. The fortresses of Badajoz and Ciudad Rodrigo are the keys to Spain. Until they fall into our hands Joseph Bonaparte is safe on his borrowed throne, but once I give those keys into Lord Wellington's hands, the might of the French armies will begin to crumble. I cannot put so much at risk for the sake of one woman.

He remembered the remedy old Jem, his father's kennelman, used to apply to quarrelsome bitches. 'Don't try to keep 'em apart,' the old man would say. 'Pen 'em up close and let 'em battle it out. Wonderful how quiet that makes 'em.'

'I shall put *la inglesa* in your charge,' he said with a straight look at Mercedes. 'You will be accountable for her health and safety.'

'I account to no one,' she snapped with a toss of her proud head.

'Then look after her to please me, *querida*,' said Harry softly.

'Her father and mine are old friends. I cannot let harm befall her.'

'I will do it if it pleases you and for no other reason,' she conceded, and he nodded.

He turned, saying in English, 'I am too busy to concern myself with you, Clio, and I am often away. Doña Mercedes will look after you, and I shall expect you to obey everything she says.'

'But, Harry –!'

'No buts. Now I must leave you.' He turned away, ignoring her pleading eyes.

'Come, *inglesa*,' said Mercedes, taking her arm in a painful grip. 'Allow me to show you the way we live here in the hills.'

Throughout that scorching summer, while the parched slopes grew yellow and then grey-brown and every stream dried to a trickle, Clio endured all the discomforts and humiliations a jealous woman could devise. Mercedes neglected no opportunity to make her prisoner miserable, treating her worse than the servants whom she bullied as she pleased. If kind Manuela intervened she was likely to be slapped for her pains.

Clio was made to gather firewood and wash linen, pound meal and carry water from the brook at the bottom of the hill, which Mercedes would sometimes spill deliberately for the pleasure of sending the prisoner to fetch more.

'We cannot feed idle mouths,' she would say. 'If you live with us, you must work.'

In spite of these taunts, it was Mercedes's frequent absences that Clio grew to dread, for when she was away Jorge the Dwarf would scuttle out of the corner where he mixed his potions and unguents. Everyone was wary of Jorge. The stunted legs which had earned him his nickname moved with stealth and surprising speed and he had the knack of blending with his background so you never knew where he would materialize. Shameless eavesdropping and spying taught him everyone's secrets. His principal value to the guerrillas lay in his skill as a medicine man, but despite his knowledge of herbs and healing he was generally disliked.

He was also adept at gathering information and spying on French movements. He had his own network of informants and correspondents; he came and went as he chose, stealthy and secretive as a spider. Once he had been caught and tortured by a French patrol. They had broken both his malformed legs and tied him to a blazing stake before riding away; but Jorge managed to escape and thereafter his implacable hatred of the French earned him the additional soubriquet of The Scorpion, the creature whose deadly sting would be turned against itself if escape was impossible.

Jorge's large head with its narrow, undershot jaw and flat black eyes was permanently hunched forward by the over-developed muscles of his shoulders, and his sinewy arms seemed disproportionately long, as if the upper part of a man's body had been carelessly linked to the nether half of an ape. As if in defiance of these physical defects, he was inordinately vain, dressed in silks and velvets, and believed himself irresistible to women.

While the *guerrilleros* and their leader were present, he was content to play the part of Court Jester, entertaining them with stories and sly jokes; but the moment the men rode away a different side of his character emerged.

At first Clio was astonished that the two old crones who cooked for the *guerrilleros* put up with his arrogant behaviour. One morning she saw him limp to the simmering cauldron and demand food, though the stew had barely been on the fire an hour and would not be ready before noon.

When Angelica ladled out a pannikin he barely tasted it before dashing it to the floor, declaring it fit only for pigs. His black eyes roamed round the cave, looking for mischief, and fastened on Clio.

'Pick up the dish, *inglesa*,' he ordered.

'Pick it up yourself,' she retorted, supposing this to be one of his jokes.

Angelica drew in her breath sharply and bent to retrieve the fallen dish, but Jorge was too quick for her. With his foot he sent it spinning across the floor towards Clio.

'Pick it up,' he repeated.

'No.'

Manuela, at work chopping onions, gave Clio a warning look. 'Do not offend him, *señorita*.'

'Why not, since he is offending me?' She raised her handkerchief to her nose, and again heard Angelica's hiss of apprehension.

'I will show you why not, *inglesa*.' Jorge moved crabwise across the cave and stood over her menacingly. 'For the last time, will you do as I ask or must I punish you?'

Clio looked round for support, but Angelica was industriously stirring the cauldron, her back turned, and Manuela kept her eyes obstinately on her work. It was clear neither was prepared to stand up to the dwarf's bullying, and Clio's own bravado ebbed.

'Oh, very well, if you insist, but you are making a great fuss about nothing,' she said crossly, and stooped to pick up the fallen pannikin.

Jorge received it with a smile that was more like a sneer. 'So the little *inglesa* is not so brave after all. What a pity. I would have enjoyed the opportunity to teach you manners. That pleasure must come another day.'

He moved away, leaving her puzzled and a little frightened. Later, on their way to fetch water, she asked Manuela why the women permitted Jorge to treat them with such contempt.

'Bad things happen to those who offend Jorge,' said Manuela sombrely.

'What kind of bad things?'

Manuela looked carefully round before replying. Then she set down her buckets and sat upon a rock, gesturing to Clio to do the same.

'Once Angelica had a dog. Just a little dog, quite young. Jorge used to play with it. One day when he was teasing it with a bone, the dog bit his hand and made it bleed. The next day when Angelica went to feed it, she found it dead.'

Clio considered the story, unimpressed. 'You think Jorge killed it?'

'*Quién sabe?*' Manuela shrugged. 'Then there was Juana. She was a good girl but – you know –' she tapped her forehead.

'What happened to Juana?'

'What happens too often to such girls. She swore the child was Jorge's and he had promised to marry her, but he denied it absolutely. Her father was angry. Everyone knows Jorge's pockets are lined with gold, but he would give her nothing.'

'Did she die, too?'

'Her father said Jorge put a curse on her. Who can tell? The doctor could do nothing. She died before her child was born.'

'And that is why you let the nasty creature bully you? You should be ashamed,' said Clio vigorously. 'I am not afraid of any dwarf.'

'I am glad of it,' said Manuela simply. 'All the same, *señorita*, take my advice. Be careful what you say to Jorge.'

She picked up her buckets and Clio followed her up the hill, mulling over what she had said.

For the next few weeks, while Mercedes remained with the guerrillas, Jorge gave Clio no cause for concern. She might have forgotten the incident with the pannikin had she not from time to time felt herself observed and, looking round, encountered his sly assessing gaze.

There came a day, however, when Mercedes and her maid left the guerrilla stronghold to return to Ciudad Rodrigo. Her husband, Don Sebastian, who had spent the past months at King Joseph's court, was expected home before the new year, and Mercedes was anxious there should be no breath of scandal concerning the child she was carrying.

El Forastero and his band had ridden off in pursuit of a French patrol, leaving Clio in the charge of the two old women, Angelica and Nuria. Jorge was absent on one of his solitary missions, and she prayed he would not return before the rest of the band.

It was a stifling October day, without a breath of wind, and as she worked with the old women preparing food, Clio glanced up from time to time, fearing she saw the hunched shadow of Jorge fall across the cave mouth.

They took their siesta late. When Jorge did appear, he approached the corner where Clio was sleeping so silently that neither of the old women stirred.

She woke as his sleeve brushed her face. 'Come, *inglesa*, this is no time to sleep. There has been a fight and many of our men are wounded. You must help me gather herbs for dressings.'

In the gloom of the cave he looked like a huge crow looming over her. 'Come,' he said again, and his talons fastened on her arm.

'Is – is Don Enrique hurt?'

'What is that to you? Come, hurry!'

The old women woke, grumbling. 'What's the matter? Can't we have a moment's peace?'

'I need fresh herbs before nightfall. The girl can help me pick them.'

Angelica rose stiffly. 'I know where they grow. I will pick them for you.'

'No, you must stay here. The men will need food.'

'It is already prepared.'

Jorge's grip tightened on Clio's arm, dragging her forward. Nuria turned away, muttering, but Angelica barred his path.

'Do not take the girl,' she said in a low voice. 'Don Enrique gave orders she was to stay with us.'

'Out of my way, old woman,' said Jorge with a malevolent glance. 'I give the orders now. Come, *inglesa*, there is no time to lose.'

Angelica watched with narrowed eyes as he pulled Clio away down the path and vanished towards the woods.

The sun was dipping towards the mountain top when Harry dismounted to water his horse at the stream a mile from the cave. He was glad to stretch his legs after long hours in the saddle. The ambush had been successful though his band had suffered a number of casualties, more or less serious. He hoped Jorge would return in time to tend the wounded.

Before tomorrow's dawn the dispatches the French patrol had carried would be in the hands of Major Colquhoun Grant, though whether they would be enough to improve Harry's bargaining position was another matter. Granto El Bueno was a hard man to deal with; despite the successful mission Harry had the uneasy feeling that he was no nearer obtaining his longed-for pardon.

This summer of 1811 had seen great changes in the state of both armies, and none more sweeping than in the French high command. Masséna, by now a weary and disillusioned old fox, had been recalled by Napoleon and in his place came Marshal Marmont, Duke of Ragusa: stern, handsome, and in high Imperial favour. In the time-honoured way of new brooms, he had set about sweeping away all his predecessor's mess and muddle.

A new spirit of efficiency, austerity and resolution reigned at Marmont's headquarters. Away went the officers' mistresses in their fancy uniforms, skittering back to Madrid as fast as their pretty ponies would carry them. Marmont revictualled the great fortresses of Badajoz and Ciudad Rodrigo and strengthened their defences. Then he turned his attention to the *guerrilleros*.

From their mountain lairs the *guerrillero* bands swooped, attacked, and vanished again, slipping like sand through Marmont's fingers and occupying large numbers of his troops in fruitless pursuit. Dispatches and movement orders seized by the *guerrilleros* filtered by devious ways into the hands of Lord Wellington's Intelligence officers, and thence to the Commander-in-Chief's own desk. Gruesomely badged with blood, these captured papers filled the gaps in the jigsaw of information his lordship needed to complete before launching his next offensive against the great fortresses that were the keys to Spain.

One vital link between El Forastero's band and Lord Wellington's headquarters was the dashing figure of Major Grant, who wore a blue cloak over his British uniform and spoke Spanish like a native. He had been quick to appreciate the singularity of Harry's position and the use he could make of it.

Grant was a shrewd and daring man, not overburdened with scruples. When he offered to secure Lord Wellington's recommendation for a pardon, Harry had no choice but to agree. The price was a constant supply of intelligence; but to Harry's dismay Grant constantly invented reasons why he could not yet approach the matter of a pardon.

In order to succeed with his lordship, I must be able to put your case in a favourable light, declared Grant's most recent letter. *Unless he is firmly convinced of the value of information supplied by you, I fear no pardon will be forthcoming.*

The damned fellow's trying to raise the ante, thought Harry gloomily, and the deuce of it is, he holds all the cards.

As the horse drank, his gaze roamed the hillside above; bare and parched though it looked from afar, closer inspection revealed small patches of colour, clumps of late-flowering thyme and lavender, the rusty red of lichen against grey rock, peeling white trunks of eucalyptus and the sheeny silver-green of wild olives.

One patch of colour that caught his eye was too bright to be natural. After a moment's puzzled attention, he took his glass from the case. Steadying his elbow against a rock, he put it to his eye.

Next instant he snapped the glass shut and began bounding up the rough slope. Raising its dripping muzzle, his horse watched him vanish over the skyline. He snorted his disapproval and forded the stream alone. Holding his head carefully to one side to avoid treading on the trailing reins, he trotted quietly away in search of his evening feed.

Oh, why didn't I listen to Mamma and pay attention to her warnings? thought Clio as she followed Jorge along a narrow path between overgrown clumps of cistus. Since leaving the cave he had said nothing more about gathering herbs; she knew with uncomfortable certainty that it had been no more than an excuse to separate her from the other women.

More than any of her sisters, Clio had chafed at the restrictions and prohibitions imposed upon girls with the object of turning them into young ladies. Now the rules and warnings she had so often rebelled against acquired a terrible relevance. So did the lecture Mrs Hardy had given to her elder daughters, warning them of perils which young girls might face in a foreign land.

'Never forget, *mes enfants*, that Man is an animal,' she had said in her pretty, accented voice. 'Like all male animals he is dangerous. You would be careful in your dealings with a bull or a wild boar, *n'est-ce pas*? You would not take liberties with a stallion? Then remember this: the human male is more to be feared than any wild beast since unlike the animals he has the power to dissemble. Be very careful to avoid putting yourself in any man's power. You may think he is tame and gentle enough to eat from your hand, but when you are alone with him it will be too late to discover your mistake. Do you understand me?'

'Oh, yes, Mamma!' they had chorused gaily, without comprehending in the least what she meant. They knew that Mamma had suffered mysteriously at the hands of a certain unscrupulous adventurer during her escape from The Terror though precisely what he had stolen from her had never been quite clear.

On their return to the schoolroom, Clio and Laura had been inclined to joke.

Laura, who had a gift for caricature, swiftly drew a furious bull pawing the ground, with puffs of steam escaping from its nostrils and Papa's features. She passed it to Clio, who giggled and handed it on.

'Look, Julia!'

Julia was not amused. She snatched the drawing and threw it on the fire.

Now Clio stole a sidelong look at her captor. It was not difficult to imagine Jorge as a ravening beast.

'There are plenty of herbs here,' she said, 'and moss as well. Shall we pick them?' Never let an animal know you fear it, she thought, and tried to suppress the quaver in her voice.

'Later.'

Clio forced a smile. 'Come, *amigo*, show me what you want. You said yourself there was little time.'

Jorge stopped. On his face was a sly twisted smile. He looked all round to satisfy himself they were alone, then grasped her hand, pulling her close.

'I will show you what I want,' he said.

Before she realized what he meant to do, one arm was round her waist, pressing her against him, while his other hand explored her breast. She shuddered with disgust and tried to push him away, but she might as well have pushed at a block of granite.

'Let me go!' she gasped, twisting to escape those cruel questing fingers.

Far from discouraging, her struggles excited him. His breathing was loud and harsh in her ear as he nuzzled her neck, trying to reach her lips.

'Forget about Don Enrique, little *inglesa!* He is not for you,' he said hoarsely. 'Come, be kind to Jorge and he will be kind to you.'

'Kind!' Clio's temper rose. Greatly as she feared this slobbering pawing creature, she was not prepared to suffer such liberties without protest. '*Demonio enano!* Take your hands off me, you filthy dog!'

'You should be flattered by my attentions,' he jeered. 'Call yourself a woman? Why, a chicken has more meat on it.'

With an instinct that was entirely primitive, Clio brought up her knee and drove it into his most vulnerable parts. Jorge grunted and doubled up, breathing hard. His eyes glinted hate.

'That was a mistake, *inglesa*. A bad mistake.'

His misshapen leg shot out, hooking round hers. She tripped and fell to the ground with his weight on top of her. Stiff fronds of thyme scratched her neck and arms, and the pungent aroma filled her nostrils as she struggled to free herself. Hands on her shoulders, Jorge pinned her down, his face not six inches from hers.

'You shall pay for that, *inglesa*,' he said softly.

'Let me go.' Desperately she tried to bargain. 'Let me go and I won't say a word to anyone.'

He laughed. 'You will say nothing to Don Enrique?'

'No, no! Let me go!'

'There is one way to make sure you tell no tales,' he said and his strong fingers fastened about her throat. Terrified, she tore at them as they began to tighten against her windpipe. Blood drummed in her ears and her senses began to swim.

'No!' she gasped. 'No.'

Dimly she was aware of a commotion among the bushes at the edge of the path, where the slope plunged down steeply to the stream.

'Ten thousand devils!'

Through fogged eyes she saw the hate on Jorge's face replaced by alarm; felt the sudden release of pressure as his fingers relaxed, but before she saw who her rescuer was, she fainted.

When Clio recovered consciousness her head was resting against Harry's shoulder. His face, pale beneath the tan and deeply scored by a long flesh-wound, was bent over her and he breathed heavily after his frenzied scramble up the hill. Of Jorge there was no sign.

'By God, Clio, can't I leave you alone for a minute without you getting into some scrape?' he demanded with the anger of one who has had a bad fright.

'Where – where is he?' Tenderly she felt her bruised throat.

'Gone – with a hiding he won't forget in a hurry. Why did you do it? Jorge, of all people! The last man I wish to make an enemy of. And now what the devil am I to do with you?'

'With me?'

'Don't humbug! You know very well I can't watch over you day and night; nor can I leave you alone after what has happened. You were lucky I was riding past. Damn it all, I thought you safe enough with Jorge. How did it happen? You must have provoked him. Have you no sense?'

'He – he attacked me, Harry. Truly, I did nothing.' Clio's teeth chattered with shock.

Harry's arms tightened about her, but his tone was still exasperated as he said, 'The trouble is, you're a great deal too free and easy for your own good. You don't know how to behave.'

'*I* don't?' The injustice of the accusation banished her shock.

She sat up, eyes blazing. 'How dare you call me free and easy?'

'Oh, I daresay you don't mean any harm, but this ain't England, you know. What does for Englishmen won't do for Spaniards at all.'

'You need not tell me *that*!'

Furious, she jumped up, ignoring the hand he stretched to help her. 'If that is your opinion of my morals, I wonder you keep me here against my will.'

'I told you before, I have no choice.'

'Why not? Why can't I go back to Papa? At least that would rid you of my unwelcome presence.'

'Impossible,' he said flatly.

'Why? His regiment is only a few miles distant.'

'Ah, but your father is not with his regiment. He has taken sick leave and returned to Lisbon.'

'Why didn't you tell me he was ill? Poor Papa!'

'Oh, don't repine. He is at least as well as you or I. It appears he prefers the society of Lisbon to that of a front-line regiment, and who can blame him? In his absence, Auguste discharges his duties – and the general opinion of his superiors is that he makes a more competent cavalry commissary than your revered parent.'

She could not help smiling. 'Poor Papa! It is hardly his *métier*. Then may I not join Auguste's establishment? He would be glad to see me, I daresay.'

'You can have little idea of the life of a commissary on active service if you suppose Auguste would be pleased to add you to his burdens,' said Harry, who knew very well that a certain handsome sloe-eyed young woman, sister to two of his *guerrilleros*, now lived on terms of the greatest intimacy with the acting deputy commissary. If Clio joined his establishment, Auguste would feel bound to distance himself from this paramour and Harry was reluctant to sacrifice such a fruitful source of information.

'You seem to know a great deal about it!' exclaimed Clio resentfully.

'It is my business to know.'

He was silent for a while, mulling over an idea that had come to him. It might answer; certainly he would have no peace of mind while Clio remained here. Thoughtfully he assessed her appearance. After months of open-air living, her skin was tanned in a way that would have horrified her Mamma. In her black, uncovered stays, loosely laced; red flounced skirt, straw sandals and fringed shawl, she looked so much the Spanish peasant girl that he smiled.

Clio tilted her chin. 'Do you find my appearance amusing?'

'On the contrary, I was thinking how well those clothes become you. You look quite the señorita.'

'Since I am obliged to dress as a peasant, it is hardly surprising if I look like one.'

'Oh, it is more than the clothes! The glance, the turn of the head: you have it to the life.'

Unable to resist the challenge, she planted one fist on her hip and held the other aloft, slowly twirling her skirt and stamping.

'*Olé!*' She struck a pose.

Harry did not smile. He said, 'I had bad news today. We have lost Manuela.'

'*Lost?*'

'Dead. It was the damnedest chance. Rochefort himself saw her crossing the bridge out of the city and recognized her. He sent his men to arrest her. She died under their questioning.'

'Oh, Harry!' Clio sat very still. After a moment she said, 'Do you think she betrayed you?'

'I cannot tell. Certainly it will be difficult for me to pass messages into the city without her assistance.' He paused, then said quietly, 'My greatest fear is that Mercedes, too, will fall under suspicion.'

Don Enrique had vanished. He was all Harry now, and as in the old days her mind leapt to meet his, guessing his plan almost before it formed.

'I could carry your messages,' she said eagerly.

Harry frowned. 'It will be dangerous.'

'I do not care for that. Please, Harry! I would so much like to help you.'

'Have you considered what might happen if you were caught?'

'Why should I be caught? You said yourself I look quite the señorita! Besides, *I* am not Mercedes's servant.'

Still he hesitated, unwilling to put her in a position of such peril, hating the necessity that drove him to employ women and children to carry messages he dared not trust to a man. Between the need to keep his own identity secret and his urgent desire to earn a pardon, he often felt like a juggler who had thrown too many balls in the air and had not hands to catch them.

Something of the knife-edge he walked communicated itself to Clio. On impulse she said, 'Why do you remain a bandit? Why fight for a people who do nothing to deserve your efforts?'

'I have no choice.'

'Could you not make a clean breast of the whole affair? I cannot see you were much to blame.'

Harry turned away to stare over the darkening valley. He said, 'I have put myself beyond the pale.'

'I believe that if Lord Wellington knew how you came to be in this situation, he would recommend your pardon,' persisted Clio, disregarding his frown.

'Then you are wrong.'

'How can you tell, unless you ask him?'

'I have asked,' said Harry with suppressed bitterness. 'A year ago I wrote my case to his lordship, begging him to intercede with the Government on my behalf. This was his reply.'

From an inner pocket he drew a paper so folded and creased it seemed likely to fall apart. Clio spread it out carefully.

Sir,
I have received your letter of 10 March, which you appear to have written under a misapprehension. You think that the Government are inclined to pardon you: so far from it, that if they can catch you, or have you caught, you will be hanged; and I therefore recommend you to keep out of the way, and to take care of yourself. In the enclosed letter I have stated the only means by which you can hope to receive a pardon for

your crimes; and I can undertake to solicit your pardon on no other terms.

In respect to your pardon, you cannot expect that it should be given to you immediately. I must be able to assure the Government that you had served your country with zeal, and given useful information.

I have the honour to be etc.
Wellington

'Hanged!' exclaimed Clio. 'Why, that is monstrous!'

Harry's smile twisted. 'In the eyes of the army it is a sufficiently monstrous crime to break parole; and assault on a superior officer is punishable by death.'

'You assaulted a superior? Why?' When he was silent she added, 'Tell me the full story, Harry, or I swear I will not lift a finger to help you.'

'You have the damnedest way of plaguing the truth out of a fellow,' he complained, but she sensed that he wished to unburden himself.

'The whole story,' she insisted. 'No saying you cannot remember the half of it. Robert told me about the charge of the 23rd at Talavera, and how he left you with the wounded. What happened after?'

'Just what you might suppose,' said Harry disgustedly. 'Our gallant ally General Cuesta withdrew the Spanish Army as soon as Lord Wellington was fairly out of sight, leaving both his own wounded and the British to the mercy of the French. Two other officers were taken at the same time as I – Major Hobhouse of the — Dragoons, and Captain Darcy of my regiment. Did you ever meet Darcy, Clio? He was at school with me – a big fellow, a year or so ahead of me.'

'I don't recall the name,' she said after a moment's reflection. 'At least you were not alone.'

'I would rather by far I had been, for I could hardly have chosen worse company! Hobhouse the kind of prosy, pettyfogging stickler for etiquette that too many cavalry regiments are cursed with, and Darcy my sworn enemy.'

'Your *enemy*? A brother officer?'

'At school Darcy was the kind of bully who stands new boys on a table and makes 'em sing for his amusement,' said Harry briefly. 'As you know, poor Rob has never been able to sing a note. I chanced to come by to find Darcy cutting with his cane at Rob's legs, saying if he wouldn't sing he should dance for him, so I took away the cane and gave him the hiding he deserved. He has never forgotten.'

She nodded. 'So you were taken prisoner. Did you give your parole then?'

'It was given for me.'

'Given for you?' she echoed, astonished.

'I was out of my mind with a fever, so Hobhouse and Darcy gave their paroles and undertook to be responsible for my good behaviour. I was mad as fire when I discovered what they had done in my name, but by then it was too late to remedy matters.'

'But then you are blameless! If you gave no parole, how could you break it?'

'Wait: you asked for the full story and the full story you shall have. As I say, we were given the degree of liberty consistent with an officer on parole, and conducted to Torrijos, on the road to Madrid. How I got there I don't know, for I remember nothing of the journey: I supposed they carried me. We were held for a week in Torrijos, waiting for an escort, and meantime I regained my senses.

'The town's Governor was a very civil fellow, and invited the three of us to dine. That was where I first met Doña Mercedes and her husband. He had been to Madrid to take his oath of allegiance to King Joseph, but as they were returning home to Ciudad Rodrigo their coach met with an accident, and the Governor of Torrijos begged them to be his guests while it was repaired.' He paused, then said, 'How well I remember that first meeting!'

Clio could picture it. Harry, lean and dashing, pale from his recent fever, looking across the room at the voluptuous dark-eyed beauty. Her head turning, feeling his gaze. . . .

'We hardly exchanged a dozen sentences, but next morning as

I walked in the garden, a monk brushed past me and pressed a folded paper into my hand. It told me to feign illness before dinner. The sentries had been bribed and a ladder placed against the wall. All I had to do was climb down. A horse and a guide would be waiting – everything was arranged. It would have been the basest ingratitude to refuse.'

'Go on.'

'All went well until as I descended the ladder, Darcy and Hobhouse entered the room, and saw at once what I was about. Hobhouse leaned out and seized my hair. He began to shout as if all the devils in Hell were after him, while Darcy ran to alert the guard.'

Clio drew in her breath sharply. 'You – you struck him?'

'Yes, for my sins. When I saw his great red face staring down into mine and knew that he alone stood in my way to freedom, I hit him with all my strength. He toppled from the window and fell.'

It was worse than she had expected. She put a hand to her mouth to stifle a moan. He went on:

'I scrambled down the ladder as fast as I could, but Hobhouse was beyond help. Poor devil – I think his neck was broken. The guards kept their bargain and paid me no heed, and I jumped on the horse that was waiting, with Don Alvaro, Mercedes's brother, to guide me. We were away before anyone answered Darcy's calls.' He shrugged. 'After that my boats were burnt. I preferred my father to believe I had perished than know the truth.'

'*I* would not have blamed you.'

'You do not understand matters of honour.'

'Thank God I do not! You wrote your case to Lord Wellington in confidence, then?'

'Yes, but Darcy had been before me,' said Harry bitterly.

Clio reflected for a moment. She said, 'His lordship's letter spoke of certain terms. What are they?'

'Nothing less than information leading to the capture of Ciudad Rodrigo. That alone will restore my honour.'

'And the guerrillas? How did you come to lead them?'

'Oh, this country has been owned by Alvaro's family ever since the Moors were beaten at Granada in the fifteenth century. Alvaro was the strangest fellow you ever met – such a master of disguise that you never knew where you would meet him. One minute he was the damnedest arrogant grandee, and the next a priest or a cowherd. He was taken by the French at last – wounded in a skirmish and cruelly murdered. His band would have scattered had not Mercedes rallied them and obliged the men to take me for their chief.'

While she took him as her lover. Clio said, 'What part did her husband play in this?'

'Why, none! As you know, Don Sebastian is *afrancesado*. He cares for nothing but his French friends, but this gives Mercedes access to much valuable information.' He paused, then said quietly, 'Without her I could have done nothing. Hers is the spirit that inspires the men . . . the courage that will save Spain. And yet. . . .'

'Yet?' she prompted, hoping for something she dared not put into words.

'Yet I am unworthy of her love.' His shuttered expression returned: before her eyes Don Enrique took the place of Harry and she knew the time for confidences was past.

She rose, brushing twigs from her skirt, wincing at the pain from scratches and bruises. 'I fear I have caused you a good deal of trouble, one way and another. You can hardly refuse me the chance to make amends! No, do not argue. If you had not in your heart wished me to take Manuela's place, you would never have told me of her arrest.'

He was obliged to admit the truth of this. 'All the same, Clio, I beg you will be careful.'

'When were *you* ever careful?'

'Promise me.'

'Very well, I promise, and in return I require a promise from you that if Ciudad Rodrigo falls you will not be too proud to reopen negotiations for a pardon.'

He gave this assurance readily enough, though an almost superstitious fear that to speak of them would make them fall through kept him from mentioning his recent dealings with Granto El Bueno.

Two days later, as the first rain of autumn began to fall in a steady drizzle, shrouding the parched foothills, he escorted Clio and old Angelica as far as the bridge that spanned the Agueda under the very walls of Ciudad Rodrigo's ancient fortress. He showed her where messages would be hidden every third day under the buttress at the water's edge where the townswomen came to wash their linen. Then he waited out of sight of the postern gate as they crossed the bridge and hammered on the studded door.

11

The moustachio'd sentry who emerged from the guard house buckling his belt fancied himself in the role of Don Juan. His gaze slid over old Angelica, burdened with her two baskets, and fastened appreciatively on Clio. Spanish girls were much to his taste, with their well-developed bosoms, neat ankles and hand-span waists. As he questioned her he was more concerned with distracting her into letting slip her veil than in examining her papers. Not that this mattered: the papers were perfectly in order. They had been prepared by Don Patricio Odonoju – born Paddy O'Donoghue of County Kerry – whose novitiate at the Irish College of Salamanca had been rudely disrupted by the war. He was a skilful forger whose services were much prized by the guerrillas. The papers identified Clio as one Consuela Arrondo, seamstress, from the town of Castelo Branco, come to Ciudad Rodrigo in search of work.

The choice of profession was Clio's own notion. All the Hardy sisters were handy with a needle, since the exigencies of the family budget had precluded the services of a dressmaker on any but the most important occasions. If Clio lacked Julia's flair for design or Laura's determined attention to detail, at least her skill was greater than that of the Spanish seamstresses, whose clothes were uniformly frumpish and old-fashioned.

'I shall be quite at liberty to call at any house I choose,' she told Harry. 'Women speak freely before their servants, and if I get commissions from French officers' wives, I may pick up useful information.'

So her papers were prepared, and two hampers full of ribbons, cottons and samples of silk were provided, to give substance to her story.

The sentry glanced briefly at the contents of the hampers, pinched Clio's cheek and laughed off the resulting slap. Finally he opened the postern to admit them.

'If the wives of our officers can't find work for you, I'll find you some myself!' he leered as they passed, and a number of well-whiskered heads looked out of the guard house to speed them with admiring whistles.

'Such manners! Those Frenchmen are no better than animals!' scolded Angelica, but she waited until they were out of the soldiers' sight before spitting in their direction.

They were careful not to approach Don Sebastian's house directly, but spent the morning wandering the streets with Clio's ribbons and silks, knocking on doors and asking if the mistress of the establishment would like to see her wares.

Twice she was invited to show them in tapestried boudoirs where the bored wives of French officers whiled away the hours with gossip and chocolate. At other houses she was shooed away by supercilious footmen, though even the most taciturn unbent a little towards the pretty dark-eyed ribbon-seller with her soft hesitant voice.

'You are from across the border?' asked one.

'*Sí, señor.* From Castelo Branco. I have come to find work, to feed Mamma and the little ones.'

'Your father is dead?'

'God rest his soul. Both my brothers, too.'

'*Pobrecita!* Try the house on the corner. You will be better received there.'

'*Muchas gracias, señor.*'

Clio enjoyed herself. It was delightful to wander where she pleased and feel her own mistress once more. She explored the town with scant compassion for Angelica's aching feet, then joined the crowd in the Plaza Mayor to watch the mules of a French foraging party stream under the arch that led to the fortress.

How often during her captivity had she gazed down at the same scene during the long lonely hours while Julia strolled in the gardens with Colonel de Rochefort! Then she had dreamed of freedom, and imagined Robert come to rescue her at the head of a storming party. Vain hope! She pictured Robert's face when Rochefort dragged her away. How miserable and wobegone he had looked! He was not suited to a soldier's life. If it had not been for Harry's urging he would probably have become an academic like her father, writing serious treatises in the comfort of his own library. Harry had forced him into a mould he did not fit, while she – Clio experienced a spasm of guilt – she had promised to marry him when she did not in the least love him. Ten minutes in Harry's company had taught her that, but Harry seemed determined to forget there had ever been any warmer feeling than friendship between them.

He is punishing me because he cannot punish himself, thought Clio, and for a moment her spirits drooped.

'Come, *señorita*. No one is watching us. It is time to find Doña Mercedes.'

Harry's mistress. I wish it had been anyone else, thought Clio, but she followed Angelica obediently to a handsome house in a side street and knocked on the ancient studded door.

The sallow sharp-faced woman with a bunch of keys at her waist who confronted them in the gloomy entrance hall was not disposed to be civil.

'Good day, *señora*,' said Clio, bobbing a curtsey. 'My mistress the Marquesa da Silveira has sent me with a letter to Doña Mercedes.'

'Give it to me.' The woman extended a yellow hand.

'My mistress insisted I should deliver it myself.'

'Nonsense. What impertinence! I will take it.'

Clio refused to be browbeaten. 'If you will not permit me to hand it to Doña Mercedes myself, I will tell my mistress.'

The woman hesitated, torn between reluctance to offend a Marquesa and unwillingness to conduct this travel-stained young woman to her mistress.

Clio returned the letter to her pouch. 'Come, Angelica.'

'No, wait. You may deliver your letter. Follow me.'

She led them through the dim high-ceilinged hall furnished in dark oak with antique weapons hung on the walls. Following close on her heels, Clio caught a whiff of rotten teeth only partly masked by oil of cloves, and wondered how Doña Mercedes came to employ so unappetizing a housekeeper.

'Wait here,' she said curtly, opening the door that led to a sheltered courtyard.

The morning rain had cleared away, and even at this season, the sun struck warm against the walls of mellow stone. A fountain flung sparkling arcs of water over the stone dolphins on the edge of a marble basin, and late flowers gave the air a delicious fragrance.

Mercedes was reclining on a bank of cushions while a pretty, delicate-featured child with long dark hair braided in a single plait read to her from a leather-bound book. Mercedes's pregnancy was now well advanced; she looked pale and listless, very different from the vital, glowing creature she had been in the mountains. Her hair, elaborately dressed under a high comb and lace mantilla, had lost its shine and her whole attitude was of despondent lethargy.

'What is it, Eugenia? I gave orders I did not wish to be disturbed,' she said languidly, barely glancing up.

'Forgive me, *señora*.' Eugenia's expression was sour. 'A woman has come, bringing a letter from your cousin the Marquesa.'

'Then why are you standing there? Give it to me.'

'The saucy baggage insists on delivering it herself.'

'Fool! Why did you not say so? Send her to me.'

Eugenia beckoned, and Clio hurried forward to curtsey at Mercedes's feet. She had hoped this meeting would be in private, but Mercedes's dark eyes rested on her indifferently without betraying a flicker of recognition.

She took Harry's letter and perused it with apparent lack of interest; then flung it aside, saying with a bitter little laugh, 'Well, Consuela! My cousin recommends you as a skilful dressmaker. What do I want with a dressmaker? Go and ply your trade about the town, but do not look to me for employment. I have enough servants to feed. Eugenia! Show them out.'

'Won't you at least examine the samples I have brought?' said Clio, taken aback by this abrupt dismissal.

Mercedes's eyes flashed. 'How dare you argue! Go, or my grooms will set the dogs on you.'

There seemed nothing for it but to obey. Clio picked up her hamper and prepared to retire.

'Continue, Amalia,' said Mercedes to the child watching round-eyed, and bent her attention on the book. But just as Clio and Angelica were about to leave the courtyard, the imperious voice called, 'Stay! I have changed my mind. I will look at your patterns after all. Take the child away, Eugenia, and finish her lessons. I cannot be troubled with her today.'

The child rose reluctantly, clasping her book. 'Will you hear me tomorrow, Mamma?'

'Perhaps. We shall see. Come here, Consuela. Show me the latest Paris fashions.'

Hardly daring to raise her eyes for fear of another rebuff, Clio knelt to unfasten the straps of her hamper. She heard the retreating footsteps of Eugenia and the child's lighter tread. Then a hand gripped her shoulder. She looked up to see the mask of indifference stripped from Mercedes's features. Her large eyes were brilliant with fear.

'Thank the saints you have come! I have been in despair. Manuela has disappeared and I have no one I can trust. That woman is Rochefort's spy.'

The story she recounted in hurried whispers confirmed Harry's fears. Since Manuela vanished, Mercedes had been virtually a prisoner in her own house.

'I should not have let her go. I fear she has fallen into Rochefort's hands. That man is a devil! Three days ago he called to commiserate over the loss of my maid. I asked what *he* knew of the matter, and he laughed in my face. Poor Manuela! She served me since we were both children.'

She twitched at her mantilla with fingers that trembled, and her big diamond ring flashed in the sun.

'Rochefort had the effrontery to recommend Doña Eugenia

to me. He threatened to denounce me to my husband if I would not take her, and I dared not refuse. The charming creature spies on me constantly. I am trapped here until my child is born.'

On the balcony overlooking the courtyard Amalia's lesson was proceeding. The drone of her reading came to their ears, but even without turning her head Clio could feel Doña Eugenia's button eyes upon them.

She searched in her hamper and drew out a book of French fashion plates, providentially captured from a baggage train. 'Examine the pages as you talk,' she whispered. 'When did Colonel de Rochefort return here?'

'Such styles! Does the Empress of France really display herself so wantonly?' In a lower tone she said, 'He came back from Madrid at the same time as my husband, bringing his new wife with him. Give me more patterns. These are not to my taste.'

As Clio bent to search in the hamper, Mercedes went on in low, rapid tones, 'I have important news for Don Enrique. Governor Reynaud has been ordered to transfer part of his garrison to Valencia, to support Marshal Suchet, and he has barely two hundred veterans left to defend the town. Food is short, and Reynaud would prefer to surrender on good terms than see Ciudad Rodrigo stormed.'

This was startling news. 'He is ready to *surrender?*'

'Hush! He told me this in private. Reynaud is Swiss, you know, and tired of this war. His brother has been appointed Vice-Master of Trinity College, Cambridge. He wishes to visit England. The time is ripe for Wellington to strike.'

'And your husband? Does he advise surrender?'

Mercedes flashed her a scornful look. The strain of the past weeks showed in tiny lines about her eyes and mouth. 'Don Sebastian fights with the winning side, but this time I shall make sure he does not escape the consequences of his crimes.'

The lesson had ended. Mercedes leaned forward, whispering, 'Rochefort leaves on Wednesday for Salamanca. I have it from a sure source. Come at the siesta hour when Eugenia is sleeping, and I will tell you more.'

'Very good, my lady.' Clio bobbed a curtsey. From the tail of her eye she saw Doña Eugenia descending from the balcony. She began to pack away her materials. Across the lid of the hamper Mercedes's eyes met hers with a look of complete understanding.

The extraordinary news that Governor Reynaud was prepared to surrender Ciudad Rodrigo for the price of a safe-conduct to England met with a degree of cynicism when it reached British military headquarters.

'Hang it all, Grant! You can't expect me to believe that. Why, the fellow must be mad as a hatter!' exclaimed Colonel Murray, Chief of Intelligence. 'It is tantamount to inviting us to march on Madrid. Reynaud may wish to surrender his fortress, but I am very sure Marmont does not.'

'My informant is a man I trust, and he was clear on the matter. He has a correspondent inside the city, and I have never found him mistaken,' said Grant in his decided way. In the past months he had acquired considerable respect for the information supplied by Harry Churchill, but he had no intention of revealing to Murray the source of his intelligence. There was a good deal more to be squeezed from that particular lemon, in Grant's view, before it became necessary to honour his own bargain. Murray was inclined to be over-scrupulous. While Harry Churchill lived in doubt of his pardon, he would work more diligently than if it was handed him on a plate.

'Smells like a trap to me.' Murray shook his head.

'Possibly. Certainly none of the dispatches we have intercepted between Reynaud and Marmont hints at such an intention. What answer shall I return to the Governor?'

'Why, tell him if he wishes to communicate with Lord Wellington he should do so through the proper channels,' said Murray impatiently. 'He cannot expect his lordship to indulge in any hole-and-corner negotiations. The matter is too serious for that. Meanwhile, tell your *guerrillero* friends to pursue their blockade with vigour. The city still has provisions for two months, and if we are to reduce it we must ensure that no further supplies are received.'

Grant saluted and withdrew. Privately he wished Murray would not look so handsome a gift horse in the mouth. If the Governor of Ciudad Rodrigo wished to surrender his stronghold, why not profit by his madness? Time enough to ponder the rights and wrongs of the matter when the city was in their hands.

Riding back to the hills through the biting frost of a December evening, he reflected on other ways of hastening the city's capitulation. He thought it might be possible, without positively going against his orders, to devise a means of killing two birds with one stone. By the time he arrived at the deserted chapel where El Forastero's messenger waited, his plan was ready to be communicated to the *guerrillero* chief.

After the scorching summer, the autumn rains turned the roads into channels of liquid mud so deep and clinging that horses, let alone carriages, found it difficult to travel, and any officer unwise enough to attempt to move artillery might be sure of bogging half his pieces in the morass.

Now winter tightened its grip on the Spanish plateau, freezing the muddy ruts and dusting the sere landscape with a deceptively sugary sprinkle of snow blown into every depression by the cutting north-east wind.

No convoys could be expected to travel in such weather. The people of Ciudad Rodrigo notched new holes in their belts and looked with hungry eyes at the two hundred cattle remaining to the garrison, which were driven out to graze every morning on the grassy slope of the glacis, or allowed to wade across to the islands in the middle of the Agueda river, where forage could still be found.

When word was brought to Governor Reynaud that the whole of this precious herd was missing, driven off by the *guerrilleros* under the very noses of the garrison, he acted with an energy that astounded those officers who thought him a fat phlegmatic Swiss who would be better employed in a counting house than commanding a front-line garrison.

'*Sacré Dieu!* Those gentlemen are becoming a trifle too

impudent. It is high time we taught them a lesson,' he declared, and ordered his horse to be saddled.

'Surely you do not intend to chase them yourself?' objected Colonel de Rochefort. He received a frosty stare from the Governor's bleak blue eyes.

'Why not, sir? Do I have to remind you that those cattle represent the whole of our meat resources until Marshal Marmont sees fit to revictual us? Certainly I shall chase them.'

Though Rochefort was careful to defer to the Governor in public, it had long been understood that any suggestions he made were nothing less than orders.

'But, sir –'

'Allow me to do my duty as I recommend you to attend to yours, Colonel,' said Reynaud crisply. He had long resented his position of subservience to Rochefort, whom he regarded as a man with the morals of an alley-cat and Lucifer's own pride. He urged his horse forward, obliging Rochefort to stand aside or be trampled and ordered his trumpeter to sound the advance. The studded double door swung slowly outward.

The column swept in a jingling wave across the bridge, with the Governor's chestnut horse in the lead. He turned in his saddle to favour Rochefort with a stiff bow. Then they were gone, streaming across the level plain in the direction of the ring of hills that marked the border with Portugal.

Rochefort long remembered the look that accompanied Governor Reynaud's bow.

When the troopers rode wearily back at sunset, the drooping heads of their horses telling their own tale, the young officer in command had more to report than failure to recover the stolen cattle.

'We found them all right, sir,' said Lieutenant Coignet, standing stiff yet crestfallen in the cobbled keep. 'The tracks were plain. They had made no attempt to cover them. We followed them all the way to El Bodón, where the houses were shuttered and empty. The cattle were penned near the slaughterhouse. When we opened the gate to drive them out, the guerrillas closed in on us from the rear. We lost six men....'

'The Governor?' interrupted Rochefort harshly.

'Captured, sir.' Coignet swallowed painfully. He was a fair-headed, fresh-complexioned boy, newly commissioned – the kind of good-looking youngster the Emperor liked to single out from the ranks as the target of some grand gesture. He had been in Spain only a couple of months: no doubt that was why Governor Reynaud had chosen him to command the escort, thought Rochefort bitterly.

'Well, what is it?' he snapped, and the boy's colour rose.

He said diffidently, 'It was strange, sir, but one might almost have said the Governor *wished* to be captured. When I saw the danger I urged him to save himself, but instead he rode towards the bandits, calling out, "I am the Governor of Ciudad Rodrigo. Take me to your leader." I heard him plainly.'

'Treachery,' muttered Rochefort, understanding the bow from the saddle. Rage rose in him as he realized he had been hoodwinked by a man he despised, and he knew instinctively where to lay the blame. Doña Mercedes Cortes was at the bottom of this; somehow she had contrived to slip a message past the spy he had placed in her household, and this was the result.

'Close all the gates and double the guard,' he ordered. 'No one is to enter or leave the city without my permission. Until a new governor is appointed, I am in command here.'

There were few festivities that year in Ciudad Rodrigo to mark the Feast of the Nativity. Without food, firewood or forage for their animals, the people huddled in icy rooms, pressed together for warmth. A few almonds and raisins, jealously hoarded, were all most households could provide to vary the monotony of lentils and sausage sliced ever thinner as the hungry winter closed in.

Cramped into a tiny house in the Calle del Viejo Obispo with Angelica and her silent husband, Tomás, Clio fared no better than the rest of the townspeople. El Forastero and his *guerrilleros* had withdrawn towards Salamanca, so there were no messages to collect from the buttress on the bridge; and Mercedes warned her to stay away since Doña Eugenia was becoming suspicious of the seamstress's frequent visits.

Sometimes when she could no longer bear the cold frowstiness of the little house, she would take her basket and with her black shawl wrapped tightly against the biting wind would make her way to the Plaza Mayor, below the cathedral, to watch the garrison's comings and goings and pick up whatever rumours were current.

Rumours there were in plenty, none of them reassuring. Governor Reynaud had been succeeded by General Barrié who, it was said, had accepted the appointment with deep reluctance. A fussy, vacillating man endowed with neither vigilance nor resolution, he was putty in the determined hands of Colonel de Rochefort.

Under Rochefort's direction, the mood of the garrison stiffened. Though it could no longer be doubted that Lord Wellington meant to attack Ciudad Rodrigo, there was no more talk of surrender.

In the first freezing days of the new year, a foraging party rode into the city, manes and moustaches stiff with ice.

The officer in command reported that a trestle bridge had been constructed at Marialva and two British divisions, believed to be the Light and the Fourth, had crossed the Agueda and occupied the villages around El Bodón.

'Decidedly they intend to besiege us,' said Tomás. He shook his head gravely. '*Ay de mi!* Less than two years since the French bombarded our walls and now we must suffer the same from the English! What sins has our poor country committed that God should punish us thus?'

'The English are our friends. They will not plunder us as the French did,' asserted Angelica, shivering as much with apprehension as with cold.

'Soldiers will always plunder. You should have stayed in the hills. A town under siege is no place for women.'

'I am too old,' Angelica cackled. 'No soldier would trouble himself to molest me.' Nevertheless she cast an anxious glance at Clio and muttered, 'Yet I fear for the young ones. If only Doña Mercedes had not dragged us back to be caught like rats in a trap!'

Too late, thought Clio, fighting down the panic evoked by

the word *trap*. Ever since as a small child she had been shut in the broom cupboard by an unkind nurserymaid to frighten her into good behaviour, she had felt a horror of confined spaces. All too vividly she pictured hand-to-hand fighting in the city's narrow streets and the rape and pillage that would follow a storming. Reynaud had wanted to negotiate a surrender to save the city from such a fate; but Reynaud was gone and Barrié, for all his pomposity, obeyed Colonel de Rochefort, who would fight to the last however unequal the odds because it was his nature to prefer death with glory to the ignominy of surrender.

Glory! thought Clio with mingled resentment and disgust. Rochefort will have the glory and we shall suffer for it. Most of the French officers had already dispatched their women to the safety of Madrid; Clio wished Mercedes would accept one of the many lifts she was offered, but this she refused to do.

'Why should I run from our allies? Why should I be driven from my home? Save yourself, if you wish, but do not ask *me* to play the coward.'

In these anxious days their relationship changed. Clio's dislike changed by degrees to a reluctant respect, and still more reluctant affection. Obstinate and high-handed Mercedes might be, but she was certainly no coward.

'I was thinking of your children,' said Clio, though she had been thinking a good deal of her own safety as well. 'Will you not send Amalia to Madrid?'

'Are your gallant countrymen such monsters that you fear they will molest my daughter?'

'No, but –'

'You are not obliged to stay. I no longer require your services. You are free to go,' said Mercedes in a disdainful drawl calculated to enrage any free-born Englishwoman. Her black eyes sparkled with malice. 'Madame de Rochefort sent a note offering me a place in her carriage. Take it, with my blessing. I would rather be alone than surrounded by croakers.'

'I am not a croaker,' said Clio fiercely, while wondering whom Rochefort's wife might be.

Mercedes laughed.

In angry silence Clio unpinned the folds of black silk in which she had swathed her patron, but even when a pin jabbed her accidentally on purpose, Mercedes would not give Clio the satisfaction of hearing her squeal.

When she had departed, however, Mercedes sighed and slumped in her chair, laying a hand on her stomach as the child changed position.

Her time was near, and the double ring of steel was tightening on Ciudad Rodrigo, inside and out. Even if Marmont returned to relieve the beleaguered fortress, a battle was now inevitable.

Despite her bold words to Clio, she was afraid.

12

Auguste's star was rising with a speed that afforded him keen satisfaction. After six months' devotion to his work in the commissariat he was well on his way to fulfilling Lord Amherst's prediction and becoming rich as a nabob. Since he scrupulously set aside for his master a proportion of all his profits, Samuel Hardy's finances – little though he troubled his head about them – were also healthier than they had been for years.

Regularly every month Auguste was able to dispatch several hundred pounds to London, to be safely invested in $4\frac{1}{2}$ per cent stock. If the sum credited to Auguste's own account was more than twice as large as Mr Hardy's, it did no more than reflect their relative exertions in earning it.

Auguste's energy and enterprise won him well-deserved popularity with Hamilton's Horse.

'Your clerk is a marvel!' the quartermaster sometimes exclaimed to Samuel, when he called to draw rations and found cheeses, hams, fresh bread and preserves in abundance while other regiments had to make do with tough beef and ship's biscuit. Auguste was equally successful in obtaining forage for the horses of the 31st, who remained plump and glossy in comparison to their brethren in less fortunate regiments.

'He is an excellent fellow. I rely on him absolutely,' Samuel would respond; and if the quartermaster privately thought it disgraceful that Deputy Assistant Commissary Hardy should accept praise for work done entirely by his clerk, he was too anxious to retain Auguste's services to broadcast this opinion.

In fact the arrangement suited Auguste perfectly. He was never happier than when running about the country in search of supplies; with commissary gold in his pockets he was adept at persuading the niggardly peasants of the Guadiana valley to reveal their hidden hoards. Where persuasion proved fruitless, the threat of cutting a farmer's corn for forage or allowing the cavalry horses to trample it was generally enough to unlock the larder doors.

Many well-to-do peasants – and convents too – thought it no shame to offer the commissary's clerk substantial bribes to save their own corn at the expense of their neighbours'. This money, needless to say, never appeared in Auguste's neatly-penned balance sheets, but went to England with the rest to swell his account.

'Good vork deserves good pay,' Auguste would mutter as he rode away in front of his laden carts.

In contrast to the cheerful, hospitable Portuguese, Spanish farmers and townsfolk alike were surly and tight-fisted. The British soldiers regarded their property as a legitimate target and suspected them, not without good reason, of being just as ready to offer aid and comfort to the French as to their sworn allies. The troopers appreciated Auguste's efforts on their behalf and even when members of his foraging parties observed his more questionable transactions, they did not feel obliged to report them.

Though the regiment changed its quarters twenty times between June and September as the opposing armies marched, countermarched and manoeuvred, their sufferings were from heat and fatigue and the mosquitoes, leeches and scorpions that infested the Guadiana basin. Thanks to Auguste's exertions, neither horses nor men went hungry.

It was therefore as great a blow for the regiment as for Auguste himself when Samuel Hardy declared that the climate was ruining his health and applied to Commissary-General Bisset for sick leave.

Auguste was in despair. Must he leave his friends and allow his profitable systems to fall into other hands? Must he abandon Josefa, the handsome sixteen-year-old daughter of a rich peasant farmer to whom he had become passionately attached? Or should he forsake his master who would certainly be robbed by untrustworthy servants on the long journey to Lisbon? What would Mrs Hardy say if her husband suffered some misfortune?

'He has no more sense zan a child,' he muttered, torn between inclination and long-established duty.

For days he wrestled with the problem. Eventually the matter was solved by the arrival of two letters.

The first was directed to Auguste himself, and had the honour to inform him that the Commissary-General in England, being satisfied with his work – 'How ze deuce 'e knows anyting of the matter I cannot say,' growled Auguste – was pleased to announce his promotion to the post of Deputy Assistant Commissary to the 11th Light Dragoons, and should report to them at once at Covilhao.

Since this town was on the way to Lisbon, Auguste's nimble wits at once perceived a way to please all parties. First he would accompany Mr Hardy to Lisbon and see him comfortably settled there before proceeding to join his new regiment.

Relieved to have his difficulty resolved so neatly, Auguste went to his master's stores depot, which happened to be in a church, and found Samuel Hardy seated at a long table right in front of the high altar. By the light of four thick wax candles stuck in a richly ornamented candelabrum he was staring at a letter which had arrived by the same courier, tears pouring down his cheeks.

'Alas, poor child! Oh, unhappy girl!' he cried, pushing the paper away with a gesture of despair.

Auguste picked it up. The letter was dated from Madrid, two months earlier, and its crumpled grimy state testified to the number of hands it had passed through before reaching its destination.

My dearest Papa,
It is with Joy and Sorrow mixed that I pick up my Pen in the

Hope that this may reach you wherever you may be.

I rejoice to know you have been delivered from Cruel Captivity, but it is with Sorrow that I write to tell you of poor Clio's death. She was Barbarously Murdered by Brigands who attacked our Convoy on the road to Madrid.

I know the Pain this must cause you, and if it were in my Power to change this Melancholy News I would. When the Shooting began, our conveyance was overturned. Clio ran from it, and was Cut Down.

My own Situation, though hardly Agreeable, is helped by the Attention of Colonel de Rochefort, who shows me every Consideration.

Though separated by the Cruel Hand of War, my Family is often in my Thoughts.

I remain, Dearest Papa,
    Your affectionate daughter,
        Julia

Auguste's emotion on reading this was scarcely less than his master's. Of all the Hardy children Clio was his particular favourite.

'"All my pretty chickens,"' moaned Samuel distractedly. 'Oh, my poor Clio! If only I had not opposed the match with young Churchill! How can I break the news to her mother?'

He picked up the letter again, saying with more composure, 'Rochefort... Rochefort.... I knew a fellow of that name when I was in Madrid. I remember he had estates in Angoulême, but he will have lost those, poor fellow, in the Revolution. Ah, what a weary world this is!'

Sunk in sorrow, he accepted without question all Auguste's arrangements for departure. When permission came for them to travel, the two took leave of their regiment and were driven to Vilha Velha, there to embark on a riverboat bound for Lisbon.

The scene in the Quinta da Rosa, one golden morning in late October when Captain Cole called to take leave of Laura, was a very pretty, domestic one. For a moment he stood in the open doorway, watching her unobserved.

Laura was wearing green ribbons in her hair and a fresh delicate muslin dress of the same colour. One dark-eyed child sat on her lap, and two more leaned against the breakfast table close to her skirts as she slowly spelled out letters on a sheet of paper.

With her glossy brown ringlets falling over either shoulder, her blooming complexion, and her serious intent gaze bent on the work, she made so charming a picture that he could not help considering how excellent a wife she would make for some lucky fellow, and wishing he could be that fellow himself.

Laura radiated the kind of serenity a man needed. She was practical, and her calm good sense smoothed away troubles as easily as children's tears. During his leave Robert had spent a good deal of time with Laura, and every encounter increased his regard for her. Together they had installed the orphans and their attendants in this handsome commodious *quinta* which he had rented.

'Papa will repay you as soon as he returns,' she said earnestly when the landlord demanded payment in advance. 'After all, if he had not brought me little Miguel, I might still be thinking of nothing but picnics and balls, as my silly friends do.'

'I am very glad you have found a more worthy cause,' he assured her. 'Pray do not trouble about repayment. I shall count it an honour to have been allowed to assist you.'

The truth was that he should very much have liked to set up house at the Quinta da Rosa with Laura and her ever-increasing family, but naturally propriety forbade it. Instead he lodged at Lahmeyer's Hotel in company with his friend Captain Coghlan, who had lost an arm at Fuentes de Oñoro and was soon to sail for England.

Now Robert had been ordered to rejoin his regiment in cantonments at Covilhao. He would have liked to express something of his admiration for Laura before departing, but was inhibited by the fact of his betrothal to her captive sister.

At that moment Laura raised her eyes. 'Robert!' she cried in as much glad surprise as if he had not called on her every day for two months. 'How very pleased I am to see you. Come and tell me the news.'

He sat down and accepted a cup of chocolate. 'Melancholy news for me, at any rate,' he said, sighing. 'I am ordered to leave at once for Covilhao.'

'Oh, I am sorry to hear it! I shall miss your company so much. How shall I manage the children without your help?'

'You know you will manage very well!' He was pleased, however; and her warmth emboldened him to say with a touch of wistfulness, 'May I hope you will think of me sometimes when I am away?'

'I shall do more than think!' she responded vigorously. 'I shall plague you with letters telling of our doings and asking your advice. Dear Robert! You can have no notion how much your help has meant to me these past weeks.'

'I wish I need not go –' he was beginning, when a commotion in the street outside made Laura put down the child and hurry to the window. A carriage had drawn up before the door, and the driver was questioning her maid.

'Whoever – ? Oh!' She drew in her breath sharply. 'It is Auguste... and Papa!'

'Would you rather I left?'

'Pray stay.' She peered from the window. 'He – he looks fatigued... and angry.'

Even at this distance Mr Hardy's short, stiff steps, abrupt turns of the head and flourishing cane betrayed strong emotion.

Laura thrust the baby into Robert's arms and ran to greet her father. Robert followed more slowly, the children close on his heels, wide-eyed and curious. As he came within earshot he heard Samuel Hardy say, 'Upon my word, miss, you have led me a pretty dance! It is too bad. As if I had not enough to endure without being made a laughing-stock by my own daughter. Wherever I go I hear tales of you. You have made enemies of half my acquaintance and put the other half to trouble and expense. Are you lost to all filial feeling that you should abandon me in this hour of need?'

'Oh, Papa – Papa! I am sorry. So very very sorry!'

Tears spilled from Laura's eyes, though in Robert's view her father's testiness was hardly cause for such distress.

'Indeed, sir, you must not blame Laura,' he said with some

force. 'She has done nothing to deserve your reproaches.'

'No, Robert, he is right. I should never have gone – never have wished.... Oh, poor Clio! Can I ever forgive myself?'

Weeping uncontrollably, she cast herself into her father's arms and buried her face in his shoulder.

'There, child. You must be brave – we must all be brave. Pray Heaven she did not suffer,' he said in a kinder tone.

More puzzled than ever, Robert turned to Auguste. 'What has happened?'

'Do not blame my master, sir. He iss not himself.' As ever in moments of stress, Auguste's accent thickened. 'Since ve heard of Miss Clio's death ve haf searched for Miss Laura to bring her ze news, but no von could say vhere she vas living.'

For a moment Robert felt stunned, unable to take in the sense of the words.

'Clio's *death?*' he said dazedly. 'I don't – I can't believe it!'

'Zose *sacré guerrilleros* haf killed her.'

'When did you hear this? Who told you?' said Robert in a low, shaken voice. Laura's distress pierced his heart. He longed to take her in his arms and comfort her but could hardly do so in the presence of her father.

Instead he drew Auguste aside, listening grim-faced to the story of Julia's letter while the familiar sense of desolation and self-criticism threatened to overwhelm him. First Harry, now Clio: two bright spirits whom he had loved. If he had acted more boldly both might still be alive. He could have disobeyed orders and carried Harry away from Talavera instead of leaving him in the hands of the treacherous Spaniards. He could have called Rochefort's bluff and braved his pistol to save Clio. Was it cowardice or self-preservation that stopped him behaving as a hero should?

I am not a man of action, he thought dismally. I think too much: see the dangers too clearly. Laura would understand. She would accept me for what I am rather than trying to change my nature. Again his glance strayed to the glossy head bowed on Samuel Hardy's shoulder. Not for the first time he cursed the impulse that had led him to join the army and prove himself as much as a man as Harry.

*

The news of Clio's death was more than a shock to Mrs Hardy. Samuel's attempts to soften the blow in his letter were unavailing and as the truth sank in something young and hopeful, a part of her own spirit, seemed to die. She knew she would never be the same again.

It had always been her pride as a mother that she had no favourites among her brood. Her clear eye saw their bad points as well as the good, and accepted her children for the individuals they were. Even Joshua, the single boy among all this galaxy of girls, she accorded no special favour on account of his gender: indeed she was peculiarly alive to the danger of his becoming spoiled, and swift to check any tendency to vaunt a male superiority over his sisters. Her beautiful eldest daughter also came in for criticism which busybody neighbours felt she hardly deserved.

'That girl is an angel. How can her mother possibly find fault with her?' Mrs Collingbourne was once heard to murmur. 'Mrs Hardy does not know how lucky she is.'

'She would be better advised to save her scolding for Miss Laura,' agreed her bosom friend Miss Parsons, who had been greatly annoyed by a dose of unsolicited advice from that forthright damsel. 'How dare she tell me Trixie is too fat and should take more exercise? As if I did not know what was good for my own dog!'

But although she was aware of this conversation, Mrs Hardy did not reprove Laura. She realized her second daughter's desire to manage the affairs of others sprang not from mere bossiness but a genuine concern for their well-being. Even her absurd obsession with marriage was merely the expression of her longing to command her own destiny. Laura had outgrown childhood more quickly than her contemporaries. Mrs Hardy could not but admire her disregard of the opinion of more conventional souls and determination to do good in the world.

Yet no matter how even-handed she strove to be, there was no doubt that Mrs Hardy's third daughter occupied a very special place in her heart. More than any of her other children, Clio was Genevieve herself when young. How can I blame her faults, knowing so well where they come from? she sometimes reflected. Recklessness was at the root of most of Clio's misdemeanours, but courage and recklessness were closely akin – who could say where one left off and the other began? Some might have called Genevieve's own escape from Revolutionary France a reckless adventure: how well she remembered the horror with which Auguste – the only one of her father's servants who had not run away – had greeted her proposal that he should carry her out of the house in a wicker hamper beneath a bundle of dirty linen. 'Remain here quietly, *petite folle*, and they vill forget you,' he had scolded. 'If you try to escape and they catch you, ve can expect no mercy. What could ve do in England, you and I, without money or friends to help us?'

But she had insisted and he had played his part loyally, despite his grumbles. Never would she forget that nerve-tingling hour hidden in the hamper while Auguste played cards with the guard; the fear that any moment the lid might be flung back. Through all the humdrum years of housekeeping and childbearing it had been a memory to cherish: that time when death had been so close she had felt more alive than ever before or since. Samuel would not have understood, but Genevieve knew in her heart that it had been the same half-fearful, half-ecstatic craving for adventure that had impelled Clio to take the place of her own maid in order to escape from home. It was very wrong of her. No right-thinking parent could condone such reprehensible conduct, yet Mrs Hardy found it... understandable.

I should have made her come back, she thought now, sitting at her bureau and staring with misted eyes at the forest of masts swaying in the brisk autumn sou'westerly. I was weak and foolish to allow her to stay because she wished it, and this is my reward. Sometimes it is cruel to be kind. Her father would have sent her home, but I overruled him...

She felt a momentary but nevertheless intense spasm of bitterness. It required no great effort of imagination to picture what her husband had been doing when Clio met her death. She should have known better than to hope he would concern himself with his daughters. All he ever thought of were his *sacré* Romans!

Yet that was hardly fair, she reminded herself, looking again at his letter. In his anxiety to spare her pain, Samuel had so obfuscated the circumstances surrounding the girls' disappearance that it was difficult for her to understand how it had come about. Julia and Clio had become separated from the convoy – that much was plain – and somehow been taken as hostages by a French officer, Colonel de Rochefort.

Rochefort? She considered the name. It woke echoes of some long-ago memory. Hadn't her grandfather fought a duel in the Jardin de Luxembourg with a certain Vicomte de Rochefort, back in the reign of Louis XV? Some business of a pledge to La Pompadour – she could not remember the details. It was all ancient history now. Probably this Rochefort Julia spoke of was a man of no better birth than the rest of Napoleon's officers. Whichever he might be, *sans-culotte* or *ci-devant aristo*, Colonel de Rochefort had commanded the convoy taking her daughters to Madrid. On the way it had been attacked by *guerrilleros*. Resolutely she tried again to picture the scene so that the fact of Clio's death might become real to her, as one bites on an aching tooth to discover if the pain is yet bearable. It was no use: her mind shied away.

If only, she thought instead. *If only* I had let her have her way over Harry Churchill. That was where her longing to escape from home started, and this is where it has led. It is all my fault.

A tap on the door interrupted these regrets. Jane entered – her pale, blotched face witness to her own distress – and announced in a subdued voice that his lordship was below and wished to speak with her.

'His lordship?'

'Lord Amherst, ma'am.'

'Great heavens! I hope you have not left him standing at the door?' exclaimed Mrs Hardy, much flustered.

'I showed him into the library, ma'am.'

Lord Amherst rose from the wing chair near the fire as Mrs Hardy entered the library a few minutes later. He bowed over her hand without speaking and she was struck by how greatly he had aged in the three years since she last saw him. His handsome aquiline features had become gaunt, the skin stretched tight over prominent bones, and though he held himself as upright as ever there was a certain stiffness to his carriage which hinted at infirmity rather than pride. He wore his own hair tied in a simple queue and it had no need of powder, being white as any wig. Only his deep-set diamond-shaped eyes under their strongly marked brows gave any indication of the fiery spirit for which he had been renowned before overwork, ill health, and the blow of losing his only son aged him prematurely.

'Terrible news, ma'am. I came as soon as I heard,' he said in his abrupt way. 'Offer my deepest sympathy, for what that's worth! No –' as she tried to reply – 'no need for pretty speeches. I can guess what you feel – only too well! Been through it myself. Only wanted to let you know I'm here to help in any way I can. Like to help, if you'll let me.'

'You are very good, my lord,' she murmured, controlling her emotion as best she could. This blunt-tongued irascible man had the reputation of being the only person in public life whom both the army and the politicians trusted. He was the vital link: a man who knew how to make Lord Wellington's demands acceptable to his opponents at Court and in Parliament. That he should have put aside his affairs in order to offer her his condolences in person touched her deeply.

'Good?' he repeated irritably. 'Of course I'm not good. Least I can do.' He took a turn across the room and halted before her, tapping the floor with his cane. 'Can't comprehend how it happened. Never should have happened. Your husband had no business to drag his daughters round at the tail of the regiment.'

She felt bound to defend Samuel, though in her heart she agreed. 'Permit me to observe, my lord, that you yourself encouraged my husband to seek a commission. You are hardly in a position to blame him for doing so.'

'I don't blame him for seeking a commission, but for dragging his daughters round like camp followers. Nothing but a damned nuisance. I can't understand why he didn't leave 'em safe in Lisbon. The front's no place for young females.'

'My husband did as he thought best,' she said stiffly. 'If anyone is to blame, it is I. I should not have allowed Clio to flout my authority and remain with her sisters.'

'Flout your authority, ma'am?'

Mrs Hardy flushed. 'I fear so. I forbade her to go with her father to Lisbon, I thought her too young, particularly after –'

'Yes, yes,' he said impatiently. 'So how did she get there?'

'She exchanged clothes with her maid and had herself smuggled on board without my knowledge.'

'Did she, by George!' His tone was half-admiring.

'I should have insisted she returned by the next boat. It is all my fault.'

'No, ma'am. You must not blame yourself. The truth is, we poor parents feel obliged to blame ourselves for whatever befalls our children, supposing ourselves in some way responsible for their actions; but if we took the trouble to trace each event to its true roots we would generally find the cause quite beyond our control.'

It was rather what she had been thinking herself.

He said musingly, 'Harry had a high opinion of your daughter, ma'am. Had it not been for this foolish business of an elopement I would have been happy enough to see them make a match of it.'

'A match!' she exclaimed, astonished. 'They were much too young.'

'No younger than Juliet when she made her choice.'

'My lord, I feel it hardly proper to apply the standards of a romance to my own child!'

'Yet you would not deny that what appears proper to one generation may be considered exceedingly improper in the next?'

Mrs Hardy raised her brows, aware that he was quizzing her. She smiled a little and shook her head but said nothing.

Lord Amherst sighed. 'My own wife, God rest her, was barely sixteen when we married. Ah well, it is too late to change matters now, but I beg you will cease to blame yourself for what you could not have prevented, and will consider me at your service in any way I can assist you. It cannot be easy for you, ma'am, with your husband away.'

Mrs Hardy acknowledged that it was not easy, but pride made her add that she and her children rubbed along pretty well. She offered refreshment.

'Alas, ma'am, my time is not my own,' he responded, and the rueful fleeting charm of his smile reminded her vividly of Harry. Soon after he took his leave and drove away towards the harbour, assuring her once more of his readiness to help in any difficulty.

'You have only to ask. My secretary is a good fellow and will make sure your message reaches me. A *bientôt*, Mrs Hardy!'

Though the pain of losing Clio remained as sharp as before, she was comforted to know that Lord Amherst had not forgotten them. She hoped she would never have occasion to remind him of his promise but it was gratifying to be assured that help was near if she needed it.

Straightening the fichu about her shoulders, she cast a critical eye about the room, annoyed to see that since the arrival of the fateful letter the housemaids had so far neglected their duties that a perceptible film of dust lay on the drum table where her husband kept his writing materials. The brass surround to the fireplace was by no means as bright as she liked it, either, and a questing finger across the chimneypiece revealed that, too, in need of soap and water.

Her withdrawal from household supervision, brief as it had been, had already allowed standards to slip. It would not do.

'Lazy sluts,' she said aloud, and the responsibilities of the chatelaine which had temporarily slipped from her shoulders settled back across them like a well-worn harness. With a rapid mental inventory of all she could see to criticize, she rang the bell to summon Eliza and Jane.

13

When Clio entered the courtyard of Don Sebastian Cortes's house on a dark, rain-swept morning of the seventh of January, 1812, she knew at once something momentous had occurred. The grooms were whistling as they wisped the carriage horses; maids chattered and giggled as they tripped across the cobbles. One and all wore an air of smiling self-congratulation.

Even the taciturn gatekeeper touched his forehead in the semblance of a salute and said, 'Good day, *señorita*. A happy day for us all.'

'What has happened?'

He was pleased to be the first to enlighten her. 'My lady has been delivered of a healthy boy, the Blessed Virgin be praised!' He paused, looking at her with concern. 'Why, *señorita*, what is the matter? You are pale as a ghost.'

'It is nothing.' Clio put a hand on the gate for support. She felt a curious floating sensation, as if her head was suspended an inch or two above her body.

'Poor child, you are cold. Come in by the fire,' said the gatekeeper with gruff kindness. 'I will send to tell the mistress you are here.'

Clio was glad to obey. The sudden weakness that invaded her limbs made it hard to drag her hamper even as far as the kitchen, where she sank on a bench, holding out her hands to the blazing range. Warmth seeped into her as she watched kitchenmaids and scullions scuttle about their duties. All was normal, yet somehow different. Harry's son, she thought, and again felt dizzy.

'Here, little one. Get this inside you.' The fat cook ladled broth from a blackened cauldron and thrust the bowl into Clio's hands. 'By the look of you you've had nothing to eat today.'

Nor last night either, thought Clio. Her teeth chattered on the rim of the bowl, but the food revived her.

'Go on, drink up. The mistress isn't one to begrudge you a meal, not like some I could mention. Such a time she had of it, poor lady,' went on the cook, plumping down beside Clio, her face alight with the special relish reserved by servants for death and childbirth. 'Her screams! You could hear her from here to the Plaza Mayor! We had five priests and two doctors, holy water, even the toe of Saint Ildefonso brought from the shrine, and Heaven knows how much *that* cost the master. More than once they thought she was gone. Don Sebastian spent all night in his cabinet, calling on the saints to spare his wife –'

'And make sure the child was a son,' put in the spit-boy, grinning.

'Naturally the master wants a son now that poor Don Alvaro is dead, God rest him! And the mistress heir to all his lands.'

'A great inheritance,' agreed Clio. The faintness was passing and she felt a strong wish to see Harry's child.

When Doña Eugenia rustled into the kitchen a few minutes later, her sharp features wore an expression that was almost agreeable, but it was soon plain this was due to her pleasure in telling the seamstress that she had wasted her journey.

'No question of permitting you to bother the mistress today. No question!' she said sharply. 'Señor Cortes has ordered complete rest.'

'Will you not tell her I am here, at least? I wished to ask her –'

'You would be better advised to let me do the asking,' snapped Doña Eugenia.

'Very well, *señora*. I will come back tomorrow for her orders.'

'You will do nothing of the kind. I will send for you when you are needed.'

'Thank you, *señora*.' Clio rose, conscious of partisan looks from the kitchen staff, who detested Doña Eugenia's assumption of power. 'May I ask you to convey my good wishes to your mistress?'

The housekeeper pursed her lips as if she considered the phrasing of this request an impertinence. She swished from the room without answering, keys jangling at her waist. Clio thanked the cook and hoisted her hamper, ready to depart.

She was re-crossing the courtyard towards the gate when an urgent hissing from a group of cypresses shading the dark cloister attracted her attention.

'Consuela! Wait!'

Peering into the shadows, she made out the form of Amalia, Mercedes's daughter, framed in a dark low entrance like an agitated mouse at the mouth of its hole. She beckoned, then put a finger to her lips.

Intrigued, Clio approached and Amalia caught her by the hand.

'I was so afraid you would pass without seeing me,' she said, her small face puckered with worry.

'What is the matter, *niña*?'

For answer Amalia pulled her inside the dark entrance which looked as if it had been designed for unloading barrels. She pushed the stout door shut behind them and shot the bolt.

'Mama wishes to see you,' she said.

'But Doña Eugenia said –'

'Doña Eugenia must not know. Leave your hamper and follow me.'

As Clio's eyes grew accustomed to the half-light, she made out a flight of steps rising steeply from the ground to first-floor level. Obediently she followed Amalia to a narrow landing and along a passage built between the outer and inner walls of the house. At intervals light filtered through holes in the wall. Amalia stood on tiptoe to put her eye to one and gestured to Clio to do the same.

The spyhole revealed a small bare room like a nun's cell, starkly furnished with a wooden bed beneath a crucifix, a dark oak chest and a table at which Doña Eugenia was engaged in checking accounts. The keys at her waist clinked gently as she rose and lifted the lid of the chest. She removed a layer of linen, and from their vantage point above her the girls saw the gleam of metal.

'See what she has stolen,' breathed Amalia, her lips close to Clio's ear.

The chest was full of silver and gold ornaments. Doña Eugenia reached beneath the rustling folds of her gown and drew out a small pair of silver candlesticks, then a necklace of glowing stones.

'Mama's rubies!'

Amalia clapped her hand to her mouth to stifle her indignation as the sour-faced woman examined the jewels, holding them close to her eyes as if assessing their value. After a careful look at each, she wrapped the necklace in a scrap of linen and stowed it in the chest. Silently Amalia plucked at Clio's sleeve and drew her on.

The secret passage led past a dozen rooms where servants were working. Amalia gave each a casual glance and hurried on; plainly the passage was a favourite haunt of hers. In places it narrowed so they could only squeeze along with difficulty; there were steps and ramps, branches, alcoves, and culs-de-sac which showed that it had been adapted by many different hands since the house was constructed. It was not so long since Clio had been a child herself. She could not help reflecting how much she and her sisters would have liked to possess such a labyrinth in their own home, though no doubt this one had been constructed for darker purposes than games of hide-and-seek. Heretics could have hidden here from the dreaded Inquisition and lovers stolen at dead of night through its twisting maze. She shivered, picturing human bones walled up behind those blank brick faces, and workmen murdered to ensure their silence.

At last Amalia stopped and listened intently. With extreme caution she moved forward again and applied her eye to a spyhole. Clio copied her and found she was looking into Mercedes's bedchamber. It was a grand, square, lofty room hung with magnificent tapestries. A stout woman swathed in a white apron stooped at the hearth, mending the fire, and beside the carved oak fourposter whose blue silk curtains were tightly drawn lay a cradle carved from polished wood. Nothing could be seen of its occupant.

Clio found she was holding her breath and let it out slowly on a sigh. Most passionately she yearned to see the child lying swaddled in that cradle.

For a few moments they waited, gazing at the silent tableau, then Amalia nodded, satisfied, and Clio heard the faint scratch as her nails felt for a hidden catch. She pressed it and smoothly a section of panelling slid aside, leaving a gap large enough for them to squeeze through.

At the movement the nurse looked up and saw them. Her hand flapped in an unmistakable gesture of warning. She shook her head, pointing to the door, and Clio's straining ears caught the murmur of voices beyond it. Amalia closed the panel quickly, leaving herself and Clio in hiding.

A peremptory hand rapped twice, and the nurse bustled to the door. She opened it, curtseying deeply.

'*Señor!*'

Don Sebastian Cortes passed her without a glance. It was the first sight Clio had had of Mercedes's husband, and she studied him with keen attention.

He was a thin man of middle height, dressed entirely in black, and carried himself with the stiff dignity of one assured of his own worth. Clio observed his pale face and dark-ringed eyes, the long obstinate jaw, surrounded by a fringe of reddish beard. 'Proud as the devil,' Harry had called him, and she could well believe it.

With measured tread he approached the curtained bed.

'Leave us,' he ordered without turning his head.

Despite the forbidding note, the stout nurse voiced a protest. '*Señor*, my lady is sleeping.'

'Then wake her.'

'But, *señor*, the doctor's orders were –'

'Do as I say.'

Before the nurse could obey, from behind the curtains an imperious voice demanded what was the matter.

'My lady, your husband is here.'

Clio sensed rather than saw Mercedes's shrug. 'Then do not stand there like a fool. Open the curtains. Well, husband? Have you come to admire your son?'

Clio heard the trace of mockery and hoped Don Sebastian did not. Baiting a Spanish hidalgo was a risky game.

'I congratulate you on your achievement. A fine boy.' Don Sebastian's deep-set eyes turned to the cradle. 'Colonel de Rochefort has brought a gift for him.'

'How civil of Colonel de Rochefort!'

'He is below with his lady.'

'I am not well enough to receive. Pray thank them and convey my regrets.'

Don Sebastian said smoothly, 'It would hardly be politic to refuse him. Consider my position.'

'Confound your position!'

'Do not be hasty. You would be ill-advised to offend Colonel de Rochefort, *señora*.'

The tone was still gentle and reasonable, but Clio shivered. There was something feline about Mercedes's husband. He valued his dignity too much to display emotion, yet she sensed a smouldering anger.

That Mercedes despised him was apparent in her expression of disdain.

'What do I care for a Frenchman's favour? You may tell Colonel de Rochefort I have no wish to be plagued with his attentions now or at any other time.'

'*Señora*, you will see them.'

Mercedes shrugged impatiently. 'Oh, very well, admit them. It is a matter of no importance,' she snapped, and Don Sebastian nodded.

'I knew you had too much sense to refuse,' he said and left the room with his soft measured tread.

The moment the door swung shut behind him, Mercedes flung aside the covers and sat up. She wrenched the bell-rope with a force that bade fair to sever it from its mooring.

'Maria! Conchita! Beatríz! Attend me, you lazy bitches!'

Maids scurried to answer the call. With a stream of orders Mercedes sent them flying back and forth. They fetched armfuls of shawls and lace mantillas from presses; mirrors, combs and brushes from the dressing table, hare's foot and rouge, jewellery from the ivory casket. The nurse watched the commotion stolidly, rocking the cradle with her foot.

In a shorter time than Clio would have believed possible, Mercedes was transformed from pale sufferer to *grande dame*. If it was art rather than nature that tinted lips and cheeks with the appearance of health and if the gloss on her high-dressed hair owed more to oil than brushing, at least the colour and shine were enough to distract attention from her restless hands and shadowed eyes.

Colonel de Rochefort coolly assessed her appearance as he bowed over her hand, murmuring civilities. The stoicism of Manuela, her maid, had been astonishing. Nothing would persuade her to say a word that linked her mistress with the guerrillas. When at last he had allowed her soul to leave her broken body, he had been no wiser than before he arrested her.

Nor had his spy within the household furnished the proofs he needed. If one was to believe Doña Eugenia – whose reports had hitherto been reliable – the lady of the house spent her days instructing her daughter, working her tapestry, and ministering to her husband. She neither entertained nor was entertained. In the two months preceding the birth of this child she had not left her house at all, nor had her servants attempted to pass the city gates.

Yet detailed information regarding the garrison's strength and dispositions was still reaching the *guerrilleros* Rochefort was convinced that Señora Cortes maintained contact with them, though he could not prove it.

Through the spyhole, Clio watched the Frenchman with a mixture of fascination and revulsion. His handsome arrogant features repelled her. She wondered how Julia could ever have allowed that thin-lipped sneering mouth to kiss her. There was a woman with him now, an extravagantly-dressed female, more doll than human, tripping into the bedchamber on Don Sebastian's arm. The poke of her ludicrous bonnet, maroon velvet banded with pleated white muslin and crowned by three nodding ostrich plumes, projected so far that her features were hidden. Her figure was sharply defined by a full-length redingote, also in maroon, cut very tight at the waist and full in the skirt. Its leg o' mutton sleeves were trimmed at the shoulders with lace epaulettes, giving a quaint, quasi-military look. The smallest of buttoned boots peeped from under a hem which was quite unsuited to winter walking, being of dagged white muslin in the same style as her cuffs and frilled collar.

She looked frivolous, fashionable and very French as she twittered and cheeped responses to Don Sebastian's gallantry, and it was a full minute before one of her elegant pirouettes brought her round to face the spyhole.

With a considerable shock Clio recognized her eldest sister.

'Ju-!' A sharp pinch from Amalia cut off the word half spoken. As if in a dream Clio watched Julia twittering civilities and cooing over the cradle. What a transformation! Julia's very nature seemed to have changed with her clothes. Her laugh was shrill, her gestures blatantly coquettish. A proper Bath Miss, thought Clio, and blushed for her.

Mercifully etiquette decreed that such a visit should be brief. Very soon Rochefort signalled to his lady to make her adieux, and Julia extended her fingertips to Mercedes in farewell. She tripped to the door: echoes of 'Adorable!' 'Most charming!' and 'The prettiest creature imaginable!' faded as the party moved away.

Intelligence returned to the face of the stout nurse, who had been standing by the cradle in an attitude of bovine stupidity. She signalled that the coast was clear.

'Come,' whispered Amalia. The panel moved smoothly back. Clio composed her features and followed her into the bedchamber.

After taking leave of Don Sebastian, Rochefort and his lady

went separate ways. She returned to the fortress in an elegant closed carriage that had once belonged to an archbishop, while her husband mounted his horse to ride on his daily tour of the outposts.

All day the problem of how to trap Doña Mercedes occupied his thoughts. He was still brooding over it when darkness fell and he came back to sup with Julia in their candlelit apartment whose grilled and shuttered windows overlooked the Agueda bridge.

This was the hour Julia loved most in all the day: the one time she could be sure of Rochefort's undivided attention as he ate and listened with an indulgent smile to her prattle of the day's events. She spent a good deal of time preparing for these precious moments, ordering his favourite dishes and dressing with care. Rochefort liked to see her *en beauté*, as he termed it, and was generous with jewels. Tonight she wore sea-green silk cut low across the bosom with a high waist, tiny puffed sleeves, and a flowing skirt. About her neck sparkled his latest gift of square-cut emeralds.

She found him abstracted this evening and disinclined for talk, so like a good wife she curbed her tongue and forebore to harass him until he had eaten. When at last his boots were removed and he stretched himself before the fire, his dark head in her lap, she asked what was troubling him.

'Did Don Sebastian's son displease you? You have hardly spoken a word since our visit.'

She smiled a little consciously, aware of certain recent changes in her own body, news of which she had not yet communicated to her husband.

Rochefort smiled and made an effort to throw off his moodiness. He knew his young wife was often lonely and homesick, an easy target for the sneers of other officers' wives, most of whom were jealous of Julia's beauty.

'On the contrary, I thought the baby very charming.'

'Like his mother?'

Rochefort frowned. 'I must own I find Don Sebastian's wife something of an enigma.'

'Why, from the frequency of your visits, I supposed you to be one of Doña Mercedes's admirers!' said Julia with an archness that did not quite conceal anxiety.

'Then you are mistaken. My visits to that house have quite another purpose than admiring Doña Mercedes's *beaux yeux*.'

'You cannot deny she is very handsome,' said Julia, relieved to learn she had nothing to fear from that quarter. 'All the same,' she added reflectively, 'I wonder Don Sebastian is not more careful of her reputation.'

Rochefort yawned and stretched, listening with half an ear. The warmth of the fire made him drowsy; he reflected how agreable it would be to take his pretty wife to bed here and now, but any moment the inevitable knock would summon him to pull on his boots once more and cross the frosty courtyard to make his report to Governor Barrié.

'Why should you suppose her reputation in jeopardy, my love?' he asked idly.

Julia gave him a bright sharp glance, far removed from her usual dreamy gaze. It reminded him disagreeably of her younger sister.

'It can hardly be enhanced by the company she keeps.'

'I did not know you were acquainted with her friends. What company does she keep?'

Intrigued, Rochefort sat up. Julia's cheeks were flushed and her eyes bright with the half-resolute, half-fearful air of one about to light the fuse that will lead to an explosion.

'Shocking company,' she said with unusual force. 'Do you recall my speaking of a woman – a lady of quality – who questioned me and Clio on our arrival in the *guerrilleros* cave? *That woman was Doña Mercedes!* The moment I set eyes on her today I recognized her.'

Rochefort was not easily surprised, but now he wondered if his wife had lost her senses.

'Impossible!'

'I assure you it is true.' Julia spoke with the calm of complete conviction. 'The face, the voice, even the ring she wore.... There can be no possibility of mistake.'

'I was there in the cave. I did not see her,' he said slowly.

'No, for she took good care you should not. When the bandits dragged you in, she vanished and we did not see her again, but I have an excellent memory for faces.'

'Yet today you made no sign?'

'I wanted to speak to you first. Don Sebastian has powerful friends, as you have told me a dozen times.' When he was silent, she went on eagerly, 'Do you not see what this means? If Don Sebastian has links with the *guerrilleros*, you have an enemy in your midst.'

Rochefort shook his head. 'I find it hard to believe Don Sebastian would play us false. He has received much favour from the Emperor and shown himself strong in our support. Doña Mercedes is a different matter.... You are right. The matter must be investigated.' He drummed his fingers against the table. 'I must approach this with care. If I accuse her directly she will certainly deny the charge, and without proof....'

'I can give you proof,' said Julia.

She rose and went to the satinwood bureau. The sketchbook she took from a drawer had suffered a good deal in its travels, being waterstained and grimy on the covers, but the drawings within were undamaged.

Rapidly she turned the leaves. There were pencil studies of peasants, drawn while journeying up-country with the supply waggons; a sketch of Clio at rest beneath a cork tree; Robert Cole's long serious face half obscured by his forage cap. She paused at the page where she had recorded her impression of the ambush, and Rochefort recognized the narrow defile between cliffs, his men sprawled in death and his own horse leaping to freedom.

'Here is your proof,' said Julia, and placed the book in his hands.

Rochefort studied the sketch and his lips pursed in a silent whistle. From the foreground Doña Mercedes's aristocratic features stared haughtily, nostrils flared and mouth scornfully curved. Behind her the *guerrilleros* crowded round the fire, bowls in hand. Beneath was the telltale caption: *In the Bandits' Lair*, and the date, *25 April 1811.*

Rochefort brooded over the portrait, his face intent with the controlled excitement of the hunter. He closed the book and slipped it in his pocket, then looked at his wife with something akin to awe. He could hardly believe this pretty foolish creature should hand him the long-desired instrument of revenge on his arch-enemy.

He was a man of impulse, and on impulse he had married Julia, charmed by her artless devotion and unable to secure her surrender by any other means. He had felt Pygmalion's urge to breathe life into this unawakened goddess, to transform Nature and make from this English wildflower a fashionable cultivated bloom who would be the envy of his friends.

In this aim he had succeeded. Frizzed and frilled and laced, Julia no longer bore the least resemblance to a wildflower. Like many a man before him, Rochefort found the woman he had created less appealing than the orginal: lately he had begun to encourage other advances and ask himself if he had not, after all, made a poor bargain.

Now he regarded her with new eyes. Brains as well as beauty! He had not expected so handsome a bonus.

'Then the child –' he mused aloud.

'Is very likely the offspring of El Forastero,' said Julia in her dreamy way. 'Certainly he does not in the least resemble Don Sebastian.'

How could such a scrap of humanity be said to resemble anyone? Rochefort's teeth flashed in a smile. He reached out to pull Julia into his arms.

'My love, you have given me what I wished for. Doña Mercedes has played her cards well, but with your trump in my hand I shall win the game! You must not fret if I am absent for a few days. When I return, you may expect good news.'

He kissed her lingeringly, then shouted for his boots. Within a few minutes he was gone, hurrying down the stone steps with a light purposeful tread, but for a long time after his steps faded into silence Julia stood where he had left her, both hands pressed to her stomach, suddenly full of fear for the woman she had betrayed.

14

News of Don Sebastian's arrest spread like wildfire through the beleaguered city of Ciudad Rodrigo. It sent flickers of fear into the cabinets of Spanish notables who secretly dreamed of running with the hare as well as hunting with the hounds. If Don Sebastian, a declared Francophile, was suspected of double dealing, who could consider his skin safe?

Clio found the market buzzing with the story, which had even diverted public attention from the muffled pounding of British cannon against the western wall. The common people took a robust view of Don Sebastian's predicament.

'He who sells his soul to the Devil must expect to be paid in the Devil's coin!' declared a brawny baker as Clio elbowed her way into his small dark shop in search of the grey bread which was all he had to sell. 'Don Sebastian opened his arms to the invader. Let him see what manner of men his new friends are.'

'That old fox is too cunning to leave any tracks,' said a customer sourly. 'He has been eating white bread and swilling good French wine while we starve. For my part, I would like to see him hang from the castle tower.'

There was a chorus of agreement.

Without waiting to complete her errand, Clio hurried to question Mercedes. Ten days had passed since the birth of her son, but she kept to her bed. Clio found her propped on pillows, weak from a recent cupping. Bright spots of colour burned on her cheekbones, and her eyes had a feverish glitter.

From a nearby room the baby wailed and was swiftly hushed.

Mercedes frowned at Clio's report. 'Rochefort is a greater fool than I thought if he supposes my husband to have any dealings with *guerrilleros*. When Marmont returns from Valencia he will discover his mistake. Pray Heaven the British break down our walls before then!'

She asked for news of the siege. Since the night of 8 January, when Colonel Colborne's volunteers had seized the Great Teson, the main outwork, British cannon had kept up a steady bombardment. Trenches dug by relays of working parties under cover of darkness crept ever nearer to the walls. As soon as those walls were breached, an assault would be inevitable.

'Surely Governor Barrié will negotiate?' said Clio.

Mercedes was quick to dash this hope.

'While Rochefort is behind him, Barrié will never surrender. He has pinned his hopes on Marmont's return, but if the *guerrilleros* do their work well, Marmont will not know of the danger until too late.' She smiled. 'Lord Wellington has the reputation of a hard taskmaster but a just one. He will not forget El Forastero's part in the capture of Ciudad Rodrigo.'

'What shall *we* do if the city is stormed?' asked Clio, trying to keep her voice steady.

Mercedes raised her eyebrows. 'I intend to remain in my own house. Surely you are not afraid of your gallant countrymen? Why should I be?'

'Will you not send your children to safety?'

'They are safe enough with me.' Mercedes laughed shortly. '*Pobrecita!* You sound like a servant girl, afraid of shadows.'

'I am not afraid,' said Clio with cold anger.

'Good. Then come closer and listen. Today you must go up on the walls and watch for Camilo's mule-cart. There should be a message for us. If you find it, bring it here without delay. When the English storm the town, none of the traitors within our walls must be allowed to escape.'

Huddled in his over-size cloak in a niche in the ramparts, legs bent and long arms wrapped round his body, Jorge the Dwarf looked like a malevolent spider as he watched the path leading from the postern to the bridge.

The winter sun had just set. This was the hour when the British guns ceased their relentless pounding and the garrison hurried to repair the day's damage. In the past forty-eight hours two sizeable breaches had been opened opposite the Santa Cruz convent on the other side of the city. It would be no more than three or four days, thought Jorge, before Lord Wellington overcame his customary caution and ordered an assault on Ciudad Rodrigo. Before that happened he wanted his revenge, on the English girl who had caused his banishment from the *guerrillero* band, and on El Forastero himself.

The bitter memory of his beating still burned in his throat like bile. I, he thought, who have served my country as well as any man alive, and nailed more French hides to trees than Don Julián Sánchez himself, to be punished like a cheating servant! All on account of that English girl. Damn her, and El Forastero with her! Any woman who puts temptation in a man's way gets what she deserves.

This was the third day he had crouched by the wall, observing the townspeople's comings and goings while the guns thundered against the Santa Cruz wall. Since the investment had begun no one was allowed to leave the city without the Governor's permission, but women still went about their daily tasks of buying food from the carts of any peasant bold enough to approach the walls. The few remaining sheep and goats were still driven to pasture on the islands in the river, and household linen was scrubbed and rinsed below the bridge.

Watching their activities, Jorge had formed the opinion that if El Forastero was sending and receiving messages they were probably carried by these women.

Earlier that day, while the guns were still booming, he had seen a cart drawn by a white mule and driven by a pretty, dark-haired, buxom young woman cross the low-lying flats to the bridge, and deposit a basket of vegetables under one arch.

At the sight of them Jorge's attention sharpened, for he recognized the girl as Josefa Barca, daughter of old Camilo and sister to two of his former comrades in El Forastero's band.

Two hours later the basket was still there, and Jorge still lurked near it, hugging his arms round his body against the bone-chilling cold. A thin drizzle soaked into his cloak. He was about to leave his post and seek shelter, when fifty yards to his right the postern gate opened, letting a finger of yellow light stream on to the path. He heard the sentry's laughter and the smack of a kiss.

'Go on, then, baggage! Pick it up and be quick about it or I'll be in trouble as well as you. Too busy fluttering your eyelashes at the guardroom to remember it sooner, I suppose!'

'Oh, *monsieur,* you have saved me! How can I thank you?' exclaimed a voice whose slight appealing hesitation betrayed a foreign origin. Jorge knew that voice. He sat motionless, straining his ears.

'My mistress would have killed me if I had gone home with no food.'

'My sergeant will kill *me* if he finds the gate unlocked at this hour,' grumbled the sentry. 'Hurry, now, before he comes down on me like a ton of bricks.'

Light feet pattered down the path. A skirt whisked past so close that Jorge could have reached out and grasped it. He clenched his teeth, knowing that with the sentry watching he dared do nothing. *La inglesa*, he thought. Like a spider who feels the fly shake his web, he yearned to stretch out his arms and seize her.

Clio caught up the basket and returned as swiftly as she had gone. Jorge heard her laughing protest as the sentry claimed his reward, then the gate clanged shut, cutting off the finger of light.

Jorge rose and stretched his cramped limbs. His hands and feet were numb, but a fierce triumph warmed his heart. He had the information he needed: all that remained was to whisper it in the right ear.

Moving at surprising speed, despite his short legs, he crossed the bridge and set off in the direction Josefa had taken. Tonight he would watch her house in the hope of intercepting further messages; tomorrow would be time enough to make Colonel de Rochefort the offer of his services.

Three miles away in the British camp at Fuenteguinaldo, candlelight gave an illusion of cosiness to the tent where Robert Cole, recently seconded to Pack's Portuguese division, sat on a camp stool with pen in hand and a scatter of botched sheets of paper round his feet. Around him the camp was astir with the tense expectancy of action. From time to time the harsh bray of a donkey was answered within the city, and the occasional fireball above the walls showed defenders hard at work repairing the breaches torn that day by the British batteries.

He must hurry. He had much to do and little time.

My dear Laura, he wrote and paused, eyeing the words with disfavour. How cold they looked! How stiff and formal! How little they revealed of the love and anguish searing his heart!

They would have to do. On each of the botched sheets he had tried a different salutation, but none was to his liking. *Beloved* was too passionate and *Very Dear* sounded patronizing. *Dearest* hinted at other Dears, while *Dear* alone seemed chilly. He would have liked to call her his Angel, his Muse, his Inspiration, even his Soul, but the English language did not lend itself to such high-flown addresses. *Alma Mía* sounded fine, and *Queridísima Mía* better still, but Laura was no linguist and might even suppose the letter to be misdirected.

My dear Laura it must be, though in letters to come he would strive to find a more satisfying form of address. That is, if I survive to write any more letters, thought Robert, his stomach sinking as it always did on the eve of battle.

He sighed and picked up his pen.

... I hasten to reply to your letter which reached me by this morning's dispatch and gave me more pleasure than I can easily express. For the past weeks my brigade has been encamped at Fuenteguinaldo, in the neighbourhood of Ciudad Rodrigo, while working parties from the Light,

> Third, First and Fourth Divisions opened a parallel to bring our batteries within range of the Lesser Teson, in the hope of effecting a breach....

Again the pen faltered and stopped. Again the paper was scrunched and thrown aside. What did Laura – or any woman for that matter – care for parallels and batteries and breaches? By writing of them he was evading the central issue: until he faced it squarely he would know no peace.

In any case, this letter was destined to reach Laura only if he failed to survive the coming conflict. Others would tell her about the battle. What they could not tell her was how much he loved her.

Robert smiled and drew up a fresh sheet of paper. This time his pen moved easily.

> My Beloved Laura,
> When you read this I shall be dead and my hopes of a future shared with you vanished for ever. For that reason I write now on the eve of battle to acquaint you with what is in my heart, and to let you know that the sweet thought of you has been my inspiration and comfort every moment since we parted....

He told her of the Will he had made in her favour and his hope that she would use his fortune to found an orphanage for the needy children of the Peninsula. Again he smiled, picturing her astonishment when his lawyer confirmed the bequest. Dear Laura! So simple and courageous. So truly good!

> ... Do not grieve for me, dearest Laura, but remember me as one whose only wish was for your happiness.
>   Ever your devoted
>   Robert Cole

He sealed the letter and addressed it, then enclosed it in a second wafer with instructions that it should be opened in the event of his death. Yawning now and shivering, he reached for his dispatch box to place the letter among his personal papers.

'Love-letters, *Señor Capitán*?' said a quiet voice at his elbow.

Robert started violently and turned. Catching up the candle he stared at the figure that had materialized from the shadows.

He saw a man of middle height, wiry and thin to the point of gauntness. A wide-brimmed sombrero screened the dark face, and his garments were cut in the easy *serrano* fashion, the breeches loose over soft leather boots, the buttons of the tunic as big as saucers. He wore a swordbelt and a wide sash in which was stuck a brace of pistols, and his chest was crisscrossed with bandoliers. All in all, an ugly customer to spring up at your elbow without warning, and Robert fought down an inclination to shout for assistance.

'Who the deuce are you?' he demanded angrily.

'Men call me El Forastero.'

'The Devil they do! What do you mean by stealing in here without leave!'

'Don't you know me, *Señor Capitán*?'

'Know you?' Robert stared at him. The voice had a teasing familiarity, and yet.... 'How the deuce should I know you?'

'Look a little closer, *señor*.'

Smothering a curse, Robert brought the candle closer to the thin, deeply tanned face. An instant later he stepped back abruptly, the candle shaking in his hand.

'Harry!' he exclaimed in a tone of disbelief. 'My God! I – I think I must be dreaming... or else quite mad.'

He sat down suddenly upon the camp stool, his face so shocked and pale that Harry was moved to grasp his shoulder. He said bracingly, 'Steady now, old fellow. You are as sane as ever you were. I am sorry to startle you so, but the truth is, my fellows are waiting outside and I can't let them guess my true identity.'

'You... *you* are El Forastero?'

'The same.'

Now that the first astonishment was beginning to pass, Robert had time to remember what he had suffered at El

Forastero's hands, and also certain unsavoury rumours connected with the death of his friend Harry Churchill. He had refused, through loyalty, to believe any slander put about by Harry's old enemy... but now, seeing him in this preposterous rig, Darcy's tale acquired a horrid plausibility.

'So Harry Churchill has become a bandit,' he said slowly. 'Upon my soul, I should never have known you.'

'Should I take that as a compliment?'

'You may take it how you please. What I would like to know is why you have returned from the dead in this fashion and why you choose to dress as a Spanish brigand instead of a British officer?'

'Because I can no longer lay claim to that title.' Harry held up his hand. 'Wait. I will explain, but first you must promise me your help... and your silence.'

'Why should I help you?'

'Call it for old times' sake.' Harry's eyes crinkled in the smile that woke so many memories. 'Come, Rob, won't you trust me? You should, you know. This is a matter that must appeal to your notions of chivalry.'

Robert sighed impatiently. He could never be angry with Harry for long. Besides, he was curious. 'Very well, you have my promise. What is this great affair?'

'Tell me first, when does tonight's attack begin?'

'At seven, as soon as it is dark enough to conceal our movement.'

Harry rubbed his chin, dark eyes brooding. 'What part will your brigade play?'

'No great part. We are to create a diversion at the Santiago gate while the Light and the Third assault the breaches.'

'Do your men carry ladders?'

'Yes. If we meet with only small resistance, we are authorized to attempt an escalade.'

'Oh, famous! Just as I hoped.'

Robert regarded him with suspicion. 'What are you up to, Harry? Unless you enlighten me I will not say another word. What is famous about our ladders, and how does the matter affect my sense of chivalry?'

Harry cast a quick glance over his shoulder to see they were not overheard, then said in a low, rapid voice, 'Listen! Within the city are two brave women who have rendered us the greatest assistance over the past months. They have kept us supplied with intelligence at the risk of their lives. Now they are in grave danger. I need your help to rescue them.'

'Permit me to take your baby to safety, I beg,' said Julia in trembling yet resolute tones. 'If you will not save yourself, at least let me care for him.'

'You presume too much, Madame,' said Mercedes haughtily. 'I need no help from Colonel de Rochefort or his wife.'

Julia winced. 'If we are overheard –'

'I am not afraid of being heard.' Under hooded eyelids, Mercedes regarded her uninvited guest. 'By what right do you come here, frightening my servants and spreading alarm? Is this another of your husband's efforts to incriminate me?'

'Oh, no – no! Nothing of the kind. Quite the contrary!' Julia's colour rose and the easy tears provoked by injustice filled her eyes. It had cost her a good deal to beard the tigress in her den. All last night after her husband's departure she had wrestled with her conscience, trying to ignore the inner voice that told her that far from being grateful for her warning, Doña Mercedes would most likely have her thrown out of the house. It seemed the inner voice had been right. Her attempt to undo her own mischief had failed and her heart sank as she realized how angry Rochefort would be to hear of this visit.

Hoping to avoid recognition, Julia had muffled herself in the thickest of hooded cloaks, yet here was Señora Cortes trumpeting her name to every interested ear. She should never have come!

'Can you deny your husband sent you here, hoping you would induce me to betray myself?'

'Certainly I deny it,' said Julia indignantly. 'My husband does not know I am here.'

'Then why are you urging me to leave my home?'

'I have made it as plain as I could. Why will you not believe me? I came because I felt it my duty to warn you that my husband has evidence of your – your liaison with El Forastero.'

'What evidence?'

Julia sighed and rose with a certain dignity. The woman was impossible. She should never have come.

'I cannot disclose the kind of evidence. If you choose to disregard my warning, that is your affair. I have discharged my duty. Farewell, *señora*. My carriage is waiting. I think it unlikely we shall meet again.'

'Stay.' Mercedes stretched out a hand. For an instant her guard dropped and Julia saw fear in her eyes. 'You are leaving for Madrid?'

'There is room in my carriage for you. Your friends will be glad to offer you a refuge, and in your husband's absence you are entitled to my protection.'

Mercedes closed her eyes. From half a mile away the muffled roar of cannon came to their ears and shock waves rattled the casement. She caught her breath, imagining the sack of the city while she lay helpless. . . .

She shook her head. 'I cannot desert my people.'

'And the child?'

Another pause, even longer. Then Mercedes said harshly, 'Take him to my mother's house in Toledo. The nurse will direct you. Leave him there to await my coming. But listen, *señora*! If any harm comes to him I will not rest until I have killed you. Do you understand?'

'I understand.'

Mercedes lay back against her pillows. 'Take him,' she whispered. 'Take him now, before I change my mind.'

'*Adios, señora.*'

Julia beckoned the stout nurse, watching silently by the cradle. 'Come!'

They left the room together; as Julia paused to close the door, she heard a long wail and then a storm of sobbing.

'Wake up, *señorita*, wake up!'

Dazed with sleep, Clio started up from her pallet, clutching the blanket about her shoulders. Like the rest of the household she slept in her clothes, but even they hardly kept out the cold. Angelica stood in the doorway, a lantern throwing shadows on the wall, but its light was eclipsed by the unearthly glow beyond the grilled window. Fireballs carved flaming arcs through the sky. It looked as if the whole city was ablaze.

'The British are attacking! *Ay de mi!* Where is Don Enrique? He promised to come to our house. What has gone wrong?'

'Hold your tongue, woman!' Tomás appeared behind her. 'We know our orders. We will carry them out. If Don Enrique is not here, I take command.'

A change had come over Tomás. He straightened his shoulders, assuming the weight of responsibility.

'Go to Doña Mercedes,' he told Clio in a tone far removed from his usual hesitant mumble. 'Tell her the traitors' doors are guarded. None shall escape. Wait with her until Lord Wellington enters the city. Go now, without delay.'

As if in a dream, Clio obeyed.

The cold bit deep as she left the house and she hugged her black shawl close about her ears, partly for warmth, partly in an instinctive effort to deaden the noise of bursting shells, screaming voices and the crash of falling masonry. The streets were weirdly bright and crowded with frightened people scurrying this way and that, clutching their valuables. Women wailed prayers while men growled curses. Ammunition carts rumbled over the cobbles, whips cracking, drivers shouting for passage. Guns boomed menacingly, coming ever nearer.

To reach Mercedes's house she had to pass the old tower which British guns had pounded to rubble. Dodging from one patch of shadow to the next, she hurried along the alley below the ramparts, cursed and shoved by men too busy to ask what she did there. Since there had been no time for the garrison to repair this gaping breach, Rochefort had ordered two cuts to be made on either side of the demolished section, with 24-pounder guns mounted on parapets where they could sweep the gap with their fire.

As the grim, smoke-blackened spearhead of British soldiers who had surmounted the ditch began to struggle up the debris-strewn slope, the guns fired, cutting a great swathe in the attackers.

Half-deafened by the din, the survivors of that first rush halted on the lip of the breach, momentarily baffled by the sixteen-foot drop on to swords embedded in stout beams, metal entanglements and the deadly spikes known as *chevaux de frise*.

Again the guns roared, and again the crest of the breach was swept clear. But now more attackers were pouring up from the ditch, struggling to the top of the glacis in a relentless wave.

'The guns, boys!' yelled a British voice. 'Spike the guns.'

The wave split to right and left, some men throwing haybags into the cut to break the fall while others jumped down on top of them. Clio saw a fierce struggle around the left-hand gun and heard a trumpet blow the order to retire.

Immediately a flash more brilliant than anything she had yet seen seared her eyeballs, followed by the crashing thump of an explosion. The ground seemed to rise beneath her feet while beams and stones flew in all directions. A heavy object struck her head: she slid into darkness punctuated by dazzling streaks of light. She lay there half-conscious while a distant cheer announced that the Light Division had carried the lesser breach.

Feet trampled past her, wheels missed her prostrate form by inches. Dreadful cries from the wounded came to her ears as the sky lightened and darkened, but she could not move.

I must get up, she thought hazily. I must go to Doña Mercedes. But the effort of pulling herself upright was too great. Her head rang with the blast and she had lost the will to stir. I will rest for a while, she thought. I will feel better when I have slept. Soon the noise and lights will stop and I can sleep.

She let her head sink, uncaring that it rested in a heap of garbage. Gradually the sounds of battle faded in the distance and the intervals between explosions lengthened. Far away she heard cheering.

Now, she thought. I will go to Doña Mercedes now. But still she could not rise.

Hands plucked her skirt. Fiery liquid splashed her closed lips and trickled in a burning stream down her chin. She coughed and spluttered, trying to push the flask away.

'Tha's t'ticket, Paddy. Gie un more o'that,' growled a drink-blurred voice.

Clio opened her eyes on two creatures of nightmare. From smoke-blackened faces their red-rimmed eyes glittered crazily. One had a black lace mantilla draped over his filthy tunic; the other sported a French staff officer's cocked hat and heavily braided uniform. It was too small, and the unbuttoned tunic hung open exposing a mat of hair on his chest. Both men reeked of spirits.

' 'Ere, *chica*. Let's take a look at yer.'

The mantilla-wearer's weight slumped against her. She felt a rough hand fumble under her skirt, pulling up the layers of petticoat. For an instant shock and outrage paralysed her: then she began to kick and shout. She dredged from her memory every term of abuse she had culled from Auguste's ragbag repertoire, and spat them at her assailants.

'*Salauds! Schweinhunden!* Sons of Belial!'

The soldiers had been drinking raw brandy ever since the breach was carried and were fortunately too fuddled to coordinate their attack. They had thought a pretty *señorita* fair game: a kicking spitting wildcat was a different matter.

A well-directed blow from Clio's wooden patten brought the affair to a close. Paddy groaned and bent double, and at once Clio wriggled free. His comrade made a half-hearted clutch at her shawl, but she evaded him and fled, leaving them staring owlishly.

'She called us sons of Belial,' mumbled Paddy. 'Where would a *señorita* be larnin' such names?'

'Ah, man, you're drunk. You're dreamin'. Stick to the liquor and leave the women alone – they're nobbut trouble.'

Clutching one another for support, they staggered towards the Plaza Mayor, where a cheering crowd of British infantrymen were engaged in looting the garrison's central liquor store. Wild with victory and alcohol, a temporary madness possessed them. Any officer trying to restrain their excesses took his life in his hands.

Seeing their allies on the rampage, even those citizens of Ciudad Rodrigo who had been preparing to welcome the victorious British thought it prudent to bolt and bar their doors. Screams and crashes punctuated by explosions told the grim fate of a city taken by storm.

After her narrow escape, Clio moved with the stealth of a hunted animal, pressing herself into the shadows whenever anyone passed, and it was with the relief of a weary vixen returning to her earth that she reached Mercedes's house and pushed open the low door of the secret passage. In the past weeks she had been at pains to familiarize herself with its twists and branches. Remembering how Theseus escaped from the Labyrinth, she had taken the precaution of running a string along the wall for guidance. With this in her hand she hurried up the first flight of steps, hoping she would find Amalia there.

The child spent much of her time flitting like a small lonely ghost from one end of the big house to the other, spying on the servants. Clio knew her own mother would have pronounced this an unhealthy pastime, but then Mrs Hardy's notions on the upbringing of children could hardly have been more different from Mercedes's, who encouraged her daughter to tell tales, particularly where they concerned her housekeeper.

Privately Clio found it surprising that Doña Eugenia's long inquisitive nose had not sniffed out the secret passage for herself: did she never wonder where Amalia disappeared for hours at a stretch?

After the tumult in the streets, the house seemed deathly quiet, as if the building held its breath in the hope of escaping notice by the rampaging mobs outside.

Passing the housekeeper's room, Clio paused to look through the spyhole, but the bare little cell was empty. Even the brass-handled chest had gone.

Had Soña Eugenia taken her loot and fled? Clio imagined the sour-faced woman hurrying through the streets clutching her booty, and hoped that she too would encounter soldiers on mischief bent.

Light filtered at intervals through the holes, but between them the passage was dark. Clio moved cautiously, senses alert, one hand outstretched before her, the other on the guiding string.

In the darkness ahead something stirred. Her nostrils caught a faint pungency: cinnamon, overlaid with something offensive – a blend of garlic, black tobacco and foul breath. The hairs rose on her neck and she stopped, eyes straining to pierce the darkness.

'C – Consuela? Is that you?' It was Amalia's voice, small and scared.

'Amalia!' she said with relief.

'Oh, you have come! I have been so frightened. I thought you would never come.'

'Where are you?'

'O–over here. We have waited so long for you.'

'We?'

In the narrow space the smell was stronger. Even before memory pinpointed its origin, instinct sent Clio whirling round, seeking an escape. Hands came from the darkness, seizing her arms and twisting them behind her back.

'Not so fast, *inglesa*,' said Jorge the Dwarf, and laughed deep in his throat.

She stood still, fighting down panic. 'Why have you come here?' she whispered.

A dark lantern was uncovered and by its dim glow she saw Amalia crouched in a niche in the wall, eyes wide in her white face.

'Didn't I say she would come? You have been a good girl,' Jorge told the child. 'Now you can run away.'

'I don't want to run away. I want to stay with Consuela. *You* run away.'

'Silence, brat!'

Astonished at this rough address, Amalia stood up, her lips quivering. 'I won't! You're a rude horrid man and I don't like your games. I won't play any more.'

'Be off with you.' He pushed her so hard she stumbled against the wall. She cowered away from him, huddling against Clio for protection. Jorge tried to shove her again, but she clung fast to Clio's cloak.

'Leave the child alone! What do you want with me?'

The memory of their last encounter was disagreeably vivid in

Clio's mind, but to her relief he relaxed his grip, saying pleasantly enough, 'Why, I have been sent by Granto El Bueno to conduct you to safety, *señorita*.'

So Jorge was working for Colonel Grant! A sudden rush of thankfulness smothered Clio's disappointment that it was not Harry who had sent for her.

'You must come at once,' he urged, but Clio hesitated.

'First I must speak to Doña Mercedes.'

Jorge shook his head. He thrust forward his long narrow jaw until it almost touched her ear, whispering, 'It would not be wise. The French could prove nothing against Don Sebastian, so they set him free. He is with the *señora* now. Come, our horses are waiting. We must not delay.'

Clio still hesitated. It was bad news that Don Sebastian had been released.

'Do not go, Consuela,' whispered Amalia, plucking at her skirt. 'Do not leave me here alone.'

'Hush, *niña*. You must tell your mamma that I have gone to Granto El Bueno. Will you do that?'

Reluctantly the child nodded and released her skirt.

'Come,' said Jorge impatiently. As she followed the dwarf's dim lantern down the passage, Clio glanced back but Amalia had vanished.

'Hurry!' He hustled her along the passage, and all the time the noise from outside grew louder. When at length they stood before the street door, the confused roaring sounded like a storm at sea.

'Wait here. I will fetch the horses.'

He slipped out and she stood alone in the stairwell, listening to the shouts and shots, screams and crashes.

Somewhere a woman was sobbing hysterically. '*Pietá!* For the love of all the saints, spare me!' For a moment she fancied it was Mercedes, but when had Mercedes ever begged or sobbed?

The door swung open on a gust of noise. Jorge was back, leading two horses.

'Quickly, *señorita*!'

She allowed him to lift her to the saddle. The night air struck cold through her cloak, but the horse moving beneath her seemed the very essence of freedom. Without exchanging a word, they crossed the bridge where British dead still lay where they had fallen, and set spurs to their horses' flanks, heading for the hills.

15

By God, our fellows are in an ugly mood! thought Harry, weaving at his best pace through the rubble-strewn maze of alleys towards the Calle del Viejo Obispo.

He wore the borrowed uniform of a Portuguese *cacadore*, in which disguise he had been able to join Major Cole's storming party at the Santiago gate.

They had been late, their approach made more difficult by craters and obstacles in the moat. It was close on eight o'clock before Robert's party reached the heavily studded door in its massive arch, but they saw at once that no attack had been expected at this point.

The garrison's strength was concentrated on the breaches. From the west side of the city came the confused roar of battle and columns of smoke rose into the reddened sky. Here it was relatively quiet. Robert's shouted demand that the gate be opened met with no response.

At once he gave the order for an escalade. Harry had been among the first on the ladders, but no sooner had his head surmounted the wall than a rough Scots voice in the street below shouted that the fight was over.

'Come doun, ye slugabeds! Come doun, ye damned dagoes! Ye've missed a bonnie fecht. The toun's ours!'

With this assurance, the Portuguese troops lost no time in shinning up the ladders and jumping into the street. They ran to the gate to admit their comrades. Harry shouted a word of thanks to Robert and set off alone, alternately praying and cursing.

Dear Heaven, let him find Mercedes and Clio before the rioting soldiers did! Damn Colquhoun Grant, who had persuaded him to send them into this trap! Damn Mercedes's own pride which would not shrink from danger.

Harry had wanted her to stay with him until the baby was born, but she would not listen.

'Why should my child be born in a cave like a pauper? Don Sebastian shall pay for the shame he has brought on me. When my son – *our* son – inherits his estates, I shall have my revenge.'

Sometimes Harry thought Don Sebastian might be less of a dupe than his wife imagined. Behind that stiff façade lay a cunning brain. Why else should Joseph Bonaparte have gone to such lengths to obtain his support?

I should never have let her return, he thought, and to send Clio after her was compounding the error.

Yet after the episode with Jorge the Dwarf, he dared not leave Clio alone. Harry knew Jorge's unforgiving nature and regretted making an enemy of him, but in the circumstances he had had no choice.

His lungs ached from running. He slowed to a walk, trying to believe that all might yet be well. In his last message he had told his correspondents to gather at Mercedes's house. The place was like a small fortress: they should be safe enough. This wild shooting and burning was the inevitable aftermath of a storming, but soon British officers would have their troops under control again. Marauding mobs would be called to order, looters punished, a few men hanged to put the fear of God and Lord Wellington into the rest. But still the niggling fear remained: what might not happen before then to an unprotected woman?

As if to lend substance to his fears, piercing screams echoed from the house he was passing. Cursing the delay, he turned towards the sound.

'Mercy, *señor*, mercy! We are your friends. Take all we have! *Ay, ay!*'

The front door was ajar. Harry bounded up the stairs and almost tripped over the body of a woman lying on the floor with two British soldiers on top of her. A third was rifling the drawers by the light of a lantern.

'Mercy!' screamed the woman, seeing what she took for yet another tormentor.

Harry seized one soldier by the collar and seat of his trousers and threw him down the stairs. His comrade scrambled up, furious, fumbling for his knife. Harry struck him a blow that sent him reeling against the wall.

'Get out,' he ordered grimly. 'Restore what you have stolen and get back to your regiment!'

The men stared to be so addressed by a humble Portuguese *cacadore*. 'Why, you bloody dago –' began the treasure-hunter thickly, swaggering across the room. The flat of Harry's sword caught him across the shoulders and he collapsed in a heap, whimpering.

'*Muchas gracias, señor*,' said the stout woman in a trembling voice full of bewilderment. 'We invited them to eat, thinking them our friends, but they would have killed us. See, they have stolen all we possess.'

'Turn out your pockets,' ordered Harry.

Shamefaced and resentful, the looters threw gold and silver into a heap. Harry surveyed them keenly, satisfied he would know them again.

'Be assured Lord Wellington shall hear of this,' he promised, and turned to their victim. 'Bolt your door, *señora*, and let no one enter before daylight. I will make it my business to see these men are punished.'

He left her calling the blessings of the saints upon him, and hurried on his way. Musket shots splintered the night. As he passed behind the Plaza Mayor he saw tongues of flame greedily licking the sky and through the drunken roars and cheers thought he distinguished the clarion tones of old Sir Thomas Picton condemning the revellers to eternal damnation.

'They have gone mad,' he muttered. 'Mad with blood and drink. No one can control them now.'

But the danger to Mercedes and Clio was less from drunkards than those calculating villains of which every army has its share. These had seen in the town's defenceless inhabitants a ready source of profit. Figures in smoke-blackened uniforms flitted about the streets on their own furtive business, stealing whatever came to hand. Wails rent the night as jewellery was wrenched from ears and fingers, and some such wails ended with ominous suddenness.

Harry was not much given to prayer, but now he begged God most fervently to keep his correspondents behind locked doors that night.

Mercedes must be near her time. Anxiety knifed afresh at the thought of Spanish doctors and midwives, many of whose medical practices belonged to the Dark Ages. It seemed an eternity before he reached the grilled iron gate that defended Don Sebastian Cortes's property from the world. This was where Tomás should have been waiting to admit him, but to Harry's consternation the gate had already been forced wide open. Within the courtyard scuffling knots of soldiers were dragging furniture from the house, fighting over their plunder like starving dogs on a carcase.

On the cobbles a great fire blazed. Harry saw a corporal of the Light Division, a great bull of a man, stagger from the cellar clasping a barrel of spirits to his chest. With a maniacal laugh he flung it on the flames.

'Plenty more where that came from, boys!' he roared, and there was a general rush for the cellar. Magically the courtyard cleared.

A movement in the arch towards the stables drew Harry's eye. A darker patch of shadow resolved itself into two horses, with a cloaked man at their heads. An urgent whisper reached him:

'Quick, my lord!'

A second muffled figure ran down the steps and mounted hurriedly. From the slight stiffness of his gait, Harry recognized Don Sebastian Cortes.

A chill touched him. What had gone wrong? Had his message gone astray or been misunderstood? Don Sebastian should now be under arrest. Where was Tomás, who should have been guarding the gate? Why was Don Sebastian stealing out of his own house like a thief in the night?

He must not escape.

Harry waited until the riders were under the gate-arch, then stepped from the shadows to seize the bridle of the leading horse.

'One moment, *señor*.'

The horse checked – but only for an instant. Don Sebastian was famous for the quality of his mounts, schooled by the old methods of Lippiza to take an active part in combat. Spurred forward against the restraining hand, the white stallion raised himself in a *levade* that snatched the reins from Harry's fingers, while at the same time Don Sebastian struck a swift vicious blow at his assailant. Still on his hind legs, the stallion launched himself through the arch, striking sparks from the cobbles, and was gone.

Cursing freely, Harry picked himself up and put a hand to his head which sang with the force of the blow. Blood trickled between his fingers. He pushed through the knots of men thronging the stairs and ran to the upper floor, stomach cold with foreboding.

At the end of the passage he saw the door ajar and he groaned aloud. Only the most determined effort of will forced him across the threshold and into the lamplit bedchamber.

It was empty.

A fire smouldered in the grate and the curtains of the great fourposter were drawn, but a single glance was enough to tell him no lusting soldiers had penetrated Mercedes's private sanctum. He felt an overwhelming relief. She had gone. At the last moment common sense must have prevailed over pride, and she had fled from her house before the sack began.

Slowly his eyes travelled round the luxuriously furnished room. The allegorical figures in the wall-hung tapestries smiled down at him, sharing his relief. Hardly aware that he moved on tiptoe, Harry crossed to the wooden cradle set in front of the fire with a nursing chair beside it. He examined it, frowning, observing the faint hollow where a tiny swaddled form might have lain. He touched the mattress. It was cold. He stepped back, his heart thundering. Why hadn't he been told of the child's birth? Messages from Clio had reached him regularly over the past ten days, but she had made no mention of this. *Something was wrong.*

Perhaps Mercedes had forbidden her to give him the news, knowing he would come through hell and high water to look at his first-born. Harry smiled reluctantly: that must be the answer. She had always said it would be running his head into a noose to enter Ciudad Rodrigo while Rochefort held sway there. She must have preferred to keep her secret until the city was safe once more in British hands.

Satisfied with this reasoning, Harry prowled the room, instinctively avoiding the curtained bed. That was where Don Sebastian claimed his rights. The thought filled Harry with revulsion. If only he had held fast to the traitor's reins! He had enough evidence to send Don Sebastian to the gallows ten times over, but what good was evidence without the man himself? Such a slippery customer would take care never to place his person within reach of British justice – one could be sure of that.

With a last glance round the room, Harry made for the door. His hand was on the latch when a small explosive sound made him turn, reaching for his sword, every nerve tingling.

A sneeze.

There could be no doubt whence it had come. Sword in hand, Harry crossed the room in two swift strides and pulled aside the silken bed-hangings.

'Come out.'

There was no answer, no movement. For a moment his eyes probed the gloom, then he uttered a choking cry and stepped back.

Sprawled in the great bed, arms stretched in supplication, eyes fixed and glassy, lay Mercedes, a jewel-hilted dagger through her heart. Blood spread in a rusty stain across the fine linen sheets and dripped into the carpet.

He touched her hand: it was still warm. In a passionate

outburst of grief he caught her to him, searching for a heartbeat, urgently calling her name.

'*Mercedes! Enamorada! Amada!*'

Her head sagged, lifeless. Tears stung his eyes as he gazed at the face he had last seen full of fire and pride. A burning fury beat so hard in his temples that he thought his head would burst.

'He shall die for this.'

He had not the smallest doubt whose hand had struck the fatal blow. Mercedes would never believe that violence lurked beneath her husband's controlled façade, but Harry had always suspected it.

'He is Bonaparte's puppet, Enrique, dancing when the Emperor pulls the strings!' she used to say with her rich laugh. 'He would be too afraid of losing face with his French friends to admit his wife deceived him.'

But it was she who had been deceived. I should never have let her return, thought Harry, shoulders bowed with the weight of his guilt.

The windows were tightly shuttered, the lamp-flame burned steadily, yet the bed-hangings stirred softly. Harry looked hard at them, then bent to feel under the bed. His hand encountered a buckled shoe. As his fingers closed on it there was a shocked gasp, a sudden stiffening and shrinking like a snail withdrawing into its shell.

'Come out, you faithless bitch,' said Harry grimly. 'Come out and see how well you have protected your mistress.'

He tugged. For a moment the shoe's owner resisted; then strength prevailed. Into the lamplight slid a pathetic bundle of skirts and thin legs: not the tiring-woman he had expected but little Amalia.

'*Niña!*' He was thunderstruck. 'What are you doing there?'

She looked up and recognized him. Her face seemed to crumple slowly and painful sobs racked her.

'Mamma! Oh, poor Mamma!'

Harry knelt and gathered her in his arms. Carrying her across to the fire, he set her on his knee, soothing her as he would his small niece when she fell and bumped herself. Amalia buried her face in his shoulder and cried as if she would never stop.

'Mamma! Oh, poor Mamma!'

He waited patiently, listening as if in a trance to the shouts and crashes in the courtyard below. They seemed to come from another world. He thought of Mercedes – not the staring-eyed body on the bed but the warm, proud vital creature he had first known, whose beauty had enchanted and enslaved him.

When had that spell been broken? When had he realized that Mercedes saw him as a weapon through which to strike at her husband, a useful tool in the liberation of Spain rather than a lover? Harry knew all too well who had turned the cold light of reality upon his romantic dream. He had imagined himself a hero like El Cid... until Clio came and called him a common bandit.

Damn Clio! Damn her clear eyes which stripped a man of his pretensions. Damn her interfering ways! Clio was to blame for the present fiasco. She must have failed to comprehend his last message, though his courier Josefa Barca reported having heard her pick it up from beneath the bridge. Perhaps – horrid thought – others had also observed her. Harry's anger evaporated. He felt very cold.

Amalia's sobs were subsiding. She raised her tear-stained face from his shoulder and he knew he could wait no longer to question her.

'Tell me, *niña*, where were you when the soldiers came to the house? Did you see Consuela the seamstress?'

She nodded, still sniffing and gulping. In the courtyard the soldiers were heaping furniture on the bonfire, which raged out of control. Tendrils of smoke had begun to creep through the bedchamber shutters.

'Tell me,' he urged.

Amalia said as if repeating a lesson, 'She has gone to Granto El Bueno. He sent a little man to find Consuela and bring her to him.'

'Who was this little man?'

'Just a man,' said Amalia with a shrug of distaste. 'I wanted Consuela to stay, but she said she must go with him.'

It was a relief to know Clio, at least, was safe. Nevertheless, it rankled with Harry that she should have been so ready to save her skin that she abandoned Mercedes. Clio had many faults, but he had not reckoned cowardice among them.

More smoke was filtering through the curtains. Like a mist it filled the room, blotting out the smiling nymphs and cupids, blurring the outline of the great fourposter.

'Come,' said Harry, and set Amalia on her feet. She hung back, dragging at his hand.

'Mamma –'

'She would wish you to be a brave girl and do as I tell you,' said Harry firmly.

He pulled open the door, but after one look at the flames licking up the stairway, hastily slammed it shut.

'No way out there. We'll try the window.'

Amalia's sharp little face was very pale, but her voice was steady as she replied, 'No, no, Don Enrique. I know a better way. Let go of my hand and I will show you. The door is behind the curtain.'

'Where are you taking me?' asked Clio when they had ridden for two hours. She had not thought the British lines so far away.

'Granto El Bueno is billeted at the Quinta Aguila. He bade me bring you there.'

'*Bueno.*' Clio allowed herself to relapse into a stupor of fatigue. The Quinta Aguila was a favourite rendezvous with El Forastero's guerrillas, and its owner, old Camilo Barca, frequently acted as go-between for Harry and his correspondents, passing on their messages.

The *quinta* had been built as the summer residence of a nobleman and enjoyed a noble site, perched above a rippling sea of olives which sloped in wave-like ridges to the very lip of the Garganta de Agueda, whose roaring waters formed the frontier between Spain and Portugal. No more than twenty miles from the fertile plain surrounding Ciudad Rodrigo, this border country was wild and barren, its serrated hills and sunless valleys a happy hunting ground for guerrillas, robbers and wolves. French patrols seldom ventured into these dangerous passes:

even the best-armed convoys made long detours rather than cross such an inhospitable region.

Square-built and commodious, the *quinta*'s original structure had been so often augmented as family needs dictated that it was hard to say to which period it belonged. Certainly there was more than a trace of Moorish influence in the pointed archways and hidden courtyards, and if the building had few pretensions to elegance, at least its thick high walls and isolated situation afforded the inhabitants comfort and privacy. In the past century it had descended the social scale and the present owner, a shrewd peasant farmer, was also a fervent patriot and Francophobe, who freely allowed guerrillas such as Don Julián Sánchez and El Forastero to billet their men at his expense, besides providing them with food and forage with a liberality few *hidalgos* would have matched.

Clio had often heard Harry declare that without Camilo's support his band's effectiveness would have been cut by half. It was therefore with perfect confidence that she followed Jorge's horse up the winding path through the olive groves and through the gate into the farmyard.

When did the first chill of foreboding touch her? Was it the silence where she had expected bustle? Even at dawn on a winter morning farmyards are full of sound and movement, but here not a cock crowed or dog barked. Where were the turkeys, the chickens and goats? The byres were empty, their doors hanging open and bedding tracked into the yard as if beasts had been driven out in haste. Around the henyard, ominous drifts of feathers told their own tale. The only animals in sight were horses tethered beneath a long roof in a manner that was unmistakably military. Clio stared hard at them. These were not the hardy agile ponies favoured by mountain *guerrilleros*, but larger, stronger beasts. She noted their long tails and her heart began to bump unsteadily. The British cavalry docked its chargers.

'The French are here,' she whispered, plucking at Jorge's sleeve. His bright malicious eyes turned on her and suddenly her mouth went dry. *He knew.*

'*Sí, señorita.*'

Clio looked round wildly. The yard gate had closed behind them. There was no escape.

Brisk steps crunched on gravel. The slim, trim uniformed figure of a French cavalry officer came smartly round the corner of the house, paused on seeing them, then approached swiftly.

'*Bravo, amigo!*' said Colonel de Rochefort, and showed his pointed teeth in a smile that stopped well short of his eyes. 'I had begun to fear the bird was already flown.'

'Flown?' Clio looked from one to the other, but there was no more pity in Rochefort's smile than in Jorge's bright gaze.

'Traitor!' she said hotly. 'Wretch! Viper! *Hijo de puta!*'

'Spare Jorge your compliments – they are wasted on him,' said Rochefort languidly. 'He did no more than carry out my orders. I need your help, Miss Hardy, and prevailed upon Jorge to bring you to me.'

'Why should I help you?'

'Because only a fool fails to see his own danger, and you are not a fool, Miss Hardy.'

'You flatter me.'

He bowed. 'I assure you it is no more than the truth.'

'What if I refuse to help you nevertheless? French chivalry would hardly permit coercion of a helpless female.'

'I consider you no more helpless than you are foolish, Miss Hardy,' said Rochefort with a certain grim amusement. 'If coercion is needed, Jorge will gladly supply it – I have no doubt it will give him the keenest satisfaction. You see, we have made a bargain, Jorge and I.'

'A – a bargain?'

'Certainly. The terms are very simple. In return for his help in bringing you to me, I have agreed to deliver you into Jorge's hands if you prove obstinate. I need your confirmation of certain matters. If you cooperate, I undertake to send you unharmed to the British lines. If you refuse, Jorge will get his reward.'

Clio whispered, 'I am your wife's sister. You would not –'

'Oh, make no mistake, I would! Julia is on her way to Madrid. She knows nothing of this, nor does your relationship weigh in the least with me.'

'But why should Jorge wish to hurt me?'

'My dear Miss Hardy, you should know by now that there is nothing in the world more delicate than a Spaniard's pride,' said Rochefort sententiously. 'In offending Jorge I fear you have made a most implacable foe. Come, follow me. No doubt you wish to wash and refresh yourself after your long ride.' His cold eyes raked her from head to foot. He added softly, 'Do not attempt to escape. My men are watching every entrance. I assure you Jorge is excessively anxious to claim his reward.'

16

Auguste hummed to the beat of his horse's hooves as he trotted with his foraging party along the road that led to the Quinta Aguila. Though his duties were heavy, with a hungry regiment to feed and the Spaniards more than ever reluctant to surrender their winter stores, his heart was unusually light, for he was in love.

Not for him (it must be admitted) the heady, reckless spontaneous emotion a younger man would have called love. Auguste was at least as much in love with his future father-in-law's well-stocked farm and well-filled moneybags as he was with Josefa's own well-rounded person. Nevertheless, for the first time in all his wandering life Auguste felt his affections seriously engaged, and he was determined to obtain the promise of his beloved's hand before the army left Ciudad Rodrigo.

A man owes it to himself to look to the future, he reflected as he jogged along. I have worked hard all my life: I deserve some warmth and comfort in my old age. I have had enough of English fog and rain. When this war is over, Spain will be a country where a man of enterprise and prudence may live agreeably, especially if he has thought to provide himself with a pretty wife and a nice little fortune. Josefa favours me, and she is Camilo's only daughter. Her brothers? Rascals, by all accounts, but what does that matter to me? The old man denies her nothing.

As he recalled the last kiss he had stolen in the moonlight, Auguste's moustache lifted in a smile. Camilo was the richest farmer in the district....

Behind him the troopers chatted, their accoutrements jingling in the crisp morning. They, too, were in high spirits.

'What's old Marmont going to say when 'e 'ears 'ow 'Ookey's stolen a march on 'im?' chuckled one. 'Poor bugger'll eat 'is baton!'

The convent of Santa Barbara which Auguste had earmarked as a likely place from which to requisition provisions lay barely half a league from Josefa's home. When they neared the encircling wall, he beckoned the corporal alongside.

'Go vith some men to the back to see nothing vill escape that vay,' he said quietly.

The corporal grinned and saluted. Six troopers wheeled their mounts and trotted quietly into the trees. The rest approached the main entrance.

The fat, florid little Abbot's expressive eyes shone with tears as he begged Auguste to seek food elsewhere.

'We are a poor house, *Señor* Commissary. We have given all we can spare. Must my people go hungry to feed your army?'

Auguste was too familiar with this plea to pay it much heed. 'Ve are fighting to save your country, Father,' he said with cheerful composure. 'As you are avare, the British Government pays for all requisitioned food. You haf only to present my promissory note to the Juez de Fora, and you vill be recompensed.'

'What use is a promissory note to men with empty bellies?' cried the Abbot, his chins wobbling with emotion.

Auguste surveyed him with a sardonic eye. 'Permit me to observe, Father, it vould not damage your own health to keep Lent early this year. No, do not argue. Direct me to your storeroom before I lose patience.'

The Abbot's woeful expression changed to one of cunning. 'A word in your ear, *señor*. Half a league distant stands a rich farm belonging to a most ungodly peasant, one Camilo Barca. There you will find everything you seek, in abundance. Food, wine, forage for your cattle – far more to the taste of your brave soldiers than our miserable fare.'

Auguste tugged his moustache, pretending to consider. 'Vhy should this peasant be more inclined than you to gif me food?'

'Oh, Camilo will cause you no trouble,' said the Abbot, delighted by this chance to do a neighbour a bad turn. He added, leering, 'It is his daughter with whom you should deal. A beautiful girl, *señor*, with a partiality for British uniforms.'

'Vhy, you snivelling priest!' exclaimed Auguste in a fine rage. 'I happen to be acquainted with Señorita Barca! How dare you insult her?'

The Abbot looked glum, though he was still prepared to argue in defence of his stores. However a loud shouting from the back of the building interrupted his discourse and next moment Auguste's foresight was vindicated by the entry of several lay brothers escorted by the corporal.

'Beg pardon, sir, but we saw these fellows driving away in a cart,' he said with the merest flutter of an eyelid.

'Ah, *señor*, that cart is of no concern to you,' said the Abbot hastily. 'A small charitable offering I wished to send to our afflicted brethren in Ciudad Rodrigo.'

'Perhaps you'd like to see what they've got in the cart, sir? There's sacks and barrels and I don't know what besides.'

'I vould indeed,' said Auguste, giving the Abbot a look of stern reproof. 'A house vich is able to send food to its *afflicted brethren* can hardly refuse to supply *my* needs. Come, Father, no more excuses. Unless you vish my men to break into your storeroom by force, you vould be vell advised to desire your cellarer to surrender his keys.'

With bad grace the Abbot complied. After Auguste had indicated exactly what his men should take from the laden shelves, he left the corporal to carry out his orders and rode alone towards the Quinta Aguila, chuckling to think how much old Camilo would enjoy the story of the Abbot's discomfiture.

As he came in sight of the farm's orange-tiled roofs, following the steep track that wound between silvery olives and dark clumps of pine trees, he heard galloping hoofs approaching. Prudently Auguste drew aside to let the traveller pass. Two bends of the track above him he saw a cloud of dust, out of which emerged the shape of a light cart drawn by a white mule, being driven at a furious pace.

That is Camilo's favourite mount! thought Auguste, recognizing the sedate animal who had certainly never been driven like this before. 'And dash my vig if that ain't Josefa herself!' he muttered, urging his horse forward to block the track.

The manoeuvre proved disastrous. The white mule skidded to avoid the unexpected obstacle and the fair driver, more intent on plying the whip than keeping her seat, was thrown off balance by the sudden swerve.

'*Du Lieber Gott!*' groaned Auguste in dismay, seeing his beloved pitch headlong over the rail and land in a flurry of shawls and petticoats. He dismounted hastily to go to her aid, but Josefa was a robust young woman and not slow to see where lay the blame for her downfall. In a trice she was on her feet again, brandishing the whip which had kept her company throughout. As mule and cart vanished round the bend in the track, she laid it about Auguste's shoulders, at the same time speculating upon his parentage and ultimate destination in terms as forceful as they were uncomplimentary.

'Gently, my dove, gently!' he protested, torn between admiration and laughter. With her hair down her back, bosom heaving and large eyes flashing, Josefa was magnificent, but he was too busy avoiding her blows to tell her so.

'A thousand pardons, *señorita*,' he cried when her tirade ceased for lack of breath. 'Pray permit me the honour of escorting you home, after which I undertake to recover your conveyance with all possible expedition.'

Josefa gasped and surveyed him more closely. 'Oh, Don Auguste, it is you! How glad I am to see you!'

'Why, so am I!' Relieved by this more propitious greeting, he took her chin between his fingers, intending to kiss her lips, but she brushed him away as if he had been a troublesome insect.

'No, *señor*! You do not understand. I must fly. The French –'

'The French, my dove?'

'They are at the *quinta*.'

Auguste stepped back, eyes narrowed. This was serious news. Old Camilo's hatred of the invaders was a local byword. If the French were in possession of his farm it would not be with his consent.

'They killed my father when he tried to resist, and my young brother too,' said Josefa tearfully. 'My poor aunt was caught and carried away with our cattle. I myself barely escaped with my life. I must go. If they find me –'

'Haf no fear, I vill protect you.' Auguste tapped his teeth, saying thoughtfully, 'How many men haf they?'

'Twenty, thirty – I cannot tell. All night I hid in the byre, fearing any moment that they would discover me. When at dawn they opened the gate to drive out our cattle, I took Father's mule from the outside stable and fled.'

'My poor child, how you haf suffered!' Auguste's thoughts went to the well-armed troopers he had left plundering the Abbot's storeroom. If only they were here! Auguste himself had no desire for glory, but a captured French patrol might have furnished him with a number of covetable items, among them an officer's sabretache and some dozens of drinkable claret.

'I must find El Forastero and warn him Jorge has betrayed us,' said Josefa distractedly, shaking off his restraining hand. 'He must not walk into a trap.'

'You vere expecting El Forastero?' said Auguste, curious to meet the famous *guerrillero* leader whose exploits formed the principal subject of conversation in every *posada* between Badajoz and Salamanca.

'He should have come to us last night,' said Josefa. 'His correspondents left messages with my father. Something is wrong, *señor*. Perhaps he has been killed.'

Auguste put an arm round her waist and was about to comfort her in the way he knew best when he felt her stiffen into an attitude of intense concentration.

'Listen!' she breathed.

At first he could hear nothing but the wind sighing in the

pines. Then it occurred to him to lay himself flat on the ground, placing one end of the ramrod of his pistol against the earth and the other in his ear. At once he heard hoofbeats.

'He is coming!'

Auguste took his horse by the bridle and tethered him in thick bushes. He and Josefa concealed themselves behind a large rock that commanded an excellent view of the path.

They had not waited many minutes before a solitary horseman came into view, cantering up the path as easily as if he and the horse were of one flesh. He wore a wide-brimmed hat shadowing his face, and a loose-cut suit of russet leather. The horse he rode was as lean and wiry as himself, and supremely sure-footed. Though the path was rough and strewn with stones, he picked his way on a loose rein with never a stumble.

'El Forastero!' exclaimed Josefa, and ran to meet him.

The horseman halted, doffing his hat and smiling.

'Why, Josefa! What are you doing here? Jump up behind and I will carry you home.'

'You cannot go there, Don Enrique –' she began breathlessly, but before she could say more she was interrupted by a strangled cry. Next moment Auguste came pelting down the track like a madman, hat and wig falling off in his haste. On his face was such a look of glassy-eyed astonishment that Josefa feared he had sat on a scorpion.

'What ails you, *señor?*' She caught at his sleeve, but he brushed past her without a word.

Dashing up to the grey horse, he placed one hand on its withers and stared fixedly into the rider's face.

'Mr Harry!' he said in tones of deep emotion. 'Devil take my soul!'

'Don Enrique Monte de Laiglesia at your service, *señor,*' said Harry. He bowed stiffly, frowning a warning.

'Monte de – ? Vell, dash my vig, if that don't beat all!'

'Hush, man.' Harry bent to whisper urgently. When he straightened again, Auguste had recovered his composure.

'Very vell, Mr Harry, if zat's your game, old Auguste vill not spoil it,' he muttered, shaking his head.

'*Señor! Señor!*'

Josefa had been too occupied with her own troubles to heed their brief exchange. Now she loosed a torrent of impassioned words, and Harry's mouth tightened as he listened. At the name of Rochefort a curious stillness came over him. For a moment he brooded, chin on chest, then turned with a quick movement to lay his hand on Auguste's shoulder.

'Where are your men, *amigo*? You did not ride here alone?'

He spoke in Spanish, and instinctively Auguste replied in the same tongue. 'At the Convent of Santa Barbara, *señor*. I left them loading provisions.'

'Damn the provisions! We can show them better sport than that. Are they game for a fight?'

There was a glinting light in Harry's eyes which, together with the tightly compressed mouth, woke uncomfortable memories in Auguste.

'British soldiers are always ready to fight, *señor*,' he said with a marked lack of enthusiasm.

'And you, you old reprobate? Are you game to fight with me?'

Auguste hesitated. Combat was no part of a commissary's duty. In all his months on the Peninsula he had studiously avoided close encounters with the enemy, having a strong desire to protect both his skin and his pocket, but with Josefa's beautiful eyes fixed on him, how could he disappoint her?

'To the death,' he said hollowly.

Harry clapped him on the shoulder. 'Good man! Off you go, then, quick as you can, and fetch your fellows here to me. If we look sharp we may catch Rochefort like a rat in a trap.'

'And Jorge?' Josefa looked up eagerly.

'That devil will wish he had never been born before I have done with him,' said Harry quietly. 'Hurry, now. Success will depend on taking them unaware.'

17

The farm kitchen was warm and dimly lit and Clio was very tired. She wished Colonel de Rochefort would stop asking questions and allow her to rest. Such absurd questions! Why should he be interested in her father's circle of acquaintance? Why was he curious to know the names of the boys he had tutored?

'Your father gave private coaching to the son of Lord Amherst?'

'Among many others.' Clio yawned and sighed, but Rochefort was impervious to hints. Her head drooped and she jerked it up again. It seemed an eternity since Angelica had woken her to the sound of cannon.

She must remain alert and keep Colonel de Rochefort in a good humour. His threat of surrendering her to Jorge lay like a black cloud on her mind, but despite her best efforts the warmth and mulled wine had made her drowsy. She had accepted the wine in the hope that it would revive her, but instead it seemed to blunt her senses, and Rochefort's questions reached her through a fog of weariness.

Crouched in a corner in his preferred manner, Jorge waited with a spider's patience. There were only so many drops to be squeezed from any lemon. When the Frenchman had squeezed his fill, it would be Jorge's turn. For that he was prepared to wait.

Rochefort watched Clio struggle against sleep and knew the

moment had come to strike. At first she had been wary and suspicious, but under his calm monotonous questioning she had gradually lost her caution. Like a skilful matador he had flourished the cape until his victim reeled with exhaustion: it was time for the fatal thrust.

'What a tale you will have to tell at home, *mademoiselle*! To have lived in the mountains with the famous *guerrillero*! Marmont's officers have the warmest admiration for El Forastero, you know. He is quite a hero in their eyes.'

Clio blinked, focusing her own eyes which had a tendency to shut against her will. 'A hero? But he is your enemy.'

'A worthy foe may be admired, *mademoiselle*. You must not suppose us French so petty-minded as to reserve our admiration solely for those who curry favour with us! I assure you El Forastero is quite the rage among our young fire-eaters. They are astonished to see a Spaniard display such courage and leadership.'

Clio stirred and opened her mouth, but said nothing.

Rochefort went on, 'Why, Lord Wellington's success is founded on El Forastero's exploits! What audacity! We never know where he will strike next. His effrontery – *incroyable*! You heard the story of how he kidnapped the Governor of Ciudad Rodrigo? One would not have supposed a Spaniard capable of such a plot.'

The corners of Clio's mouth lifted but she remained silent.

'I am quite out of conceit with myself,' admitted Rochefort ruefully. 'I believed I knew the Spanish character through and through, but this man confounds all my preconceptions. Why do you smile, *mademoiselle*? I assure you it is true. He even forbids his men to torture prisoners. A merciful Spaniard! Do you not find that remarkable?'

'Only half a Spaniard,' she corrected, smiling more widely.

Not by the smallest change of expression did Rochefort show his sudden intense interest. Indeed, he shrugged slightly, as if the fact was well known to him.

'True,' he said indifferently, 'but when a man has been reared in the *hidalgo* tradition of barbarism it is rare – I would say unique – for him to reject it.'

'Barbarism!' The word struck Clio as supremely ridiculous. 'You have it wrong. Harry is no barbarian!'

'*Harry?*'

Too late she saw the gleam of satisfaction.

'Harry Churchill,' he said lingeringly. 'The son of Lord Amherst, whom your father used to teach. So simple: I cannot understand why I failed to see this before.'

Clio had gone very pale. 'You are mistaken. Lord Amherst's son was killed at the battle of Talavera.'

'Was *captured* at Talavera, and escaped after breaking his parole. Thus Harry Churchill becomes Don Enrique Monte de Laiglesia. Now I see it all.'

He pulled a sheet of paper towards him and selected a quill from the inkstand. Clio watched, wishing she could tear out her tongue. One word, one ill-considered word, and she had damaged Harry beyond repair.

Rochefort's pen moved swiftly. He dusted the ink and read it over, then passed the paper to her, saying, 'Now, *mademoiselle*, you will oblige me by setting your signature to this, after which I will be happy to send you on your way.'

Clio took the paper. The damning sentence seemed to burn itself on her brain.

> *I, Clio Hardy, do hereby affirm that Don Enrique Monte de Laiglesia, also known as El Forastero, is an Englishman, by name Captain the Honourable Henry Churchill, late of His Majesty's Twenty-Third Hussars, who was captured at Talavera and escaped after breaking his parole.*

'Sign, *mademoiselle*.'

Clio pushed the paper back. 'I cannot.'

'You will not leave here until you have signed that paper.'

Clio wondered how she could ever have thought him handsome. His narrow face wore an expression of sneering triumph that made her long to strike it.

'Give it to me.' She stretched out a hand and took the paper, then screwed it into a ball and flung it in the fire.

The smile left Rochefort's mouth. 'That was foolish, *mademoiselle*. Very foolish.'

'I have a singular abhorrence for setting my name to a lie,' she said in a shaking voice. 'Colonel de Rochefort, you have brought me here under false pretences, and you have no right to detain me any longer. I have answered your questions as well as I can. Now I must insist you keep your promise to release me.'

'Have you forgotten that I also made a promise to Jorge?' said Rochefort in a voice soft with menace.

'You are a French officer. You would not stoop so low.'

'Do not deceive yourself, *mademoiselle*. There is nothing – *nothing* – to which I would not stoop if by doing so I could make an end of El Forastero. You can have no conception of the damage his activities have caused us if you think I will let any chance to discredit him slip through my fingers.'

He rose abruptly and stood for a moment looking down on her. 'I shall leave you to reflect on what I have said. I hope I may return to find you in a more obliging humour.' At the door he paused with his hand on the latch. 'Jorge!'

The spider stirred in his corner. '*Sí, señor?*'

'I am told you have particular powers of persuasion, *amigo*. I wish you will use them to convince *la inglesa* of the wisdom of obeying me.'

'Most willingly, *señor*.'

'In ten minutes I will return.'

'*Bueno, señor.*'

He means it, thought Clio, and a cold dew of terror broke out on her forehead. He is going to leave me in the hands of this vile creature whose mind is as warped as his body.

'Colonel de Rochefort!' The cry was wrenched from her without conscious thought.

'You have something to say to me, *mademoiselle?*'

'For the love of God, do not leave me alone with that devil.'

'Will you sign?'

Clio was silent.

'You give me no choice, *mademoiselle*.' He went out softly, closing the door.

Clio sat very still. She heard a sharp click as the door bolt shot home, then the shuffle of Jorge's feet behind her. The miasma of garlic and rotten teeth enveloped her in an evil cloud and his hands crawled over her shoulders, kneading and caressing.

'Don't touch me.' She shuddered, pulling her cloak around her.

'Did you not hear the Colonel?' he mocked. 'You are mine. I may do as I please with you.'

'If you hurt me he will be angry.'

'Who spoke of hurting you?' His voice took on a beggar's whine. 'All I seek is a little pleasure, a little compensation for the times you and your countrymen have sneered at poor Jorge. How many times have I risked my life for your proud officers? They were glad enough to make use of me, but they would never stoop to share a crust with a miserable dwarf. They laughed behind my back and called me evil names. You shall pay for that laughter, *inglesa*.'

Dear Heaven, he is deranged, she thought in terror, remembering every horrid tale she had heard of Spanish cruelty. He blames *me* for all the slights he has suffered at our hands.

'Call Colonel de Rochefort,' she said as firmly as she could. 'Tell him I will sign his paper.'

'Oh no! You cannot escape that way.'

'Call him back.' When he did not move, she jumped up and ran to the door, beating on it with her fists.

'*Colonel de Rochefort!*'

At once, to her relief, she heard his voice the other side of the door.

'*Mademoiselle?* You will sign?'

'Yes – oh, yes!'

Her voice was suddenly smothered as Jorge dropped thick folds of cloak over her head and wound it tightly about her neck. She clawed at the heavy material, suffocating in the muffling softness.

'*Mademoiselle?* You are there?' Rochefort rattled the handle. 'Devil take it, he has locked the door! Open at once, you wretch! How dare you disobey me?'

'Shout all you please, *señor*,' muttered Jorge. He swung Clio off her feet with casual ease and carried her across the room. Laying her on the table, he set to work to bind her ankles to its legs, ignoring Rochefort's increasingly angry demands for admission.

'All in good time, *Señor Coronel*,' he muttered, sawing away with his dagger.

He means to kill me, thought Clio as the cord tightened cruelly on her skin. Blindly she struck at him, hardly conscious of the cord biting into her leg as she flung herself to and fro. Strong as he was, Jorge could not restrain her movement enough to secure his knots.

'*Mil demonios!*' he growled. With the edge of his hand he struck her a stunning blow at the base of the neck, and grunted in satisfaction as he felt the struggling, squirming body go limp. Deftly he completed the task of securing her ankles and wrists, then with careful, almost finicky precision slit her clothing from neck to hem and peeled it aside as one might expose the flesh of an orange.

Stepping back, he surveyed his prize. Clio moaned faintly beneath the cloak that shrouded her head. She made small ineffectual movements as if trying to shield her body from his gloating gaze.

The rattling at the door had ceased. Doubtless Rochefort had realized the futility of beating against its stout panels and had gone to seek another entrance. Jorge grinned. The second entrance to the kitchen was one known only to El Forastero and his band, who had sometimes been obliged to leave hurriedly through the trapdoor concealed behind the dresser. It led to the cellar and thence through a series of storerooms to the open hillside. That was the way Jorge himself planned to depart when he had settled old scores.

'You may have her when I have finished with her, *Señor Coronel*,' he muttered with savage glee. 'It may be you will not find her greatly to your taste.'

Clio was stirring. He allowed her time to regain full consciousness and discover that she was helpless, before divesting himself of his nether garments and approaching the table. He ran the tip of his dagger lightly the length of her body. A thin red line followed its passage.

'*Vamos!*' he exclaimed, and straddled the table like some grotesque Priapean effigy, so intent on his revenge that he did not hear the faint creak as the trapdoor behind the dresser was stealthily raised.

Harry, climbing silently through the opening, froze into immobility as he recognized the hunched outline of the dwarf in the firelight's glow. An icy anger filled him. Whispers and veiled hints from the women in his band had warned him of Jorge's sadistic leanings, but he had not expected to find him tormenting a servant girl under Rochefort's very nose.

'Leave that woman alone!' he growled, and sprang forward to seize Jorge by the collar, dragging him off his victim. Only then did Harry see that the woman was bound, and Jorge had a knife in his hand.

Taken by surprise, the dwarf kicked and struggled, spitting curses, then struck with a vicious backhand thrust at his unseen assailant.

Harry felt a searing pain as the blade sliced through his thigh. Like a man who has swatted a hornet believing it to be a fly, he realized he had seriously underestimated his opponent. Jorge was fighting mad and out for blood. There could be no question of throwing him aside: it was a case of kill or be killed.

'Quiet, fool! It is I. Where is Rochefort?'

Instead of answering, Jorge launched another attack, his prehensile arms flailing as the dagger sought a vital spot.

'Traitor! *Englishman!*' he gasped, and stabbed again.

'Why do you call me that?'

'It is true. *La inglesa* told me. You have lied to us all.'

'Where is she?'

Jorge's lips drew back from his teeth. Again the dagger seared Harry's thigh.

'Tell me, damn you.' He tightened his grip on Jorge's collar, forcing his head back until his breath rasped and his bolting bloodshot eyes stared into Harry's own.

He would not speak. He would go to his death leaving Harry uncertain whether or not Clio was safe in the British lines. Quietly, almost regretfully, Harry pressed both thumbs against the base of Jorge's skull, at the same time bending back his spine. The dwarf's neckbone cracked. His body slumped limply and the dagger clattered to the floor.

Harry released his grip and stood a moment breathing hard, looking down at the crumpled body. He remembered the days when Jorge had been his trusted lieutenant; the many dangers they had shared. Clio's coming had ended that. After she made her appearance nothing had been the same, either between himself and Jorge or in his relations with Mercedes. Clio had reminded him he was an Englishman, a fact that for nearly two years he had been able to forget.

Damn Clio. Damn all trouble-making females. There was no place for them in a theatre of war. Samuel Hardy should have kept his daughters at home at their needlework instead of bringing them to the war-torn Peninsula.

The woman on the table stirred, recalling him to the present. Harry glanced quickly at her, then away. The slender defenceless body spreadeagled on the table, its head shrouded, was a blatant invitation to lust. It woke a dark excitement he was ashamed to acknowledge for it offended every principle instilled in an English gentleman.

He bent and retrieved Jorge's dagger, using it to sever her bonds, then curtly bade her cover herself. He had no time to waste on her. By the looks of it, he had arrived in time to prevent the wench suffering any great damage. Perhaps she would choose her company more carefully in future.

His own business was with Rochefort. He must be found, and quickly, before Auguste's men stormed the farm. They must be creeping forward now, hidden among the olives, waiting for the signal to attack. Any moment the French sentries might become aware of their approach. He must not delay.

Harry stepped past Jorge's body and quietly eased back the bolt on the kitchen door. Beyond lay a smaller room, sombrely yet comfortably furnished with a handsome carved armchair, a bureau and two fine antique lacquered chests with brass handles. Here old Camilo used to transact business and smoke his long cigars.

The winter sun fell on the map spread out across the bureau. Steam rose from a bowl of chocolate and the carved chair was pushed back at an angle as if the occupant had risen in haste.

Cautious as a cat, Harry approached the bureau. A sheet of paper lay on the map, the ink still glistening. He picked it up and scanned the few lines, then laid it gently back as anger flared up in him – anger and a bitter sense of betrayal.

I, Clio Hardy, do hereby affirm....

That his jealously guarded secret should have been given away to the enemy by Clio herself was something he would not have believed without incontrovertible evidence. Here was the evidence... where was Clio?

His mind darted here and there, fitting what he knew to what he suspected, coming up with a dreadful hypothesis. According to Amalia, Grant had sent 'a little man' to fetch Clio. Had that man been Jorge? Had he brought her here, only to find the farm in French hands? That woman....

Harry stiffened as a footstep sounded in the passage. The back of his neck tingled in sudden awareness of danger.

'Good day, Captain Churchill,' said a silky voice he knew all too well. 'Turn to face me, if you please, and raise your hands above your head. Do not be tempted to do anything foolish, unless you wish me to blow out your brains.'

Slowly Harry turned. The barrel of a pistol confronted him, held steadily at the level of his eyes.

Rochefort smiled. 'So we meet again. May I say how delighted I am to see you, Captain Churchill? I had begun to fear you would disappoint me.'

'Who told you my name?'

'Who but your friend Miss Hardy? A charming girl. She and I had a most interesting discussion.'

'I wonder you should believe anything told you by that empty-headed chit,' said Harry scornfully. He measured with his eye the distance beween the desk and window: it was too far to jump with the gun so close to his head.

'Ah, but I do believe her and so, I am convinced, will the

Spaniards you have deceived so shamelessly. I do not think you will find them so ready to offer you assistance when they hear the truth about you.'

'Where is Miss Hardy?' With all his self-control, Harry could not prevent the edge of anxiety from sharpening his voice. Rochefort's smile widened.

'Pray be seated, Captain Churchill. There are many things I wish to ask you before we leave, and we have little time.'

'Damn you, what have you done with her?'

'Patience, my dear sir. First you will oblige me by answering certain questions. After that we will consider the question of Miss Hardy. I assure you she is in safe hands.'

'I should have listened to Pedro. He said none but a fool gave a scorpion a second chance to sting,' Harry observed, still covertly scanning the room in search of anything that might serve to level the odds a trifle. Auguste's troopers must be in position now. Any moment they would launch their attack. His own best chance of escape lay in the first confusion of the skirmish. He glanced out of the window but in the farmyard all was quiet, the French soldiers sipping soup round their fires, the tethered horses lazily swishing their tails.

'What do you want to know?'

'The names of your correspondents here and in Salamanca,' said Rochefort with the confidence of one who knows he has the whip hand. 'Unless you furnish me with a complete account of them, I must warn you that you will not see Miss Hardy again.'

'Be serious, man! You cannot expect me to betray the names of those who have helped us,' protested Harry, but the response was mechanical for all of a sudden his concentration had become focused on the door behind Rochefort – the door leading to the kitchen.

He had pushed it shut when he entered Camilo's business room. Now – dim though the light was in that corner – he could swear that the door had begun to move, opening by infinitesimal degrees just wide enough for a ghostly shadow to flit through the aperture and vanish behind a screen.

Had he imagined it? Harry held his breath, waiting for Rochefort to give some sign that he, too, was aware of an intruder, but he said nothing.

Then, from the sea of olives surrounding the farm, faint but unmistakable rose the plangent note of a bugle sounding the Charge, followed by startled shouts and running feet.

'*Sacré Dieu!*' growled Rochefort, but the pistol did not waver from its aim.

'*Aux armes! Les Anglais sont ici!*' Snatching up their weapons, the French scurried to their posts, and the insistent throb of a drum mingled with the clatter of approaching hoofs.

Auguste's troopers charged up the hill with the abandon of foxhunting squires.

'Gone away!' screamed Cornet Harris, sitting back with a long rein as his bay charger flew the farmyard wall. Sparks flew from the cobbles as horse after horse dashed into the yard and the demoralized French ran hither and thither in their haste to escape.

Rochefort took a single long step forward to press the barrel of the pistol against Harry's temple, but before he could complete the movement a number of things happened with bewildering speed.

Out of the shadow of the screen loomed a menacing black crow, which wrapped its wings around his head; while at the same moment Harry, ducking swiftly out of the line of fire, dived at Rochefort's knees in a flying tackle. Together they crashed to the ground. Rochefort's head hit the stone flags with a crack. He groaned, tried to rise, and slumped back on one elbow, blood streaming from his wounded skull.

Harry removed the pistol from his grasp and stood up, breathing hard. Pale as a ghost, Clio confronted him.

'You damned fool!' Relief mingled with fear made his voice shake. 'Of all the stupid, reckless, *imbecile* things to do! You might have been killed.'

'Don't scold, Harry. He was going to shoot you. I could not stand by –' Her voice broke. Wordlessly she held out her arms and he caught her, hugging her tightly, looking over her bent head at his fallen enemy while the blood drummed a relentless rhythm in his ears: *Kill, kill, kill!*

Only a fool gave a scorpion a second chance to sting. Rochefort had been given two chances; he should not have a third. Mercedes's violent end, Clio stripped and humiliated, these were memories that would remain with him until expunged with Rochefort's own blood.

The Frenchman was watching him. As if aware of what was passing through Harry's mind, he gave a little shrug and fumbled at the hilt of his sword.

'Captain Churchill, I must ask you to accept my surrender.'

'Never.'

The sword clattered on the floor. Harry did not even glance at it.

'Come, Captain Churchill. By the rules of war you cannot refuse it.'

'I am bound by no rules,' said Harry through clenched teeth. 'As you were good enough to remind me, an officer who breaks his parole puts himself outside the law.' He pushed Clio gently to one side as she tried to intervene, and took Rochefort by the elbow. 'On your feet, Colonel. There is no rule that says a prisoner who tries to escape may not be shot.'

'I have not the least desire to escape,' said Rochefort, determinedly remaining supine. 'Miss Hardy, I appeal to you to witness the surrender of my sword.'

In the farmyard, the brief skirmish was over. Rochefort's men, herded into a byre, looked on with sullen bewilderment as Auguste strutted here and there, self-important as a rooster, supervising the collection of enemy baggage and provisions. When this task was completed to his satisfaction, he would come to make his report. Before that happened, Rochefort must be killed.

'Leave us, Clio.'

'No, Harry.'

'Go.'

'You cannot do such a thing.'

'Don't tell me what to do.'

Again he bent and tried to haul Rochefort upright, but the Frenchman lay limply.

'If you shoot me, Captain Churchill, it must be in cold blood. I have no intention of providing you with an excuse to kill me.'

'You deserve to die.'

'Maybe. But will El Forastero kill a helpless prisoner? Is he capable of such a crime? His reputation will be destroyed when word of my murder gets about.'

'It is already destroyed.'

Footsteps crunched across the yard. Auguste's head passed the little window, and a moment later they heard his brisk tattoo on the farmhouse door.

'Don Enrique, are you zere?' he called. 'Ve haf searched everywhere but Rochefort is not to be found. I fear he has escaped us.'

Harry cursed softly. He levelled the pistol at the reclining Frenchman, who stared steadily back at him, defying him to pull the trigger. Slowly Harry's finger tightened.

'No, Harry!' screamed Clio. She ran forward to kneel beside Rochefort, shielding him with her body. 'Help!' she called. 'Come quickly! Colonel Rochefort is here.'

But before Auguste could respond to the summons, Rochefort's arms clamped round Clio's own waist, pinning her arms to her sides. She gasped and tried to struggle free, but like a wounded leopard, Rochefort changed in an instant from a defeated suppliant to a dangerous foe. Using her as a living prop, he scrambled to his feet and then, her body interposed between himself and the pistol, bent to retrieve his rejected sword.

'Call your men off, Captain Churchill,' he said coolly. 'If anyone tries to stop me, Miss Hardy dies.' He began to retreat backwards towards the door, careful to allow Harry no chance to shoot without injuring Clio. As he reached it, the door swung open to reveal Auguste with the troopers drawn up behind him.

'Stop him!' shouted Harry; but after one glance at Rochefort's grim face and the half-fainting girl he held as a shield, Auguste stepped back, waving to his men to give the French officer passage.

'Stop him,' repeated Harry furiously.

'I – I dare not.'

In frozen stillness they watched Rochefort drag his hostage across the yard to where the horses were tethered. There he hoisted Clio across the saddlebow of Auguste's handsome bay charger, and sprang up behind her.

'My horse!' groaned the hapless commissary, but valued his skin too much to intervene.

'*Adiós, Don Enrique!*' Rochefort raised his sword in a mocking salute. Then he clapped spurs to the horse's flanks and cantered out of the yard.

'Fools! Damned fools! Why didn't you stop him?' raged Harry.

'For ze same reason you did not shoot him,' retorted Auguste, mopping his brow. 'I tell you plain, I vould rather lose a dozen prisoners than put a voman's life in danger.'

'I am going after him,' said Harry hurriedly. 'You will oblige me, old friend, by saying nothing of my part in this. Have I your promise?'

'But Mr Harry –'

'Don Enrique.'

Auguste shrugged and sighed. 'As you vish. But vhere am I to get a new horse, answer me zat!'

'Oh, I daresay Josefa may help you there,' said Harry and Auguste brightened a little.

He shook his head. 'Zat voman! Strange how ze mind plays tricks. For von moment I thought ... I believed....' He turned away, muttering, and Harry wasted no more time. He ran to the byre where he had hidden his horse, and less than a minute later was galloping down the track through the olive grove on Rochefort's trail.

Every discomfort Clio had endured in the Peninsula paled into insignificance beside that ride. Bundled across Rochefort's saddle, her ribs crushed against the unyielding pommel and her legs dangling helplessly, she suffered almost as much from fear of what might be in store as from bodily pain. Her lungs ached from the effort of drawing breath only to have it jolted out by the horse's next stride, her head ached from the after-effect of Jorge's blow, but most of all her heart ached to know that she had been the instrument of Rochefort's escape.

Yet how could she have stood by and allowed Harry to damn himself for ever? No hope that he would forgive her now. With his enemy free to spread the tale of El Forastero's true identity, Harry's influence over his *guerrilleros* would wane as swiftly as it had grown. Nor were they likely to be slow in avenging this slight on their national pride. Harry had been keenly aware how slender was the knife-edge on which he balanced. If Spanish generals would not accept the authority of Lord Wellington himself, the anger of the haughty mountain chiefs when they discovered they had been duped into taking orders from an English officer – and a very junior officer at that – could readily be imagined.

Rochefort rode fast, sparing neither his prisoner nor his horse in his determination to shake off pursuit. But Auguste's charger had already done a fair day's work and his strength was not without limit. When he felt the beast begin to stagger under the double burden, Rochefort drew rein on the bank of a stream and allowed Clio to slide to the ground.

'I believe I need trouble you for your company no longer, *mademoiselle*,' he said with mock courtesy, his narrow eyes laughing down at her.

She struggled to rise, but her cramped stiff limbs would not obey. 'Where are you going?'

'Why, to join my wife, who should by now have reached Madrid in safety. Have you any message you wish me to give her? As for you, I shall leave you here.'

'Here?' she echoed in dismay. 'You cannot leave me here in the middle of nowhere!'

'Do not be afraid. I am sure Captain Churchill will discover you soon enough,' he said heartlessly. 'He may even have some emphatic remarks to make on your behaviour! I am sorry to have been obliged to handle you a little roughly. May I offer a word of advice?'

'Offer it if you must but I will not undertake to observe it,' snapped Clio. She felt the keen resentment of the dismounted for the mounted. If only I could topple him from that horse and leave *him* here for Harry to find! she thought, but knew it was a fantasy.

'Well, what is it?' she demanded, disliking him more every minute.

'Only this: that I recommend you not to interfere in men's affairs in future, *mademoiselle*. You have escaped unscathed this time; you can hardly expect to be so fortunate again.'

'*Fortunate!*'

Rochefort bowed, laughing at her indignant face. 'I consider you have been extremely fortunate. Now with your permission I have the honour to bid you adieu.'

Still smiling, he rode away and Clio, relieved at last of any need to conceal her emotions, rested her aching head against the trunk of a tree, and abandoned herself to tears.

18

Crying all alone is an unsatisfying exercise, and before long Clio's natural optimism reasserted itself. At least I am alive, she thought, and I have not after all a great deal to reproach myself with.

Encouraged by this reflection, she wiped her eyes, then looked about her – only to discover that very far from being in the middle of nowhere, as she had supposed, a church spire dominated the landscape at no great distance from where she sat, and round it smoke rose from the chimneys of a sizeable town.

The proximity of other humans provoked in her the normal feminine reaction of wondering how she could improve her appearance before encountering them, and a glance in the stream left her in no doubt there was room for improvement. With her tangled elflocks, pale dirty face and ruined clothes, she looked what Laura would with justice have described as 'A Fright', and she set to work to remedy this as far as possible. She washed her face and braided her hair, and was engaged on the ticklish task of securing the two halves of her mutilated dress with a sash torn from its hem when a shadow fell across the rock on which she sat.

'Well, Clio,' said Harry. 'I trust you are proud of yourself.' He dismounted and dropped the reins over his mount's head. 'Stand, Francisco,' he said, and walked towards her.

As he approached she saw the weariness in his face and

guessed how bitter it had been for him to lose such a prize as Rochefort. Her own reproaches for his conduct fled from her mind, and she said simply: 'Oh, Harry!'

'Is that all you can say? So you know what your foolishness has cost me?'

Clio's back stiffened. She said, 'I am sorry to have been the cause of Colonel de Rochefort's escape, but I cannot regret preventing you from killing him.'

'The world would be a better place without vermin. You should not have interfered.'

'But he was your prisoner! He surrendered his sword.'

'I did not accept it.'

'How would you have explained the death of a prisoner?'

Harry shrugged. 'These things happen. It would have been accepted.'

'What about your reputation?'

'That has already gone, along with any chance of a pardon.'

'But, Harry –'

'Grant made the capture of Rochefort, *alive or dead*, the final condition of his intervention with Lord Wellington on my behalf,' he said in a harsh, clipped voice. 'I am not likely to get another such chance.'

'Colonel Grant had no right to set conditions! His price is too high,' she said indignantly.

'He is a Scot.'

'Rochefort's horse was nearly foundered. He cannot have gone far.' Even as Clio spoke, she realized the futility of searching for him in country he knew so well. A man like Rochefort must be stalked, not hunted.

'Why did you interfere? I thought you had better taste than to lose your heart to a Frenchman,' said Harry bitingly.

'Lose my heart? Indeed I have not! He is Julia's husband!'

'Julia's husband?' It was Harry's turn for surprise. After a moment he began to laugh reluctantly. 'If that don't beat all! What a dull place the Peninsula would be without the Hardy sisters! My father used to say that soldiers' wives were the deuce for the trouble they caused among the men, but a commissary officer's daughters make humble camp followers seem models of decorum. How the Devil did Julia contrive to snare that slippery rascal? By all accounts he has had more *affaires du coeur* than Don Juan himself, yet always avoided the trap of matrimony. Why, the last I heard, he was paying court to pretty Paulette, and that is a sure road to advancement!'

Seeing him laugh, she began to hope he had recovered his spirits, but a moment later the black mood returned.

'I must go,' he said, 'but first I want you to promise you will never speak of Harry Churchill's part in this.'

'How can I promise such a thing?'

'You must, for my life will depend on your silence. Harry Churchill no longer exists,' he said sombrely. 'He was a foolish fellow and died after Talavera.'

'It is not true!'

'It must be true. Come, Clio, will you give me your promise?'

Wordlessly she shook her head. Tears spilled suddenly from her eyes. She turned away, but not before he heard her whisper, 'I loved him.'

The tight control he had maintained over his feelings deserted him and with a stifled exclamation he stepped forward and caught her in his arms, murmuring endearments.

'Clio! Little darling! Don't cry.'

For the space of a minute they clung together, their differences forgotten, and Harry knew with wrenching certainty that any other love would always be second best.

'Let me come with you,' she pleaded. 'I promise I wouldn't trouble you or – or hinder you. Only let me come!'

Even before he spoke she read the refusal in his face.

'Oh,' she said flatly. 'Mercedes. I had forgotten.'

'Mercedes is dead,' said Harry.

'Dead! But how? Did our soldiers –?'

He shook his head. 'She was stabbed to death by her own husband.'

'Oh Harry! How dreadful. I am truly sorry.' She saw his look of disbelief and hastened to add, 'I know we were not always good friends, but in these last months I came to entertain the warmest regard for her courage. That she should suffer such an end!'

'Someone betrayed her,' said Harry grimly. 'Someone who knew of our liaison – I cannot understand whom. Not Rochefort, of that I can be certain. She was careful never to appear unveiled when he was my captive.'

'It could have been Julia,' said Clio after a moment's thought.

'Julia?'

'We both saw Mercedes unveiled when we first arrived at your cave. Julia has an artist's memory. She would not have forgotten anyone so striking.'

Harry was hardly listening. He said in a tone of burning self-reproach, 'I should never have allowed her to return. I suspected Don Sebastian would be dangerous, especially if he suspected her fidelity.'

Clio hardly dared put her next question but it had to be asked. 'What of her children? Amalia...?'

'Safe with my friends.'

'And the baby?'

'What baby?'

'Your son!'

The baby hardly seemed real to Harry. He shook his head, saying vaguely, 'I don't know.'

She turned the subject, asking if he would not trust to Lord Wellington's clemency. 'No one can deny the services your *guerrilleros* have rendered him! Colonel de Rochefort himself said you must be worth a division at least.'

Harry's face fell into the lines of stubborn pride that she had come to regard as his 'Spanish look'.

'Clemency! You do not know the Beau if you suppose clemency to play any part in his dealings. Justice, yes – but not clemency. Besides, Darcy has so poisoned his mind against me that I would not be admitted to his presence, let alone granted a fair hearing.'

'Harry Churchill afraid to face the music! I would not have believed it.'

If she hoped to provoke him she was disappointed. 'I shall face the music in my own time and my own way. First I have scores to settle.'

'No, Harry.'

'Yes, Clio.'

'If you kill Julia's husband I will never forgive you,' said Clio fiercely, and he smiled.

'Go back to Robert. Your happiness lies with him, not me. Remember, Harry Churchill is dead.'

'No!'

He took her hands and pressed them to his lips, kissing each finger in turn. 'One day you will be glad I did not let him ruin your life as he did his own. Now I must go.'

'Take me with you,' she begged, but he walked quickly to the waiting horse.

'Try to forget me, Clio,' he said, staring down from the saddle with sombre eyes. He looked every inch a Spaniard now, but she knew the Englishman was still there if only she could set him free.

'I shall never forget you.'

He shook his head. 'Robert will make you happy as I never could, and your happiness is the most important thing in the world to me.'

She turned away, not wishing his last sight of her to be in tears. 'Go, then,' she said, and held her head high and her back straight until she knew from the silence that he was out of sight.

A grief too heavy for weeping descended on her spirit. Clouds had blown up from the west, blotting out the bright morning, and a keen raw wind blew down off the mountains, carrying the hint of snow to come. Clio shivered and huddled in her cloak, her thoughts as bleak as the January sky. For that one brief time when he held her in his arms she had known the old Harry was alive – the one she loved and who loved her – then that beloved image had dissolved once more into the proud cold mask of Don Enrique. There could be no going back. Harry himself had said so but until now she would not believe it....

'Over there! Look!'

The shout startled her into the present. A small party of horsemen had trotted out of the trees and halted. Waving his gold-laced hat, the leader spurred towards her, and flung himself off his horse.

'Miss Clio! Alive! A miracle!'

Beneath his halo of fluffy grey curls, Auguste's rubicund face beamed at her, inviting her to share his delight.

'Zat mad boy said ve should find you here but I did not believe him. Truly, a miracle! Ve never thought to see you alive again.'

'I wish I was dead,' said Clio.

His smile faded, replaced by a look of concern. He put his arm round her shoulders, hugging her as if she was a child again. '*Pauvre petite! Comme tu as soufferte!* Come, mount my horse. Your troubles are over now and old Auguste vill take you home.'

The beam that crashed from a blazing roof in Ciudad Rodrigo and temporarily deprived Major Cole of his senses also broke his collarbone and several ribs and blotted out all recollection of the storming.

When he recovered full consciousness two days later, his one clear memory was of the letter he had written to Laura, and he resolved to lose no time in asking her to marry him. Attended by his faithful servant Joachim, he returned to Lisbon in the company of other officers whose wounds were slight enough to permit of travelling and, finding Lahmeyer's Hotel too full to give him a room, repaired at once to the Quinta Rosa where he received a rapturous welcome.

'How very thankful I am to see you alive!' Laura declared when she had finished exclaiming in horror over his battered state. 'Of course you must stay here until you are fully recovered. Father and I would not hear of you going elsewhere. You can have no idea how much the children have missed you! Even the smallest pray for your safety every night.'

'I am very grateful to them,' he said, smiling. 'And you? Have you missed me?'

Laura blushed rosily. 'How can you ask?'

With her large brown eyes and statuesque figure, she seemed to Robert's dazzled eyes to have acquired a new radiance.

'I have thought of you constantly. There has hardly been a moment since we parted when you were out of my thoughts,' he said breathlessly. 'Laura, I am a plain sort of fellow, as you know, and not much of a hand at pretty speeches, but if you will do me the honour of becoming my wife, I shall be the happiest man alive.'

It was the moment she had long dreamed of. Laura did not hesitate. 'Oh, Robert! Yes, with all my heart,' she whispered, and lifted her lips for his kiss.

Samuel Hardy, entering the room to find them thus engaged, had no difficulty in divining what had just been said. He waved away Robert's apologies.

'No need to be sorry, my boy! We were all young once, you know. Of course you may have her, with my blessing. Upon my soul, Laura, how pleased your dear mother and sisters will be!'

Mention of her sisters cast a cloud over Laura's happiness. Her face fell. Gently she removed her hand from Robert's clasp, saying confusedly, 'Oh! Of course. It is impossible. I had forgotten.'

'What are you talking about? What is impossible?' inquired her father testily.

Laura's eyes filled with tears. 'I am sorry. I was wrong even to think of marrying when Julia is a captive and poor Clio –'

'Nonsense! Putting off your wedding and making yourself unhappy won't bring 'em back,' said Samuel robustly. Laura's charitable activities had badly damaged her chances of marriage and were rapidly becoming as irksome to him as they had been to Hugh Arbuthnot, for whom Samuel felt a good deal of sympathy. He had no intention of allowing so desirable a son-in-law as Robert to slip through his fingers a second time.

'But Papa, convention demands –'

'Convention is a luxury we poor mortals must sometimes be prepared to sacrifice,' said Samuel firmly. 'Who can tell how long this war will last or when Robert will be required to rejoin his regiment? What do you say, Robert? A simple drumhead wedding as befits an officer on active service, or would you rather wait a year or so for a society affair in England?'

Faced with such a choice, Robert had no hesitation in agreeing to the former, and if he guessed at Samuel's wish to spare his own pocket, he was too well bred to say so.

Laura was less accommodating. Simple the ceremony might be, but she wished all their acquaintance to be there. With Lady Arbuthnot's connivance she planned to make her wedding the most talked-of affair of the season.

At first it was hoped that Mrs Hardy might attend, but the mailboat brought disappointment with the news that an epidemic of measles among the younger children made it impossible for her to leave them. This was a blow, but Laura was equal to it. No hole-and-corner marriage for her. Having smarted from the gibes of some ladies who considered her work among destitute children a betrayal of her country and class, Laura had an understandable desire to show off her matrimonial prize. She issued invitations with a lavish hand even to those who had been loudest in their condemnation of her orphans. Certain haughty ladies might well have sent regrets had it not been for the staunch efforts of good-natured Lady Arbuthnot to support her god-daughter.

'Everyone of any note will be there,' she assured waverers. 'I understand Lord Wellington himself has promised to attend. I declare I would not miss it for the world!' And so great was her influence over British society that few dared question her.

Arriving in Lisbon one sunny morning in March, Clio found the household in a state of happy confusion. She was shown into the morning room where Laura, flushed and bright-eyed, knelt amid a stack of cardboard boxes, rummaging through their layers of tissue paper with the eager absorption of a terrier digging out rabbits.

'Well, Laura! Have you had a birthday?'

Laura turned and her mouth dropped open. The blood

drained from her face, leaving it very pale, and she pressed a hand against her heart as if about to faint.

'You!' she gasped.

Even from a sibling, this greeting seemed lukewarm.

'Don't be alarmed! I am not a ghost, I assure you.' Clio could not help smiling. 'Well, is that all you have to say to your long-lost sister?'

At this Laura jumped up and embraced her, but there was still a constraint in her manner which Clio could hardly fail to notice.

'Whatever are you doing with all this paper?' she asked, hoping to relieve the tension, but the question served only to increase Laura's confusion.

'I – you see – we had no notion – Julia's letter...' she gabbled, nervously pushing back the hair that had escaped from its ribbon. A card fell on the carpet and Clio stooped to retrieve it.

'*To Laura, with every good wish for your happiness,*' she read, and the matter at once became plain.

'You are to be married!'

Laura's mouth opened and shut silently. She looked around as if to escape, but at that moment the door was flung wide and Robert entered wearing civilian clothes, a snuff-coloured plain frock-coat and narrow trousers, his arm bound up in a sling.

He was evidently in the grip of strong agitation, and strode across the room to where Laura stood without seeing Clio, who had stepped back a little to avoid the swinging door.

'My love, I have just heard – Is it true?' he demanded, grasping Laura's hands.

She nodded, mutely gesturing, and Robert turned to see Clio standing by the door.

'I see I have to felicitate you both,' she said in a strained voice.

Robert stared at her, glassy-eyed as a sleep-walker. 'I thought.... We were told.... Julia's letter....' His voice trailed away into silence. He looked beseechingly at Laura as if for inspiration.

'You thought I would never return? Well, you can hardly be

blamed for that,' said Clio, but nevertheless the betrayal cut deep. It was no use telling herself she had not valued Robert's devotion; to find his affections so rapidly transferred from herself to Laura was unexpectedly bitter.

'I am sorry if my reincarnation causes you distress,' she said a little unsteadily; and at that Laura's good nature overcame her dread of losing Robert.

'No, no! You must not think that! We are only a good deal surprised! You see, Julia wrote to tell us the dreadful bandits had killed you. I am so glad – so *very* glad – to know she was wrong. Where in the world have you been all this time? You are so thin! I would hardly have known you. Wait while I find Father and tell him the happy news!'

She ran through the french window into the garden, leaving Robert and Clio alone.

'You must think me a low, despicable fellow,' he said in an agonized tone, standing as rigid as if he had swallowed a poker.

'Why should I? You have done nothing to merit such a description.'

He would not meet her eye. 'To propose marriage to you, and then –'

Poor Robert, always so correct! She took pity on his wretchedness and said the first thing that came into her head. 'I am sorry, I lost your ring. I don't know where. So much has happened.'

'My ring? Oh! It does not signify.' He looked a little reassured, but still said mournfully, 'What must you think of me? Can you ever find it in your heart to forgive me?'

She found his hangdog mien more irritating than pathetic but strove not to hurt his feelings. Taking his hand, she said with all the briskness she could muster, 'My dear Robert, there is nothing to forgive. Only consider! The circumstances of our betrothal were so ... so singular that no one could blame you for acting as you have. You must not reproach yourself.'

'But I do. I think I always shall. Yet how can I make amends to you without doing Laura the gravest wrong?'

'Amends? What nonsense!' His determined self-castigation

was becoming decidedly tiresome. He should be comforting her, not the other way about. She said firmly, 'I have already said there is nothing to forgive. I wish you and Laura most happy. There! Let us say no more about it.'

'But you must understand –'

'Not another word.'

To her relief the uncomfortable interview was terminated by the entry of Samuel Hardy, whose uncomplicated pleasure in having his favourite daughter restored to him did much to revive her spirits. He hugged her, pinched her cheek, and hugged her again while tears poured unchecked down his face.

'Well, Puss! A fine time you have given us, worrying what had become of you,' he exclaimed, pulling out a large silk handkerchief and noisily blowing his nose. 'What do you mean by it, hey? Here you are again, bright as fivepence, just in time to see your sister married. What do you think of that? Your sister has stolen a march on you, Miss Puss! You'll have to start looking round for a husband yourself if you're not to find yourself left on the shelf!'

'Clio has become very strange,' complained Laura a week later, seeking out her father as he sat sketching in his favourite arbour. 'This morning I asked if I should wear a bonnet or a chip hat to be married, and she said it made no difference. No difference! Do you think her sufferings have affected her mind?'

'I doubt it very much,' said Samuel without removing his gaze from his view of the harbour. He wished Laura would go away and leave him in peace. In fact, he wished everyone would leave him in peace. He had so much to do, so many antique remains to record and classify in order to incorporate them in his great work, yet from morning until night people pestered him with frivolous demands on his attention. Only yesterday he had received a curt communication from the Assistant Commissary-General, suggesting it was time he returned to his regiment. Had the fellow no notion of what was important?

A new worry had begun to preoccupy him. Would the war last long enough for him to accumulate all the material he needed? Ciudad Rodrigo had not belied its reputation. Once in possession of this key, other doors had begun to open for Lord Wellington. After half a decade of more or less unavailing campaigning, his star was unmistakably in the ascendant and it had begun to seem not only possible but probable that he would succeed in expelling Bonaparte's armies from the Peninsula within the year.

If that should happen, Samuel might find himself obliged to return to England with his work incomplete; and now Laura would persist in following him about, seeking his opinion on such trivial matters as the extent of her trousseau and who should be asked to attend the wedding.

Samuel sighed for his dear wife, who would have handled these affairs without allowing him to be troubled, but alas, Genevieve was far away and the answers Clio gave her sister generally provoked more friction than satisfaction.

Still, of all the people round him, Clio seemed the only one not bent on plaguing the life out of him. It was true that her adventures – of which she seldom spoke – had left her a good deal quieter, but on the whole he thought he preferred the new reflective Clio to the old exuberant one. All young animals grow up, he thought. Puppies, kittens, lambs – in time they all achieve a certain gravity. Clio's new-found gravity was not unbecoming. Certainly she seemed less interested in quarrelling with Laura than of old.

For Clio, the weeks preceding Laura's wedding were not happy ones. She found Laura's air of triumph very hard to bear. She seemed unable to utter two sentences without a reference to her coming marriage.

'Major Cole... Robert... my husband to be... after we are married....'

At times this constant refrain so exacerbated Clio's nerves that sisterly affection barely sufficed to keep her from strangling Laura; though to be fair, she was not the only one to harp on the matrimonial theme. Romance – like victory – was in the air that spring. There seemed to be hardly a young lady of their acquaintance who was not recently betrothed and planning her wedding. Clio was soon heartily tired of all the talk of settlements and trousseaux and bridesmaids, and took to making long solitary walks along the river bank, or riding alone into the surrounding hills. At this time of year the countryside was breathtaking in its beauty, the meadows verdant with velvet grass so thickly embroidered with wild flowers that it resembled a Persian carpet, heavy-scented racemes of lilac and white laburnum festooned in the untrimmed hedgerows, and bright-plumaged birds, finches and orioles, cuckoos, quails and hoopoes, filling the air with their song. She longed for a companion to share her pleasure in these sights, but most of the convalescent officers preferred to spend their time lounging the streets or ogling the pretty laundresses by the Tagus.

'You should not ride alone and expose yourself to vulgar insult,' scolded Laura, on discovering the solitary nature of these promenades.

'Be easy! No one has shown the least inclination to insult me,' said Clio, laughing despite herself. 'If they did, I hope I should know how to send them to the rightabout.'

'Then have a care for *my* reputation, even if you have none for your own,' said Laura with a sniff. 'People will think it very odd to see you go about unattended, and everyone knows you are my sister. I would have thought you had made yourself conspicuous enough already, without courting notoriety in this way.' She saw Clio's melancholy look and added consolingly, 'When I am married and have time to call my own, *I* will ride with you about the countryside as much as you please – that is, if Major Cole has no objection.'

'I cannot for the life of me see why he should,' murmured Clio, 'and until that moment comes I shall ride as I please.'

But Laura had already dismissed the subject from her mind and returned to the more absorbing business of planning her wedding.

In common with most of his countrymen, Samuel Hardy made few concessions to local custom in the matter of diet, and breakfast at the Quinta Rosa was always a substantial meal. When Laura heard her father give a strangled cry – half oath, half choke – and saw him stare fixedly at his plate, her first thought was that the devilled kidneys were too hot and she must speak to the cook.

Then she saw that he was staring at the letter he had just opened which lay beside his plate. The kidneys were innocent.

'Vandal! Benighted Philistine! Is nothing sacred?' he demanded, plucking the wig from his head and throwing it to the ground.

'What is the matter, Papa?'

'Matter? I'll show you what is the matter!'

He passed her the offending letter. With only the curtest preamble and in terms barely polite, the clerk to the Assistant Commissary-General ordered Mr Hardy to report with all speed and 'without encumbrances' to the depot at Retaxo, on the road to Castelo Branco, there to relieve Mr Whitmore, a commissary officer whose services were needed at the front. He further had the honour to inform Mr Hardy that in the event of his failing to arrive on the appointed day, the Commissary-General in Lisbon would be happy to accept his resignation from the service.

'The insolent jackanapes!' Samuel snatched back the letter and read it again, simmering with indignation. 'I am *ordered!* Not desired, or requested, mark you, but ordered! Not a hint that I might be engaged in more important work than baking biscuit and weighing out beef. And so soon! Even if I leave at once –'

'Papa! You cannot leave before my wedding!' cried Laura tragically, seeing her cherished hopes dissolve like melting snow.

Samuel glanced at her stricken face and said with unusual resolution, 'No, indeed. Not at all the thing.' He frowned at the letter again. 'But I must go soon after.'

'Shall I come with you, Papa?' asked Clio, rousing from her abstraction.

He shook his head. 'No, Puss. You have been abroad long

enough. It is time you returned home to your Mamma and learned to behave like a young lady again.'

'But, Papa –!'

'No arguments, Puss. My mind is made up. When Laura and Robert are married you will not want to be a burden on them.' Seeing her disconsolate expression he added in a kinder tone, 'After all, I daresay you will find it pleasant to be back among your own friends.'

She thought it sounded very tame, but Laura was nodding approval and it was true she had no wish to form an unwanted third in the young couple's household.

'I could stay with Lady Arbuthnot,' she began hopefully, but for once Samuel was proof against cajolery.

'No, Puss. I shall have quite enough to worry me without fretting over what mischief you are in. I will go down to the harbour this very morning and secure you a passage.'

Against this verdict there was no appeal, and in any case Clio lacked the spirit to argue further. Indeed, as the last days before the wedding slipped away she began to feel stifled by the little world of British society in Lisbon, where it was impossible to make an observation without hearing it repeated a dozen times, or dance more than once with the same man without exciting rumours of an engagement. At home, she thought, at least she would be accorded a degree of freedom, though the memory of Harry would remain a perpetual source of regret, an open wound nothing would heal.

If only! she thought, and sighed. Crying over spilt milk never helped, and given the same circumstances she knew she would have acted in the same way. Deny it as he might, she understood Harry too well to doubt that if he had killed an unarmed, helpless prisoner – no matter what the provocation – he would have found it hard to forgive himself. Better that he should blame her... and yet....

She sighed again and tried to concentrate on weaving wreaths of wildflowers for the headdresses of Luisa and Estrella, the pretty orphans chosen by Laura as her bridesmaids. Her thoughts kept returning to Harry. Hoping for news of him, she had lingered in Ciudad Rodrigo as long as Auguste's regiment was stationed there, though Auguste himself urged her to leave.

'You should go to your father, *petite*. It vill do no good to vait. Mr Harry vill not come.'

'How can you tell?'

He shook his head, smiling. 'Major Cole loves you, *petite*. He vill make you happier zan zat mad boy.'

'Just one more week,' she said stubbornly. 'After I have been away so long, what difference will one more week make?'

But the week had stretched to two, and become a month before news that El Forastero had moved south to harass the convoys on the road to Badajoz finally banished her hopes. Auguste was right; Harry had cut her out of his life, and she must do the same to him.

And, after all, that lost month had made a difference. If she had returned to Lisbon sooner, Robert might not have committed himself irrevocably to Laura. Even that chance of happiness had slipped through her fingers and she had no one to blame but herself. All she could do now was put the best face she could on her sister's triumph.

Triumphant indeed was Laura's bearing as she tripped briskly up the aisle on her father's arm; returning with her veil flung back to show her radiant smile, she might have posed for a portrait of Victory. Happiness improves the looks of even the plainest bride, and Laura was far from plain. Her handsome features softened into something approaching beauty as she paused on the church steps, arm in arm with her bridegroom, to savour the admiration of the throng before entering the carriage decked with flowers and ribbon love-knots. It was her moment of glory. She meant to extract the very last ounce of pleasure from it.

'Your turn next,' she whispered to Clio, embracing her warmly while the guests pressed round to offer their good wishes. She picked up her rustling skirts and stepped into the carriage with Robert at her side. The crowd cheered and threw flowers. The coachman raised his whip.

'Catch, Clio!'

Laura flung her bouquet high in the air but Clio's hands remained clasped before her, and it was a giggling Miss Ellison who snatched the flowers and pressed them to her bosom as the bridal carriage rumbled away.

After the last guest had departed somewhat top-heavily down the *quinta*'s steps, the house seemed eerily quiet. Samuel Hardy supped early with an abstracted air and soon retired to his study. He had ordered his horse to be saddled at first light and meant to spend the intervening hours writing up notes for Clio to carry back to England.

'I may not see you before I leave, Puss,' he said, pausing in the hall to bid her good night.

'Goodbye, then, Papa.'

'You have my letters to your mother?'

'Yes, Papa.'

He studied her with a little smile. 'Good girl. Now, you must not repine, eh, Puss? I think I know how you are feeling, but it is for the best, you know. Robert Cole will do very well for Laura, but you would soon have found him a sad prose. Good night then, Puss.'

'Good night, Papa.'

She watched the study door close behind him, then made her way across the scented courtyard to the children's quarters where all was equally quiet. Worn out with excitement and rich food, the orphans had subsided into sleep without protest. After making a tour of the silent nurseries as she had promised Laura, Clio returned to her own room which wore the desolate air of one soon to be vacated.

Cabin trunks and hat-boxes were stacked in one corner; a carpet-bag and other impedimenta still to be packed lay about in disorder. Evidently her maid had found it more entertaining to watch the wedding guests than attend to her mistress's packing.

Clio rang the bell to summon her back to her duties. Shaking pins from her hair with a sigh of relief, she picked up a comb to tease out the tangles. Presently she heard the murmur of voices in the passage.

'Come in!' she called in response to a tap on the door. 'You may leave the rest of my packing until the morning. Come and undress me now.'

'If only I might!'

Clio swung round on her stool, cheeks aflame. '*Harry!*'

He stood there in the doorway like an apparition conjured up by her dreams. Hair ruffled, eyes bright, still wearing his shabby *serrano* suit of well-worn leather and crumpled turned-down boots, laughing at her astonishment.

He's different, she thought. More... more *alive* – triumphant, even, as if some affair has been settled to his satisfaction. A chill touched her. It needed little imagination to guess what that affair might be.

'Stop!' she said breathlessly as he took a step towards her. 'Why have you come here? How dare you steal up on me like this?'

'I've paid my debts, Clio.'

'Debts?' she repeated blankly. '*Debts?*' Words, insults, half-formed questions jumbled and tumbled in her brain, blocking her tongue. The pent-up excitement emanating from that tense, triumphant figure in the doorway infected her too, setting her pulses racing.

'I thought – Why didn't –?'

He took a long step forward and clasped her hands. She tried to pull back but he held firm. 'I have come to my senses, Clio,' he said seriously. 'I only pray I am not too late.'

Her eyes narrowed. She knew that intent pleading look and braced herself to resist it. 'Too late for what?'

'To tell you I love you. To ask you to marry me.'

'Marry you? Are you mad?' For a moment the sheer effrontery of the proposal robbed her of speech. Then her temper rose and the impulse to wipe that look of satisfaction off his face overcame all prudence. Her eyes blazed. 'Oh, that is very fine! Now you have had enough of galloping about paying off old scores you think it is time to find a wife. Well, you can look elsewhere. If you think *I* care to be treated in such a way you are sadly mistaken! I am not one of your adoring Spanish señoras, Harry!'

'You don't have to tell me that.'

The laughter in his voice fanned her wrath. 'Go away,' she said hotly. 'Go back to your fighting and your women and leave me alone. I am returning to England. I never want to see you again.'

'Balderdash! Didn't you beg to come with me? Said you wouldn't mind the discomfort so long as life was exciting? Well, that's what I'm offering you now. Life! Excitement! Come on, Clio. Admit that's what you really want.'

'You are too late,' she said flatly and had the satisfaction of seeing him blink, just as if she had struck him across the face. He took a step backward, frowning.

'What do you mean? How can I be too late? I came just as soon as I saw that damned announcement of your wedding. Miss Hardy to wed Major Cole – I never had such a shock in my life! I started back at once and here I am.'

'Too late.'

'Don't do it, Clio,' he said earnestly. 'Robert is the best fellow in the world, but you must take my word you would not suit.'

'Why shouldn't we suit? What do you know of the matter? You sang a different tune when you urged me to marry him. Can you blame me for taking your advice?' Her voice shook a little; it was becoming difficult to control her laughter. Rarely had she known Harry at a loss and she savoured every second of his discomfiture.

He dropped his head on his hands and groaned. 'You are the most obstinate and perverse creature in the world! I only said that –'

'Why say it? Why tell me something you didn't mean?'

'To be honest, I thought it the one sure way of preventing the match,' he admitted. 'When have you ever taken my advice?'

'Then you are hoist with your own petard. We were married today,' said Clio, but her triumph was short-lived. With a sudden pounce, Harry possessed himself of her hands and pulled her close to him.

'In that case I shall be obliged to abduct you by force,' he growled, and Clio gave a little shriek. The game had gone too far.

'Let me go. Robert will be angry....'

'Liar!' said Harry cheerfully, and released her. 'It was Laura who married Robert, deny it if you can.'

'Who told you?' She rubbed her wrists, eyeing him balefully.

'Why, someone whose word can always be relied on – in short, your father.'

'*Papa?*'

He laughed at her astonishment. 'Do you suppose me such an ill-bred fellow that I would make you an offer without the consent of your father? While you were at supper, I spent a very agreeable hour in his study, admiring the treasures of antiquity. Truly a remarkable scholar, your father!'

Confounded by this evidence of men's duplicity, Clio was in no mood to listen to eulogies of a parent who had played her such a shabby trick.

'What did he say to your proposal?' she inquired in tones heavy with sarcasm. 'I hope he had the good sense to show you the door!'

'On the contrary, he congratulated me on my courage and said an elopement would do very well for you since a second marriage such as he endured for Laura's sake would certainly kill him.'

She had to laugh. 'Poor Papa! I daresay he will be glad to be rid of us all.'

'Then you will marry me?'

'Wait. You go too fast. I have said nothing of the kind,' said Clio, though her heart had begun to race. 'How do I know Harry Churchill will not vanish again? I tell you I have no wish to find myself married to a stiff-necked *hidalgo*.'

'No fear of that,' said Harry quietly. 'El Forastero has settled his accounts. He will not come back.'

He walked to the open window and stood for a moment

breathing the warm lilac-scented air. 'Don Sebastian was caught by my fellows on the Madrid road.'

'Did they kill him?'

'He offered them a king's ransom to let him go. That may or may not have made his end more painful.' He paused, then added with a perceptible effort, 'Mercedes is avenged.'

'And Colonel de Rochefort?'

The grim lines of his face relaxed. He said almost gaily, 'Oh, that is another matter! I saw Rochefort ten days ago, when I had occasion to congratulate him on the beauty and charity of his wife.'

'To *congratulate* him?'

'That surprises you? Listen. I shared a bench with your sister for a stage or two in the diligence that runs from Toledo to Madrid. Neither she nor her husband recognized me for I was disguised as a friar, but I could not help admiring her devotion to the noisy infant she was burdened with and who, I must confess, made the lot of the other passengers perfectly intolerable. In the end I was forced to sit up with the coachman to escape the din.'

'A baby? Julia?' Clio frowned, trying to grasp what he was telling her. 'But, surely –?'

'Oh, she informed us all that the child was not her own. She had merely undertaken the duty of conveying him to the care of his grandmother. It appeared,' said Harry, watching her closely, 'the infant had been confided to her in Ciudad Rodrigo by a noble Spanish lady, one Doña Mercedes Cortes... was that not a strange chance?'

'Oh, Harry! What did you say to her?'

'What should I have said? That child will inherit two great estates, those of his mother and Don Sebastian's too. Would it have been a kindness to cast doubts on his legitimacy?'

There was a roughness in his voice that told how the matter had affected him.

'No,' said Clio firmly. 'You did the right thing. All the same....'

'Regrets are something no outlaw can afford. Come, Clio, I

have answered your questions. Now you must answer mine. Will you marry me?'

'Tell me first whether Lord Wellington will have you pardoned. You cannot remain an outlaw all your life.'

'Oh, Clio! Don't you see that is part of my strategy? The Beau has an eye for a pretty woman. If I am obliged to face the music I would rather do it with you at my side,' said Harry, straight-faced. 'Why else should I risk marrying you?'

'Coward!'

'I don't deny it. All the same, I have reason to believe my chances are fair. Grant himself said as much. There, does that satisfy you?'

'Oh, Harry!' She allowed him to draw her into his arms. The touch of his lips woke memories, recognizable but subtly changed, like a reflection in running water. The boy whose kisses she remembered had become a man, that most dangerous and unpredictable animal.

He drew back, placing his hands on her shoulders. 'I thought I had lost you,' he said seriously. 'When I saw Robert's ring about your neck I made sure you had forgotten me. What became of my locket?'

'Oh! I gave it to my maid,' she confessed.

'Faithless!'

'I had to. She was afraid of losing her character for letting me take her place aboard *Niobe*, and nothing would satisfy her until I gave her your locket.'

'Then I must consider it well lost.' He kissed her again, and laughed a little wryly. 'I love you so. Try as he might, even Don Enrique could not help loving you.'

'He had a charming way of showing it!'

'He dared not show it. It was as much as his life was worth.'

He drew her close again. A new urgency entered his kisses and she met them with the pent-up passion of the missing years. Time passed unheeded.

Dimly she became aware of a disturbance outside, wheels on cobbles and the jingle of harness. Then came a loud attention-seeking cough and the sibilant whisper: 'Ze horses, Mr Harry! Must ve vait here all night?'

Reluctantly he released her. 'We must go. Auguste's patience is wearing thin.'

'*Auguste?*'

He laughed at her surprise. 'Who do you suppose brought me here? He is mightily concerned that this time our elopement should be done in proper style.'

'You mean –?'

'He is waiting outside with a carriage and pair. If I am to deprive you of a splendid wedding by carrying you off in this dastardly fashion, at least the elopement will give people enough to gossip about.'

'Harry, you mad thing!'

'Don't deprive me of my fun, I beg! Your maid is party to the plot. All you have to do is climb down the ladder and we will be gone.'

'A ladder! Is there nothing you have forgotten?'

He shook his head, smiling. 'You are thinking of the sorry mess I made of the business before! Well, I can't blame you, but they say a fool learns from his own mistakes. At least on this occasion you may be sure I have enough in my pocket to pay the coachman!'